THIS FREEDOM

THIS FREEDOM

BY

A. S. M. HUTCHINSON

BOSTON

LITTLE, BROWN, AND COMPANY

1922

"With a great sum obtained I this freedom."

—ACTS xxii, 28.

CONTENTS

PART ONE

HOUSE OF MEN

THIS FREEDOM

CHAPTER I

ROSALIE's earliest apprehension of the world was of a mysterious and extraordinary world that revolved entirely about her father and that entirely and completely belonged to her father. Under her father, all males had proprietory rights in the world and dominion over it; no females owned any part of the world or could do anything with it. All the males in this world — her father, and Robert and Harold her brothers, and all the other boys and men one sometimes saw — did mysterious and extraordinary things; and all the females in this world — her mother, and Anna and Flora and Hilda her sisters, and Ellen the cook and Gertrude the maid — did ordinary and unexciting and generally rather tiresome things. All the males were like story books to Rosalie: you never knew what they were going to do next; and all the females were like lesson books: they just went on and on and on.

Rosalie always stared at men when she saw them. Extraordinary and wonderful creatures who could do what they liked and were always doing mysterious and wonderful things, especially and above all her father.

Being with her father was like being with a magician or like watching a conjuror on the stage. You never knew what he was going to do next. Whatever he suddenly did was never surprising in the sense of being startling, for (this cannot be emphasised too much) nothing her father did was ever surprising to Rosalie; but it was surprising

in the sense of being absorbingly wonderful and enthralling. Even better than reading when she first began to
read, and far better than anything in the world before the
mysteries in books were discoverable, Rosalie liked to sit
and stare at her father and think how wonderful he was
and wonder what extraordinary thing he would do next.
Everything belonged to him. The whole of life was
ordered with a view to what he would think about it. The
whole of life was continually thrown off its balance and
whirled into the most entrancing convulsions by sudden
activities of this most wonderful man.

Entrancing convulsions! Wonderful, wonderful father
with a bull after him! Why, that was her very earliest
recollection of him! That showed you how wonderful he
was! Father, seen for the first time (as it were) flying
before a bull! Bounding wildly across a field towards her
with a bull after him! Wonderful father! Did her
mother ever rush along in front of a bull? Never. Was
it possible to imagine any of the women she knew rushing
before a bull? It was not possible. To see a woman
rushing before a bull would have alarmed Rosalie for she
would have felt it was unnatural; but for her father to be
bounding wildly along in front of a bull seemed to her
perfectly natural and ordinary and she was not in the
least alarmed; only, as always, enthralled.

Her father, while Rosalie watched him, was not in great
danger. He came ballooning along towards Rosalie, not
running as ordinarily fit and efficient men run, but pro-
gressing by a series of enormous leaps and bounds, arms
and legs spread-eagling, and at each leap and bound always
seeming to Rosalie to spring as high in the air as he
sprung forward over the ground. It would not have
surprised Rosalie, who was then about four, to see one
of these stupendous leaps continue in a whirling flight
through mid-air and her father come hurtling over the

gate and drop with an enormous plunk at her feet like a
huge dead bird, as a partridge once had come plunk over
the hedge and out of the sky when she was in a lane
adjacent to a shooting party. It would not have surprised
her in the least. Nothing her father did ever surprised
Rosalie. The world was his and the fulness thereof, and
he did what he liked with it.

Arrived, however, from the bull, not as a ballooning
bird out of the sky, but as a headlong avalanche over the
gate, Rosalie's father tottered to a felled tree trunk,
and sat there heaving, and groaned aloud, "Infernal parish; hateful parish; forsaken parish!"

Rosalie, wonderingly regarding him, said, " Mother
says dinner is waiting for you, father. "

Her mother and her sisters and the servants and the
entire female establishment of the universe seemed to
Rosalie always to be waiting for something from her
father, or for her father himself, or waiting for or upon
some male other than her father. That was another of
the leading principles that Rosalie first came to know in
her world. Not only were the males, paramountly her
father, able to do what they liked and always doing wonderful and mysterious things, but everything that the
females did either had some relation to a male or was
directly for, about, or on behalf of a male.

Getting Robert off to school in the morning, for instance. That was another early picture.

There would be Robert, eating; and there was the entire
female population of the rectory feverishly attending upon
Robert while he ate. Six females, intensely and as if their
lives depended upon it, occupied with one male. Three
girls — Anna about sixteen, Flora fourteen, Hilda
twelve — and three grown women, all exhaustingly occupied in pushing out of the house one heavy and obstinate
male aged about ten! Rosalie used to stand and watch

entranced. How wonderful he was! Where did he go to when at last he was pushed off? What happened to him? What did he do?

There he is, eating; there they are, ministering. Entrancing and mysterious spectacle!

Robert, very solid and heavy and very heated and agitated, would be seated at the table shoving porridge into himself against the clock. One of his legs, unnaturally flexed backward and outward, is in the possession of Rosalie's mother who is on her knees mending a hole in his stocking. The other leg, similarly contorted, is on the lap of Ellen the cook, who with very violent tugs, as if she were lashing a box, is lacing a boot on to it. Behind Robert is Anna, who is pressing his head down with one hand and washing the back of his neck with the other. In front of him across the table is Hilda, staring before her with bemused eyes and moving lips and rapidly counting on drumming fingers. Hilda is doing his sums for him. Beside him on his right side, apparently engaged in throttling him, is Gertrude the maid. Gertrude the maid is trying to tear off him a grimed collar and put on him a clean collar. Facing Gertrude on his other side is Flora. Flora is bawling his history in his ear.

Everybody is working for Robert; everybody is working at top speed for him, and everybody is loudly soliciting his attention.

"Oh, do give over wriggling, master Robert!" (The boot-fastener.)

"'Simon de Montford, Hubert de Burgh, and Peter de Roche.' Well, *say* it then, you dreadful little idiot!" (The history crammer.)

"Oh, master Robert, do please keep *up!*" (The collar fastener.)

"Keep *down*, will you!" (The neck washer.)

" Four sixes are twenty-four and six you carried thirty! " (The arithmetician.)

" Robert, you *must* turn your foot further round! " (The stocking-darner.)

" ' The Barons were now incensed. The Barons were now incensed. The Barons were now incensed.' *Say* it, you ghastly little stupid! "

" Do they make you do these by fractions or by decimals? . . . Well, what *do* you know, then? "

Entrancing spectacle!

Now the discovery is by everybody simultaneously made and simultaneously announced that Robert is already later in starting than he has ever been (he always was) and immediately Rosalie would become witness of the last and most violent skirmish in this devoted attendance. Everybody rushes around hunting for things and pushing them on to Robert and pushing Robert, festooned with them, towards the door. Where was his cap? Where was his satchel? Where was his lunch? Where were his books? Who had seen his atlas? Who had seen his pencil box? Who had seen his gymnasium belt? Was his bicycle ready? Was his coat on his bicycle? Was that button on his coat?

With these alarums at their height and the excursions attendant on them at their busiest, another splendid male would enter the room and immediately there was, as Rosalie always saw, a transference of attendance to him and a violent altercation between him and the first splendid male. This new splendid male is Rosalie's other brother, Harold. Harold was eighteen and him also the entire female population of the rectory combined to push out of the rectory every morning. Harold was due to be pushed off half an hour later than Robert, and as he was a greater and more splendid male than Robert (though infinitely lesser than her father) so the place to which

he was pushed off was far more mysterious and enthralling than the place to which Robert was pushed off.
A school Rosalie could dimly understand. But a bank!
Why Harold should go to sit on a bank all day, and why
he should ride on a bicycle to Ashborough to find a bank
when there were banks all around the rectory, and even
in the garden itself, Rosalie never could imagine. Mysterious Harold! Anna had told her that men kept money
in banks; but Rosalie had never found money in a bank
though she had looked; yet banks — of all extraordinary
places — were where men chose to put their money! Mysterious men! And Harold could find these banks and
find this money though he never took a trowel or a spade
and was always shiningly clean with a very high collar
and very long cuffs. Wonderful, wonderful Harold!

Robert was due to be pushed off half an hour before
Harold was due to be pushed off, but he never was; the
two splendid creatures always clashed and there was always between them, because they clashed, a violent scene
which Rosalie would not have missed for worlds. A
meeting of two males, so utterly unlike a meeting of two
females, was invariably of the most entrancingly noisy or
violent description. When ladies came to the rectory to
see her mother they sat in the drawing-room and sipped
tea and spoke in thin voices; but when men came to see
her father and went into the study, there was very loud
talking and often a row. Yes, and once in the village
street, Rosalie had seen two men stand up and thump one
another with their fists and fall down and get up and
thump again. When two women, her sisters or others,
quarrelled, they only shrilled, and went on and on shrill-
ing. It was impossible to imagine the collision of two
women producing anything so exciting and splendid as
invariably was produced by the collision of two males.

As now ——

In comes Harold in great heat and hurry (as men always were) with his splendid button boots in one hand
and an immense pair of shining cuffs in the other hand.

" Haven't you gone yet, you lazy young brute? "

" No, I haven't, you lazy old brute! "

Agitated feminine cries of " Robert! Robert! You
are not to speak to Harold like that. "

" Well, he spoke to me like that."

" Yes, and I'll do a jolly sight more than speak to you
in a minute if you don't get out of it. Get out of it, do
you hear? "

" Shan't! "

" Robert! Robert! Harold! Harold! "

" Well, get him out of it, or he'll be sorry for it. Why
is he always here when I'm supposed to be having my
breakfast? Not a thing ready, as usual. Look here,
where I'm supposed to sit — flannel and soap! That's
washing his filthy neck, I suppose. Filthy young brute!
Why don't you wash your neck, pig? "

" Why do you wear girl's boots with buttons, pig? "

Commotion. Enthralling commotion. Half the female
assemblage hustle the splendid creature Robert out of the
door and down the hall and on to his bicycle; half the
female assemblage cover his retreat and block the dash
after him of the still more splendid Harold; all the female
assemblage, battle having been prevented and one splendid
male despatched, combine to minister to the requirements
of the second splendid male now demanding attention.

Busy scene. Enthralling spectacle. There he is, eating; shoving sausages into himself against the clock just
as Robert had shovelled porridge into himself against the
clock. One ministrant is sewing a buttton on to his boot,
another with blotting paper and hot iron is removing a
stain from his coat, divested for the purpose; one is pouring out his coffee, another is cutting his bread, a third is

watching for his newspaper by the postman. And suddenly he whirls everything into a whirlpool just as men, if Rosalie watches them long enough, always whirl everything into a whirlpool.

"Oh, my goodness, the pump!"

Chorus, "The pump?"

"The bicycle pump! Has that young brute taken the bicycle pump?"

"Yes, he took it. I saw it."

Commotion.

"Catch him across the field! Catch him across the field! Where are my boots? Where the devil are my boots? Well, never mind the infernal button. How am I going to get to the bank with a flat tyre? Can't some one catch him across the field instead of all standing there staring?"

Away they go! Rosalie, seeking a good place for the glorious spectacle, is knocked over in the stampede for the door. Nobody minds Rosalie. Rosalie doesn't mind — anything to see this entrancing sight! Away they go, flying over the meadow, shouting, scrambling, falling. Out after them plunges Harold, shirt-sleeved, one boot half on, hobbling, leaping, bawling. Glorious to watch him! He outruns them all; he outbellows them all. Of course he does. He is a man. He is one of those splendid, wonderful, mysterious creatures to whom, subject only to Rosalie's father, the entire world belongs. Look at him, bounding, bawling! Wonderful, wonderful Harold!

But Robert is wonderful too. If it had been Anna or Flora or Hilda gone off with the pump, she would have been easily caught. Not Robert. Wonderful and mysterious Robert, wonderfully and mysteriously pedalling at incredible speed, is not caught. The hunt dejectedly trails back. The business of pushing Harold out of the house is devotedly resumed.

And again — enthralling spectacle — just as the reign of Robert was terminated by the accession of Harold, so the dominion of Harold is overthrown by the accession of father. Harold is crowded about with ministrants. Nobody can leave him for a minute. Rosalie's father appears. Everybody leaves Harold simultaneously, abruptly, and as if by magic. Rosalie's father appears. Everybody disappears. Wonderful father! Everybody melts away; but Harold does not melt away. Courageous Harold! Everybody melts; only Harold is left, and Rosalie watching; and immediately, as always, the magnificent males clash with sound and fury.

Rosalie's father scowls upon Harold and delivers his morning greeting. No " Good morning, dear," as her mother would have said. " Aren't you gone yet? " like a bark from a kennel.

" Just going."

Wonderful father! A moment before there had been not the remotest sign of Harold ever going. Now Harold is very anxious to go. He is very anxious to go but, like Robert, he will not abandon the field without defiance of the authority next above his own. While he collects his things he whistles. Rosalie shudders (but deliciously as one in old Rome watching the gladiators).

" Do you see the clock, sir? "

" Yes."

" Well, quicken yourself, sir. Quicken yourself."

" The clock's fast."

" It is not fast, sir. And let me add that the clock with which you could keep time of a morning, or of any hour in the day, would have to be an uncommonly slow clock."

Harold with elaborate unconcern adjusts his trouser clips. " I should have thought that was more a matter for the Bank to complain of, if necessary. I may be wrong, of course —— "

"You may be wrong, sir, because in my experience you almost invariably are wrong and never more so than when you lad-di-dah that you are right. You may be wrong, but let me tell you what you may not be. You may not be impertinent to me, sir. You may not lad-di-dah me, sir."

"Father, I really do not see why at my age I should be hounded out of the house like this every morning."

"You are hounded out, as you elegantly express it, because morning after morning, owing to your disgustingly slothful habits, you clash with me, sir. My breakfast is delayed because you clash with me, and the house is delayed because you clash with me, and the whole parish is delayed because you clash with me."

"Perhaps you're not aware that Robert clashes with me."

"Dash Robert! Are you going or are you not going?"

He goes.

"Bring back the paper."

He brings it back.

Wonderful father!

Rosalie's father gives a tug at the bell cord that would have dislocated the neck of a horse. The cord comes away in his hand. He hurls it across the room.

Glorious father!

There was a most frightful storm one night and Rosalie, in Anna's bed with Flora crowded in also and Hilda shivering in her nightgown beside them, too young to be frightened but with her sister's fright beginning to communicate itself to her, said, "Ask father to go and stop it."

"Fool!" cried Flora. "How could father stop the storm?"

Why not?

CHAPTER II

FLORA's sharp and astounding reply to that question of Rosalie's was recalled by Rosalie, with hurt surprise at Flora's sharpness and ignorance, when, shortly afterwards, she found in a book a man who could, and actually did, stop a storm. This was a man called Prospero in a book called " The Tempest."

She was never — that Rosalie — the conventional wonder-child of fiction who reads before ten all that its author probably never read before thirty; but she could read when she was six and she read widely and curiously, choosing her entertainment, from her father's bookshelves, solely by the method of reading every book that had pictures.

There was but one picture to " The Tempest, " a frontispiece, but it sufficed, and at the period when Rosalie believed the ownership of the world to be vested in her father and under him in all males, " The Tempest," because it reflected that condition, was the greatest joy of all the joys the bookshelves discovered to her. She read it over and over again. It presented life exactly as life presented itself to the round eyes of Rosalie: all males doing always noisy and violent and important and enthralling things, with Prospero, her father, by far the most important of all; and women scarcely appearing and doing only what the men told them to do. Miranda's appearances in the story were indifferently skipped by Rosalie; the noisy action and language in the wreck, and the noisy action and language of the drunkards in the wood were what she liked, and all the magic arts of Prospero were what she thoroughly appreciated and understood.

That was life as she knew it.

Rosalie's father, when Rosalie thought the world belonged to him and revolved about him, was tall and clean-shaven and of complexion a dark and burning red. When he was excited or angry his face used to burn as the embers in the study fire burned when Rosalie pressed the bellows against them. He had thick black eyebrows and a most powerful nose. His nose jutted from his face like a projection from a cliff beneath a clump of bushes. He had been at Cambridge and he was most ferociously fond of Cambridge. One of the most fearful scenes Rosalie ever witnessed was on one boat-race day when Harold appeared with a piece of Oxford ribbon in his buttonhole. It was at breakfast, the family for some reason or other most unusually all taking breakfast together. Rosalie's father first jocularly bantered Harold on his choice of colour, and everybody — anxious as always to please and placate the owner of the world — laughed with father against Harold. But Harold did not laugh. Harold smouldered resentment and defiance, and out of his smouldering began to maintain " from what chaps had said " that Oxford was altogether and in every way a much better place than Cambridge. In every branch of athletics there were better athletes, growled Harold, at Oxford.

Rosalie has been watching the embers in her father's face glowing to dark-red heat. Everybody had been watching them except Harold who, though addressing his father, had been mumbling " what chaps had said " to his plate.

" Athletes! " cried Rosalie's father suddenly in a very terrible voice. " Athletes! And what about scholars, sir ? "

Harold informed his plate that he wasn't talking about scholars.

Rosalie's father raised a marmalade jar and thumped it down upon the table so that it cracked. "Then what the dickens right have you to talk at all, sir? How dare you try to compare Oxford with Cambridge when you know no more about either than you know of Jupiter or Mars? Athletes!" He went off into record of University contests, cricket scores, running times, football scores, as if his whole life had been devoted to collecting them. They all showed Cambridge first and Oxford beaten and he hurled each one at Harold's head with a thundering, "What about that, sir?" after it. He leapt to scholarship and reeled off scholarships and scholars and schools, and professors and endowments and prize men, as if he had been an educational year-book gifted with speech and with particularly loud and violent speech. He spoke of the colleges of Cambridge, and with every college and every particular glory of every college demanded of the unfortunate Harold, "What have you got in Oxford against that, sir?"

It was awful. It was far more frightening than the night of the storm. Nobody ate. Nobody drank. Everybody shuddered and tried by every means to avoid catching father's rolling eye and thereby attracting the direct blast of the tempest. Rosalie, who of course, being a completely negligible quantity in the rectory, is not included in the everybody, simply stared, more awed and enthralled than ever before. And with much reason. As he declaimed of the glories of the colleges of Cambridge there was perceptible in her father's voice a most curious crack or break. It became more noticeable and more frequent. He suddenly and most astoundingly cried out, "Cambridge! Cambridge!" and threw his arms out before him on the table, and buried his head on them, and sobbed out, "Cambridge! My youth! My youth! My God, my God, my youth!"

Somehow or other they all slipped out of the room and left him there, — all except Rosalie who remained in her high chair staring upon her father, and upon his shoulders that heaved up and down, and upon the coffee from an overturned cup that oozed slowly along the tablecloth.

Extraordinary father!

Rosalie's father had been a wrangler and one of the brilliant men of his year at Cambridge. All manner of brilliance was expected for him and of him. He unexpectedly went into the Church and as unexpectedly married.

His bride was the daughter of a clergyman, a widower, who kept a small private school in Devonshire. She helped her father to run the school (an impoverished business which, begun exclusively for the "sons of gentlemen," had slid down into paying court to tradesmen in order to get the sons of tradesmen) and she maintained him in the very indifferent health he suffered. Harold Aubyn, the brilliant wrangler with the brilliant future, who had begun his brilliance by unexpectedly entering the Church, and continued it by unexpectedly marrying while on a holiday in the little Devonshire town where he had gone to ponder his future (a little unbalanced by the unpremeditated plunge into Holy Orders) further continued his brilliance by unexpectedly finding himself the assistant master in his father-in-law's second-rate and failing school. The daughter would not leave her father; the suitor would not leave his darling; the brilliant young wrangler who at Cambridge used to dream of waking to find himself famous awoke instead to find himself six years buried in a now third-rate and moribund school in a moribund Devonshire town. He had a father-in-law now a permanent invalid, bedridden. He had four children and another, Robert, on the way.

It was his father-in-law's death that awoke him; and he awoke characteristically. The old man dead! Come, that was one burden lifted, one shackle removed! The school finally went smash at the same time. Never mind! Another burden gone! Another shackle lifted! Dash the school! How he hated the school! How he loathed and detested the lumping boys! How he loathed and abominated teaching them simple arithmetic (he the wrangler!) and history that was a string of dates, and geography that was a string of capes and bays, and Latin as far as the conjugations (he the wrangler!) how he loathed and abominated it! Now a fresh start! Hurrah!

That was like Rosalie's father — in those days. That way blew the cold fit and the hot fit — then.

The magnificent fresh start after the magnificent escape from the morass of the moribund father-in-law and the moribund school and the moribund Devonshire town proved to be but a stagger down into morass heavier and more devastating of ambition. He always jumped blindly and wildly into things. Blindly and wildly into the Church, blindly and wildly into marriage, blindly and wildly into the school, blindly and wildly, one might say, into fatherhood on a lavish scale. Blindly and wildly — the magnificent fresh start — into the rectory in which Rosalie was born.

It was " a bit in the wilds " (of Suffolk) ; " a bit of a tight fit " (£200 a year) and a bit or two or three other drawbacks; but it was thousands of miles from Devonshire and from the school and schooling, that was the great thing; and it was a jolly big rectory with a ripping big garden; and above all and beyond everything it was just going to be a jumping-off place while he looked around for something suitable to his talents and while he got in touch again with his old friends of the brilliant years.

It was just going to be a jumping-off place, but he never jumped off from it; a place from which to look around for something suitable, but instead he sunk in it up to his chin; a place from which to get in touch again with his friends of the brilliant years, but his friends were all doing brilliant things and much too busy at their brilliance to open up with one who had missed fire.

The parish of St. Mary's, Ibbotsfield, had an enormous rectory, falling to pieces; an enormous church, crumbling away; an enormous area, purely agricultural; and a cure of a very few hundred agricultural souls, enormously scattered. Years and years before, prior to railways, prior to mechanical reapers and thrashers, and prior to everything that took men to cities or whirled them and their produce farther in an hour than they ever could have gone in a week, Ibbotsfield and its surrounding villages and hamlets were a reproach to the moral conditions of the day in that they had no sufficiently enormous church. Well-intentioned persons removed this reproach, adding in their zeal an enormous rectory; and the time they chose for their beneficent and lavish action was precisely the time when Ibbotsfield, through its principal land-owners, was stoutly rejecting the monstrous idea of encouraging a stinking, roaring, dangerous railway in their direction, and combining together by all means in their power to keep the roaring, dangerous atrocity as far away from them as possible.

It thus, and by like influences, happened that, whereas one generation of the devoutly intentioned sat stolidly under the reproach of an enormous and thickly populated area without a church, later generations with the same stolidity sat under the reproach of an enormous church, an enormous rectory and an infinitesimal stipend, in an area

in which a man might walk all day without meeting any
other man.

But the devout of the day, not having to live
in this rectory or preach in this church or laboriously
trudge about this area, did not unduly worry themselves
with this reproach.

That was (in his turn) the lookout of the Rev. Harold
Aubyn — also his outlook.

He is to be imagined, in those days when Rosalie first
came to know him and to think of him as Prospero, as a
terribly lonely man. He stalked fatiguingly about the
countryside in search of his parishioners, and his parishioners were suspicious of him and disliked his fierce,
thrusting nose, and he returned from them embittered
with them and hating them. He genuinely longed to be
friendly with them and on terms of Hail, fellow, well
met, with them; but they exasperated him because they
could not meet him either on his own quick intellectual
level or upon his own quick and very sensitive emotional
level. They could not respond to his humour and they
could not respond, in the way he thought they ought to
respond, to his sympathy.

He once found a man — a farm labourer — who in
conversation disclosed a surprising interest in the traces
of early and mediæval habitation of the country. The
discovery delighted him. In the catalogue of a second-
hand bookseller of Ipswich he noticed the " Excursions
in the County of Suffolk, " two volumes for three shillings,
and he wrote and had them posted to the man. For days
he eagerly looked in the post for the grateful and delighted letter that in similar circumstances he himself
would have written. He composed in his mind the phrases
of the letter and warmed in spirit over anticipation of
reading them. No letter arrived.

When he came into the rectory from visiting he was always asking, " Has that man Bolas from Hailsham called? " Bolas never called. He furiously began to loathe Bolas. He was furious with himself for having " lowered himself " to Bolas. Bolas in his ignorance no doubt thought the books were a cheap charity of cast-off lumber. Uncouth clod! Stupid clod! Uncouth parish! Hateful, loathsome parish! For weeks he kept away from Hailsham and the possible vicinity of Bolas. One day he met him. Bolas passed with no more than a " Good day, Mr. Aubyn." He could have killed the man. He swung round and pushed his dark face and jutty nose into the face of Bolas. " Did you ever get some books I sent you? "

" Ou, ay, to be sure, they books ——— "

He rushed with savage strides away from the man. All the way home he savagely said to himself, aloud, keeping time to it with his feet, " Uncouth clod, ill-mannered clod, horrible, hateful place! Uncouth clods, hateful clods, horrible, hateful place! "

That was his attitude to his parishioners. They could not come up to the level of his sensibilities; he could not get down to the level of theirs.

With the few gentle families that composed the society of Ibbotsfield he was little better accommodated. They led contented, well-ordered lives, busy about their gardens, busy about their duties, busy about their amusements. His life was ill-ordered and he was never busy about anything: he was always either neglecting what had to be done or doing it, late, with a ferocious and exhausting energy that caused him to groan over it and detest it while he did it. In the general level of his life he was below the standard of his neighbours and knew that he was below it; in the sudden bounds and flights of his intellect and of his imagination he was immeasurably above the intellects of his neighbours and knew that he was immeasurably above them. Therefore, and in both moods, he commonly hated and despised them. "Fools, fools! Unread, pompous, petty!"

At the rectory, among his family, he seemed to himself to be surrounded by incompetent women and herds of children.

He was a terribly lonely man when Rosalie first came to know him and thought of him as Prospero. He is to be imagined in those days as a fierce, flying, futile figure scudding about on the face of the parish and in the vast gaunt spaces of the rectory, with his burning face and his jutting nose, trying to get away from people, hungering to meet sympathetic people; trying to get way from himself, hungering after the things that his self had lost. In his young manhood he was known for moods of intense reserve alternated by fits of tremendous gaiety and boisterous high spirits. ("A fresh start! Hurrah!" when release from the school came. "What does anything matter? Now we're really off at last! Hurrah! Hurrah!") In his set manhood, when Rosalie knew him, there were substituted for the fits of boisterous spirits paroxysms of violent outburst against his lot. "Infernal parish! Hateful parish! Forsaken parish!" after the ignominy of flight before the bull. "Blow the dinner! Dash the dinner! Blow the dinner!" after wrestling a soggy steak from his pocket and hurling it half a mile through the air. These and that single but terrible occasion of "Cambridge! Cambridge! My youth! My God, my God, my youth!"

A terribly lonely man.

CHAPTER III

The Aubyn family occupied only a portion of the enormous rectory. There was a whole floor upstairs, and there were several rooms on the ground and first floors, that were never used, were unfurnished except for odds and ends of lumber left behind by the previous vicar, and were never entered. Rosalie once explored them all, systematically though very fearfully, and also very excitedly. She was searching for some one, for two people.

In the household she knew her father and her mother, her brothers and sisters and the servants; but there were two mysterious inhabitants of whom she often heard but whom she never saw and never could find. It used to frighten her sometimes, lying awake at night, or creeping about the house of an evening, to think of those two mysterious people hidden away somewhere and perhaps likely to pounce on her out of the dark. What did they eat? Where did they live? What did they do? What *were* they?

One of these two eerie and invisible people was heard of from her father. Several times Rosalie had heard him, when talking to persons not of the family, speak of " my wife." The other eerie and invisible creature was heard of from her mother: " My husband."

Where were they? Of all the mysterious things which Rosalie used to wonder over in those days, this undiscoverable " wife " and " husband " were the most mysterious of all, and more mysterious than ever after that day on which, walking on tiptoe for fear of coming upon them suddenly, holding her breath and pausing in fearful apprehension before entering the untenanted rooms upstairs, she explored the whole house in search of them. She got to know all sorts of little odds and ends about them; that the wife felt the cold very much, for instance, for she had heard her father say so; and that the husband did not like mutton, for her mother told that to Mr. Grant the butcher; and she was often hot on their tracks for she had heard her father say, " My wife is upstairs " and had rushed upstairs and searched; and her mother say, " My husband is in the garden," and had run into the garden and hunted. But all these clues only deepened the mystery. They were never to be found.

It *was* mysterious.

Then one day the wife (she heard) fell ill, and through her great concern about that — for she was profoundly interested in these people and used to feel awfully sorry for them, hidden away like that perhaps with no fire and nothing to eat but mutton — the mystery was explained.

With the family she was going towards church one Sunday morning and she heard her father tell a lady that " my wife " was not very well that morning and couldn't come. Rosalie during the service prayed very earnestly for the wife's recovery and took the opportunity of praying also that she might be permitted to see the wife " if she is not very frightening, O Lord, and the husband too, if possible, for Jesus Christ's sake, amen."

And at lunch, having thought of nothing else all the morning, there was suddenly shot out of her the question, " Father, is your wife any better now? "

Rosalie commonly never spoke at all at meals; and as to speaking to her father, though it is obvious she must have had some sort of intercourse with him, this famous question (a standing joke in the house for years) was the single direct speech of those early years she ever could remember. She spoke to her father when she was bidden to speak in the form of messages, generally about meals being ready, or relative to shopping commissions he had been asked to execute; but he was far too wonderful, powerful and mysterious for conversation with him on her own initiative. " Father, is your wife any better now? " stood out in her later recollection, alone and lonelily startling.

There was from all the company an astounded stare and astounded gasp; all the table sitting with astounded eyes, forks suspended in mid-air, mouths half open in astonishment, and Rosalie sitting in her high chair wonderingly regarding their wonderment. *What* were they staring at?

There was then an enormous howl of laughter, led by Rosalie's father, and repeated, and louder than before, because it was so very unusual for the family to be laughing in accord with father. Gertrude the maid fled hysterically from the room and laughter howled back from the kitchen.

Rosalie's father said, " You'd better go and ask your mother." Her mother had stayed in bed that day with a chill.

Robert " undid " Rosalie — a wooden rod with a fixed knob at one end went through the arms of her high chair and was fastened by a removable knob at the other end — and Rosalie slid down very gravely, and with their laughter still echoing trod upstairs to her mother's bedside and related what she had been told to ask, and, on inquiry, why she had asked it. " I only said ' Father, is your wife any better now? ' " and on further inquiry explained her long searching after the undiscoverable pair.

Rosalie's mother laughed also then, but had a sudden wetness in her eyes. She put her arms about Rosalie and pressed her to her bosom and cried, " Oh, my poor darling! " and explained the tremendous mystery. Wife and husband, Rosalie's mother explained, were the names used by other people for her father and her mother. A man and a woman loved one another very, very dearly ("as I loved your dear father") and then they lived together in a dear house of their own and then God gave them dear little children of their own to live with them, said Rosalie's mother.

This thoroughly satisfied Rosalie and completely entranced her, especially about the presentation of the dear little children. She would have supposed that naturally it thoroughly satisfied Anna and Harold and Flora and the others; and the point of interest rests here, that Rosalie's mother also believed that this explanation of marriage and procreation completely satisfied Anna at sixteen and Harold in the Bank at eighteen. She never gave them any other explanation of the phenomenon of birth; and it is to be supposed that, just as she instructed them that God sent the dear little children, so she believed that God, at the right time, in some mysterious way, communicated the matter to them in greater detail. Years and years afterwards Flora told Rosalie that when Rosalie was born all the children were sent away to stay with a neighbour and not allowed to return till Rosalie's mother, downstairs, was able to show them the dear little sister that God had surprisingly delivered at the house, as it were in a parcel.

One is given pain by a state of affairs so monstrous; but one suffers that pain proudly because one belongs, proudly, to a day in which nothing but stark truth may go from mother to child, not even fairy stories, not even Bible stories. Rosalie's mother is gone and her kind is no more, and in the graces and the manners of this day's generation one perceives, proudly, the inestimable benefits of the passing of her kind. Lamentable specimen of her kind, she had no interests other than her home and her husband and her children and the pleasures and the treasures and the friends of her husband and her children. She belonged to that dark age when duty towards others was the guiding principle of moral life; she came only to the threshold of this enlightened age in which duty to oneself is known to be the paramount and first and last consideration of life as it should be lived.

Rosalie's mother, whose name had been Anna Escott, kept at the bottom of a drawer five most exquisite little miniatures. They were in a case of faded blue plush, and they had been in that case and at the bottom of one drawer or another ever since the girl Anna Escott, aged twenty, had placed them in the case, then exquisitely blue and new and soft, and given up painting miniatures forever, in order to devote her whole time to looking after her invalid father and the failing preparatory school that was his livelihood.

Rosalie was herself nearly thirty when she first saw the miniatures. She was come back to the rectory from the pursuits that then occupied her to visit, rather impatiently and rather vexedly, her mother on what proved to be her death bed. She was tidying her mother's drawers, impatient with the amazing collection of rubbish they contained and hating herself for being impatient, while her mother, on the bed, patiently watched her; and she came upon the case and opened it and stared in astonishment and admiration at the beauty of the five miniatures.

She asked her mother and her mother told her she had painted them. " I used to do that when I was a girl," said Rosalie's mother.

All Rosalie's impatience was drowned and utterly engulfed in a most dreadful flood of emotion. She set down the case on the bed and flung herself on her knees beside her mother and clasped her arms about her.

" Oh, mother, mother ! Oh, beloved little mother ! "
But that is out of its place.

Yes, that girl Anna Escott, who had an exquisite talent,
and all sorts of fond dreams of its development, gave it
up wholly and entirely and forever when her mother died
and her father said, " I would like you, Anna dear, to
give up your painting and come and look after me and
the school now."

Anna said, " Of course I will, Papa. It's my duty.
Of course I will."

Girls did that, and parents and husbands asked them to
do that, in the days when Rosalie's mother was a girl.

Rosalie's mother gave away everything, first to her
father, then to her husband, then to her children. She
believed the whole of the Bible, literally, as it is written,
from the first word of Genesis to the last word of Revela-
tions. She taught it as literal, final and initial truth to all
her children, and one knows how wickedly wrong it is now
considered to teach children that the Bible-stories are
true. She taught them the whole of the Bible from books
called " Line Upon Line," and " The Child's Bible," and
in stories of her own making, and from the Bible itself.
Regrettably, the ignorantly imposed-upon children loved
it ! Till each child was eight she taught them everything
at her knee. All the nursery rhymes, and all the Bible,
and reading out of " Step by Step," and then " Reading
Without Tears," and then, in advancing series, the
" Royal Readers "; and writing, first holding their hands,
and then — first in pencil and afterwards with pens having three huge blobs to teach you how to place your fingers
properly — in copybooks graded from enormous lines
which had brick-red covers to astoundingly narrow little
lines enclosing pious and moral maxims which had severe
grey covers; and the multiplication tables and then simple

arithmetic; and General Knowledge out of " The Child's Guide to Knowledge," which asked you " What is sago? " and required you to reply by heart, " Sago is a dried, granulated substance prepared from the pith of several different palms." " Where are these palms found? " " These palms are found in the East Indies."

Likewise history out of Mrs. Markham and " Little Arthur "; also, at a ridiculously early age, how to tell the time and how to know the coinage of the realm and its values; also, whether girl or boy, the making of kettle-holders by threading brightly coloured wools through little squares of canvas; also very many pieces of poetry: " Oft had I heard of Lucy Grey," and " It was the Schooner Hesperus " and hymns — also learnt by heart and sung while Rosalie's mother played the piano — " We are but little children weak," and " Gentle Jesus, meek and mild."

All these things were taught at her knee to each child in turn by Rosalie's mother, and each was taught out of the self-same books, miraculously preserved by Rosalie's mother; the backs of most of them carefully stitched and re-stitched, and marked all through by the dates of each child's daily lesson, written in pencil by Rosalie's mother. The dates ranged from 1869 when Harold was being taught and when the books were fresh and clean, and Rosalie's mother fresh and ardent with her first-born, to 1884, when Rosalie was being taught, and the books very old and thumbed and most terribly crowded with pencil marks, and Rosalie's mother no longer fresh but rather worn, but teaching as fondly and earnestly as ever, because it was her duty. Literally at the knee of Rosalie's mother these things were taught. On her knee with one of her arms about you for the Bible teaching; and standing at her knee, hands behind you, for the teaching of most of the rest. Yes, that was the early education, and the manner of the education, of Rosalie and of her brothers and sisters; and one perceives with indignation the spectacle of a mother wasting her time like that and wasting her children's time like that.

Rosalie's mother did everything in the house and she was always doing something in the house — for somebody else. She never rested and she was always worried. Her brows were always wrinkled with the feverish concentration of one anxiously doing one thing while anxiously thinking of another thing waiting to be done. She had a driven and a hunted look.

Now Rosalie's father had a driving and a hunting look.

Rosalie's father in his youth threw away everything. Rosalie's mother throughout the whole of her life gave away everything. Rosalie's father was a tragic figure dwelling in a house of bondage; but he was at least a tragic king, ruling his house and venting his griefs upon his house. Rosalie's mother was a tragic figure and she was a tragic slave in the house of bondage. The life of Rosalie's father was a tragedy, but a tragedy in some measure relieved because he knew it was a tragedy and could wave his arms and shout and smash things and hurl beefsteaks through the air because of the tragedy of it. But the life of Rosalie's mother was an infinitely deeper tragedy because she never knew or suspected that it was a tragedy.

Still, that is so often the difference between the tragedy of a woman and the tragedy of a man.

CHAPTER IV

THE very great difference between her father and her mother maintained in Rosalie that early perception of the wondrousness of her father. She loved her mother, but in the atmosphere surrounding her mother there was often flurry and worry and there was nothing whatever in her mother to mystify and entrance by sudden and violent eruptions of the miraculous. She did not love her father for he was entirely too remote and awe-ful for love, but he entranced her with his marvellousness. This maintained in her also her perception of the altogether greater superiority of all males over all females.

Rosalie came into her family rather like a new little girl first entering a boarding school. When she was about four, and first beginning to realise herself, the next in age to her was Robert, who not only was at the immense distance of ten, but was of the male sex and therefore had a controlling interest in the world. Then was Hilda who was twelve, then Flora fourteen, then Anna towering away in sixteen, and then Harold utterly removed in the enormous heights of eighteen, second only to Rosalie's father in ownership of the world and often awfully disputing that supreme ownership.

So they were all immeasurably older than Rosalie; and they were not only immeasurably older but, which counted for much more, they all had their fixed and recognised places in their world just as girls of several terms' experience have their recognised places in their school, and for Rosalie there seemed to be no place at all, just as for new girls there is no place. Her brothers and sisters all had their fixed and recognised places, their interests, their occupations, their friendships: they all knew their own places and each other's places; they had learnt to respect and admit each other's places; they knew the weight of one another's hand in those places; they were accustomed to one another; they tolerated one another.

It was all very strange and wonderful and mysterious to Rosalie.

She was, as it were, pitchforked into this established and regulated order and to find a place for her was like trying to fit a new spoke into a revolving wheel. It cannot be done; and with Rosalie it could not be done. The established wheel went on revolving in its established orbit and the new spoke, which was Rosalie, lay outside and watched it revolve. Intrusions within the circumference of the wheel commonly resulted in a sharp knock from one of the spokes. No one was in any degree unkind to Rosalie, but there was no proper place for her and everybody's will was in authority over her will. She rather got in the way. To be with her was not to enjoy her company or to enjoy battle with her and the putting of her company to flight. To be with her was to have to look after her; and in the community of the rectory every member, when Rosalie came, was fully occupied in looking after itself and defending itself from the predatory excursions of any other member.

What happened was that in time, just as a slight and negligible body cannot be in the sphere of a powerful motion without being affected by it, so Rosalie began to move sympathetically to the wheel but on her own axis. She moved round with the wheel but she was not of the wheel and she never became really incorporated with the wheel. The spokes were revolving with incredible rapidity when she first began to notice them and they always remained relatively faster. There she was, sitting and

watching and wondering; and the twig grows as it is
bent or as it is left to bend. She looked on and absorbed
things; and the first and by far the deepest of her settled
perceptions was that, though she was subject to all powers,
all girls and women were themselves subject to the power
of all boys and men.

Up to the age of eighteen, six years represents an
enormous gulf in the relative ages of brothers and sisters.
You have only to figure it out in the case of Rosalie to
realise how far behind she was always left, and why,
though one of a family of six, she occupied a position
outside the group and was a watcher of them rather than
a sharer with them. She was four when Robert the next
above her was ten, which is a baby against a sturdy and
well-developed giant; when she was eight Robert was
fourteen, which is a greater gulf than the first; when she
was twelve Robert was eighteen which, from eighteen's
point of view, is as the difference between an aged man
and an infant; and when she was sixteen Robert was
twenty-two, which is a schoolgirl against one of the oldest
and most experienced periods of life. She came in as a
new little girl in a big school; when she had been there
eight years — counting from four, when first she was
conscious of arrival — she was still relatively the same:
there she was, twelve, with Robert eighteen and the others
twenty, twenty-two, twenty-four and twenty-six.

But there she is at eight when she had had four years'
experience from the day of first seeing her father leaping
before the bull and thinking it was perfectly natural that
he should leap before the bull. She had learnt a tremendous lot in that second four years. She knew at eight
that the world did not belong to her father and that on
that night of the storm Flora was right to call her a fool
for believing that he could stop the storm. She knew he

was not nearly so wonderful as she used to think he was; but he was still enormously wonderful and, which she thought rather curious, she began to see that he rather liked showing her how wonderful he was. He could sharpen a pencil wonderfully, and he could eat a herring wonderfully. The thing discovered was that he was very proud of how wonderfully he could sharpen a pencil or eat a herring. Strange father!

" Who sharpened that pencil? Your mother? H'nf! I should think so! No woman can sharpen a pencil. Now look at me. Watch. I hold it in my left hand, see? Arm supported against my body. Now look how I cut at it. Bold, strong strokes, see? No niggling at it as if a mouse was nibbling it; long, bold sweeps, slashes. See? Look at that. Ah, drat! That's because I was holding it down for you to see. Watch again. There! There, that's the way to sharpen a pencil. Look at that. Do you see that long firm point? See how clean and long those strokes are? That's the way to sharpen a pencil. Show that to your mother."

He was as pleased with himself and as proud as if he had turned the pencil into gold.

Funny father!

Or how to eat a herring.

" Herrings! Well, a herring is one of the most delicious fish, if it's eaten properly. There's a right way to eat a herring and a wrong way. Now watch me and I'll show you how to eat a herring. Rosalie, watch."

" Rosalie, dear," (from her mother) " watch while your father shows you how to eat a herring."

All eyes on father demonstrating how to eat a herring!

And Rosalie used to notice this about the watching eyes. Her mother's eyes — most anxiously and nervously upon the operation, as if watching a thing she would soon be called upon to perform and would not be able to perform;

the eyes of Robert (14) sulkily; of Flora (18) admiringly (it was getting to be a complaint in the family circle that Flora "sucked up" to father); the eyes of Anna (20) wearily; the eyes of Harold (22) contemptuously.

The herrings (a very frequent dish at the rectory, so much cheaper than meat) came headless to the table. First father nipped off the tail with a firm, neat stroke. Then he deftly slit the herring down the stomach. It fell into two exact perfectly divided halves. Then he lifted out the backbone, not one scrap of flesh adhering to it, and laid it on the side of his plate. Then four firm pressures of his knife and the little lateral bones were exactly removed and exactly laid on the backbone. Next a precise insertion of his fork and out came the silvery strip known to Rosalie as "the swimming thing" and was laid in its turn upon the bones, exactly, neatly, as if it were a game of spillikins. "Now pepper. Plenty of pepper for the roe, you see. There. Now."

And in about six mouthfuls father's plate would be as clean as when it was brought in, decorated rather than marred by the exquisitely neat pile of the backbone, the tail, the little bones, and the silvery swimming thing. "There! Delicious! That's the way to eat a herring"; and he would direct a glance at the plate of Rosalie's mother. Rosalie's mother made a herring into the most frightful mess it was possible to imagine. She spent the whole of her time in removing bones from her mouth; and her plate, when she was half-way though, looked to contain the mangled remains of about two dozen herrings. "Very few women know how to eat a herring," Rosalie's father would say.

Wonderful father! How to sharpen a pencil, how to eat a herring, how to do up a parcel, how to undo a parcel, how to cut your finger nails, how to sit with regard to the light when you wrote or read, how to tie a knot, how to untie a knot. Clever father, natty father!

Yes, still enormously wonderful father; but also rather strangely proud of being wonderful father. Rosalie now was constantly being struck by that. It began to give her rather a funny sensation. She couldn't describe the sensation or interpret it, but it was a feeling, when father was glowing with pride over one of these things he did so wonderfully well — a feeling of being rather uncomfortable, shy, ashamed — something like that. She contracted the habit when father beamed and glowed and looked around for applause of giving a sudden little blink.

And it was the same in regard to Robert and the same in regard to Harold. Robert at the height of his exhibitions of his wonderfulness caused the funny feeling and the blink in her; and Harold at the height of his exhibitions of his wonderfulness caused the funny feeling and the blink in her. And the wonderfulness of Robert was always being shown off by Robert, and the wonderfulness of Harold was always being shown off by Harold. Men liked showing off how wonderful they were. . . .

When Rosalie was about nine she one day was permitted to have Lily Waters in to tea with her. Lily Waters was the Doctor's little girl, also nine. For a great treat they had tea together out of Rosalie's doll's tea service in the room called the schoolroom. Robert came home unusually early from school and came into the schoolroom and began to do wonderful things before the two little girls. He spoke in a very loud voice while he did them. He stood on a footstool on his head and clapped his boots together. He held his breath for seventy-five seconds by the clock. He took off his coat and made Lily and Rosalie tie a piece of string around his biceps and then he jerked up his arm and snapped the string. Wonderful Robert! Lily screamed with delight and clapped her hands, and the more she screamed and clapped, the louder Robert talked. He did still more wonderful things. He held a cork to the flame of a match and then blacked his nose and blacked a moustache with the cork. He did a most frightfully daring and dangerous thing. He produced the stump of a cigarette from his pocket and lit it and blew smoke through his nose. Wonderful Robert! Lily went into ecstasies of delight. Rosalie also went into ecstasies but also strongly experienced that funny feeling. While Robert held his breath till his eyes bulged and till his face was crimson, and while he danced about with his nose blacked, and while he held the cigarette in his fingers and puffed smoke through his nose — while he did these things Rosalie glanced at Lily (squealing) and felt that funny feeling of being rather shy, uncomfortable, ashamed; something like that; and blinked. Wonderful though Robert was, she felt somehow rather glad when at last he went.

And just the same with Harold. At supper one night, Rosalie's father not being present, Harold talked and talked and talked about a call he had paid at the house of some ladies in Ashborough. Wonderful Harold, to pay a call all by himself! It appeared that he had been the only man there, and when Rosalie's mother said, " I wonder you didn't feel shy, Harold," he said with a funny sort of " Haw " sound in his voice, " Not in the least. Haw! Why on earth should I feel shy? Haw." He had evidently very much entertained the party. The more he talked about it the more Rosalie noticed the funny " Haw." " They must have been very glad you came," Rosalie's mother said.

Harold put the first and second fingers of his right hand on his collar and gave it a pull up. " I rather — haw — think they were," Harold said. " Haw."

Rosalie gave that blink.

Years afterwards, when she was grown up, a grown man boastfully said something in her presence, and in a flash were recalled father dissecting a herring, Robert holding his breath till he nearly burst, Harold hitching up his collar and with the "haw" sound saying, "I rather think they were." In a flash those childhood scenes, and instantly with them interpretation of the funny feeling and the blink that they had caused: they had been the rooting in her of a new perception added to the impregnably rooted impression of the wonder and power of men, — the perception that men knew they were wonderful and powerful and liked to show off how wonderful and powerful they were.

They were superior creatures but they were apt to be rather make-you-blinky creatures; that was the new perception.

On the day after her eighth birthday, the birthday itself being a treat and a holiday, Rosalie began to do lessons with Hilda. Hilda, at sixteen, had " finished her education " as had Anna and Flora at the same age. Harold, who had been a boarder at a Grammar School, had stayed there till he was eighteen; and Robert, ultimately, continued at Helmsbury Grammar School till he was eighteen. It was apparent — and it was another manifestation of the greater importance of males — that boys had more education to finish, or were permitted longer to finish it, than girls.

The school at which Anna, Flora and Hilda thus in the eight years between leaving their mother's knee at eight and completing their education at sixteen, learnt everything it was possible to know, was kept by two very thin ladies called (ungrammatically) the Miss Pockets. The Miss Pockets were daughters of the former vicar of St. Mary's and inhabitant of the rectory, and on their father dying and Mr. Aubyn coming, they established themselves in a prim villa near-by and did what they called "took in pupils." They were very thin, they had very long thin noses, they were always very cold, and from the sharp end of the long thin nose of the elder Miss Pocket there always depended, much fascinating Rosalie, a shining bead of moisture.

Rosalie's chief recollection of the Miss Pockets was of being constantly met by them as she approached the age of eight, and of them always, on these occasions, fondling icy hands about her neck and saying to her father or her mother, " And when will our new little pupil be coming to us?"

But no direct reply was ever given to this question, either by Rosalie's mother, who was always made to look uncomfortable when it was asked by the Miss Pockets, or by Rosalie's father who always seemed to jut out his nose at it and make the Miss Pockets look thinner and colder than ever.

On the morning of her eighth birthday Rosalie received from the Miss Pockets by post an illuminated text provided with a piece of red cord for hanging on the wall and inquiring, rather abruptly,

Who Hath Believed Our Report?

Rosalie thought at first this was a plaintive question directly from the Miss Pockets in their capacity as school-teachers and therefore as licensed makers of reports; but immediately afterwards saw "Isaiah" printed under it in discreet characters —

Who Hath Believed our Report?
—Isaiah.

and concluded that it was Isaiah who had believed it. On the back was written in the tall, thin handwriting of the Miss Pockets, "To our dear little pupil Rosalie, on her eighth birthday, from Agnes and Lydia Pocket."

In the afternoon the Miss Pockets called at the rectory and there was evidently some high mystery about their visit. Rosalie was in the study looking for a drawing pin wherewith to affix her illuminated card to the wall. Hilda ran in. "The Miss Pockets. Where's father? Come out," and Rosalie was hurriedly run out and shut into the dining-room, leaving the vindication of Isaiah in the matter of the report on the table. Opening the door to a chink, Rosalie saw the Miss Pockets, shivering, the permanent decoration on the nose of the elder Miss Pocket very conspicuous and agitatedly swinging, ushered into the study, and presently her father follow his jutty nose into the study after them, and very shortly after that the Miss Pockets driven out as it were by the jutty nose and looking thinner and colder than ever before. Miss Lydia Pocket, who had lost the appendage to her nose and looked curiously undressed and indelicate without it, was saying feebly, "But it was *understood*. We always thought it was *understood*."

They shuddered away; and when Rosalie went into the study immediately afterwards to recover her card, there was upon the word Isaiah, as though somebody had literally thrown doubt upon his belief of the report, a large damp spot.

On the following day Rosalie began lessons with Hilda.

CHAPTER V

The lessons with Hilda period lasted till Rosalie was twelve. " Take her off your mother's hands. That's what you've left school for," was her father's instruction to Hilda; and so there was Rosalie, put out from her mother's knee to the schoolroom like a small new ship out from the haven to the bay; and there was that small mind of hers come in to the company of Hilda and of Flora and of Anna with the obsession that men were infinitely more important and much more wonderful than women. She knew now that the world did not belong to men in the literal sense, but belonged, as her mother had instructed her, to God; but she knew with the abundant evidence of all that went on about her that everything in the world was done for men and that women were largely occupied in doing it; and she knew, from the same testimony, that men were much more interesting to watch than women, rather in the way that dogs were much more interesting than cats. Men, like dogs, were much more *satisfactory:* that was it. Her mind was throwing out feelers towards the wonders of the world and this was the feeler that was most developed. She came to her sisters very highly sensitive to the difference between men and women. And her sisters showed her the difference.

Anna was twenty then. Anna had " finished her education " four years ago. She had left school " to help your mother in the house " ; and when Flora, two years later, finished her education and left school for the same purpose, she found Anna grooved in the business of helping her mother in the house and she was not in the least anxious to help Anna out of the grooves and herself become imbedded in them.

This annoyed Anna.

Rosalie used to hear Anna say to Flora a dozen times a day, " I really don't see why you should be the one to do nothing but amuse yourself all day long. I really don't."

Flora used to say, " Well, you've always done it " — whatever the duty in dispute might be — " so why on earth should I ? "

Then either Anna's face would give a twitch and she would walk out of the room, or her face would get very red and there would be a row.

Or sometimes Flora to Anna's " I really don't see why — " would say enticingly, " Don't you ? "

" No, I don't."

" Then ask the Pope," and Flora would give a mocking laugh and run away out of the reach of Anna's fury.

The sting in this was that Anna was suspected of having Roman Catholic tendencies.

Flora was very pretty and had a gay, bold way. Anna was not pretty. She had a great habit of compressing her lips, especially in encounters with Flora, and somehow her face gave the impression that her lips always were compressed. That was the expression it normally had; it was only when Rosalie saw Anna actually compress her lips that she realised they had not been compressed before. It was as though she was always annoyed about something and then, when she compressed her lips, a little more annoyed than usual. She had also a permanent affliction which much puzzled Rosalie. Young men friends of Harold's frequently called at the rectory, and one afternoon, when two of them called, Anna was the only one at home to entertain them (except Rosalie). Flora and Hilda rushed into the drawing-room directly they came in and shortly afterwards Rosalie saw Anna come out. Anna stood in the hall quite a long time with her lips compressed, and then went into the dining-room and sat down, but almost at once got up again and went back into the drawing-room, and Rosalie heard Flora call out, " You can't join in now, Anna. You can't join in now. We're in the middle of it." Shrieks of laughter were going on. When the young men went Flora and Hilda, who had their hats on, walked away with them. Anna was left at the door. When the girls came back Anna said to Flora, " I do think you might have told me you'd arranged to go with them to see it."

Flora said, " Oh, darling, I thought the Pope had told you."

They had the worst row Rosalie had ever heard them have. Anna did not come down to supper. After supper, when Rosalie was in the room with only Harold and her father and mother, her mother spoke of the scene there had been between Anna and Flora and it was then that Rosalie heard for the first time of Anna's most strange affliction. Harold said, " Of course, the fact of the matter is that ever since Flora left school, Anna's had her nose put out of joint."

Rosalie felt most awfully sorry for Anna. Often after that she used to stare at Anna's nose and the more so because there was nothing visible the matter with it. Anna's nose was a singularly long and straight nose; now if it had been Flora's nose that was out of joint! — for Flora's nose turned up in a very odd way. Rosalie slept in Anna's room and that same night, Anna's disjointed nose and every other part of her face and head being covered with the clothes when Rosalie went up to bed, Rosalie, unable to sleep for curiosity and sympathy,

got out of bed and lit the candle and went across to look
at Anna's nose, and very gently felt it with her finger.
Absolutely nothing amiss to be seen or felt! But the
lashes of Anna's eyes were wet and there were stains of
tears upon the upper side of the mysterious nose. It was
true, then, for obviously it hurt. And yet no sign!

Rosalie got back into bed feeling of her own nose
rather anxiously.

Rosalie used formerly to sleep in Hilda's room and
Flora with Anna, but she was changed one day by her
sisters (without being consulted or given any reason)
and the new arrangement was continued. Anna was
very devotional. She used to say enormously long
prayers night and morning. She prayed in the middle
of the night also, Rosalie used to think at first, awakened
and hearing her voice, but later found out that Anna
was talking in her sleep, a thing that was mysterious to
Rosalie and frightening. The room of Flora and Hilda,
adjoined Anna's and often at night, when Rosalie was
awakened by Anna undressing and lay watching her at
her immense prayers, the chattering voices of Flora and
Hilda could be heard through the wall and shrieks of
high laughter. At that Anna's shoulders used to shudder
beneath her nightgown and she used to twist herself
lower on her knees. For some reason this also used
rather to frighten Rosalie.

Sometimes, but very seldom, Flora and Hilda used to
quarrel; sometimes, and more often, Hilda and Anna;
nearly every day, as it seemed to Rosalie, Anna and
Flora. Rosalie got to dislike these quarrels very much.
They went on and on and on; that was the disturbing
unpleasantness of them. The parties to them would sit
in a room and simply keep it up forever, not arguing all
the time, but between long pauses suddenly coming out
with things at one another; or they wouldn't speak to

one another sometimes for days together, and all sorts of small enterprises of Rosalie's were interfered with by these ruptures of relations. Innumerable things in Rosalie's life seemed to her to depend on the mutual good will of two quarrellers; many books, some old toys, walks, combined games with Carlo who was Anna's and Rover who was Flora's; innumerable delights with such seemed to be unexpectedly stopped because of " Oh, no, if you prefer to be with Anna you can stay with Anna "; or, " Oh, no. If you like Flora's paints so much you can use Flora's brushes; these are my brushes." A quarrel would in any case produce a strained atmosphere in which everything became unnatural and this strained atmosphere went on and on and on.

And the thing that Rosalie noticed was the complete difference between these quarrels of her sisters and the quarrels between Harold and Robert. Robert was rising between the years of fourteen and eighteen in those days and Harold between twenty-two and twenty-six. Most violent quarrels sometimes sprung up between them but they were physically violent, that was the point, and after swift and appalling fury, and terrible kicks from Robert and horrifying thumps from Harold they were astonishingly soon over and done with and forgotten. On one awful day Rosalie saw Robert and Harold rolling on the floor together. Robert bumped Harold's head three most frightful bumps on the floor and said between his teeth, " There! There! There! " Harold twisted himself up and hurled Robert half across the room and then rushed at him and punched him with punches that made Robert go, " Ur! Ur! Ur! "

Rosalie, at her age, ought to have cried with grief and dismay or to have run away screaming; but instead she only watched with awe. With terrified awe, as with the terrified awe that an encounter of tigers or of elephants at the Zoo might arouse; but with awe and no sort of grief as her sole emotion. Men were different. There it was again! They did these fearful things, and these fearful things were much more satisfactory to behold, not nearly so disturbing and aggravating to watch, as the interminable bickerings of the quarrels of her sisters.

Her brothers' quarrels were entirely different in all their aspects. In the quarrels of her sisters one or the other invariably cried if the bickering went far enough. These two men, though Robert especially might have been excused for bellowing, just solidly and only, with fearful gasps, thumped and clutched and strove. Not a tear! Her sisters' quarrels were always carried by one or the other to her mother or her father. How extraordinarily different Robert and Harold! Their sole anxiety was that neither father nor mother should be told! If any one threatened to tell, the two, sinking their private heat, would immediately band together against the tale-bearer. Extraordinary men! To that particularly ferocious struggle that has been described Anna and Hilda had been attracted by the din, when Robert, overpowered, was receiving terrible chastisement, and with cries and prayers had somehow separated them. Behold, the very first coherent thing these two men did was, while they still panted and glared upon one another, to unite in a mutual threat.

" And look out you don't go telling father or mother," panted Harold to the girls.

" Yes, mind you jolly well don't," panted Robert.

Anna said she certainly would.

Both the extraordinary creatures unitedly rounded on Anna. It might have been thought that the battle had been, not between them, but between them and the sisters who had saved them one from another. Astounding men! And most astounding of all to Rosalie was that at supper, little more than an hour later, Harold and Robert presented themselves as on exceptionally good terms of friendship. They talked and laughed together. They had a long exchange of views about some football teams. Harold laid down the law about the principle of four three-quarters in Rugby football instead of three and Robert listened as to an oracle. They had not been so friendly for weeks. And an hour before — !

Yes, men *were* different.

And Rosalie found that her sisters, too, knew how different and how superior men were. Flora and Hilda seemed to Rosalie always to be talking about men. Flora used to come into the schoolroom while Rosalie was at her lessons and talk to Hilda. Rosalie was very fond of her lessons and Hilda was an uncommonly good teacher and took a great interest in leading Rosalie along the paths she had herself so recently followed. But directly Flora came in, Hilda's interest was entirely diverted to what Flora had to say and to what she had to say to Flora, and it was always about men, — boys or men. Rosalie would at once be put to learning passages or working out exercises and Flora and Hilda would go over to the window and talk. They talked mostly in whispers with their heads close together; they laughed a good deal; they showed one another letters. Often they came over to the table and wrote letters. And they used to look up from their whisperings and say, " Go on with your lessons, Rosalie."

But it was very difficult to go on while they whispered and laughed and it was also very troublesome to have Hilda's most interesting explanations suddenly cut short by the entrance of Flora. Rosalie began to have the habit of saying " Oh, dear ! " and going " Tchk ! " with her tongue when Flora came in. Also restlessly to say

" Oh, dear ! " and go " Tchk ! " when the whisperings and the laughing about men went on and distracted her attention while she tried to do her exercises.

A new aspect of men began to grow out of this. Rosalie began to feel rather aggrieved against boys and men. They *interfered*.

And this went further. Just as boys and men spoilt lessons so they began to spoil walks. While Hilda attended the Miss Pockets' school and Rosalie was taught by her mother, it was always her mother with whom Rosalie took walks. Anna " never cared to go out " and Flora, whose position in the house was more like that of Harold and Robert, did much as she liked, and " dragging Rosalie about for walks " as she expressed it, was not one of the things she liked. Rosalie therefore went out with her mother until Hilda took her off her mother's hands, when the taking off included not only education but exercise. At the beginning Hilda showed herself as enthusiastic and as entertaining a walker as she was teacher. She was ready for jolly scrambles through woods and over fields, she was as keen as Rosalie on damming little watercourses, and exploring woodland tracts, and other similar delights, and she had a most splendid knowledge of the names of plants and flowers and birds and insects and delighted to tell them to Rosalie. Rosalie had loved the walks with her mother, always holding her dear hand, but she loved much more, though in a different way, the walks with Hilda.

Then men began, in Rosalie's private phrase, to " ruin " the walks.

First Flora took to joining the walks and she and Hilda talked and talked together and always, as it seemed, about men, and Rosalie just trailed along with them, their heads miles above hers and their conversation equally out of her reach. But even that was not so bad as it became. At least there were only her sisters and sometimes they did talk to her, or sometimes one or other would break off from their chatter and cry "Oh, poor Rosalie! We've not been taking the least notice of you, have we? Now, what would you like to do?" And perhaps they would run races, or perhaps explore, or perhaps tell her a story, and Rosalie's spirits would come bursting out from their dulness and all would be splendid.

Not so when on the walks men, from being talked of, began to be met.

There were at Robert's Grammar School certain young men who were in no way connected with the school but were the "private pupils" of the headmaster and were reading for the universities. One day Hilda started for the walk in her church hat and Flora also in her church hat and her church gloves. They walked very fast; Rosalie could hardly keep up. And then at a corner of a lane they suddenly started to walk very slowly indeed, and suddenly again at a stile two of these young men were met.

The young men raised their hats much farther than Rosalie had ever seen a man raise his hat and one of them said, "Well, you *have* come then?"

Flora said, "Well, we just happened to be strolling along this way." Then she said, "You needn't imagine we came to see you!" which Rosalie thought very rude; but the young men seemed to like it and all of them laughed a great deal.

Presently they all started to walk together, Hilda and Flora in the middle and one of the young men on either side. The walk lasted much later than the walks usually lasted and the whole way Rosalie trailed along behind; and on the whole afternoon the only words addressed to Rosalie by her sisters came just as, the young men having taken their leave a mile away, they were turning in at the rectory gate. Flora then said, " Rosalie, darling, don't tell mother or father or any one that we met any one." And Hilda said, " Yes, remember, Rosalie, you're not to say anything about that."

After that the young men were met, and the four walked, and Rosalie trailed, nearly every day.

One of these young men was called Mr. Chalton and the other Mr. Ricks. Like all men, and even more so, they were splendid and wonderful. They had silver cigarette cases and smoked a lot, and they wore most handsome waistcoats and ties, and some of their conversation that came back to Rosalie, trailing behind, was of very wonderful and exciting things they had done or were going to do. Mr. Holland, the headmaster of the Grammar School, was the terror of Robert's life, but it appeared that Mr. Chalton and Mr. Ricks were not in the least afraid of Mr. Holland, and they talked a great deal of what they would do to him if he ever tried to interfere with them and a great deal of what they did do in the way of utterly disregarding him. They were undeniably splendid and wonderful, but they utterly ruined Rosalie's walks and they greatly intensified Rosalie's new feelings towards men and boys, — that men and boys were a great nuisance and spoilt things.

Time went along. Other young men were met. In the holidays quite a number of young men came for their vacations to their homes in Ibbotsfield and the surrounding district. Certain of these, unlike the Grammar School private pupils, called openly at the rectory on one pretext or another, but they were nevertheless also met secretly by Flora and Hilda, ruined the walks precisely as Messrs. Chalton and Ricks had first ruined them, and were on no account to be mentioned by Rosalie to her father or mother.

The reason for this secrecy was never explained to Rosalie and the secrecy oppressed Rosalie. It took not only the form of being a thing she was not able to tell to her mother, and Rosalie was in the habit of telling everything she did to her mother, but it took also the form of mysterious and vaguely alarming perils during the walks. An immense watchfulness was kept up against chance encounters with people. One of the party would often cry, " Look! Who's this? " and the young men would separate from the girls and appear as if they were walking by themselves. Sometimes they would break right away and run off and not be met again. Very often Rosalie would be sent on ahead to a turning and told to come back at once if anybody was to be seen and then would be examined as to who the person was. Sometimes she was posted to keep watch while the girls and the young men slipped off somewhere, over a gate or into a barn. She got to know by sometimes rushing in with warnings that Flora and Hilda on these occasions smoked the young men's cigarettes. Then when they got home they would rush up to their room and wash their teeth and put scent on themselves. And invariably when the young men took their leave at the end of a walk there would be long and close whisperings in which were always to be heard the words, " Well, say you were — "; or " Look here, we'll say we were — " and generally, " Go away, Rosalie. There's nothing for you to listen to."

It all had the effect of making Rosalie feel unhappy and rather frightened. She sometimes asked, " Why mustn't I say anything to mother? " She was always told, and only told, " Because father doesn't like us meeting men."

No reason why father should not like them meeting men was ever given, and Rosalie, ceaselessly disturbed by the concealment, could never imagine what the reason could be. There could be no reason that she could imagine; and she was thus immensely taken aback when one evening at supper her father made a most surprising statement: " The girls have no chance of ever meeting men in this infernal place."

Amazing!

Rosalie's father had been abusing Ibbotsfield and everything that pertained to Ibbotsfield. Some question of expenses had started him. He was storming in his wild way, addressing himself to Rosalie's mother but haranguing at large to all, everybody sitting in silence and with oppressed faces, avoiding looking at one another and avoiding especially the eyes of father. They were literally ground down with poverty, Rosalie's father was saying. He didn't know what was going to happen to them all. " It's all this place, this infernal, buried-alive place. The girls ought to be moving about and seeing people. How can they? Very well. My mind's made up. There's my brother Tom in India. He could have one of the girls. There's your sister Mrs. Pounce in London. She's Rosalie's godmother. What's she ever done for Rosalie? Very well. My mind's made up. I shall write to Tom and I shall write to Belle. I shall tell them how we are situated. It's humiliating to have to tell them but what's humiliation? I'm accustomed to humiliation. Ever since we came here I have eaten the bread and drunk the water of humiliation. Now the children are growing up to share it. What can they do in this loathsome and forsaken and miserable place? What chance have the girls got? Can you tell me that? "

He glared at Rosalie's mother. It was clear that he regarded her as to blame. Rosalie thought that her dear mother must be to blame. Her mother looked so beaten and frightened. There was glistening in her eyes. Rosalie's heart felt utterly desolated for her mother. She wished like anything she could say something for her dear mother. Then most amazingly the chance to say something came.

" Can you tell me that? " cried Rosalie's father. " What chance have the girls of ever meeting men in this infernal place? "

Rosalie burst out, " Oh, but father, nearly every day — "

" Rosalie, don't interrupt! " cried Flora very sharply.

" Rosalie, be quiet! " cried Hilda.

Father glared and then went on and on.

It was the beginning of a chain of most startling upheavals. It was also, and the upheavals were also, a new manifestation to Rosalie of the all-importance of men. After supper, in the first place, Flora and Hilda, taking Rosalie very severely to task for her perilous outburst, explained to her that the men they met were not the kind of men that father meant they ought to meet. It was necessary, it was essential, they explained, for every girl to meet men she could marry. That was what every girl had to do. Men — surely you understand that, Rosalie — had all the money and everything and met girls and asked them to marry. Those men sometimes met on walks, you little stupid, were too young and had no money yet. " There, that's enough," they explained. " Anyhow, we shan't be meeting them much more. One of us is probably going to India; you heard what father said, didn't you? . . . Well, of course you can't understand properly. You will when you're grown up. Surely that's quite enough for you to understand at present. . . . How can a woman live if she doesn't marry, stupid? She must have money to live and it is men who have the money. . . . Well, of course they do because they earn it; look at Harold; and Robert will have money when he's a little older. . . . Well, how *can* women? Now, I said that's enough and it is enough."

It was enough and most satisfactorily enough for one purpose. It was the first explanation of men as a race apart from women that Rosalie had ever received and it precisely bore out all that she had conceived about them. It affirmed her perception of the wonder and greatness of men as compared with women. It intensified that perception.

Wonderful men! Marvellous and most fortunate men!

And then the chain of most startling upheavals began. Father wrote to Uncle Tom in India. Father wrote to Aunt Belle, Mrs. Pyke Pounce, in London. What he wrote was not to be known by Rosalie, outside the rectory wheel. The others knew, for father, with enormous pride at his wonderful epistolary style in his voice, was heard reading the letter to them. But the others, of course, knew also what Rosalie never realised, the grinding poverty of the rectory. She knew no other life than the herrings, the makeshifts, and the general shabbiness of the rectory. It was not till long afterwards that, looking back, she realised the pinching and the screwing that served — almost — to make ends meet.

So father wrote. India was far, London was near. Aunt Belle's reply came while the letter to Uncle Tom was still upon the sea. Such a reply! Wonderful father to win such a reply from Aunt Belle! "You see what it is to be able to write a telling and forceful letter!" cried father. Such an exciting reply! Aunt Belle was coming on a visit " to talk it over and see what she could do."

Aunt Belle came.

Oh, a red carpet, a red carpet for Aunt Belle, Mrs. Pyke Pounce, to come into the story! And if at the end of the red carpet there could be an "At Home" in the splendid drawing-room of Aunt Belle, Mrs. Pyke Pounce, at Pilchester Square, Notting Hill, an At Home with about sixty-five ladies crammed into it, all of them wives of most successful and well-off men, mostly retired from the Indian Army and the Indian Civil Service, and all of them chattering ecstatically, and nibbling, and pluming themselves, and tinkling their teacups, and Aunt Belle, Mrs. Pyke Pounce, enthroned in their midst, and owning everything and seeming to own her five and sixty guests, and chattering and nibbling and pluming and tinkling more ecstatically than any; and then if there could come into them beautiful cousin Laetitia (when about fifteen) with sleek black hair beautifully ribboned behind, and with pale, fine brow, and wearing the sweetest white frock, and if she could move delightfully about among her mother's guests, and then play the sweetest little trifle on the pianoforte to the delighted murmurs of the five and sixty guests of her mother ("She's under Pflunk. The great Pflunk!"); and then if there could come in from the City Uncle Pyke, Colonel Pyke Pounce, R.E., (retired) now director of several highly important companies, and if Uncle Pyke, Colonel Pyke Pounce, R.E., could stand on the hearthrug with his massy jowl and his determined stomach, and grunt, and rattle the money in his pockets, and grunt again; and if then there could come in the new parlour maid of Aunt Belle, Mrs. Pyke Pounce, with her tallness and her deftness and her slight, very slight, insolence of air, and all the five and sixty gazing upon her as haughty but envious patricians gazing upon a slave, and when she had gone swishing out if Aunt Belle, Mrs. Pyke Pounce, could tell all the sixty and five of her tallness, her deftness and her slight, very slight, insolence of manner ——

Oh, if there could be this and these and a fine red carpet, how exactly and how fittingly would Aunt Belle, Mrs. Pyke Pounce, step upon the scene!

" Dear thing ! " That was Rosalie's portrait and thought of her in long after years. Dear thing! The drawing-room of her crowded triumphs is now the shabby drawing-room of a second-rate boarding house; the jolly horse bus she used so commandingly to stop in the Holland Park Avenue and so regally to enter (whip-waving driver, cap-touching conductor) long has given place to a thundering motor saloon that stops whosoever it listeth and wherein Aunt Belles and old-clothes women fight to hang by a strap.

Dear thing! Her ownership of five and sixty guests is exchanged for ownership of not more than seven and fifty inches of cold earth in Brompton Cemetery. She is passed and Uncle Pyke, Colonel Pyke Pounce, R.E., is grunted past to lay himself beside her. They are passed. Upreared upon her and upon him is a stupendous granite chunk (in a way not unlike Uncle Pyke on his hearth-rug) erected by their sorrowing daughter. She is passed; she came into Rosalie's life and Rosalie crossed her life and she never forgave Rosalie.

Dear thing! Lie lightly on her, stones!

She came to the rectory " to talk it over and see what can be done " for a week's visit, and she stepped out of the cab, all the family assembled to greet her, a new and most surprising figure such as Rosalie had never seen before. She was dressed in startling fashions of a most wonderful richness, and she had immense plumes in her hat that nodded when she moved and trembled when she stood still, and she was herself either always nodding with glittering animation or straightening her back and quivering as if straining at a leash and just about to burst it and go off. She was like Rosalie's mother and yet not a bit like her. She was older and yet terribly brisker and stronger. Those were the days when frosted Christmas cards were of the artistic marvels of the age, and Aunt Belle beside Rosalie's mother somehow made Rosalie think of a frosted card beside one of the plain cards. When Rosalie's mother was in a room you often might not know she was there; but when Aunt Belle was in a room there seemed to be no one there except Aunt Belle. She began to talk, in a voice as high as the house, while she was still descending from the cab on her arrival, and the only time Rosalie ever saw her not talking was during service in Church on Sunday, when she was alternately glittering or whispering or else bending down so extraordinarily low that Rosalie thought she was going to lie prone upon the floor.

Dear thing! She was so kind to Rosalie and so kind to them all, and yet —— And yet they all, except Rosalie who was too small (then) to appreciate the resented quality in Aunt Belle's kindness, and Rosalie's mother who was too gentle to resent anything, and yet they all, save Rosalie and her mother, loathed and abominated Aunt Belle. It was her way of doing things. She gave kind gifts, but it was the way she gave them. She admired everything and everybody in the rectory, but it was the way she admired. She said most kind and affectionate things, but it was her way of saying them.

"Why, how very nice indeed!" That was her insistent comment upon everything in the rectory. But the tone was, "How very nice indeed—for *you*."

That was the trouble. That was what made Harold (who at twenty-six was getting very like his father) hurl about a thousand miles over the garden wall the three apples Aunt Belle gave him as his share of the "very best apples from the Army and Navy Stores" which she brought down with other "goodies" for "the dear children"; and made him grit his teeth after she had been in the house two days and cry, "Dash her! Poor relations; that's how she treats us! I'm dashed if I'm a poor relation. I'm earning three pound ten a week at the Bank and I bet that appalling old Uncle Pyke didn't get it or anything like it at my age!"

Dear thing! "She meant it kindly." That was the sweet apologetic excuse with which Rosalie's mother followed the track of the storms Aunt Belle aroused and with which she sought to abate them. "She means it kindly. She means it kindly, dear."

It should be Aunt Belle's epitaph. It ought to be graven upon that granite chunk in Brompton Cemetery. "She meant it kindly!"

Issuing from the cab, Aunt Belle began by kissing Rosalie's mother in a most astonishing series of kisses that whizzed from cheek to cheek so that it was a miracle to Rosalie that the two noses did not collide and her dear mother's be knocked right off; and then most enthusiastically kissed all the family, applying to each the phrase with which she began on Harold "Well, well, so this is Harold!" (As if it were the most astounding and unexpected thing in the world that it was Harold.) "So this is Harold! Why, what a great big clever fellow, and what a comfort to your dear mother, I am sure!" And then gazed rapturously upon the house and said to

Rosalie's mother and to them all, " Well, well, what a very, very nice house, to be sure!"

("For *you!*")

She meant it kindly. Her manner of talking about herself and about her possessions was not that of bragging or of conscious superiority; it was, to the whole rectory family, and to all poorer than herself wherever she met them, that of one entertaining a party of children — of a kind lady telling stories to a group of round-eyed infants. When she first had tea on the afternoon of her arrival she gazed upon the silver teapot as it was carried in and exclaimed, " Well, well, what a very, very handsome teapot! And hot-water jug to match! How very, very nice! Now how ever do you think I keep *my* water hot at tea? I have a very nice service all in silver gilt! It looks just like gold! And there's a kettle to match with a spirit flame under it. The maid brings in the kettle boiling and we just light the spirit with a match and there it is gently boiling all the time!"

Dusk drew in and the lamps were lit. "Lamps!" ecstatically exclaimed Aunt Belle! "*How* nice! And Hilda keeps the lamps clean, does she? What a dear, helpful girl and how very, very bright and nice they are! Now what do you think? In my house, everywhere, even in the kitchen, we've got this new electric light! Your kind uncle Pyke had it put in for me. *Installed,* as they call it. Now, just fancy, all you have is a little brass knob by each door, and you just touch a little switch, and there's your light! No matches, no trouble, just click! and there you are. Of course it was very expensive, but your Uncle Pyke insisted upon my having it. He always will insist upon my having everything of the best."

Dear thing! The echo of her ceaseless tongue brings her exactly to life again — glittering, chattering, pluming, presenting, praising — her servants! her house! her parties! her friends! her daughter! her husband! — Oh, yes, a red carpet! a red carpet for Aunt Belle, Mrs. Pyke Pounce, to come into the story, and so (at the end of her visit) into Rosalie's life like this:

" And Rosalie is going away to school! To a boarding school in London where there will be ever so many very nice playmates of her own age, and such romps, and such good wholesome food, and such nice, kind, clever mistresses! Why, what a lucky, lucky girl! There, Rosalie, what do you think of that? You are my godchild, and I and your kind uncle Pyke are going to send you to school and pay for your education because of course we are well off and can afford it and your dear mother and father can't. There! Now isn't that delightful? Come and give me a nice kiss then. The dear child! "

Tremendous moment! Supernal upheaval! First and greatest upheaval of the chain of upheavals! Rosalie was to go away to school!

That was at the rectory breakfast table on the last morning of the visit, and that was Aunt Belle, Mrs. Pyke Pounce, coming into Rosalie's life. " Come and give me a kiss then "; that was kind, kind Aunt Belle, inviting acknowledgment of her kindness and the kindness of Uncle Pyke (with a cheque) and the kindness of Cousin Laetitia (with a box of beautiful cast-off clothes that would do beautifully for Rosalie's school outfit). " The dear child! " That was Aunt Belle's acknowledgment of Rosalie's most dutiful and most affectionate and most delighted kiss. (Most amazed and excited and rather fearful Rosalie! Going to school! Going away to a boarding school in London!)

" The dear child!" Such a warm and loving kiss from Rosalie! And time was to prove it the kiss of Judas! Yes, in a few years, " I've done everything for you!" Aunt Belle was to cry. " Everything! And this is the return I get! "

CHAPTER VII

NEXT, in its turn, and exactly a fortnight before the beginning of the term at which Rosalie was to join the boarding school in London, came the letter from Uncle Tom in India, and with it the beginning of the second upheaval in the chain of upheavals.

All of this upheaval was very bewildering to Rosalie. She never understood it properly. At the beginning it had nothing at all to do with Anna, and yet Anna from the very first reading of Uncle Tom's letter — All that Rosalie understood of it was this.

First the letter came. Tremendous excitement! Father in wild excitement, Flora and Hilda in frantic excitement, every one in highest excitement. Father read the letter aloud at breakfast to Rosalie's mother and to the girls. Such a splendid letter, said father. Really, Tom was a splendid fellow, said father. He had wronged Tom. He had thought Tom selfish in his wealthy indifference. By Jove, Tom wasn't. "By Jove, the way Tom wrote almost brought tears to your eyes. Listen to this. Listen, mother. Listen, you girls."

Uncle Tom, said the letter, would by all means, old man, have one of the girls. He'd no idea that things were so bad with you. Poor old man! Why didn't you tell us before? He was sending home a small draft to Field and Company, his bankers, to help towards the girl's outfit and her passage money. " ' Which girl shall you send? ' you ask. Well, it's no good asking us, old man. You must decide that for yourselves. She'll be abundantly welcome, whichever it is, and we can promise

her a jolly good time. We are at Simla most of the year.
If you want my advice which girl to send, send the
pretti — "

Father stopped reading.

Rosalie was staring at Anna. Anna's face, which
had been pale, suddenly went crimson. The suddenness
and the violence of it was extraordinary. One moment
she had been pale. In the next she was burning red.
It was exactly as if a crimson paint had suddenly been
dashed over the whole of her face. It was extraordinary. Whatever was it? That nose of hers, perhaps?
a sudden frightful twinge like Rosalie once had had a
sudden most awful jump in a tooth? But Anna didn't
say anything and no one but Rosalie seemed to notice it.
They were all intent upon father. So intent! Flora's
eyes were simply shining!

And Flora's eyes soon after that were shining more
than ever. She was wild with excitement. Rosalie
heard the news just before tea. Flora was going to India
to Uncle Tom!

" Oh," cried Flora, " I'm so excited I simply don't
know what to do with myself! " It was all arranged.
Father had settled it. She was to go in about six weeks'
time. Very shortly she was to go up to London with
father and buy heaps of clothes and all sorts of things.
They were going to stay at a hotel. " Not with Aunt
Belle, thank goodness! " said Flora. " At a hotel! Fancy
that! " Mother wasn't going and Flora was glad
mother wasn't going. She would have a much better
time with father. Father had decided everything. He
had decided that mother couldn't leave him in the rectory
with all the housekeeping to look after, and the change
would do him good, and Aunt Belle would be able to
help with the shopping. They were going to see some
theatres and all kinds of things and were going to have

a most splendid time and then, soon afterwards — India!
" Oh, I shall go mad with excitement in a minute! " cried
Flora.

The next thing was in the evening. Rosalie, searching
for her mother to ask her something, could not find her.
She went into her mother's bedroom and there was the
most surprising thing. There was Anna on her knees by
her mother and her head on her mother's lap and Anna
was sobbing; and she was crying in her sobs, " But it's
my right! I'm the eldest. It's my right! "

Rosalie stood there, unnoticed, amazed. Whatever
was it?

Rosalie's mother stroked Anna's head and spoke very
softly, " My darling! My darling! " She said, " My
darling, your father has decided. Your father knows
best. Men always know best, my darling."

" It's my right, mother. It's my right. It's always
Flora. Oh, why should it always be Flora? "

" Dear Anna. Poor Anna. You must be reasonable,
dear Anna. We women must always be reasonable.
Don't you see that your father thinks of me? He thinks
my eldest girl — my dear eldest girl — ought to stay at
home to look after her mother. It's on my account, dear
Anna. He thinks of me."

" Oh, mother, what's the good of telling me that? A
lot he thinks of you or ever has! Why is he going up
to London with Flora when it's your place to go? A lot
he thinks of you! You say we must be reasonable. You
can be. You've been unselfish all your life. I can't be.
Not in this. I've never had a pleasure in my life; I've
never had a chance; I've never had anything done for
me. Ever since I can remember it's always been Flora,
Flora, Flora. Now there's this. I'm getting on, mother.
I'm nearly twenty-four. What have I got to look forward to? Flora's younger, Flora's different. She'll

have lots of chances of enjoying herself. This is my right. It's my right, mother."

" My dear Anna. My eldest girl. My first dear, sweet girlie. How could I do without you? How happy we've been. How happy we will be."

Rosalie crept away.

After a time Flora and her father went away on the great visit to London. They were to be away over two Sundays. A clergyman was coming from Ashborough to take service at the church. Rosalie's father went off in spirits as high and youthful as the spirits of Flora. For days before he was quite a different man. Everybody was asked to choose a present which he would bring back. Everybody chose with much excitement and chaffing except Anna, who said she could not think of anything. At meals father kept on saying how he wished he could regularly make a point of getting up to town for a bit, it made all the difference being able to get away from this infernal place for a bit. When herrings were on the table he actually came round and did her herring for Rosalie's mother and Rosalie's mother was able to eat the whole of it and said how delicious it was and how clever father was.

It was all splendid. Rosalie had never known such a jolly spirit in the house. The only thing that spoilt Rosalie's happiness in the new jolly spirit was the nights in Anna's room. Anna was most frightening to Rosalie. She prayed now longer than ever, her shoulders moving beneath her nightgown as if she was shuddering all the time she prayed. And at night she talked more than ever in her sleep; also she used to get out of bed at night and walk about the room and talk aloud to herself. It was frightening.

Then Flora and father were in London and tremendous long letters came from Flora to her mother and to

Hilda — all they were buying, heaps of dresses and underclothes and white drill coats and skirts and a riding habit and goodness knows what all. "A regular trousseau!" wrote Flora with about seventeen marks of exclamation after the word. And all they were seeing — they had been to the Lyceum Theatre and seen Mr. Henry Irving and Miss Ellen Terry and to the Savoy and seen "The Mikado." Every moment of the day was taken up and half the night. Oh, this was a change from Ibbotsfield!

Anna would never listen to the letters. When they were read out she either would put her fingers in her ears or go out of the room. And yet, curiously, she often later in the day would say in a funny constricted voice, "Let me see Flora's letter. Give it to me, will you please?" And would take it away and read it by herself.

Anna was stranger and stranger in her manner and in her behaviour at night. Rosalie came quite to dread the nights. Anna began to pray out loud. She used to pray over and over again the same thing: "It's not that I'm jealous, O Lord. O purge my heart of jealousy. It is that I see what could be and what ought to be for me and what never will be for me. I've nothing to look forward to, nothing, nothing, nothing, nothing. It *is* hard for women. O God, thou knowest how hard it is for women."

It *was* frightening.

Then came the second Sunday of the absence in London. In the night of Saturday Rosalie was again awakened by the sounds of Anna and again heard her praying and again heard "It *is* hard for women. O God, thou knowest how hard it is for women."

She had heard it so often! Anna seemed to have stopped praying. There was a light in the room and Rosalie saw that Anna, on her knees, had her head and

arms thrown forward on the bed more as if she were
asleep than praying. " It *is* hard for women." Rosalie
had heard Anna say that so often. And she was going
to be a woman one day. And she had always known that
men were the important and wonderful people of the
world. Now Anna said that for women it was hard and
that God knew it was hard. Why? She peered across
again. Anna certainly had done her prayers. She said,
" Anna. Anna. Why is it hard for women?"

Anna started to her knees and turned her body round.
" Rosalie! Why are you awake? You've no right to be
awake."

" No, but I am. I woke up. Anna, why is it hard for
women?"

" You weren't meant to hear. You couldn't understand."

" But I would like to know, Anna."

Anna got up and came across to Rosalie's bed; and by
her manner, and by her voice, and by the tall white figure
she was, frightened Rosalie. She said, " Go to sleep.
You can sleep. Why don't you when you can? One day
perhaps you'll be like me and can't."

It reminded Rosalie of " Sleep on now and take your
rest " in the Bible, and frightened her. Anna said, " It's
hard for women because men can do what they like but
women can't." She turned away. She stood still and
said with her back to Rosalie, "I've got a longing *here*."
Her hands were clasped and she brought them up and
struck them against her breast with a thud. " And I always have had and I always will have. *Here*. Burning.
Aching. And when you've got a longing like that you
must — you must — " Then she said very violently, " I
hate men. I hate them. I hate them." Then she went
very quickly to the candlestick on the dressing table and

fumbled with it to blow it out, and it fell on the ground and broke and the room was black.

The next day was Sunday. Anna said she would not go to Church as she had a headache. Rosalie had been invited to spend the day with the little girl of Colonel and Mrs. Measures and she had lunch and tea there and then came home. The path from the gate to the house was bounded by a thick hedge. On the right was the rectory paddock and through the hedge Rosalie saw that something very strange was going on in the paddock. Away in the corner where there was a little copse with a pond in the middle was a crowd of people, some men from the village and her mother and Robert and some others. Whatever was it? While she peered Harold came running out of the group towards the house. His coat was off, and his waistcoat; and his shirt and trousers looked funny and he ran funnily. He came near Rosalie and she saw that he was dripping wet. Had he fallen in the pond? Then two men came round from the back of the house carrying something, and Harold ran to them and they all ran with the thing to the pond. It looked like the door of the shed they were carrying. Rosalie scrambled through the hedge and ran towards the pond. Some one called out " Here's Rosalie." Hilda came out from among the people and waved her arms and called out, " Go back! Go back! You're not to come here, Rosalie! You're not to come here!" Rosalie stood still.

People were stooping. They had the door on the ground and Harold and a man were stooping and walking backwards over the door, carrying something. Presently there was more stooping, and then Harold and Robert and three men were carrying the door between them and walking as if the door were very heavy. Whatever was happening? Hilda came running to Rosalie.

She was crying. " Rosalie, you're to keep away. You're not to come into the house yet. I'll tell you when you can come. Go and stay in the garden till I tell you."

Rosalie wandered about by the drive. Whatever was the matter? Robert appeared with his bicycle. Harold came out after him. " Go to Ashborough station with it, you understand. See the station master. Tell him it must be sent off at once. Tell him what has happened." Robert was sniffling and nodding. Away went Robert, bending over the handle bar of his bicycle, riding furiously.

Evening began to come on. Rosalie was wandering at the back by the stables when Hilda came out through the kitchen door. " Rosalie, I've been looking for you. Rosalie, Anna is — dead."

They went in through the kitchen. On the big kitchen clothes rail before the fire were clothes of Anna's. They were muddy and sopping wet and steam was rising off them.

Rosalie ran to her mother to cry.

" Ran to her mother to cry." That's a thing not to pass over without a stop. Lucky, lucky Rosalie to have one to whom to take her grief! You can imagine her small heart's twistings by those days of sorrow, of terrifying and mysterious and dreadful things that the child never could clearly have understood; of grief, of mourning; of atmosphere most eerie made of whispers, of tiptoe treading, of shrouded windows, of conversations, as of conspirators, shut off with " Not in front of Rosalie." " Hush, not now. Here's Rosalie."

Yes, twisting stuff that; but in that " ran to her mother to cry " something that much more dreadfully twists the heart than those. Those were for Rosalie — they are for all — but frets upon the sands of time that each most kind expunging day, flowing from dawn to sunset like a tide, heals and obliterates. There are no common griefs, and death's a common grief, that can be drawn above that tide's highwater mark. But there's that sentence: "Rosalie ran to her mother to cry." That's of the aching voids of life, deep-seated like a cancer, that no tide reaches. That twists the heart to hear it because — O happy Rosalie! — the aching thing in life is *not* having where you can take your weariness. Your successes, your triumphs, there are a hundred eyes to shine with yours in those. Oh, it is the defeats you want where to tell — some one you can take the defeats to, the failures, the lost things; the lamps that are gone out, the hopes that are ashes, the springs that spring no more, the secret sordid things that eat you up, that hedge you all about, that draw you down. Those! To have some one to tell those to! Yes, there's a thought that comes with living: Let who may receive a man's triumphs; to whom a soul can take its defeats, that one has the imprint of Godhood. They walk near God.

Awfully frightening days followed for Rosalie. There wasn't a room that wasn't dark and frightening with all the blinds down, and wasn't a voice that wasn't dark and frightening, all in whispers; and then came this that closed them and that was like a finger pressed right down on Rosalie.

There was that Rosalie in the church at the funeral service. She sat at the inner end of the pew with Hilda beside her. The coffin had stood before the altar all night, with the lamps lit all night, and Rosalie believed her father had stayed with it all night. He was struck right down by what had happened, Rosalie's father. She had heard him, when Anna lay on the bed, and he crouched beside her, crying out loud, "I hated my lot! O God, I was blind to this my child that shared my lot!"

Well, there was that Rosalie in the pew beside Hilda, and while she waited for her father to begin (ever and ever so long he was upon his knees at the altar, his back to them) while she waited she turned back the leaves of her prayer book from the burial service and noticed with a curious interest the correctness of the order in which the special services came. There, in its order, was the complete record of life. Rosalie must have had an imagination and she must have had budding then what was a strong characteristic of her afterwards, — a very orderly mind. She appreciated the correctness of the order of the services and she turned them over one by one and could imagine it, like a story : that record of a life. First the service of Baptism; you were born and baptised. Then the Catechism; you were a child and learnt your catechism. Then the Order of Confirmation; you were getting older and were confirmed. Then the marriage service; you were married. Then the Order for the Visitation of the Sick; you were growing old and you were ill. Then the Burial Service; you died. Born, brought up, growing up, married, ill, dead. Yes, it was like a story. Rosalie turned on. The next service was called The Churching of Women. It was new to Rosalie. She had never noticed it before. " Forasmuch as it hath pleased Almighty God of His goodness to give you safe deliverance . . ." Rosalie had heard the word deliverance used in the Bible in connection with death. She thought this must be a service special to the burial of a woman — of Anna. She read the small print. " The woman at the usual time after her delivery shall come into the church decently apparelled. . . ." Decently apparelled? Anna was in one of those nightgowns in which Rosalie so often had seen her praying. ". . . and there shall kneel down in some convenient place." Kneel down? How *could* she? . . .

There came upon the book while Rosalie pondered it the long, black-gloved forefinger of Hilda. It turned back the thin leaves to the burial service and then pushed over one or two of the thin leaves and indicated certain places. Then Hilda's new black hat was touching her own new black hat, and Hilda whispered, " Where it says ' brother ' and ' his ' father will say ' sister ' and ' her.' It's written for men, do you see? "

Always for men! Even in the prayer book!

And it was because of men that Anna had drowned herself in the pond. Over and over again Rosalie had thought of that, wondering upon it, shuddering at the thought of men because of it. How she came to know that Anna had not died as ordinary people die, but had drowned herself in the pond she never could remember. No one told her. Rosalie was twelve then but the others were all so much older, and were so accustomed to treating Rosalie as so very much younger, that the pain and mystery of poor Anna's death was outstandingly of the class of things that were kept within the established wheel of the rectory by " Not in front of Rosalie," or " Hush, here's Rosalie."

The effect was that when Rosalie somehow found out, she felt it to be a guilty knowledge. She was not supposed to know and she felt she ought not to have known. And sharing, but secretly, the others' knowledge that Anna had drowned herself in the pond, she supposed that they equally shared with her her knowledge of why poor Anna had drowned herself in the pond — because of men. She overheard many conversations that assured her in this belief. " Some man we knew nothing about," the conversation used to say. " What else could it have been? Hush, here's Rosalie." And again, after they had all been out of the house to attend what was called the inquest, " You heard what the coroner said — that there was almost invariably something to do with a man in these cases. Poor Anna! Poor darling Anna. If she had only told us. What else could it have been? Harold, hush! Not in front of Rosalie!"

Of course it was nothing else. It was that. It was men. Anna had said so. "I hate men. I hate them." Yes, men had done this to Anna.

Her mind went violently, as it were with a violent clutch of both her hands, as of one in horrible dark clutching at means of light, to the thought that next week she was to be away at school — to be right away and in the safe middle of lots and lots of girls, and only girls. She had a frightening, a shuddering, at the thought of men who caused these terrible things to be done, who mysteriously and horribly somehow had done this thing to Anna.

The long, black finger poked at the page again. "There. 'This our brother.' Father will say 'This our sister.' Do you see, Rosalie? This our sister."

A shower of tears sprang out of Rosalie's eyes and pattered upon the page.

She wiped them. She set her teeth. A new and most awful concern possessed her. 'This our sister.' Would father remember? When he came to brother would he remember to say sister? And when 'his' would he remember to say 'her?' She searched for the places. A most frightful agitation seized her that father would forget. What would happen if he forgot?

And at the very first place father did forget!

They were come from the church to the grave. They were grouped about that most terrible and frightening pit. Rosalie was clutching her mother's dear hand, and in her other hand held her prayer book. There it was,

the first place for the change. Brokenly her father's
voice came out upon the air, and at his very first word —
the fatal word — Rosalie caught her breath in sharp and
agonized dismay.

" *Man* that is born of woman hath but a short time
to live and is full of misery. . . ."

She called out — she could not help it — " Father ! "
Her mother's hand, squeezing hers, restrained her.

The broken voice went on ". . . cometh up and is cut
down like a flower."

She heaved relief. No one had noticed it. It was
all right. No one else had heard the terrible mistake.
It was all right. But it was very wrong. Above all other
places this was the place that should have been changed.
Woman . . . that is full of misery. How could it ever
be Man? Anna, in almost her last words, had said it.
" It *is* hard for women "; and that God knew it was hard
for them — " O God, thou knowest how hard it is for
women."

In the next week she went away to school.

PART TWO

HOUSE OF WOMEN

CHAPTER I

WHAT anybody can have nobody wants; but what only one person can have there's a queue to get.

This is an elementary principle of the frailty of human nature, and knowledge of it, and experience of its mighty truth, used to cause, during the three holiday periods of the year, a standing advertisement to appear on the front page of the *Morning Post*.

"High-class Ladies' School for the Daughters of Gentlemen of the Professions has UNEXPECTED VACANCY for ONE ONLY pupil at reduced terms — Mrs. Impact, Oakwood House School, St. John's Wood, London.

ONE ONLY pupil! That was the magic touch.

The very first words addressed to Rosalie by a fellow boarder at Oakwood House were from a short, sharp-featured girl of her own age, which then was twelve, who said to her sharply, "You're a One Only. I can see you are. Aren't you a One Only?"

"Well, I'm by myself," said Rosalie, not understanding but most anxious to say the right thing.

"Stupid, you're not," said the sharp girl, "because I'm with you. Did your mother see the advertisement in the *Morning Post?* The advertisement of this school?"

It happened that Rosalie knew her mother had seen it for Aunt Belle had shown it to her and to them all. "One of the very best schools," Aunt Belle had said. "You see, it's only quite by chance there was a vacancy."

"Yes, she did," said Rosalie.

"She's the cat's grandmother," said the sharp girl.

" Never say ' she ' for a person's name. Well, if your
mother saw the advertisement then you are a One Only
at reduced terms, and I knew you were directly I saw
you. Now, tell me. Don't blink — unless of course
you're an idiot; all idiots blink. Tell me. Was that
dress made for you or was it cut down? "

" It was my cousin Laetitia's," said Rosalie.

" Of course it was," returned the sharp girl very triumphantly. " Every One Only's clothes are cut down
for her. Poopers! Do you know what a pooper is? A
pooper is half a poop and half a pauper. Every One
Only's a pooper. Well, now you know what *you* are.
You see that girl over there. Do you know what she is? "

Rosalie said she did not.

" She's a Red Indian."

" Is she? " said Rosalie, much surprised, for the girl
did not look in the least like a Red Indian.

" Ask her," said the sharp girl. " Do you know what
I am? "

Rosalie shook her head.

" Answer," said the sharp girl.

" No, I don't," said Rosalie.

" I'm a Sultan," said the sharp girl. " All the nice
girls are Sultans and the school belongs to them. Do I
look nice? "

" Very," said Rosalie, though she did not think so.

" Then why didn't you know I was a Sultan? The
school belongs to the Sultans. The One Onlys and the
Red Indians are interlopers, especially the One Onlys.
Always shudder when you see a Sultan. Shudder now."

Rosalie wriggled her shoulders.

" Again, poop."

Rosalie repeated the wriggle.

" Vanish, poop," said the sharp girl, and herself sprung
away with mysterious crouching bounds, her head thrust

forward, looking very like Gagool, the witch, in King Solomon's Mines; and was seen by Rosalie to pounce upon another small girl who was probably a One Only and, from her forlorn aspect, certainly a sad and desolated new.

One Onlys, Red Indians, Sultans. They were the three castes into which the girls divided themselves: One Onlys the poopers brought by the advertisement; Red Indians the daughters of parents resident in India; Sultans the proud creatures who paid full fees and took their title from the nickname of the headmistress—the Sultana. This Oakwood House School in which Rosalie now found herself was one of those very big old houses with a spacious, walled-in garden that probably was occupied in the Fifties somewhere, when St. John's Wood was out in the country, by a wealthy old City merchant who rode in to business two or three times a week, never dreaming that one day London was going to stretch miles beyond St. John's Wood, and his imposing residence go dropping down the scale of fashion eventually to become a school for young ladies who on their crocodile walks would huddle, giggling, along the kerbstone while the dangerous traffic roared up and down the Maida Vale highway.

Those crocodiles! There was a news agent's shop just opposite where the crocodile used to cross when it went out every morning, and one of the great excitements of the walk was to get around the corner and see what the newspaper bills had to tell. There were about forty girls at the school — a crocodile twenty files long — and on the days of sensational events the news from the placards used to come flashing back in emotional little screams from the head of the crocodile, gazing with goggling eyes, to the tail of the crocodile pressing deliriously up behind. " The Maybrick Case "; " Jack the Ripper

Again "; " Death of the Duke of Clarence "; "Loss of
H.M.S. Victoria "; Rosalie never afterwards could hear
those terrific things referred to without recalling instantly
the convulsions of the crocodile and experiencing within
her own bosom the tumults that contributed their share
to the convulsions.   She was in the writhing tail of the
crocodile when " Jack the Ripper Again " caused it almost
to swoon, and she was in its weeping head when " Death
of the Duke of Clarence " and " Loss of H.M.S. Victoria " struck its orderly coils into a tangled and hysterical
knot.

Mrs. Impact, who kept this school, was a massive and
frightening figure of doom who wore always upon her
head, and was suspected of sleeping in, a strange erec-
tion having the appearance of a straw beehive.   She was
called the Sultana and her appearance and her habits
seemed to Rosalie precisely the appearance and habits
that would belong to a sultana.   The Sultana appeared
virtually never among the girls.   The direction of the
discipline and education of the pupils was in the hands of
the chief of the Sultana's staff of badly paid and much
intimidated mistresses.   This chief of staff, by name Miss
Ough, but called the Vizier, appeared from and disappeared into the quarters occupied by the Sultana, and was
popularly supposed to be kept there in a dungeon.   If
you were near the door through which the Vizier passed
from public gaze there was unquestionably to be heard
shortly afterwards a metallic clank.   This was the portal
of the Vizier's dungeon being closed upon her and was
very shuddering to hear.   The Vizier, moreover, like
one long incarcerated, was skeletonized of form, cadaver-
ous and sallow of countenance, and grew upon her face,
as all right prisoners in royal custody grow, a thick cov-
ering of greyish down.

A second known inhabitant of the Sultana's quarters

was Mr. Ponders, her butler, who sometimes slid into the classrooms in a very eerie way with messages and whom Rosalie came to know strangely well; a third, but he did not exactly live in the awful regions, was the Sultana's husband. The Sultana's husband lived in two rooms over the stable. From the front classroom windows he was to be seen every morning disappearing through the front gates at about eleven o'clock; very shiny top hat; very tight tail coat; very tight grey trousers; very tight yellow gloves; very tight grey-yellow moustache; very tight pasty face; curiously constricted, jerky gait as though his boots, too, were very tight. Precisely the sort of chronic, half-tipsy hanger-on one used to see in billiard rooms or eating cloves in West End bars. By association of ideas with the orientalism of Sultana he was called by the girls the Bashibazook.

Junior to Miss Ough, the vizier, were four or five other mistresses, all known by nicknames. Children are exactly like savages in their horrible sharpness at picking out physical peculiarities and labelling by them. One would imagine these governesses, judged by their nicknames, a deplorable collection of oddities. Actually they must have been a presentable enough and a capable enough set of spinsters, though sicklied o'er by the pale cast of indifferent personalities, — indifferently housed, indifferently fed, indifferently paid; all anæmic, all without any prospects whatsoever, all dominated by and domineered over by the masterful personality of the Sultana.

Only one of them contributed to the life of Rosalie and this was " Keggo," Miss Keggs, who taught mathematics. This Keggo was rather like Anna in appearance, Rosalie thought, and was most popular of all the mistresses with the girls, partly because of her bright moments in which she was a human creature and an entertaining creature;

partly because of her curiously supine periods in which she would be utterly listless, allow her class to do anything they liked provided they kept perfectly quiet, and would make no attempt whatsoever to correct idleness or to impart the lesson of the hour. Miss Keggs had been known to knock over the inkpot on her desk and sit and watch the ink dripping in a pool on to the floor without making the least attempt even to upstand the vessel. No one knew why Keggo had these moods. But it was known that for her to come into class looking rather flushed was a sign foreshadowing them.

She appeared to take a fancy to Rosalie from the first, and Rosalie to her, probably by reason of the fancied resemblance to Anna. She invited Rosalie to her room and Rosalie loved to go there because the One Onlys were in a very weak and humble minority in Rosalie's first term and were rather hunted by the Sultans who were then particularly strong in numbers and rich in apparel, in pocket money and in friends. The poor little One Onlys led rather abashed lives and they had no chance at all around the playroom fire where the Sultans stretched their elegant legs and warmed their shapely toes.

One evening in her first few weeks Rosalie had to take an exercise up to Miss Keggs, and Miss Keggs's room was warm, and Miss Keggs like Anna, and Rosalie lingered and was invited to linger; after that Rosalie sought and invented reasons for going up to Miss Keggs's room and Miss Keggs would nearly always say, " Well, you may stay a little, Rosalie, as you're here."

Miss Keggs's room was right at the top of the house where were also the servants' room and the room shared by Miss Downer and Miss Frost. It was a long, narrow room with sloping ceiling and the window high up in the ceiling. In the winter it was warmed with a small oil stove which smelt terribly when you first went in but to the smell of which you almost at once got accustomed. It was curious to Rosalie that even in summer when there was no oil stove there was nearly always a very strong smell in Miss Keggs's room. Miss Keggs used eau de Cologne for bathing her forehead and temples on account of the very bad headaches from which she said she suffered and the smell was like eau de Cologne but with an unpleasantly harsh strong tang in it, like bad eau de Cologne, Rosalie used to think. However, you almost at once got accustomed to that also. These headaches of Miss Keggs were a symptom of the very bad health from which she suffered, and on the occasions of Rosalie's visits to her room Miss Keggs was very communicative about her ill health. It was the reason, she told Rosalie, why, alone of all the mistresses, she had a room to herself instead of sharing one. The Sultana had granted her that privilege, provided she would use this remote and rather poky attic, because it was so essential she should be quiet and undisturbed.

"Don't you have any medicine, Miss Keggs?" said the small Rosalie, in one part genuinely sympathetic and in the other eager to discuss anything that would prolong her stay by the warm oil stove.

"Nothing does me any good," said Miss Keggs wearily. After a minute she added, "But I really am feeling very bad to-night. Mr. Ponders very kindly gives me some medicine that relieves my bad attacks. I wonder, Rosalie, if you could find your way down to Mr. Ponders and give him this medicine bottle and ask him if he could very kindly oblige me with a little of my medicine?"

"Oh, I'm sure I could, Miss Keggs," cried Rosalie, delighted at the opportunity of doing a service.

Miss Keggs became extraordinarily animated with the

feverish animation of one who, having made up her mind after hesitation, furiously tramples hesitation under foot.

"Go right downstairs," directed Miss Keggs, "right down below the hall into the basement. You know the basement stairs?" She proceeded with her directions, detailing them most exactly. She accompanied Rosalie to the door and when Rosalie was a little down the passage sharply called her back. "And, Rosalie! If you should meet any one — if you should meet any one, on no account say where you are going or where you have been. On no account. If it should be known how ill I continue to be, I might be sent away. They might think I am not strong enough to continue my work here. Say you have lost your way if you should be met. You are a new little girl and it is easy to lose your way in this big, rambling house. Keep the bottle in your pocket and remember, Rosalie, on no account to tell. On no account." And so dismissed her.

A creepy business, going down to interview Mr. Ponders! The Sultana's butler was only seen by the girls on momentous and thrilling occasions. He opened the hall door when new little girls arrived with their mothers, and he would sometimes appear in a classroom and walk thrillingly to the mistress and thrillingly whisper. This always meant that for some fortunate girl a parent or an aunt had arrived and that the presence of the fortunate girl was desired by the Sultana. He was a shortish, dingy man with a considerable moustache. As he walked between the desks to deliver his message, his eyes were always glancing from side to side as though furtively in search of something, and always as he left the room he would stand a moment with his hand on the door as though meditating some statement and then suddenly determining to disappear without making it. A rather mysterious and thrilling man.

Come into the basement, Rosalie walked as bid along the passage, then to the right and then past two doors to the third, whereon she tapped gently, and when a man's voice said " Come in," quaked rather, and went in. The walls of Mr. Ponders' room were completely surrounded by narrow shelves. Beneath the shelves were the closed doors of low cupboards and on the shelves were ranged many glasses, china and silverware. At one end beneath the window was a sink with two taps, both dripping. On the right-hand side was a fire before which in a wicker armchair sat Mr. Ponders smoking a pipe and reading a newspaper.

" What do *you* want? " inquired Mr. Ponders.

Rosalie said, " If you please, Mr. Ponders, Miss Keggs is not feeling at all well and would you be so very kind as to give her some of her medicine, please? "

Mr. Ponders rose and regarded Rosalie from the hearthrug. " So it's going to be you coming for the medicine now, is it? " he said. He looked rather a mean little man, standing there; not thrilling as when he appeared in the schoolrooms for there was an unpleasing familiarity in his air, but still decidedly mysterious, for though he smiled and looked snakily at Rosalie, he still glanced from side to side as though furtively looking for something and he still, before committing himself to an action, paused as though meditating a statement and then suddenly performed the action as though he had made up his mind not to speak — yet.

" You're Rosalie, aren't you? " inquired Ponders, putting his hands in his pockets and stretching out his stomach like one much at his ease. " Rosalie Aubyn. You come with your Auntie. What's your Pa? "

" A clergyman, Mr. Ponders."

"Oh, he's a clergyman, is he?" Mr. Ponders's eyes slid from side to side, rather as if he had somewhere in the room some confirmation or some refutation of Rosalie's statement that he could produce if he could catch sight of it, and continued thus to slide with the same suggestion while he playfully put Rosalie through a further examination relative to her "Auntie," her "Ma" and her brothers and sisters. He appeared then to be meditating a question of some other order but instead suddenly straightened himself, withdrew his hands from his pockets and said, "Well, you'd better be running along with the medicine."

He took from Rosalie the bottle Miss Keggs had given her and from his pockets a bunch of keys. In the lock of one of his cupboards he fitted a key, paused a meditative moment, then with a decisive action opened the cupboard and from a tall black bottle very carefully and steadily filled the medicine bottle. The medicine was dark red. It first ran in a fine dark red cloud around the inner shoulders and sides of the bottle and then plunged in a steady stream direct from the larger receptacle to the smaller.

Rosalie, watching, was moved to say, "How well you pour it, Mr. Ponders."

"I've poured a tidy drop in my time," said Mr. Ponders, completing the operation and corking the medicine bottle. He held it towards Rosalie, paused in his mysteriously deliberative way, and then suddenly handed it to her. "And a tidy fair drop for Miss Keggs at that," he added. He went to the door, again paused as though uncertain whether to open it, then opened it for Rosalie to pass out. "Good night," said Mr. Ponders.

Lucky Mr. Ponders to have for his own a cosy room like that — men, always for some reason, with the best of everything again! Unpleasing Mr. Ponders to look at you like that and to speak to you like that — men, always horrible again! Rosalie, thus thinking, made a swift and unobserved climb to the attics. Miss Keggs must have heard her coming. The door was pulled sharply from Rosalie's hand and there was Miss Keggs and the bottle almost snatched away from Rosalie. "How long you've been! But you've got it! And no one saw you?" Miss Keggs went very swiftly to the washstand and took up a small tumbler. Clear that she wanted her medicine very badly. She toppled in the contents of the bottle, its neck clinking against the glass, the dark red medicine splashing and some spilling, so differently from Mr. Ponders's performance of a far more difficult operation, and with the bottle still in her hand held the glass to her lips and drank deeply.

Yet there was a funny thing about the draught. It seemed to Rosalie that Miss Keggs with that eager draught yet did not swallow at once but only filled her mouth to its capacity. She then swallowed very slowly and with movements of her cheeks as though she was sucking down the medicine and tasting it in every portion of her mouth. Colour came into her cheeks. The medicine certainly appeared to do her immense good.

Miss Keggs's friendliness towards Rosalie was settled and established from that night. Thereafter it became a very regular thing for Rosalie to visit the room of Miss Keggs of an evening; and at intervals, sometimes twice a week, sometimes not three times in a month, to descend to the den of Mr. Ponders for the dark-red medicine which did Miss Keggs so much good and which she always took in that peculiar sucking way from a full mouth. She would be so long sometimes in swallowing a mouthful, beginning a sentence and then drinking and then all that time in swallowing before she completed the sentence, that she several times, by way of apology, explained the reason to Rosalie. " I have to swallow it very slowly like that," explained Miss Keggs, " because that's the way for it to do me good. It's my doctor's orders."

" It seems a business," was Rosalie's comment.

" Yes, it is a business," Miss Keggs agreed.

Rosalie added, " How very lucky it is, Miss Keggs, that Mr. Ponders keeps your medicine."

" Yes, it's certainly very lucky," Miss Keggs agreed.

The effect of her medicine was always to make her very complaisant.

CHAPTER II

ONE seeks to give only the things in Rosalie's life that contributed to her record, as time judges a record. Of her years at Oakwood House, so far as Oakwood House itself is concerned, only that friendship with Miss Keggs thus contributed. The rest does not matter and may be passed. Rosalie was happy there. It naturally was all very strange at first but she soon shook down and found her place and formed friendships. The thing to notice is this — that even in the strangeness of her first few weeks the place was actively felt by her to be a haven. There is to be recalled that aching desire of hers, when poor Anna lay dead, to get right away from men: men who (though still pre-eminently wonderful) caused her by their showing off to blink and have a funny feeling; and by their distasteful presence spoilt her walks and her lessons; and by the frightening things they did had brought that frightening death to Anna. Thus had accumulated that aching desire to get right away from men and be only amongst girls; and the feeling remained most lively in Rosalie at the Sultana's, and intensified. Those men! She used to see the Bashibazook and shudder at him; and Mr. Ponders and shudder at him; and sometimes Uncle Pyke, and because of ways he had, feel quite sick to be near him. Men still were wonderful. The Bashibazook, Mr. Ponders, Uncle Pyke, Uncle Pyke's friends — all were infinitely superior and did what they pleased; but, oh, not nice, *frightening*. It *was* safe and nice to be only with girls. Girls were in heaps of ways extraordinarily silly and unsatisfactory. Men, though not nice, unquestionably did everything better and *could* do things. Unquestionably theirs was the best time in life. Unquestionably they were to be envied. But — not nice, *frightening.*

It was like that that her ideas at Oakwood House were shaping.

And all this time, most important and much contributory to the life of Rosalie — Aunt Belle. Tremendous occasions in those years were the visits to the Sultana's of Aunt Belle. Frequently on a Saturday kind Aunt Belle used to call at Oakwood House for Rosalie and take her to a tea shop for tea. Beautiful cousin Laetitia would accompany her, and kind Aunt Belle would always invite Rosalie to bring with her another little One Only. Kind, kind Aunt Belle! Aunt Belle used to sit by in the tea shop, affectionate and loquacious as ever, while the two schoolgirls stuffed themselves with cakes (not beautiful Laetitia who just nicely sipped a cup of tea and nicely smiled at the two gross appetites) and always kind Aunt Belle brought a small hamper of sweets and cake and apples — " The very best goodies from the Army and Navy Stores, dear child. They know us so well at the Army and Navy Stores. Your Uncle Pyke has a standing deposit account there. We can go in without a penny in our pockets and buy anything we please. Fancy that, dear child! " And always half a crown for Rosalie, as kind Aunt Belle was leaving.

Once in every term, also, Rosalie spent a week-end at the magnificent house in Pilchester Square. Such luxuries! Fire in her bedroom and palatial late dinner! Breakfast in bed on Sunday morning (" Just to let you lie as a little change from school, dear child.") and Laetitia's maid to do her hair! Rosalie immensely im-

pressed and Aunt Belle immensely gratified at Rosalie's
awe and appreciation and gratitude.

A curious manifestation there was of Aunt Belle's attitude in this regard. On that famous visit to the rectory
she had treated every one like children. Here, in her
own house, while Rosalie was still a child, twelve, thirteen and fourteen, she was treated by Aunt Belle and
shown off to by her much as if she were a grown-up
woman. About her servants, and about prices, and about
dress, and about her dinner parties, Aunt Belle chattered to Rosalie; and about Uncle Pyke, what he liked,
and what he didn't like, and what he did in the City, and
what he did at his club, and about her hosts of friends and
their matrimonial experiences, Aunt Belle chattered to
her, confiding in her and telling her all kinds of things
she but dimly understood precisely as if she were a
grown-up young woman.

Then as Rosalie grew older, sixteen, seventeen and
getting on for eighteen, was reversion by Aunt Belle to
the rectory manner. The child had been treated as a
young woman; the budding maiden was treated precisely as if she were a small child or a small savage to
be entertained by mere sight of the wonders all about
her in Pilchester Square and by having them explained
to her in words of one syllable.

"There, Rosalie," (Rosalie at seventeen) "do you
know you're eating with a solid silver spoon! Feel the
weight of it! Balance it in your hand, dear child. We
usually only use this service for our dinner parties and
your uncle Pyke keeps it locked up and carries the key
about with him. Show Rosalie the key, Pyke. But I
got it out for you to-day because I knew you would like
to see real solid silver plate. Dear child!"

Dear thing! Lightly on her, you Brompton Cemetery
stones!

Uncle Pyke never would produce the key or whatever he might be asked to show. Uncle Pyke would grunt and go on with his soup with enormous noise as though having a bath in it. Uncle Pyke never spoke at all to Rosalie on these week-end visits except, always, to put her through examination on what she was learning at school. Rosalie, though horribly frightened of Uncle Pyke, always had pretty ready answers to the examination — she did uncommonly well at school — but there never was from Uncle Pyke any other mark of appreciation than a grunt. A grunt! Those Pyke-ish, piggish men! The outstanding characteristic Rosalie came to see in Uncle Pyke and in the other husbands (his cronies) of Aunt Belle's friends was that they thought about nothing else but their food, their wine and their cigars. They disliked having about them anybody who interfered with their enjoyment of their food, their wine and their cigars. They were affectionately regarded by their wives as tame, necessary bears to be fed and warmed and used to sit at the head of the table and awe the servants. That was what Rosalie saw in them — and shuddered at in them. Hogs!

Cousin Laetitia all this time was living at home, attending a very exclusive and expensive day school. Only twelve girls at beautiful Laetitia's school and more masters and mistresses than pupils — mostly " visiting " masters — Italian, French, painting, singing, music, dancing. Laetitia was about two years older than Rosalie. Very pretty in an elegant, delicate fashion, and growing up decidedly beautiful in a sheltered, hothouse, Rossetti type of beauty. Always very affectionate to Rosalie and glad to see her; not patronising in the way she might have been patronising and yet, as the two grew older, patronising in a conscious effort to dissemble a conscious superiority.

Rosalie never could remember how early in their acquaintance it was she first understood that the great aim of Laetitia's life, and the great aim of Aunt Belle's life for Laetitia, was to "make a good match"; but she seemed to have known it ever since she first heard of Laetitia, certainly at a point of her childhood when too young exactly to understand what "good match" meant. Later on, when Laetitia had left school and was within sight of putting up her hair, "good match" was openly spoken of by Aunt Belle in her crowded drawing-room or alone in company of the two girls and Uncle Pyke.

"And soon dear Laetitia will be making a good match, a splendid match"; and beautiful Laetitia would faintly colour and faintly smile.

There began to come to Rosalie, growing older, an acute and an odd feeling of the physical and mental difference between herself and beautiful Laetitia — a feeling in Laetitia's company that she was a boy, a young man, in the company of one most pronouncedly a young woman. Rosalie was always very plainly dressed by comparison with Laetitia; her voice was much clearer and sharper, her air very vigorous against an air very langorous. Her hands used to feel extraordinarily big when she sat with Laetitia and her wrists extraordinarily bare. She would glance down at her lap sometimes and could have felt a sense of surprise not to see trousers on her legs.

That was how, as they grew older, Rosalie often felt with Laetitia.

Her last term came. She was nearly eighteen. She was going to earn her own living. That was decided. Exactly how was not decided; but Rosalie had decided it. There was an idea that she should remain at the Sultana's as a junior teacher, but that was not Rosalie's idea. "Oh, don't be a schoolmistress, Rosalie," Keggo had said when Rosalie told of the suggestion (propounded, through the Sultana, by Miss Ough and warmly endorsed by Aunt Belle and grunted upon by Uncle Pyke). "Oh, Rosalie, don't be one of us. Don't you see how we are just drifting, drifting? Don't do anything where you'll just drift, Rosalie."

"No, I'm not going to drift, Keggo," said Rosalie. (Miss Keggs, in the little room, had been "Keggo" a long time then.) "I'm not going to drift. I'm going to have a man's career. I'm going into business! Keggo, that's the mystery of that book I'm always reading that you're always asking me about: 'Lombard Street' — Bagehot's 'Lombard Street.' Oh, Keggo, *thrilling.*"

She began to tell Keggo her stupendous enterprise. . . .

There is in the study of man nothing more curious or more interesting than the natural bent of an individual mind. An arrow shot to the north and another from the same bow to the south spring not apart more swiftly or more opposedly than the minds of two children brought up from one mother in the same nursery. The natural bent of each impels it. Art this one, science that; to Joe adventure, to Tom a bookish habit. Rosalie's natural bent declared itself in "figures"; in the operations, as she discovered them, of commerce; in the mysterious powers, as they appealed to her, developed in countinghouses and exerted by countinghouses. The romance of commerce! A mind double-edged, with inquisitiveness the one edge and acquisitiveness the other (as certainly Rosalie's) is a sword double-edged that will cut through the tough shell and into the lively heart of anything. No more is required than to give the young mind a glimpse of the lively heart that is there. Rosalie's young mind was already beating with half-fledged wings against the shell about that side of life wherein, in her experience, (of her brothers, of Uncle Pyke, of Uncle Pyke's friends) men did the things that earned them livelihood and gave them independence. Along, by happy chance, buried in dust in the rectory study and found one holiday, came "Lombard Street" and Bagehot, and that was the book and Bagehot was the man to give pinions to those fledgling wings. She saw romance, and thrusted for it, in the business of countinghouses. It was fascinating to her beyond anything the discovery that money was not, as she had always supposed, a thing that you took with one hand and paid away, and lost, with the other. Not at all! It was a thing that, properly handled, you never lost. Enthralling! Thrilling! You invested it and it returned to you; you expended it and propped it up with fascinating things called sinking funds, and, although you had spent it, there it was coming back to you again! It was the most mysterious and wonderful commodity in the world. She got hold of that and she went on from that.

The romance of business! That ships should go out across the seas with one cargo and sell it, not, in effect, for money, but for another and an entirely different cargo; that cheques passing between countries, and cheques circulating about the United Kingdom, should be traded off one against the other in magic conjuring palaces called Clearing Houses with the result that thousands of little streams merged into few great rivers and only differences need be paid; that money (heart and driving-force of all the mysteries) should have within itself the mysterious and astounding quality of ceaselessly reduplicating itself — " the only thing in the world," as Rosalie quaintly put it to Miss Keggs — " the only thing in the world that people, business people, will take care of for you without charging you for storage or for

trouble " — that these mysterious and extraordinary
things should be thrilled Rosalie as the mysterious and
extraordinary things of science or of nature or the mysterious and beautiful things of art or of literature or of
music will thrill another.

That natural bent of her mind! That Bagehot that
ministered to her natural bent! Fascinated by Banks,
fascinated by the Exchange, fascinated by the Pool of
London, where, obedient to the behests of the countinghouses, floated the wealth that the countinghouses made,
— fascinated by these was Rosalie as maidens of her
years commonly are fascinated by palaces, by the Tower
and by the Abbey. Remember, it is not what their eyes
see that fascinates these romantic young misses. A dolt
can see the Tower walls and see no more than crumbling
bricks and stone. It is what their minds see that fascinates the ardent creatures. Well, Rosalie's mind saw
strange romance in countinghouses.

That Bagehot!

And then must be picked up — and were with time
picked up — others of the magic man's enchantments.
" Literary Studies," but she passed over that, the burning subject was not there. " Economic Studies "; it
much was there. " International Coinage." She read
that! It approached the subject of a Universal Money
and her thought was, " Why, what a splendid idea to have
one coinage that would go everywhere! " And then,
opening a new field, and yet a connected field and a field
profoundly engrossing to her, " The English Constitution." *How* laws came; *how* laws worked; the mysteriousness (her word) within the Council chambers that
produced governance as the mysteriousness within the
countinghouses produced wealth! The mysterious quality within precedent and necessity and change that repro-
duced itself in laws as the mysterious quality within

money caused money to reproduce itself in wealth; the *romance* of governance.

It was like that that her interests were shaping.

It was very easy, it was utterly delightful, to tell all this to Keggo. It was not at all easy, it was very terrible, to tell it before Uncle Pyke. It was appalling, it was terrific, to break to the house in Notting Hill that she desired to earn her living, not as a teacher, but in business — like men.

It was at dinner at the glittering table in the splendid dining-room of the magnificent house in Notting Hill, Rosalie there on the half-term week-end of her last term, that the frightful thing was done. At dinner: Uncle Pyke Pounce bathing in his soup; beautiful Laetitia elegantly toying with hers; Aunt Belle beaming over her solid silver spoon at Rosalie. " Try that soup, dear child. It's delicious. My cook makes such delicious soups. Lady Houldsworth Hopper — Sir Humbo Houldsworth Hopper, you know he's in the India Office, you must have heard of him — was dining with us last week and said she had never tasted such delicious soup. It was the same as this. I asked cook specially to make it for you. Now next term, when you are one of the mistresses at Oakwood House and living at their table and you have soup, you'll be able to say — for you must speak up when you are with them, dear child, and not be shy — you'll be able to tell them what delicious soup you always get at your Uncle Colonel Pyke Pounce's. Be sure to mention your Uncle by name, Colonel Pyke Pounce, R.E., not just ' my uncle,' and that he was a great deal in India where he was entirely responsible for the laying of the Puttapong Railway and received an illuminated address from the Rajah of Puttapongpoo, such a fine old fellow, not being allowed of course to take a present, which you have seen many times hanging in his study in his fine house in Pilchester Square, Notting Hill (some of them are sure to have heard of Pilchester Square, though never visited there, of course); your uncle will show you the address again after dinner; that will be nice, won't it, dear? Won't you, Pyke?"

(F-r-r-r-r-r-*rup!* from the splendid holder of the illuminated address from the Rajah of Puttapongpoo, bathing in his soup.)

"Be sure to speak up for yourself like that, dear child, and let them know who you are and that though you are poor and have to earn your living you have wealthy relations (though of course we are only comfortably off and do not pretend to be rich) and are not at all like ordinary governesses. Be sure to, dear. There; now you've finished that soup and wasn't it delicious, just? You will have another helping, I know you will. A second helping of soup is not usual, dear, and Laetitia or any one at any of our parties would never take it, but it's quite different for you, and I do love to see you enjoy the nice food I get for you. More soup for Miss Aubyn, Parker."

Now for it!

"Aunt, I won't have any more soup. I won't really. It was delicious. Delicious, but really no more. Really. Aunt. . . . About the governesses there and being one of them. I wanted to say . . . Aunt, I don't want to be a pupil-teacher. Aunt . . ."

Fr-r-r-r-*rup!* Frr-r-*roosh!* *Woosh!* Wr-r-r-*roosh!*

It is the holder of the illuminated address from the Rajah of Puttapongpoo most terribly and fear-strikingly struggling up out of his soup. "Don't wanto bea pupil teacher? Wat d'ye mean? Wat d'ye mean?"

"Why, Rosa*lie, dar*ling!" It is the exquisitely beautiful daughter of the holder of the illuminated address from the Rajah of Puttapongpoo.

" Never mind them, Rosalie. The dear child! Why, how crimson she is. Let the dear child speak. What is it, dear child? " It is kind Aunt Belle.

" Aunt Belle. Aunt Belle, I don't want to earn my living like that. I want to earn it like — like a man. I want to — well, it's hard to explain — to go to an office like a man — and have my pay every week, like a man — and have a chance to get on like men, like a man. I want to go into the City if I possibly could, or start in some way like going into the City. I know it sounds awful — telling it to you — but girls are doing it, a few. They're just secretaries and clerks, of course. They're just nothing, of course. But, oh, it's something, and I *do* want it so. To have office hours and a — a desk — and a — an employer and be — be like men. I don't mean, I don't mean a bit, imitate men like all that talk there is now about imitating men. I hate women in stiff collars and shirts and ties and mannishness like that; and indeed I hate — I dislike men — I can't stand them, not in that way, if you understand what I mean — "

" *Ros*alie! " (Laetitia.)

" Oh, Laetitia, oh, Aunt Belle, I'm only saying that to show I don't mean I want to be — . It is so fearfully difficult to explain, this. But Aunt, you do see what I am trying to mean. It's just a man's work that I mean because I'd love it and because I don't see why — . And it's just that particular kind of work — in the City. Because I believe, I *do* believe, I would be sharp and good at that work. Figures and things. I *love* that. I'm quick at that, very quick. And I've read heaps about it — about business I mean — about — "

Uncle Pyke Pounce : Uncle Pyke Pounce, holding his breath because he is holding his exasperation as one holds one's breath in performance of a delicate task : Uncle Pyke Pounce crimson, purply blotched, infuriated, kept from

his food, blowing up at last at the parlourmaid: "Bring
in the next course! Bring in the next course! Watyer
staring at? Watyer waiting for? Watyer listening to?
Rubbish. Pack of rubbish."

The parlourmaid flies out on the gust of the explosion.
Rosalie finishes her sentence while the gust inflates again.

"Read heaps about it — about business — about trade
and finance and that. It fascinates me."

The gust explodes at her.

"Wat d'yer mean read about it? Read about *what?*"

"Uncle, about money, about finance and things. I
know it's extraordinary I should like such things. But
I do. I can't tell why. It's like — like a romance to
me, all about money and how it is made and managed.
There's a book I found in father's study at home. 'Lombard Street' by Bagehot. That's all about it, isn't it?
I can't tell you how I have read it and reread it."

"Never heard of it. 'Lombard Street?' *Bagehot?*
Who's *Bagehot?*"

"I think he was a banker, Uncle."

"I think he was a fool!"

It comes out of the red and swollen face of the holder
of the illuminated address from the Rajah of Puttapongpoo like a plum-stone spat at her across the table.
Rosalie blinked. These beastly men! Violent, vulgar,
fat, rude beasts! Uncle Pyke the worst of them! But
she came back bravely from her flinch. "If he wasn't
a banker, he knew all about banking. Oh, that's what I
would be more than anything — that's what I *do* want
to be — a banker — in a bank!"

The holder of the illuminated address from the Rajah
of Puttapongpoo as if, having expectorated the plum-
stone, he desired to expectorate also the taste thereof, spat
out an obscene sound of contempt and disgust. "Fah!
I say the man, whoever he was, was a fool. And I say

this, Miss. I don't often speak sharply, but I say that I think I know another fool — a little fool — at this table. Fah! Enough of it! What's this? Trout?"

Aunt Belle to the rescue! If Uncle Pyke and Aunt Belle had kept house in Seven Dials instead of Notting Hill, Uncle Pyke would have beaten Aunt Belle and Aunt Belle would have taken the blows without flinching and then have wheedled Uncle Pyke with drops of gin. As it was, Uncle Pyke was merely boorish or torpidly savage towards Aunt Belle and Aunt Belle's way with him — as with all combative men — was to rally him with a kind of boisterous chaff and to discharge it at him as an urchin with an armful of snowballs fearfully discharges them at an old gentleman in a silk hat: backing away, that is to say, before an advance and advancing before a retreat. Uncle Pyke usually retreated, either to eat or sleep.

Aunt Belle had blinked, as Rosalie had blinked, at that horrible epithet " Little fool! " across the table. The lips that uttered it were immediately stuffed with trout and Aunt Belle immediately rushed in in her rallying way to the rescue. " Why, you great, big stupid Uncle Pyke! " cried Aunt Belle vivaciously. " It's you who don't know what you're talking about, you unkind old thing, you. Why, many, many girls, quite nice girls, are going into business now and being secretaries and things and doing very, very well indeed. Why, I declare it would do you good to have a lady secretary yourself in that big, dusty office of yours in the City, never dusted from one year's end to another, I'm sure! Laetitia, wouldn't it do your father good, the cross, grumpy old thing? Give your master some more of the sauce, Parker. Isn't that trout delicate and nice, Pyke? Trout for a pike! And I'm sure very like a nasty, savage old pike the way you tried to gobble up poor Rosalie, the dear child. Now, Rosalie,

dear child, I think that's a very, very good idea of yours
to go into business. I think it's a splendid idea, and more
and more quite nice girls will soon be doing it. Now
we'll just see what we can do and we'll make that cross
old uncle help and ask all his cross old friends in the
City, just to punish him. A young Lady Clerk, or a
young Lady Secretary! Now I think that's the very,
very thing for you. *Just* the thing, and a dear, clever
child to think of it. *Yes!*"

Kind, kind Aunt Belle! Victory through Aunt Belle!
Accomplishment! A career like a man! Aunt Belle had
said it and Aunt Belle would do it! A career like a man!
Oh, ecstatic joy! "Lombard Street" had been brought
with her in her week-end suitcase. Directly she could
get to bed she rushed up to it and took it out and read,
and read. It was all underlined. She underlined it more
that happy, happy night!

Ah, never underline a book till you are forty. Never
memorialise what you were, your lovely innocence, your
generous heart, your ardent hopes, lest the memorial be
found one day by what you have become. Rosalie, finding that "Lombard Street," unearthed from lumber, in
long after years, turned over the pages and from the pages
ghosts rushed up and filled the room, and filled the air,
and filled her heart, and filled her eyes; and she rent the
book across its perished binding and pushed it from her
with both her hands on to the fire and on to the flames
in the fire.

CHAPTER III

INCREDIBLY soon, so stealthy swift is time, came this
last term of Rosalie's at the Sultana's. Time does not
play an open game. It's of the cloak and dagger sort.
It stalks and pounces. Rosalie was astonished to think
she was leaving; and now the time had come she was
sorry to be going. Not very sorry; very excited; but
having just enough regret to realise, on looking back,
that she had been very happy at school and to realise,
actively, happiness in this last term. One knows what it
is. It's always like that. One always *was* happy: one so
seldom *is*. Happiness to be realised needs faint perception of sadness as needs the egg the touch of salt to manifest its flavour. Flashes of entertainment may enliven
the most wretched of us; but that's pleasure; that's not
happiness. One comes to know the only true and ideal
happiness is happiness tinctured with faintest, vaguest
hint of tears. It is peace; and who knows peace that
has not come to it through storm, or knoweth storm
ahead, or in storm past hath not lost one that would
have shared this peace?

So that girl's last term was (in her words) " tremendously jolly." She was just eighteen, and she was
leaving, and responsive to this the harness of the school
was drawn off her as at the paddock gate the headstall
from a colt. She was out of lessons. She did some
teaching of the younger girls. She was on terms with
the mistresses. She had the run of Keggo's room.

Such talks in Keggo's room. . . . She was out from
the cove of childhood; she was into the bay of youth;

breasting towards the sea of womanhood (that sea that's sailed by stars and by no chart) ; and she was encountering tides that come to young mariners to perplex them and Keggo could talk about such things with the experience that so enraptures young mariners and of which young mariners are at the same time so confidently contemptuous, so superiorly sceptical. Nearer to press the simile, youth at the feet of experience is as one, experienced, climbing a mountain with the young thing panting behind. " Go on ! Go on ! " pants the growing young thing. " This is ripping. Go on. Show the way. But I don't want your hand. I can do it easily by myself — better." And one evening while Rosalie stumblingly explained, and eagerly received, and sceptically doubted, " But look here, Keggo," she cried, and stopped and blushed, abashed at her use of the nickname.

Miss Keggs laughed. " Don't mind, Rosalie. Call me Keggo. I like it. It's much more friendly. I'm very fond of you, Rosalie."

They were by the oil stove, Miss Keggs in her wicker armchair, Rosalie on the floor, her back propped against Miss Keggs's knees. One of Miss Keggs's hands was on Rosalie's shoulder and she moved it to touch the girl's face. " Are you fond of me, Rosalie? "

Rosalie turned towards her and spoke impulsively. " Oh, awfully — Keggo."

The woman stooped and kissed the growing young thing, hugging her strongly, pressing her lips upon the lips of Rosalie with a great intensity. " Oh, I shall be sorry when you go, Rosalie."

" We can still be friends, Keggo dear."

Miss Keggs shook her head. " Ships that pass in the night."

" O Keggo ! "

Miss Keggs smiled, a wintry smile. " O Rosalie ! "

she mimicked. She sighed. "Oh, my dear, it's true —
true! Don't you remember how the lines go —

' Ships that pass in the night and speak each other in
         passing;
 Only a signal shown and a distant voice in the darkness.'

Just remember that in a few years. You'll hail again
perhaps. 'O Keggo!' Or I — it is more likely — will
hail 'O Rosalie!' Just remember it then." Her hand
came down to Rosalie and Rosalie took it. It was so
cold; and on her face a strained and beaten look as though
hand and face belonged to one that stood most chilled
and storm-beat upon the bridge, peering through the
storm. Her fingers made no motion responsive to Rosalie's warm touch. She said strangely, as though it was
to herself she spoke, "Does it mean anything to you,
Rosalie, a vision like that? Can you see a black and
violent night and a ship going by full speed, and one
labouring, and through the wind and the blackness a hail
— and gone, and the wreck left foundering?"

Ah, that most generous and quickly moved and loving
Rosalie — then! How she twisted to her knees and
stretched her arms about that poor Keggo, sitting there
so drooped! How readily into her eyes her young and
warm and ardent sympathies pressed the tears, their flowers! How warm her words! How warmly spoken! "O
Keggo! Keggo, dear! Keggo, why do you talk like
that? How can you? After all the kindness you've
shown me, accusing me that I'll forget and not mind!
Keggo, you shan't. You mustn't."

Then Keggo responded, catching her arms about Rosalie and straining Rosalie to her as though here was some
cable to hold against the driving sea. "O Rosalie!"

And after a little Rosalie said, "You won't again say

I ever shall forget, or hail and pass by. Oh, that was cruel, Keggo!"

Keggo was gently crying. "Natural. Natural."

"Unnatural. Horrible. And you? Why do you say such things about yourself? You didn't mean it? It's nothing? How can you ever be a wreck, foundering?"

Keggo dried her eyes and by her voice seemed to put those things right away. "No, nothing. Of course not. Darling girl, only this — you're young — young and so of course you are going by full sail as young things do. Full sail! O happy ship! Rosalie, go on telling. Go on asking. I love it, Rosalie."

She was always "Keggo" after that; and the things that Rosalie told and asked!

Such things! It is to be seen that now there were bursting into blossom out of bud within that Rosalie those seeds planted in her by the extraordinary ideas of her childhood. About men. First and always predominating, about men as compared with women — their wonder, their power, their importance, their infinite superiority; then about men in their relations with women — their rather grand and noisy ways that made Rosalie blink; their interfering presence that spoilt lessons and spoilt walks; those sinister attributes of theirs, arising somehow out of their freedom to do as they liked in the world, that somehow left the world very hard for women. Grotesque ideas, but masterful ideas, masterfully shaping the child mind wherein they germinated; burrowing in clutchy roots; pressing up in strong young saplings. Agreed the child is father of the man, but much more the girl is mother of the woman. It is the man's part to sow and ride away; conception is the woman's office and that which she receives she tends to cherish and incorporate within her. Of her body that function is her glory; of her mind it is her millstone. Man always rides away, a tent dweller and an Arab, with a horse and with the plains about him; woman is a dweller in a city with a wall, a house dweller, storing her possessions about her in her house, abiding with them, not to be sundered from them.

So with that Rosalie. Those childhood ideas of hers were grotesque ideas but she had received them into her house and they remained with her, shorn of their grotesqueness, as garish furniture may be upholstered in a new pattern, but tincturing her life as the appointments of a room will influence the mood of one that sits therein. Father owned the world — all males had proprietorship in the world under father — all men were worshipful and giants and genii. That was the established perception and those its earliest images. The perception remained, deepening, changing only in hue, as a viscid liquid solidifies and darkens in a vessel over the fire. It remained, persisted. Time but steadied the focus as the wise oculist, seeking for his patient the perfect image, drops lenses in the frame through which the vision chart is viewed. In a little the perfect image is found. There was that Rosalie, come to maidenhood, come to the dizzy edge of leaving school, with the perfect image of her persistent obsession; with the belief no longer that men were magicians having the world for their washpot and women for their footstool, but unquestionably that they "had a better time" than women and that they secured this "better time" by virtue of their independence.

"And, Keggo," (she is explaining it) "I'm going to be like that. I'm going to be what a man can be. Why shouldn't I? Why shouldn't a woman?" She paused and then went on. "Why, that's the thing that's been with me all my life, ever since I can remember. I've always known that men were the creatures. Always. Since

I was so high. Oh, I used to have the most ridiculous ideas about them. You'd scream, Keggo. And I've always had the same attitude towards them — towards them as contrasted with women, I mean. First awe, then envy, then, since I've been growing up here, just as having a desirable position in life, as having *the* desirable position in life, independence, a career, work, freedom, a goal — yes, and a goal that's always and always a little bit in front of you, always something better. That's the thing. That's the thing, Keggo. Just look at the other side. Take a case in point. Take my painful cousin, Laetitia, sweet but in lots of ways very painful. What's her goal? A good match! A good match! Did you ever hear anything so futile and sickening? Sickening in itself, but I'll tell you what's really sickening about it — why, that she'll get it — get her goal and then it's done, over, finished, won. Settle down then and get fat. Oh, I don't want a goal I can win. I want a goal I can't win. One that's always just in front."

She suddenly realised the intensity of her voice and laughed and shook her head sideways and back. She had just recently put her hair up and it still felt funny and tight and the laugh and the shake eased away the tightness of voice and of hair. She said thoughtfully, " You know, I believe I'm rather like a man in many ways, in points of view. It's through always thinking them better, I daresay. The ideas I've had about them!" and she laughed again. She said slowly, " Though mind you, Keggo, they *are* better in many ways. They can get away from things. They don't stick about on one thing. And they're violent, not fussing. When they're angry they bawl and hit and it's over and they forget it. They don't just nag on and on. Oh, yes, they're better."

She extended her palms to the oil flame, and watching the X-ray-like effects of the light and shadow upon her

fingers, she added indifferently, as one idly letting drop
a remark requiring no comment, negligently with the
voice of one saying " Tomorrow is Tuesday," or " It's
mutton today," — " Of course they're beasts," she added.

" Of course they're beasts." It was the adjusted image
to which she had brought that other perception of men
which, running parallel with the perception of their superior position, had permeated her childhood years.

CHAPTER IV

SHE'S left the school! She's living in the splendid house in Pilchester Square looking for a post!

She's found a post! She's private secretary to Mr. Simcox!

She's left the splendid house in Pilchester Square! She's living an independent life! She's going to Mr. Simcox's office, *her* office, every day, just like a man! She's living on her own salary in a boarding house in Bayswater!

What jumps! One clutches, as at flying papers in a whirlwind, at a stable moment in which to pin her down and describe her as she jumps. One can't. The thing's too breathless. It's a maelstrom. It's an earthquake. It's a deluge. It's a boiling pot. It's youth. What it must be to live it! One thing pouring on to another so that it's impossible anywhere to pick hold of a bit that isn't changing into something else even as it is examined. That's youth all over. Always and all the time all change. What it must be to live it!

What it must be! Why, when youth comes bursting out of tutelage there's not a stable thing beneath its feet nor above its head a sky that stays the same for two hours together! Every stride's a stepping-stone that tilts and throws you; every dawn a sudden midnight even while it breaks, and every night a blinding brilliance when it's darkest. New faces, new places; new dresses, new dishes; new foes, new friends; new tasks, new triumphs; never a pause, never a platform; every day a year and every year a day — not life on a firm round world but life in the heart of a whirling avalanche. How youth can live it! And all the time, all the time while poor, dear youth is hurtling through it, there's age, instead of streaming sympathy like oil upon those boiling waters, standing in slippered safety, in buttoned dignity, in obese repose, bawling at tumbling youth, "Why can't you settle down! Why can't you settle *down!* Why do you behave like that? Why can't you do as I do? Why can't you be like your wise and sober Uncle Forty? Or like your good and earnest Auntie Fifty? Why can't you behave like your pious grandmother? Why can't you imitate your noble grandfather? Oh, grrrr-r, why *can't* you, you impious, unnatural, ill-mannered, irresponsive, irresponsible exasperating young nuisance, you!" Is it any wonder poor youth bawls back, or feels and behaves like bawling back, "How to goodness can I behave like my infernal uncle or my maddening aunt when I'm whirling along head over heels in the middle of a roaring avalanche?"

Oh, poor youth, that all have lived but none remembers!

One clings, *faut au mieux,* to the intention to tell of her life only the things in her life that contributed to her record, as records are judged. There shall be enormous omissions. They shall be excused by vital insertions.

She shall be glimpsed, first, in the splendid house in Pilchester Square, in the desperate business that getting a place for a woman in a business house was when women were in business houses far more rare than are silk hats in the City in 1922. It *was* desperate. Uncle Pyke and Uncle Pyke's friends were the only channel of opportunity; and Uncle Pyke and Uncle Pyke's friends refused to be a channel of opportunity. They had never heard of such a thing and they desired to bathe in their soup and smack over their wine and not be troubled with such a thing.

Aunt Belle rallied them and baited them and told them they were "great big grumpy things"; and Aunt Belle, in her crowded drawing-room, loved talking about the search for work and did talk about it. "Has to earn her own living," Aunt Belle would chatter, "and is going into business! Oh, yes, ever so many girls who have to earn their own living are going into business now. She'll wear a nice tailormade coat and skirt and carry a little satchel and flick about on the tops of buses, in the City at nine and out again at six and a nice plain wholesome lunch with a glass of milk in a tea shop. Oh, it's wonderful what girls who have to earn their own living do nowadays. Quite right, you know. Quite right (for them). Come over here, Rosalie. Come over here, dear child, and tell Mrs. Roodle-Hoops what you are going to do. The dear child!"

But nothing done.

Just that glimpse and then comes Mr. Simcox.

Mr. Simcox was first met by Rosalie while walking with Aunt Belle and beautiful cousin Laetitia in the Cromwell Road. He came along carrying a letter in his hand with the obvious air of one who will forget to post it if he puts it in his pocket and probably will forget to do so in any case. He was as obviously "a man of about fifty-six": that curiously precise figure, neither a ten nor a five, always used for men who look as Mr. Simcox looked and always continued to look while Rosalie knew him, and probably always had looked. Men of "about fifty-six" — one never says "about thirty-six" or "about sixty-six"; it would be "about thirty-five" or "about seventy" — men of "about fifty-six" are almost certainly born at that age and with that appearance and they seem to continue in it to their graves.

Mr. Simcox was like that, and was short and had two little bunchy grey whiskers, and wore always a pepper and salt jacket suit, unbuttoned, the pockets of which always bulged and the skirts of which, containing the pockets, always swayed and flapped. When he talked he was always talking — if that is understood — and when he was busy he was always frantically busy and looking at the clock or at his watch as if it were going to explode at a certain rapidly approaching hour and he must at all costs be through with what he was doing before it did explode. He talked in very rapid jerks, always seeming to be about to come to rest and then instantaneously bounding off again, rather like a man bounding along stepping-stones, red-hot stepping-stones that each time burnt his feet and set him flying off again.

He had been in the Bombay house of a firm of indigo merchants and there had known Aunt Belle and Uncle Pyke. He had retired and settled in London and he now came very briskly up to Aunt Belle, to Rosalie and to beautiful Laetitia, greeting them and bursting into full stream of chatter while he was yet some distance away; and, having been introduced to Rosalie and snatched at her hand precisely as if doing so while shooting in mid-air between one red-hot stepping-stone and the next, whizzed presently to " I really came out to post a letter " and flapped the letter in the air as if it were a bothersome thing stuck to his fingers and refusing absolutely to be stuffed into a post-box.

" Why, there's a pillar-box just there; you've just passed it," cried Rosalie.

" Why, so there is! " exclaimed Mr. Simcox, jumping round to stare at the pillar-box as if it had stretched out an arm and given him a sudden punch in the back, and then spinning towards Rosalie and staring at her rather as if he suspected her of having put the pillar-box there while he was not looking; and while Mr. Simcox was so exclaiming and so doing Rosalie had said, " Do let me just post it for you. Do let me," and had snapped the obstinate letter from his fingers, and posted it and was back again smiling at Mr. Simcox, whom she rather liked and who reminded her very much of a jack-in-the-box.

Indeed with his quick ways, his shortness, his bushy little grey whiskers and his pepper and salt suit with its flapping pockets, Mr. Simcox was very like one of those funny little jack-in-the-boxes they used to sell. He said to her, regarding her with very apparent pleasure and esteem, " Well, that's very nice of you. That really is very nice of you. And it's most wonderful. It is indeed. Do you know, I must have walked more than a mile looking for a letter-box and I daresay I should have walked another mile and then forgotten it and taken the letter home again." He addressed Aunt Belle: " It's a most astonishing thing, Mrs. Pyke Pounce, but I cannot post a letter. I positively cannot post a single letter. When I say single I do not mean I can post no letter at all. No, no. Far from it. I mean I can post no letter singly, by itself, *solus*. My daily correspondence, my office batch, I take out in a bundle, perhaps in a table basket. That is simple. But a single letter — as you see, a clever young lady like this has to find a box for me or I might carry the thing for days together. Astonishing that, you know. Astonishing, annoying, and mind you, sometimes serious and embarrassing."

" Why, you busy, busy person, you! " cried Aunt Belle with her customary air towards a man of shaking her finger at him. " You very busy person! Fancy a basket full of correspondence! Why what a heap you must have! "

Mr. Simcox said he had indeed a heap. " Sometimes I think more than I can manage."

" Indeed," agreed Aunt Belle, " you don't seem to have much time to spare. Why, I haven't seen you in my drawing-room for quite a month (" You busy little creature, you," expressed without being stated). " I expect you're getting very rich and disagreeable." (" You rich little rascal, you!")

Mr. Simcox declared that as to that his business wasn't one to get rich at. " In no sense. Oh, no, in no sense. It keeps me occupied. It gives me an interest. That's all. No more than that." As to Mrs. Pyke Pounce's delightful drawing-room, most certainly he had been there less than a month ago and most certainly he would present himself again on the very next opportunity. To-morrow, was it? He would without fail present himself there to-morrow, " and I hope," said Mr. Simcox, taking his leave, " I hope I may have the pleasure of seeing my postmistress there again." He smiled very cordially at Rosalie and went flapping away up the street at the pace and with the air, not of one who had come out to post a letter and had posted it, but of one who had come out to post a letter, had dropped it, and was flying back to look for it.

" Oh, isn't he an ugly little monster!" cried Aunt Belle, resuming the walk.

" But I think he's nice," said Rosalie. " What *is* his business, Aunt Belle?"

Aunt Belle hadn't an idea. " He's an agent," said Aunt Belle, " but an agent for what I'm sure I don't know. He's a very mysterious, fussy, funny little person. We knew him in Bombay where he had a very good position, but he retired and what he does now I'm sure I can't say. But he's very busy. You heard him say how busy he is. Rosalie, he might know of something for you.

We'll ask him, dear child.   The funny, ugly little monster!
We'll ask him.   He might help."

He did help.   A very short while afterwards Rosalie
received the appointment of Private Secretary to Mr.
Simcox; twenty-five shillings a week; one pound five
shillings a week!   Office hours ten to five!   Saturdays
ten to one!   Holiday a fortnight a year!   A man's work!
a man's weekly salary! a man's office hours!   The ecstasy
of it! the ecstasy!

The matter with Mr. Simcox was that, in India a man
of affairs, in England he found himself a man of no affairs and a man who had "lost touch."   On a leave
from the Bombay house of the indigo firm he had been
prevailed upon by his mother and his maiden sister to
remain at home and look after them and he had done it
and gone on doing it, and they had died and he had never
married, and he had now no relatives, and by this and by
that (as he told Rosalie early in her installation) he had
dropped out of friendships and, as he expressed it "lost
touch."   He owned and occupied one of those enormous
houses in Bayswater.   It had been his mother's and he
lived on in it after her death and the death of his sister,
alone with a housekeeper.   The housekeeper resided in
the vast catacombs of the basement of the enormous
house; Mr. Simcox resided in the immense reception
rooms, miles above, of the first floor; the three suites
above him, scowling gloomily across a square at the
twin mausoleums opposite, were unoccupied and un-
visited; on the first floor Mr. Simcox had his office.   The
business done in this office, which Rosalie was now to
assist, and why it was done, was in this wise and was
thus explained to Rosalie.

Mr. Simcox, more than ever dropped out and more
than ever having lost touch after the deaths of his sister

and mother, found himself irked more than anything else
by the absence of correspondence. He had been accustomed in India to a big receipt of letters — a big *dhak,*
as he called it, using the Hindustani word — now he received no letters at all; and he told Rosalie that when
you are in the habit of getting a regular daily post, its
gradual falling off and then its complete cessation is one
of the most melancholy things that can befall a man. A
nice bunch of letters in the morning, he said, is like a cold
bath to a young man, a stimulant and an appetiser; and
a similar packet by the night delivery is an entertainment
to look forward to from sunset till it arrives and the
finest possible digestive upon which to go to bed. Mr.
Simcox found himself cut off from both these necessities
of a congenial life and it depressed him beyond conception. Dressing in the morning he would hear the postman come splendidly rat tatting along the square and
would hold his breath for that glorious thunder to come
echoing up from his own front door — and it never did.
Only the sound of the footsteps came, hurrying past —
always.

Set to his solitary dinner in the evening, again would
come along that glorious, reverberating music, and again
Mr. Simcox would hold his breath as it approached and
again — ! Oh, particularly in the winter, it was awful,
Mr. Simcox told Rosalie. Awful; she wouldn't believe
how awful it was. In the winter, in the dark nights,
there is, Mr. Simcox said, about the sound of the postman banging along the doors something that is the sheer
essence of all the mystery, and all the poetry, and all the
life, and all the comfort, and all the light and all the
warmth in the world. Often on winter nights Mr. Simcox would get up quickly from the table (He couldn't
help it) and go tiptoe (Why tiptoe? He didn't know.
You *had* to. It was the mystery and the aching atmos-

phere of the thing) tiptoe across the room to the window, and draw an inch of the heavy curtain and peer out into the darkness and towards the music. There would be the little round gleam of the postman's lantern, bobbing along as he hurried. And flick! it was gone into a doorway, and rat-tat, flick, and there it was again — coming! Flick, rat-tat! Flick, flick, rat-tat! Coming, coming! Growing larger, growing brighter, growing louder! Next door now. They always get it next door. Flick, rat-tat! What a crasher! You can feel it echo! Flick! Now then! Now then! How it gleams! He's stopped! He's looking at his letters! He's coming in! He is — ah, he's passed; he's gone; it's over; nothing . . . nothing for here. . . . Rat-tat! That's next door. The party wall shakes. The lustres on the mantelpiece shake. Mr. Simcox's hands shake. He sits down, pushes his plate away. . . .

It is absurd; it is ridiculous, of course it is; but it was pathetic, it was moving, as it was received from Mr. Simcox by that young and most warm-hearted Rosalie. Her eyes positively were caused to blink as she listened. She had an exact vision of that funny little jack-in-the-box figure up from the table and tiptoeing across the enormous dining room in his little pepper and salt suit with the pockets swaying, not flapping, as he trod along, and opening that inch of the heavy curtain and pressing out his gaze through the black window pane, and watching the gleam and the flick and then the crash and the gleam again, and then holding his breath and hearing his heart go thump, and then dropping the curtain, and back again, with his hands shaking a little and hearing the lustres tinkle. . . .

Yes, very moving to that Rosalie in her youth and warmth. She had actually to touch her nose (high up, between her eyes) with her handkerchief and she said, "Oh, Mr. Simcox. . . . Yes, and then what?"

"Then what? Ah! 'Then what' is *this.*" They were seated in Mr. Simcox's great office on the ground floor. The office of a man of many affairs. A very large writing table furnished with every conceivable facility for writing, not only note papers and envelopes racked up in half a dozen sizes, but sealing waxes in several hues, labels, string, "In" basket, "Out" basket, "Pending Decision" basket, all sorts of pens, all sorts of pencils, wafers, clips, scales, letter weights, rulers — the table obviously of a man to whom correspondence was a devotional, an engrossing, an exact art, and an art practised on an expansive, an impressive, and a lordly scale. There were also in the office a very large plain table on which were spread newspapers, a basket containing clippings from newspapers, an immense blue chalk for marking newspapers and a very long, also a very short, pair of scissors for cutting out clippings from newspapers. A range of filing cabinets stood against one wall; a library of directories and catalogues occupied shelves against another wall.

"'Then what' is *this,*" said Mr. Simcox, indicating these impressive appointments of the room with a wave of his hand. "You ask me 'then what?' 'Then what' is all this. 'Then what' has grown now to be *you.* I'll tell you."

It was this — the oddest, most eccentric notion (not that Rosalie it thought so). Mr. Simcox, cut off from letters, had determined that he must *get* letters. He *would* get letters. If the postman would not come of himself (so to speak) then he must be forced to come. And Mr. Simcox set about forcing him to come by answering advertisements. Not employment advertisements; no; the advertisements to which Mr. Simcox replied were the advertisements that offered to send you something for nothing — that implored you to permit them to send you something for nothing. They are common objects of the periodical press. Every paper is stuffed with them. " Write for free samples." " Catalogues." " Trial packet sent post free on application." " Write for our beautifully illustrated art brochure." " Descriptive booklet by return." " Write for full particulars." " Free sample bottle sufficient for seven days' trial." " Approval gladly. Postpaid." " Plans and particulars of the sole agents." " Superbly printed art volume on receipt of postcard."

The advertisement columns of every paper are stuffed with them and soon the letter-box of Mr. Simcox was stuffed with them. The postman who never stopped at Mr. Simcox's house now never missed Mr. Simcox's house. He went on a lighter and a brisker man after having dealt with Mr. Simcox's house. The agitation with which his approach was heard was now exchanged for a superb confidence as his approach was heard. The deliveries that for Mr. Simcox had never been deliveries were now, not deliveries, but avalanches. They roared into the letter-box of Mr. Simcox. They cascaded upon the floor of the hall of Mr. Simcox.

A mail thus composed does not perhaps sound interesting. Mr. Simcox, once he had got into the full swing of the thing, discovered it to be profoundly and exhaustively interesting. It possessed in the highest degree the two primary essentials of a really good mail, — surprise and variety. There would always be two or three fascinating little parcels, there would always be two or three handsome packets, there would always be two or three imposing looking letters. No common correspondence could possibly have had the number of attractively boxed gifts, the amount of handsomely printed literary and illustrated matter, and certainly not the unfailing persistency of flow, that constituted the correspondence of Mr. Simcox.

The mine once discovered proved to be a mine inexhaustible and containing lodes or galleries of new and unsuspected wealth. Mr. Simcox took in but two daily papers, and two penny weekly papers, and they might well have sufficed. But an appetite whetted and an eye opened they did not suffice. There thundered from the Bayswater free library a positive babel of cries from advertisers in the score of journals there displayed, howling for Mr. Simcox graciously to permit them to contribute their toll to his letter-box; and there were at the news agents periodicals catering for every specialised class of the community and falling over themselves to put before Mr. Simcox the full range of the mysteries, the luxuries and the necessities of every trade and profession and pursuit, from shipbuilding to cycling and from ironmongery to the ownership of castles, moors, steam yachts and salmon fisheries.

Mr. Simcox, entirely happy, one of the busiest men that might be found in the metropolis, struck out new lines. Hitherto he had received his correspondence interestedly and pleasurably but passively. He began to take it up actively and sharply. He began to write back, either graciously approving or very sharply criticising his samples, his specimens and his free trials; and the advertisers responded voluminously, either abjectly with regret and enclosing further samples for Mr. Simcox's esteemed trial, or abjectly with delight and soliciting the very great favour of utilising Mr. Simcox's esteemed letter for publicity purposes. This, however, Mr. Simcox, courteously but firmly, invariably refused to permit.

The engagement of Rosalie was a development of Mr. Simcox's hobby as natural as the development of any other hobby from rabbit breeding to china collecting. The craze intensifies, the scope is enlarged. To have a secretary made Mr. Simcox's mail and the work that produced his mail even more real than already it had become to him. Following up the personal touch that had been discovered by the criticism of samples, Mr. Simcox had opened up a line that produced the personal touch in most intimate degree: personal touch with schools and with insurance companies. He created for himself sons, daughters, nephews, nieces, wards. He endowed them, severally, with ages, with backwardness, with brilliancy, with robustness, with delicacy, with qualities that were immature and required development, with absence of qualities that were desirable and required implanting, with unfortunate tendency to qualities that were undesirable and needed repression and nipping in the bud. He placed these children, thus handicapped or endowed, before the principals of selected schools; he desired that terms and full particulars might be placed before him to assist him in the anxious task of right selection. They were placed before him. " Your backward nephew Robin " (to take a single example) engaged the personal attention of preparatory schoolmasters from Devonshire to Cumberland and from Norfolk to Carnarvon. Similarly with insurance companies. Again dependents and friends were created, by the dozen, by Mr. Simcox. Male and female created he them, cumbered with all imaginable risks, and darkly brooding upon all manner of contingencies; and male and female, cumbered and perplexed, they were studied and advised upon by insurance companies earnest beyond measure to show Mr. Simcox what astounding and unparalleled benefits could be obtained for them.

At the time when Rosalie joined him, Mr. Simcox's attention was in much greatest proportion devoted to this development of his pursuit. Under the instruction of a friend, long since dropped out and lost, who had held a considerable position in a leading assurance company, he had acquired a sound working knowledge of the principles and mysteries of insurance. The subject had greatly interested him. In the phrase he used to Rosalie he had " taken it up "; and in the phrase that so often sequels and rounds off a thing suddenly " taken up " he had suddenly " dropped it." He now, by way of the new development of his correspondence, approached it again. It received him as a former habitation receives a returned native. Mr. Simcox (if the metaphor may be pursued) roamed all about the familiar rooms and corridors of the house of the principles and mysteries of insurance. His knowledge of its possibilities enabled him to develop an astonishing ingenuity in creating cases ripe and yearning for the benefits of provision against contingencies, and as he very easily was able to prove to Rosalie, and found immense delight in proving, he had under his finger, that is to say in his exquisitely arranged filing cabinets, also in his head, a range of insurance companies' literature which enabled him to work out for any conceivable case the most suitable office or offices and the finest possible cover for his risks. " Different companies specialize," said Mr. Simcox, " in different classes of risk. A man should no more walk into one of the leading offices just because it happens to be one of the leading offices and there take out his policy or policies than he should walk into and take for occupation the first vacant house he sees, merely because it is, as a house, a good house. It may be a most excellent house but it may not be in the least the house most suitable to his requirements."

Rosalie nodded intelligently. " But how is a man to find out, Mr. Simcox?"

" Why, I suppose only by going round to every company and choosing the best, just as I make out and send around these cases of mine. But of course no one does that — the trouble for one thing, and ignorance for another, and inability to realise their real requirements and to state them clearly if they do realise them for a third. That's what it is."

Rosalie's intelligent nodding had not ceased. She had a trick, when Mr. Simcox was explaining things to her, of maintaining, with eyes fixed widely upon him, a slow, affirmative movement of her head rather as though she were some engine, and her head the dial, absorbing power from a flow of energy. The dial never indicated repletion. Mr. Simcox delighted to talk to Rosalie, to watch that grave movement of her head, and to hear the short occasional " Why's ? " and comments that came like little spurts or quivers as of the engine in initial throbbings pulsing the power it stored.

She *was* absorbing power. The months were going on. The earlier initiation into Mr. Simcox's business might have had a tinge of disappointment were it not that, whatever the nature of her work, manifestly work it was, paid for, with regular hours, with an office to attend, such as a man might do. The tinge of disappointment, if she had suffered it, would have stung out of the thought: Where, in this manufactured correspondence, in this pretence at a business which was in fact no business at all, where in all this was Lombard Street? Where the romance and mystery of finance? Where the touch with the power that was made in countinghouses and with the exercise of the power exerted from those countinghouses?

But it happened for Rosalie, first, that this thought could not come because she was too busy with the glorious novelty of being in an office and learning office ways; then, when the novelty had worn, that it could not come because a new and a real element arrived to nullify it. In the early days there was no realisation of sham because there was the real business, to herself, of learning business methods and the whole theory and practice of office routine. She could have had no better instructor than Mr. Simcox, she could have had no better training than the handling, the sorting and the filing of his curious and various correspondence. She had become an efficient and a singularly apt and keen office clerk when, more leisured because she had mastered her duties, she might first have had time for realisation that Lombard Street was not here nor all the romance and mystery with which she had invested the power of countinghouses within a thousand miles of this house of most elaborate pretence. And then, at once to prevent that realisation and to dissipate its cause, came Lombard Street to her in Mr. Simcox's new absorption in (to her) the mysteries and the romance and the astounding possibilities of the business of insurance. How the mammoth companies, whose names soon were as household words to Rosalie, accumulated their enormous funds and invested them; how, while provisioning for to-day, they must calculate against liabilities falling due in a to-morrow generations ahead; how they would put their money into property the leases of which would fall in and the estate become marketable again perhaps a hundred years hence, when officers of the company yet unborn would be looking to the prudence of those now reigning to maintain the inflowing tide; how risks were calculated and vital statistics and chances and averages studied — all this, delightedly and delightfully narrated by Mr. Simcox (watching that gravely nodding head and those wide intelligent eyes) was sheer fascination to the mind that had found romance and mystery in " Lombard Street " as commonly romance and mystery are found in poetry and music.

Then one day she took a step towards applying the fascination that she found.

It was the day of the conversation that has been recorded. How, Rosalie had asked, was the seeker after insurance to find the policies best suited to his case? Rosalie had asked; and had been told — he must go round but he never does; he must know what there is to be had but he never does know; he must realise exactly what he really wants but he never does realise it; and if he does realise it he must be able to state it clearly but he never can state it clearly.

Mr. Simcox, detailing this, permitted himself an amused contempt. The public were ignoramuses, mere children; they knew nothing whatever about insurance.

Rosalie said in a voice consonant with the grave measure of her nods: " Of course, if it was a man, as you said, looking for a house, he'd go to an agent. A house agent would tell him of houses best suited to his needs that he could choose between. Well, there are insurance agents. You've told me about them."

" Ah, but not the same thing, not the same thing," corrected Mr. Simcox. " An insurance agent, the ordinary insurance agent, is agent for a particular company. He only knows what his own company can do and he only wants his own company to do it. *That's* no good to the kind of man in the position we're speaking of. He wants some one who can tell him what all the companies will do for him. Some one who can hear his case, analyse it, put it before him in the right light and advise him the best way of placing it. That's what he wants. Exactly the same as these letters I send out — as you and I send out, I should say. Why, I've had practical examples of it. There was a young fellow I met at your aunt's house. There've been three or four cases of it for that matter but this happens to be some one you know — ".

He proceeded to tell her of a visitor at Aunt Belle's, a young man home on leave from the Indian army and recently married, with whom he had got into conversation on the subject of insurance and had most ably helped. The young man had a certain policy in view. Mr. Simcox had put an infinitely better before him. " If he had come to me before his marriage when he was first taking out a policy in his wife's favour, I could have saved him and gained her hundreds, literally hundreds," said Mr. Simcox. " He'd made a most awful mess of the business. As it was I helped him very considerably. He was very grateful, devilish grateful. He went straight to an agent of the office I recommended and did it."

" There must be hundreds like him that would be grateful," said Rosalie.

" Thousands," said Mr. Simcox. " Tens of thousands. Every single soul who insures, you may say."

" Who got the commission? " said Rosalie.

" The agent, of course," said Mr. Simcox.

" Oh," said Rosalie.

" Why? " said Mr. Simcox.

" Nothing," said Rosalie. " Only ' oh '."

CHAPTER V

THERE's much virtue in an If, says Touchstone; and there's much virtue in an " Oh " — a wise, a thoughtful, a speculative, a discerning " Oh " such as that " Oh " pronounced by Rosalie to Mr. Simcox's information that agents, and not he, drew the commissions for the insurance policies which, out of his knowledge and experience, he had advised. There followed from that " Oh " its plain outcome : her suggestion to Mr. Simcox of why not make a business, a real business, of expert advice upon insurance, and (out of the make-believe intercourse with schools) a business, a real business, of expert advice upon schools? And there shall follow also from that " Oh " a sweeping use of the intention that has been mentioned to tell only of her life that which contributed to her life. We'll fix her stage from first to last, then see her walk upon it.

This was her stage : Her suggestion was adopted. It has, astonishingly soon, astonishing success. Advice upon insurance, advice upon schools, commissions from each, are found wonderfully to work in together, each bringing clients to the other. Aunt Belle's swarms of friends, their swarms of friends, the swarms of friends of those swarms of friends, and so on, snowball fashion, are the first nucleus of the thing. It succeeds. It grows. Real offices are taken. " Simcox's." Advertisements, clerks, banking-accounts. Appearance of Mr. Sturgiss, partner in Field and Company — " Field's " — the bankers and agents. Field's is a private bank. Its business is principally with persons resident in the East, soi-

diers, civil servants, tea planters, East India merchants.
Field's is in Lombard Street. (Lombard Street!) Later
Field's opens a West End office. Field's is frequently
asked to advise its clients and their wives on all manner
of domestic matters, — schools for their children, holiday homes, homes for clients over on leave, insurance,
investment, whatnot, a hundred things. Comes to this
Sturgiss, partner in Field's, an idea of great possibilities
in this advisory business if developed as might be developed and run as might be run. Tremendously attracted by Rosalie as the person for the job. Makes her
an offer. She declines it. Mr. Simcox's death. Sturgiss comes along again. Ends in Rosalie going to Field's.
Lombard Street! Room of her own in the big offices.
Glass partitioned. Huge mahogany table. Huge mahogany desk. Field's open the West End office, in Pall
Mall. More convenient for wives of clients. Rosalie is
moved there. Manager of her own side of the business.
The war comes. Sturgiss goes out. Other important
officers of the bank go out. Her importance increases
very much in other sides of the bank's business than her
own. Press scents her out and writes her up. " The
only woman banker." " Brilliant woman financier."
Contributes articles to the reviews. Very much a leading
woman of her day. Very much a most remarkable
woman.

That's her stage. Thus she walked upon it :

The beginning part — that tumult of youth, those
dizzy jumps that we have seen her in — was frightfully
exciting, frightfully absorbing. She was so tremendously absorbed, so terrifically intent, so tremendously
eager, that the transition from the Sultana's to Aunt
Belle's, and the start with Mr. Simcox, and the transition
from Aunt Belle's to independence in the boarding house,

was done with scarcely a visit — and then a rather grudged and rather impatient visit — to the rectory home.

No, the absorption was too profound for much of that: indeed, for much of home in any form. Letters came from Rosalie's mother three and four times a week. In the beginning, when fresh left school and at Aunt Belle's, Rosalie always kissed the dear handwriting on the envelope, and kissed the dear signature before returning the letters to their envelopes; and she would sit up late at night writing enormously long and passionately devoted letters in reply. But she wasn't going back; she wasn't going down; no, not even for a week-end, " my own darling and beloved little mother," until she had found an employment and was established on her own feet, " just like one of the boys." *Then* she would come, oh, wouldn't she just! She would have an annual holiday, " just as men have," and she would come down to the dear, beloved old rectory and she would give her own sweet, adored little mother the most wonderful time she ever could imagine!

Rosalie would sit up late at night writing these most loving letters, pages and pages long; and her mother's letters (which always arrived by the first post) she would carry about with her all day and read again before answering.

And yet. . . .

The fond intention in thus carrying them on her person instead of bestowing them in her writing case was to read them a dozen times in the opportunities the day would afford. And yet . . . Somehow it was not done. The day of the receipt of the very first letter was generous of such opportunities and at each of them the letter was remembered . . . but not drawn forth. Rosalie did not attempt to analyse why not. Her repression, each time, of the suggestion that the letter should now be taken out and read again was not a deliberate repression. She merely had a negative impulse towards the action and accepted it; and so negligible was the transaction in her record of her thoughts, so mere a cypher in the petty cash of the day's ledger, that in the evening when, gone up to bed, the letter was at last drawn out and kissed and read and answered, and then kissed and read again, no smallest feeling of remorse was suffered by her to reflect that the intended reading in the dozen opportunities of the day had not been done.

And yet . . . Was it, perhaps, this mere acceptance of a negative impulse, a cloud no bigger than the size of a man's hand upon the horizon of her generous impulses? There is this to be admitted — that the letters, accumulating, began to bulk inconveniently in her writing case. What a lot dear mother wrote! Room might be made for them by removing or destroying the letters from friends who had left the Sultana's with her, but about those letters there was a peculiar attraction; they were from other emancipated One Onlys who watched with admiration the progress in her wonderful adventure of brilliant, unconventional Rosalie, and it was nice thus to be watched. Or room for her mother's letters might be made by removing or destroying letters that began to amass directly touching her desire for employment — from city friends of Uncle Pyke, from Mr. Simcox. But, no, unutterably precious those! Unutterably precious, too, of course, those accumulating bundles of letters from her dear mother; but precious on a different plane: they belonged to her heart; it was to her head, to the voice in her that cried " Live your life — *your* life — *yours!* " that these others belonged.

She was tingling to that voice one night, turning over the employment letters; and, tingling, put her mother's letters from her case to her box.

Yes, upon the horizon of her generous impulses perhaps the tiniest possible cloud. And then perhaps enlarging. You see, she was so very full of her intentions, of her prospects. She had read somewhere that the perfect letter to one absent from home was a letter stuffed with home gossip, — who had been seen and who was doing what, and what had been had for dinner yesterday and whence obtained. But she did not subscribe to that view. She was from home and her mother's letters were minutest record of the home life; but she began to skip those portions to read "afterwards." One day the usual letter was there at breakfast and she put it away unopened so as to have "a really good, jolly read" of it "afterwards." In a little after that she got the habit of always, and for the same reason (she told herself) keeping the letters till the evening. One day she gave the slightest possible twitch of her brows at seeing the very, very familiar handwriting. She had had a letter only the previous day and two running was not expected; more than that, this previous letter had slightly vexed her by its iteration of the longing to see her and by very many closely written lines of various little troubles. She was a little impatient at the idea of a further edition of it so soon. She forgot to open it that night. She remembered it when she was in bed; but she was in bed then . . . When, next day, she read the letter it *was,* again, an iteration of the longing to see her and, again, more, much more, of the little troubles: the residue was of the gossipy gossip that Rosalie already had formed the habit of skipping till "afterwards." Altogether a vexatious letter.

After that, when the letters were frequent, it was frequent for Rosalie to greet the sight of them with just the swiftest, tiniest little contraction of her brows. Nothing at all really. Meaning virtually nothing and of itself absolutely nothing. Possessing a significance only by contrast, as a fine shade in silk or wool will not disclose a pronounced hue until contrasted with another. The contrast here, to give the thing significance, was between that swiftest, tiniest contraction of the brows at the sight of her mother's letters and the eager spring to them, the quick snatching up, and the impulsive pressing to her lips when first those letters began to come. Likewise answering them, that had been an impulsive outpouring and brimming over, now was a very slightly laboured squeezing. The pen, before, had flooded love upon the page. Now the pen halted, paused, and had to think of expressions that would give pleasure.

The change did not happen at a blow. If it had, Rosalie would have noticed it. It slipped imperceptibly from stage to stage and she did not notice it.

CHAPTER VI

THERE was a thing she said about men once (in the boarding house now) and often repeated. "They're very fond of saying women are cats," she once said. "Fools! It's men that are the cat tribe: tame cats, tabby cats, wild cats, Cheshire cats, tomcats and stray cats! Aren't they just? And look at them — tame cats are miserable creatures, tabby cats the sloppy creatures, wild cats ferocious creatures, Cheshire cats fool creatures, tomcats disgusting creatures, stray cats — on the whole the stray cats are the least objectionable, they are bearable: at the right time and for a short time."

This characterisation of men as Rosalie, in sequent development of her attitude towards men, had come to regard them was delivered to the girl with whom (for cheapness) her room in the boarding house was shared. Rosalie went from Aunt Belle's to this boarding house to assert and to achieve her greater independence. A man, Rosalie debated, would have gone into bachelor rooms; but young women did not go into bachelor rooms in those days and the singularity of Rosalie's attitude towards life is rather well presented in the fact that she never set herself against conventions inhibitory of her sex merely because they were inhibitory of her sex. When the years brought those violent scenes and emotions of what has been called the suffragette campaign, Rosalie, who might have been expected to be a militant of the militants, took no part nor even interest in it whatever. She did not desire the privileges of men merely because they were the privileges of men; she desired a status which happened to be in the right of men and she went towards it without seeking to change the established order of things, just as, from one field desiring a flower in another field, she would have gone to fetch it without changing her dress.

A man, anxious for full independence, would have gone into bachelor rooms; but young women did not go into bachelor rooms. They achieved their independence perfectly well, and far more cheaply, by going into a boarding house. She therefore, very excitedly, went into a boarding house.

There was no difficulty about leaving Aunt Belle's. Once Rosalie was established in business with Mr. Simcox, tied to business hours, and earning a weekly salary, she no longer occupied in Aunt Belle's house the position of dependence which was in Aunt Belle's house the first, and indeed the only, qualification for all who occupied her house. Aunt Belle's guests had to *be* guests: wealthy guests who could be entertained from early morning tea (beautifully served) to bedtime and made graciously to admire; or if poor guests, and particularly poor relations, guests who could be even more impressed and were naturally much more enthusiastically delighted and profoundly admiring. Rosalie, in business, could not be entertained and did not sufficiently admire. She had to have a special early breakfast; she disappeared; she was not in to lunch or tea; she was not sufficiently impressed by what cook had prepared but had rather too much to say about what she had been doing, at dinner; and she excused herself away to early bed on the ground of fatigue or of having certain books to study. Rosalie, in business, was not a guest at all in Aunt Belle's sense of the word: indeed there came an occasion — Rosalie twice in one week late for dinner — when Aunt Belle said awfully, " My house is not a hotel, Rosalie. I cannot have my nice house turned into a hotel."

It was the nearest thing to an unkind word ever spoken
by Aunt Belle to Rosalie, and it was so near that it
brought Aunt Belle up to Rosalie's bed that night — solicitude in a terrific dressing gown of crimson silk — to
express the hope that Rosalie was not crying (she was
not; she had been sound asleep) at anything Aunt Belle
"might have said." "But you see, dear child, there are
the servants to consider, all that delicious soup and all
that most tasty turbot *au gratin* to be kept warm for you,
and there is your kind Uncle Pyke to consider; men do
not like their meals to be . . ."

The boarding house, which Rosalie, with qualms as to
its reception by Aunt Belle, had for some time been secretly meditating, came easily after that. The boarding
house had moreover for Aunt Belle a double attraction.
It not only removed Rosalie in her capacity of one threat-
ening to turn Aunt Belle's nice house into a hotel; it also
restored Rosalie in her capacity of overwhelmed, grateful and admiring poor relation. Rosalie was now invited
from the boarding house just as previously she had been
invited from the Sultana's; the table and the appointments of Aunt Belle's house were now lavishly displayed
in contrast to the display and the table endured by
Rosalie at the boarding house; Aunt Belle was again
supremely happy in Rosalie and abundantly kind; dinner
each Saturday night was a standing invitation and frequently for these dinners Aunt Belle arranged "a little
dinner party for you, dear child, just one or two really
nice people that it is nice for you to meet and that you
can tell your friends at the boarding house about, dear
child."

Aunt Belle helped Rosalie to choose the boarding house
and saw that it was "nice." Nice people went there and
the proprietress, Miss Kentish, was nice. Miss Kentish
had a grey, detachable fringe which became, and re-

mained, semi-detached immediately after breakfast, and
a mobile front tooth which came out surprisingly far
when she talked and went in with a sharp click when she
stopped. She had for newcomers a single conversational
sentence — " My name is Kentish, though funnily
enough we come from Sussex " — and, for all purposes,
a single business principle, that of willingness " to come
to an arrangement." " I am afraid I cannot remedy your
water not being hot at eight o'clock," she would say to a
boarder, " but I will gladly come to an arrangement with
you. Ten minutes *to* eight or ten minutes *past* eight "
(click). She would come to an arrangement on anything. She became very fond of Rosalie in course of
time and once told her that though her duties never permitted her to attend church she had " come to an arrangement " with the vicar and felt that she had " come to an
arrangement with Our Lord " (click). She came to an
arrangement with Rosalie in the matter of tariff, receiving her and a Miss Salmon, who also sought arrangement, as " two friends as one." This was two persons
sharing a room at the tariff of a person and a half. Living was very cheap in those days. Rosalie, at the beginning, with Miss Salmon, paid 18/6 a week, and out of
the twenty-five shillings paid her, at first, every Friday
by Mr. Simcox there remained what seemed to Rosalie
great wealth.

She set herself to save on it and her first purpose in
thus saving was to accumulate money on which she could
draw so as to be able to pay for a room private to herself.
That would have taken some time. Her successive increases in her earnings, as Mr. Simcox's hobby developed
into a business, brought privacy, and in time what
amounted to luxury, by much swifter process. Rosalie
was a very long time at the boarding house. From being
two friends as one she passed to a small remote room of

her own, then to a larger and more accessible room, then
to a bed-sitting-room, finally to a very delightful arrangement. There was on the second floor a fine roomy apartment having a dressing-room opening out of it. Rosalie,
by then in much favour with Miss Kentish, not only secured the suite but " came to an arrangement " with Miss
Kentish by which the furniture and fittings were removed
from the rooms and Rosalie permitted to fit, decorate
and furnish them herself. Rosalie never knew happier
hours than in the furnishing of those two rooms into a
little kingdom of her own: she never in all her life knew
days as happy as the days there spent.

But at the beginning, two friends as one with Miss
Salmon and first contact with life from the angle presented by some twenty various individuals met at meals
and in the public rooms. Miss Salmon was a pale, fussy
creature with pince-nez in some mysterious way set so
far from her eyes that she always appeared to be running
after them as if to keep them balanced. Whenever anything of which she did not approve was being said to
Miss Salmon or was being done before Miss Salmon, she
maintained throughout it, moving about in pursuit of her
pince-nez, a rather loud, constant, tuneless humming.
When her moment came she would always begin " Well,
now " and then swallow forcibly as though the swallowing gave her pain. " Well, now " (gulp). This introduction was always precedent to speech by Miss Salmon, whether after humming or not. Rosalie frequently
went to Sunday church service with her and there was
an occasion in the Litany on which Miss Salmon, who
either had been wandering or sleeping, suddenly came to
herself at the correct moment and said: " Well, now " —
(gulp) — " We beseech thee to hear us, O Lord."

Miss Salmon was employed as a daily nursery governess by a family resident across the park who, not hav-

ing room for her, had "come to an arrangement" with
Miss Kentish for her accommodation at the boarding
house; and with her fussiness, her nose pursuit, her humming and her general ineptitude of habit and of thought,
she was as it were a fated companion for Rosalie; and it
was the case that all the other inmates of the boarding
house were, in regard to Rosalie, equally and in the same
sense fated. Miss Salmon and they were fated, or fatal,
to Rosalie, in the sense that it would have been well then
for Rosalie, as always well for any developing young
thing, to have been among companions who drew upon
her sympathies and called for her consideration. The
contrary was here presented to her. She was ripe to be
intolerant for she was very full of purpose and purpose
is a motive power of much impatience. Miss Salmon,
who would have made a saint impatient, made Rosalie,
who was not a saint, very impatient and the virus of this
impatience was that very soon Rosalie made no attempt
to conceal it. It seemed to Rosalie that whenever she
projected any plan to Miss Salmon — as to "do" a pit
at a theatre — or any theory — as that men and not
women were manifestly the cat tribe — it seemed to her
that Miss Salmon *always* hummed with the maddening
humming denotive of disapproval, and *always* prefaced
stupendously stubborn idiocy with the "Well, now" and
the gulp that alone were sufficient to drive enthusiasm
crazy.

"Mmmmm — mm. Mmm — mmmm — mm — mm,"
would go Miss Salmon, following her pince-nez up and
down the little bedroom. And then, the pince-nez poised,
"Well, now" (gulp).

And Rosalie came to cry, "Oh, never mind. Never
mind, for goodness' sake. I know exactly what you're
going to say so what is the good of saying it?" Miss
Salmon nevertheless would say it, in full measure, pressed

down at intervals in solid lumps with reiterated " Well, now " (gulp). And then Rosalie would hum to show she was not listening and thus in time to the position that Rosalie, beyond the ordinary changes of everyday conversation, took not the slightest notice of Miss Salmon but busied herself in their room, or came into it or went out of it, precisely as if Miss Salmon, who with her gulps, her fussiness and her balancing was very much there, was in fact not there at all. When Rosalie for the weekly dinner at Aunt Belle's used to dress in the evening frock of Laetitia's given her for the purpose by Aunt Belle, she used, at first, to say to Miss Salmon, " There, how do I look, Gertrude? Can you see that mend in the lace? "

" Well, now — " (gulp).

Very soon she was dressing (at the common dressing table) with no more regard for Miss Salmon or for the continuous humming of Miss Salmon (signification of Miss Salmon's disapproval of the monopolisation of the dressing table) than if Miss Salmon had been an automaton wound up to balance a pince-nez around the room, to hum, and at intervals to gulp.

This was a small thing, but it was an important small thing. Rosalie was entirely insensible to the opinions and the existence of Miss Salmon, and it followed that she became entirely insensible to the feelings of Miss Salmon. To begin by ignoring a person with whom you are in daily contact is certainly to end by not caring at all what happens to that person. It was the misfortune of Miss Salmon to suffer periodically and acutely from biliousness (which she called neuralgia). In an attack she took instantly to her bed and lay there flat on her back, absurdly and unnecessarily poising her pince-nez, and looking, unquestionably, very unpleasant. Rosalie, who believed that Miss Salmon on these occasions had

overeaten herself, the attacks invariably coinciding with
pork in winter and with a fruit trifle known in the boarding house as " Kentish Delight " in the summer, of both
of which Miss Salmon was avowedly fond, was at first
warmly sympathetic and attentive on their occurrence,
anointing the fevered brows with eau-de-Cologne, nipping the unnecessary pince-nez off the pallid nose, dark-
ening the room, and stealing about on tiptoe. In time her
attitude came to be expressed by her reception of the
sight of Miss Salmon prone, stricken, yellow, pince-nez
poising. " What, *again?* "

" Well, now —— " (Gulp).

But Rosalie would be gone.

And it came to be the same with all the other fellow
inmates of the boarding house, alike the men and the
women. Rosalie, in a colloquialism of to-day not then
coined, " had no use for them." There was in none of
them anything that aroused her esteem; there was in each
of them, in degree greater or less, much that provoked
her scorn. The result was as resulted from Miss Salmon — she did not bother about them; and not bothering
about them she suffered an inhibition of her sympathies.
To repeat the thing said, her environment here was, as it
were, fated or fatal. In her eagerness for her career her
generous emotions were likely to be laid aside and to
wither; and the environment of the boarding house in no
way drew upon her sympathies.

This was not good for Rosalie.

Moreover, the community of the boarding house served
Rosalie ill on another point. She came there with all
those grotesque ideas of her childhood on the respective
positions of men and women precipitated through her
older years to the perception given to Keggo: women
were this, women were that; in their commonest char-
acteristics they contrasted very badly with men; men did

things better than women; they had by far the better lot in life than women; unquestionably men were the creatures; of course — off-handedly — they were beasts. She came to the boarding house with these ideas and the boarding house presented these ideas to her in living fact and assured her in her ideas. She came there very susceptible to the qualities she believed to be rooted with their sex in men and women and she saw those qualities there at once. The boarding house might have been all her ideas of women and of men taken away by an artist and put into an exact picture. It was her words to Keggo in terms of actual life. Its population, little varying, was always round about twenty; the proportion in sex always in the region of fifteen women to five men. The figures were always constant and the characters, when they changed, seemed always to Rosalie to be constant; the names changed, the personalities did not change. Even the faces did not change: there are certain types of faces that either are produced by permanent residence in boarding houses or that go instinctively to boarding houses for their permanent residence. There is a boarding-house mould. There would always be two husbands with wives and three men without wives. The men were never spoken to by any of the women but with a certain archness which Rosalie detested; and they never spoke to the women but with a certain boisterousness, a kind of rubbing together of the hands and a " Ha! What miserable weather, Mrs. Keeley. How does it suit you? Ha!" which Rosalie equally detested. It was as though the women, leading boarding-house lives, knew that the men (who were never in to lunch and sometimes absent from dinner) did not lead boarding-house lives but secret, dashing and mysterious lives; and as though the men knew that they lived secret, dashing and mysterious lives but condescended to the women who lived only boarding-house lives; and the archness on the one side and the boisterousness on the other implied tribute and worthiness of tribute. This implication Rosalie also detested.

Men — as she now saw men and women — she dismissed; generally as " of course they're beasts," severally and in the groups to which they belonged, as cats — of the cat tribe — tame cats, wild cats, Cheshire cats, tomcats and stray cats. But she dismissed them. That was her attitude, as it developed, towards men. They had been, in her regard, owners of the earth, possessing and having dominion over the round world and all that therein is, as a stage magician owns and dominates his stage; they had next been wonderful things but apt to be troublesome and braggart things whose braggadocio caused you to blink and have a funny feeling; they had then been sinister and frightening things that caused poor Anna to say it *was* hard for women; they became, at last, creatures that had the best of life, that is to say the better time in life, not because they merited it, but because it was theirs by tradition and they stepped into it, or were put into it, as naturally as a man child is put into trousers; and they had, when all was reckoned up, the better qualities — largeness, tolerance, directness, explosiveness (as opposed to smouldering-ness) — not, Rosalie thought, because they were males, but because they had the position that males have, just as by the habit of command is given to small boys in the Navy and very young men in the Army the air and the poise of command.

Yes, certainly men were, as they had always been, the creatures; but the eyes that formerly saw them as magicians, as by a savage is seen only the mystery of the moving hands, the tick, and the strike of a clock, now looked inside the case and saw the works. No mystery. No exclusiveness of natural power. Nothing abnormal.

Men, on their estimable qualities and position, were what they were merely because, as the works of a watch, thus and thus the wheels were made to go round. Easy. Nothing in it. On the contrary. On the contrary, men were the more despicable in that, dowered as by tradition they were dowered, they yet were — what they were! The eyes that had been caused to blink by Robert blowing smoke through his nose and by Harold pulling up his collar and speaking with a " haw! " sound, blinked from a contempt yet more profound (because now known for contempt) at the exhibition, seen all about her, of men's unlovely side. And she dismissed them. They did not attract her in the smallest degree. All that they had in them to esteem, whether of qualities or of position, they had — here was the parallel — in common with drones in a hive. They had the best of everything; they were blundering, blustering, noisy, careless, buccaneering owners of the world, and to her — as all the roystering swarm to any individual worker bee — to her, negligible: she was a worker bee, busy, purposeful.

There is a special function belonging to drones in a hive. That special function of men in regard to women was repellant to Rosalie. All that pertained to it was repulsive to her. She loathed to think of men in that capacity and she loathed to see women ensnared in that regard by men. Beautiful cousin Laetitia and the " good match " that obviously had been found for her: she detested seeing those two together: it made her feel sick.

Men! By this and by that in passage of time she was in contact with a good number and a good variety of men. There was the frequently changing male contribution to the boarding-house community; there were clients met in the development of her work at Simcox's; there were the men of the circle of Uncle Pyke Pounce; there were the men of the circle of cousin Laetitia, brought to the little Saturday-dinner parties. A very fair average, a rather wider than the normal average of contact with men; and she dismissed them. They had not any attraction for her at all. If, rarely, she met one whose superficial points were superficially attractive, his contribution to her attitude to men was to make her blink (inwardly) the more, albeit on a different note. That one so exceptionally dowered should find pleasure in, for instance, dalliance of sex! Contemptible! Oh, sickening and contemptible! One Harry Occleve, of Laetitia's circle, so obviously "the good match," was outstandingly such a case. It was thought upon him, scornful and disgusted thought, that made her, walking back from one of the Saturday-evening parties — he was always there — arrange her experiences with men in that analogy between men and cats which, as related, had been delivered to Miss Salmon.

Like a tame cat! She never had met a man she despised so much. You'd think a man like that couldn't help but be above such things as Cousin Laetitia and Aunt Belle made of him. "Occleve." The very name that he owned had a nice sound; and he was brilliantly clever and looked brilliantly clever. He was a barrister and Aunt Belle, who was forever talking about him, had said that evening, just before his arrival, that some famous counsel had declared of him that he was unquestionably the most brilliant of the young men of the day at the Bar. So he was talented, had a great future before him, had a strong, most taking presence, a commanding air, a voice of uncommon charm — and was in bonds to Laetitia! Looked sickly at her! Mouthed fatuous nothings with her! Was obviously marked down to be that "good match" that Laetitia was to make; and was content, was eager, to be the tame cat of her languishing glances and of Aunt Belle's excessive gushings! Was to be seen in a future not distant mated with Laetitia and sharing with her an atmosphere of milk and silk and babies and kisses! Tame cat! What an end to which to bring such qualities! What a desecration of such qualities to set them to win such an end! Tame cat!

But they all were cats of one kind or another. Yes, men are of the cat tribe! Tabby cats — the soft, fattish kind, without any manlike qualities, that seemed to be by far the greater proportion of all the men one saw about in buses and in the streets and met in business; tabby cats — sloppy, old-womanish creatures. Cheshire cats — the kind that grinned out of vacuous minds and that never could speak to a woman without grinning; the unattached men at the boarding house invariably were of the Cheshire-cat cats. Tomcats — the beastly ones with lecherous eyes that looked at you. "Of course they're beasts." It had been a large experience of the tomcat cats that had made her add that final summary of men to Keggo. The Bashibazook, once or twice encountered in her last terms at the Sultana's, though never spoken with, had looked at her in a horrible way, not understood, but felt to be frightening and horrible; Mr. Ponders, on a dreadful occasion after handing over the medicine for Miss Keggs, had horribly said, "Well, now, wouldn't a kiss be nice? I think a nice kiss would be very nice." She had managed to get away without being touched; the nausea in her eyes perhaps had frightened him. It was nausea she felt, not fear, a horrible physical sickness; and finally to round off the "of course they're beasts" of men as then experienced and now to fill up the schedule of tomcat cats the friends of Uncle Pyke Pounce's circle and Uncle Pyke Pounce himself and the men like the men of his circle — tomcats something past their prime as lechers (but at a hint only more lecherous for that) but in the full prime of their beastliness as guzzlers, who with guzzle eyes eyed their food. She had come across a word in Carlyle's " French Revolution " that instantly brought Uncle Pyke Pounce and his friends to her mind and that always thereafter she applied to the elderly tomcat encountered or passed in the street — " atrabilious." Atrabilious! The very word! She looked it up in the dictionary, was disappointed to find it did not mean exactly what she thought it meant, but gave it her own meaning, and applied it to them. It *sounded* like them. They had small beady eyes, set in yellow; no apparent eyelids either above or below, just an unblinking eye set in a puffy face like a currant in a slab of cold pudding that gloated or glared at everything and everybody as if it was a thing to be devoured; guzzlers who gloated upon their food and wallowed in their soup, always with little streaks of red veins and blue veins in their faces. Atrabilious! Tomcats!

Wild cats — the roamers, the untamed ones, the ones with cruel and with wicked faces that made you not sick, but frightened; mostly they were dressed in rough clothes, men hanging about the streets who patently were thieves or worse, who looked at you and at once looked all around as if to see if any were about that might protect you; but often dressed in gentle dress and then with the cruel and wicked look more cruel and more wicked, to make your shudder to think of a woman having to belong to *that*.

Stray cats — on the whole the only really bearable ones; the lonely ones that seemed to have lost something or to be lost, that seemed to need looking after, that made you have a funny tender feeling towards them, a wanting as it were to pick them up and carry them home and be sharp with them because they couldn't take care of themselves, and to be kind to them also because they couldn't take care of themselves; yes, the only bearable ones: Mr. Simcox was precisely one.

All cats, of the cat tribe. There wasn't one you couldn't place. There wasn't one, save dear little Mr. Simcox and the stray cat ones you sometimes saw, that was not in some trait contemptible. The only thing to be said for them was that it was their nature. They were created like that. You just shrugged your shoulders at them and let them go at that, negligible entities. Active disgust was only felt of them when one of their traits was manifested directly towards you; or, much more, when the sight was given of such a one as this Harry Occleve making such an exhibition of himself and enjoying it, delighting in it, asking nothing better than to be philandering with Laetitia, or escorting Laetitia, or gazing at Laetitia. That did make you angry enough with a man to hate a man. It was like seeing a good book — as it might be " Lombard Street " — used to prop a table leg; or a jolly dog — as the dearest Scotch terrier once brought to the boarding house — led for a walk on a leash by an old maiden mistress and wearing a lapdog's flannel coat with ribbon bows at the corner. Her aversion to Harry Occleve was such that, in their rare passages together, she was almost openly rude to him. It seemed there was even no physical quality he had but he used it to abase himself or to make an exhibition of himself. He had noticeably long, strong-looking arms, but the sickening thing to see him once using those arms to hold silk for Laetitia while she wound it! He had a striking face that she named, from a line in Browning, a " marching " face — " one who never turned his back but marched breast forward " — but to see that face bent fatuously towards Laetitia! There radiated from the corners of his eyes towards his temples those little lines that sailors often have, " horizon tracks," she called them; but to see them deeply marked while he mouthed earnest nothings with Laetitia! There was an odd, nice smell about him, of peat, of tobacco, of soap, of heather with the wind across it, of things like that most agreeably mixed, and actually she had heard Laetitia say to him in the babyish way she spoke to him, " You smoke too much. You do." And he, like a moon calf: " Oh, you're not going to ask me to give up smoking, are you? " And she with a trailing eye and hint of a blush, " Perhaps I shall — some day." And he — a sigh! Positively a love-sick sigh straight out of a novel! Ah, positively she could detest the man! She came to discover it as an odd thing that, while commonly she was entirely indifferent to men, always after a Saturday meeting with Laetitia's Harry she had for quite a day or two an active detestation of them.

But it was the women at the boarding house — to instance the boarding house — the fifteen women, the immense, straggling army of women as they looked to be when they came trooping in to dinner or went trailing out again, that had Rosalie's sharpest observation and that best pointed her youthful estimates. Unlike men who had fallen woefully from her childhood estimate of them, the women maintained and intensified her early estimate of women. The women in the boarding house showed Rosalie what women come to. A few were emphatically old; the rest, with the single exception of Miss Salmon, were emphatically not old; on the other hand they were emphatically not young. They were at pains to let you see they were not old and the pains they were at rather dreadfully (to Rosalie) emphasised the fact that they were not young. The thing about them, the warning, the proof that they exhibited of all Rosalie's ideas about the inferiority of women, was that they were, in her phrase,

derelicts — not wanted; abandoned; homeless; or they
would not be here.   Yes, *derelict;* and what was worse,
derelict not in the sense of desuetude of powers or of
powers outworn, but with the suggestion of never having
had any powers, of having been always the mere vessels
of another's powers — some man's; and now, with that
power withdrawn — the man, whether father, brother,
lover or husband, gone — derelict as a ship, abandoned
of crew, rudderless and dismasted, is derelict; as an obscure habitation, cold of hearth, crazy of walls, abandoned to decay, is derelict.   She summed them all up as
having arrived at what they were precisely because in
their earlier years they had been what in her childhood
she had supposed women to be: inferior creatures at the
disposal and for the benefit and service of men.   What a
warning never to be that!   There they were — *manless.*
And therefore derelict.   And because derelict for such
a reason, therefore testimony to a social condition that
was abominable, and because seen to be abominable never,
never herself should enfold.   Never!   Manless.   Hus-
bandless.   There they were, the straggling mob of them,
— deserted by husbands, semi-detached from husbands,
relict of husbands fallen out with a stitch in the side in
the race for husbands.   Urh!

She was very young, Rosalie.

" Despised and rejected of men," she said to Miss
Salmon, holding forth in their bedroom on her subject.
" That's what I call them.   Despised and rejected of men.
Oh, don't hum louder than ever.   It's not irreverent to
say that.   It describes a condition, that's all, and I'm using it because it describes this condition, their condition,
exactly.   It does.   You can hum; but it does.   They've
never done anything, they've never meant to do anything,
they've never tried to do anything except hang round
after some man.   That's all.   They've either caught him

and now lost him; or they've missed him and now go on missing him. That's their lives. That's nearly any woman's life. It's not going to be mine. If anything were wanted to make the whole idea of marriage and all that repulsive to me — and nothing is wanted — that would. Despised and rejected of men! I used to think and to say I intended to be like a man and to do a man's work and have a man's share. I tell you that even getting so close to a man as that — I mean as close as intentional emulation of him — even getting as close as that makes me feel sick now. It's my own life I'm going to have, my own place, my own share; not modelled on any one else's. If it were conceivable that I ever met a man I cared tuppence about — but it isn't conceivable; that's a quality that's been left clean out of me, thank goodness — but if it were conceivable, what I'd offer would be just to share; to go on living my own way and he his — Oh, your humming! I mean after marriage, of course; I think this free-love business they talk about is even more detestable than the lawful kind — just animalism. That's all I'd do. Me my life; he his life; meeting, as equals, when it was convenient to meet. I'd like to bring all these poets and people who write about love into our dining-room to see those people. That'd teach them!

> Man's love is of his life a thing apart;
> 'Tis woman's whole existence.

What an existence! "
 " Well, now — " (gulp).

CHAPTER VII

"You have pretended to dislike and to despise men, but it was a *pretence* to *deceive* me and you are a *liar.*"

This was the astounding opening of an astounding letter, pages and pages, to Rosalie from Miss Salmon. Pages and pages, having the appearance, each one, of a battlefield or of a riot: a welter of thick, black underscores strewn about like coffins or like corpses, and a bristling pin-cushionful (black pins) of notes of exclamation leaping about like war-dancing Zulus or staggering about like drunken or like wounded men. A welter you had to pick your way through with epithets rushing against you at every step like units of a surging mob hounding and charging against an unfortunate pedestrian caught in the trouble.

Miss Salmon had two months before introduced " a gentleman friend " to the boarding house. He was a clerk in some big business firm. His name was Upsmith and he bore upon a fattish face a troubled, beseeching look, rather as though something internal and not to be mentioned was severely incommoding him and might at any moment become acute. Miss Salmon called him Boo, which Rosalie considered grotesque but not unsuitable, and it was communicated to the boarding house that the twain were at a mysterious point of affinity called, not an engagement, but an understanding.

Rosalie had by this time taken the second step in her upward progression of comfort in the boarding house. She had moved into a separate room, leaving Miss Salmon to become half of another two friends as one, and she and Miss Salmon therefore saw much less of each other. But Rosalie still sat at the same table as Miss Salmon at dinner and there Mr. Upsmith joined them.

The thing may be hurried along to its astounding conclusion in the astounding letter. It was not in itself an event of any sort of moment to Rosalie. She was in no way outraged by being called a liar. There is no hurt at all in being called a liar when you know you are not a liar. The accusation has sting only if you are a liar; and indeed it is comforting evidence of some inner self within us that only when we have ourselves debased that inner self become we open to wounds from without. That citadel is never taken by storm; only by treachery. No, the significance of the astounding letter reposed in the fact that her reception of it opened to Rosalie a glimpse of a quality rising beneath her to carry her forward as a wave beneath a swimmer. It has been perceived in her but Rosalie had not perceived it.

A great triumph and a great happiness swelled within Miss Salmon with the arrival of Mr. Upsmith and with the circulation about the boarding house that there was an understanding between herself and Mr. Upsmith. Her humming took on a loud, defiant quality, as of triumph; she pursued her pince-nez with a certain eagerness, as of confidence of balance and certitude of capture. Her note and her air seemed to say that she was Boo's and Boo hers and she gloried in it with that exalted and yet something fearful glory that is to be seen, pathetically, on the faces of very plain young women, or of distinctly ageing young women, who have got a Boo but for whom the Boos of this world are elusive to capture and slippery to hold. The look is to be seen a dozen times on any Sunday afternoon when the young couples are out.

At dinner time Miss Salmon would talk much to Boo in whispers and then would look up and hum across at

Rosalie in triumph, as of one that knew things that Rosalie could not know and that had a thing that Rosalie did not possess. Mr. Upsmith looked also much at Rosalie, in no triumph, but in an apparent great excess of his unfortunate complaint. He stared, troubled and beseeching, at her at meals, and he stared, troubled and beseeching, at her when he encountered her away from meals. The longer he sojourned in the boarding house the more troubled and beseeching, when Rosalie happened to notice him, did his fattish countenance appear to become. That was all. There scarcely ever was exchanged between them even the courtesies customary between dwellers beneath the same roof; they never, that Rosalie could remember, were a minute alone together and yet on a day in an August, Miss Salmon a week away on a month at the seaside with the family to which she was nursery governess, Rosalie was being told in the violent opening sentence of one letter that she had pretended to despise and dislike men but had only done it to deceive Miss Salmon and was a liar; and in the impassioned sentences of another which had been enclosed and had fallen and to which bewildered she stooped and then read, that the heart of Boo was at her feet (" your proud, sweet little feet that I would kiss in my adorance ") that he had adored her ever since he had first set eyes on her, that he treasured " like pearls before swine " every encouragement she had given him from her divine eyes and from her proud little lips, that he had had no sleep for a fortnight and felt he would go mad unless he wrote these few lines (nine pages), that he earned " good money," and that he was, in conclusion, to which Rosalie amazedly skipped, " ever and ever and imperishably always her imperishably adoring Boo."

Two days previously Rosalie had received, but not read, another slightly mysterious letter. It had been in her receptacle in the letter rack in the hall, addressed to her in an unfamiliar writing and deposited by hand, not through the post. It had begun " Dear Miss Salmon, re our friendship I have to inform you — " Rosalie had turned to the end, " B. Upsmith." She had replaced it in its envelope, written upon the envelope, " This is evidently for you, but addressed to me, as you see — R." and had placed it in another stamped wrapper to be forwarded by Miss Kentish. She had only thought of it as in funny style for a love letter, proper no doubt to the niceties of an " understanding." And what had happened was that the vile, egregious, and infamous Boo, writing to break off one understanding and establish another, had placed them in the wrong envelopes. The outpourings of his bursting heart to Rosalie had been received by Miss Salmon; the information " re our friendship " had gone to Rosalie.

Of itself, as has been said, the whole incident was nothing at all in the life of Rosalie. It came with the crash, but only startling and quite harmless crash, of an unexpected clap of thunder, and it passed as completely and as passively, doing no damage, leaving no mark. Miss Salmon never returned to the boarding house; the vile, egregious and infamous Boo haply incisively informed by Miss Salmon of what he had done, incontinently, and without speech to Rosalie, fled from the boarding house. They were gone, they were nothing to Rosalie; the correspondence was destroyed, it was nothing to Rosalie.

But the significance of the matter was here. There was in Miss Salmon's letter to Rosalie one paragraph that Rosalie read a second time. She had received the letter when coming in just before dinner. Not at all injured nor in any way discommoded by the hurtling epithets, the terrific underscores intended to be as bludgeons, or the leaping exclamatory notes set there for stabs, she had put the thing away in a drawer and gone down to her meal. The passage alluded to came more than once into her mind. When she was about to get into bed that night she destroyed the letter, first reading that paragraph, and only that, again. Sole in the violent welter of those sheets it had no underscores nor any exclamations. It was added as a postscript. It said:

"Well, now; Boo and I met the first time in a crowd watching a horse that had fallen down. It kicked and I stepped back quickly and trod on his foot. It made him put his hands on my arms and I looked around to apologise and there was his dear face smiling at me, although in great pain, for I had trodden on a corn he has; and I knew at once it was the face I had looked for and longed for all my life and had found at last; and I loved him from the first and we went out of the crowd and talked. Well, now; I clung to him in all our happy, happy months together, in a way you can never understand, because I loved him, and because I am not the sort that men like because I am only plain, and I knew that if ever he left me I could never get another. Well, now; you have taken him away from me. You could get dozens and dozens of men to love you, but you have taken mine, and I never, never can get another."

The thoughts of Rosalie, not sequent, but going about and amounting thusly, were thus: "That is very pathetic. That is horribly sad and pathetic. Coming at the end like that and without any strokes and flourishes, it is as if she was exhausted of her hate and rage and just put out an utterly tired hand and set this here like a sigh. *That's* pathetic, the mere look of it and that thought of it. And then what she says. The dreadfully simple naïveté of the beginning of it. Staring at a fallen horse in the street. It's just where they would be, both of them. They'd stand there for hours and just stare and stare. And then she steps back on his foot and there's 'his dear face' smiling at her; ah, it's pathetic, it's poignant! I can see it absolutely. Yes, I can. As if I were in the crowd around the horse, watching them. There they are, the horse between us, and all the doltish, staring faces round about; and their two dull and stupid faces; and as their eyes meet that sudden look upon their foolish faces, as of irradiation out of heaven, that would make a clown's face beautiful and cause the hardest heart to twist. But it doesn't cause mine to twist. That's the odd thing. I remember perfectly when a thing like that would have given me a little blinky kind of feeling. I've always been awfully quick to notice things like that. I've often seen them. Quite recently, so little, I believe, as a year ago, things like that, things like this, would have moved me a lot. They somehow do not now. That frightful ending of hers: 'You could get dozens and dozens of men to love you, but you have taken mine and I can never, never get another.' That is most terribly pathetic. I think that is the most poignant thing I have ever heard. Well, I can realise its utter pathos; I can realise it but I cannot feel it. It does not move me. 'And I never, never can get another.' It's frightful. I could cry. But I do not a bit want to cry. I must have somehow changed. I am not a bit sorry if I have changed. I would be sorry to go back and be as, if I have changed, I must have been — sentimental. I *have* changed. I believe I can look back and see it. About the time I left the Sultana's, mother's letters, and keeping them and answering them, began to be — yes they *did* begin to be a little tiny bit of a nuisance to me. Yes, it was beginning then, *this*. And I expect earlier, if I worked it out. There's nothing in it to regret. It's just a growing out of a thing. It's not, when I see a thing that's pathetic, that I've grown blunt or blind and

can't see it for pathetic. It's just — I know what it is
— it's just that it doesn't appeal to me in the same way.
It's like seeing a dish of most tempting food in front of
you, not that I ever remember my mouth, as they say,
watering at anything; but say strawberries and cream —
I'm fond of strawberries and cream — it's like seeing a
dish of strawberries and cream in front of you, and knowing it's good and knowing it's delicious, and knowing
you're awfully fond of it — and just not being hungry;
turning away and leaving it there, not because it's not
everything that it ought to be, but just because — you
don't want it. I should say that's how it is with me about
these — these pathetic things. I know they're pathetic.
I don't want them."

That is how it was, how it had become, with Rosalie.
That was just her first recognition of it, as the swimmer,
intent on his own making of his progression, recognises
not, till he has been borne some distance by it, the cur-
rent that also is carrying him along.

Visits home to the Rectory were further manifestations to her of this arising symptom.

There were appeals that should have arisen to her out
of her home; and they did arise; and she recognised them;
but they did not appeal to her — not in the old way.
She went home very rarely for occasional week-ends,
always for her annual holidays, always for Christmas; and the discovery she made was that she liked
her home very much better when she was away from
it than when she was in it. When a visit was in
prospect she desired her home, that is to say her
mother, most frightfully. But when the visit was in
being the joy she had promised herself she would spread
somehow was not at her command; the love she had
yearned to show somehow was chilled within her and not

forthcoming. It was the tempting dish in a new illustration — rushing eagerly to it, avid of its delights; coming to it and finding, after all, one was not hungry.

Strange!

Her mother was ageing rapidly. She could have wept to see the ageing signs; but somehow, seeing them, did not weep; was not moved; received the impression but was not sensitive to it; felt the tug but did not respond to the pull. Rather, indeed, was apt to be a little impatient. Returned to London and to her engrossing work and longed to be back with her mother; came back to her mother — and was not hungry.

Strange!

Then she began to analyse the strangeness of it and found it was not, after all, so strange; at least it was not a thing to be distressed about, nor bearing conviction of unnatural qualities, of hardness, of unkindness. There was a line she knew that came in a verse:

> There was a time when meadow, grove and stream,
> The earth, and every common thing
>   To me did seem
>   Apparelled in celestial light,
> The glory and the freshness of a dream.
> It is not now as it hath been of yore.
>   Turn wheresoe'er I may
>   By night or day,
> The things which I have seen I now can see no more.

" The things which I have seen I now can see no more." That was the line. " The things which used to appeal to me now appeal no more — or rather not quite in the same way. I think I used to be very sentimental. It is stupid and useless to be sentimental. People must grow old. There's nothing sad in that. It is natural. It is life. It is life and one must accept life. The unnatural thing, the foolish and wrong thing, is to remain a sentimental child for ever, with a child's ready foolish tears at what are common, necessary facts of life. I can be much kinder, much more really kind, by seeing things clearly and in their right perspective than by occluding them with false compassions. I am always my dear, my darling mother's devoted daughter, ever at her disposal, and she knows it and loves me for it. When I am to her or to any friend but as ships that pass in the night — Keggo's phrase — then let me take myself to task."

Keggo's phrase! Keggo was being intermittently seen at this time and these thoughts of Rosalie's were very close to the occasion when finally she lost sight of Keggo. It could be said like this — that Keggo here made a contribution to Rosalie's life that passed Rosalie on her way.

They had kept touch for quite a time after their separation as governess and pupil. They then lost touch.

"Why, it must be more than a year!" cried Rosalie, suddenly encountering Miss Keggs near the Marble Arch one evening and delightedly greeting her. It was in the summer and Rosalie had gone out from the boarding house after dinner for some fresh air in the park. She was enormously glad to see Keggo again and carried her greeting straight on into excuses for her share in their long sundering. "More than a year! You know, the fact is, Keggo, that when I first left the Sultana's, and for quite a time afterwards, I used to gush. I did! I was so frightfully full of all I was doing and it was all so new and so wonderful and I was so excited about it that it was sheer letting off steam — gush — to write you reams and reams of letters about it as I used to do. Then it got normal and the — the tumultuousness of it wore off and I was just — I am, you know — just absolutely absorbed in it and there was no more steam to let off; all the energy went into the work, I suppose. So gradually, I suppose, without quite realising it, I gave up writing. But, oh, if you knew how glad I am to see you now!"

Miss Keggs to all this presented only a fixed smile. A smile belongs much more to the eyes than to the lips. The lips, but not the eyes, can counterfeit a smile. False coin is "uttered" as they say in law; and the lips utter. Not so the eyes. All metal that the mouth issues is to be tested there. The expression in Miss Keggs's eyes was not at all in consonance with that of her mouth. The expression of her eyes was rather oddly vacant as you may see on the face of a person who is apparently attending to what you are saying but really is listening to another conversation in the same room. "Not listening" as it is called. "An absent look" as they say.

Nevertheless she joined dove-tailed response to Rosalie's words. "To tell you the truth," said Miss Keggs, speaking very slowly and repeating the preamble. "To tell you the truth I wouldn't have received your letters if you had written them."

"You wouldn't? Why not?"

"To tell you the truth —" there had been a pause before she first spoke; a pause again before this reply and then again a beginning with this phrase about which there was nothing odd in itself but something odd in the manner of its use by Miss Keggs. "To tell you the truth, I've left the school."

"Left the Sultana's!"

Miss Keggs nodded with slow inclinations, like grave bows, of her head.

"Whatever for? Keggo, when, why?" And then Rosalie, impelled by some apprehension that suddenly pressed her, put a quick hand on Keggo's arm and cried sharply, "Keggo! There is something very strange about you. What has happened to you? Something has happened. You can't keep it from me."

But Keggo could. At that quick gesture of suspicion of Rosalie's, animation sprung to meet it as a cat, at a sudden start, will leap from profound slumber to a place of safety and to arched defence. Miss Keggs, in their first exchanges, might have been as one drowsily answering questions from a bed. She was suddenly, in her instant casting away of her absent air, as that one flinging away the bedclothes and leaping upright to the floor. What had she been saying? She had been quite lost in something she was thinking of when Rosalie came up. She scarcely had recollected her. She had been very, very ill with " this influenza " and still was only convalescent. Why, how very, very glad she was to see her dear Rosalie again! And how Rosalie had developed!

" Why, Rosalie, you are beautiful! You are! And you don't blush or simper to hear it! Yes, you are beautiful."

There was a little room in a street somewhere off the Harrow Road that Miss Keggs now occupied. It was a forbidding street. It was one of those derelict streets frequent in certain quarters of London, in Holloway, in Kentish Town, in Kilburn and all over South London, all about which life teems and roars but where, along their own pavements, no life is. They are most characteristic of themselves, these streets, when, as often to be seen, there is no soul along them but a sad drab that is an itinerant singer that drifts along wailing, at every few paces shuffling her body in complete turns to scan the windows she has passed and the immediate windows on either hand. She has no home and these are not homes to which she wails. There is no flicker of life at any window. She's a sad drab, repulsive within; and they are sad drabs, not nice within. At night, but not before dusk, forlorn things flicker in and out of them like drab ghosts had on the strings of a puppet show. By day there sometimes is an old man crawling in or crawling out; sometimes a woman, always with a parcel or a net bag, fleeting along, expressionless. The high houses, all of one pattern, appear to have no pattern. They are like dead walls and the place they enclose like a vault, and the itinerant drab like a thing in drab cerements (they trail the dust) that ought to be dead wailing for entrance to things, tombed in those walls, that are dead. There is no life at all in these streets. There is nothing active or positive. There is just passivity and negation. There is just nothingness. They are not habitations, which connote life; they are repositories, which connote desuetude. They are the repositories of creatures, not that have done with life, for the sheer fact of living acknowledges service to life, but with whom life has done.

These came to be Rosalie's thoughts of this street — Limpen Street — but they could not have been hers when she was first going there to spend evenings with Miss Keggs, for it was in her earlier visits there to Keggo that she cried there. When she could cry for pure compassion for another she was still too — too ardent for Limpen Street to be seen as it has been presented. From the first it affected her disagreeably but she would have felt, then, a sympathy for its state, and a belief that it could be aroused out of its state, and a wish so to arouse it; and in her earlier visits she had ardently this sympathy, but it was raised to a profound compassion; this belief, but it was a conviction; and this wish, but it was a resolution, in regard to Keggo.

For Keggo was *drinking*.

Keggo had been drinking for years and years and now Keggo had walled herself away in Limpen Street to drink and drink, still secretly with the sharp cunning of the secret drinker, but now with cunning only necessary when of her own wish she met the world. At the Sultana's, (only Mr. Ponders in her secret, and in her pay; " that vile man " as, after the revelation, she always spoke of him to Rosalie) at the Sultana's and in all her life of that period she was, as it were, as one whose life is threatened, dwelling among spies; that breastplate of her cunning never could be laid off then; now, as one threatened, but secure in a castle, the breastplate only was needed when sallies forth were made. There was at the Sultana's the need of constant care to inhibit her cravings; there now was none to save her — unless Rosalie did.

There is no need at all to tell all this and all that by which Rosalie was led to this most terrible discovery and Keggo impelled to her most painful revelation. There was deceit and its exposure; lies and their crumpling in the hand; mystifications and their sinister interpretations; contingencies and their ugly dissolutions. These would be all beastly to tell. Beastly is a vile word but this is a vile thing. There was about it all, all the time, a tainted and unwholesome atmosphere. There was always in the little room in Limpen Street that strange disagreeable smell of bad eau-de-Cologne that always had hung about the little room at the Sultana's.

Beastly things. . . .

But they were not felt to be beastly by Rosalie, then. They are said here to be beastly, for they were beastly, only in excuse for Rosalie afterwards. They only were to her, then, intensely sad, most deeply pitiful, intensely increasing of her love for Keggo as pure love is increased by seeing its object in tortures that may not be helped because they will not be confessed. If only Keggo would tell her! Once or twice she said to Keggo, speaking with an entreaty that must have made obvious to Keggo her knowledge, " Keggo, haven't you something to tell me; something that you'd like to tell me? " The occasion was always when she was leaving after a visit that had found Keggo very unwell, very dejected of spirits, and that Keggo had at last terminated by saying, " I think perhaps you had better go, Rosalie. I think perhaps I'd be better lying down." But Keggo's answer always was, " Something to tell you? No, nothing at all! What should I have to tell you? "

And then one day something said brought them very near to the matter between them. Miss Keggs came nearer yet. She said, " The fact is, Rosalie, I sometimes get so I simply cannot make an effort, the smallest effort. I believe when I'm like that if a thousand pounds were offered me for the going out and asking of it, and God knows I want it badly enough, I simply could not make the effort to do it. I'd simply let it pass and know that I was letting it pass and not care. That's how it's got with me, how it is sometimes with me, Rosalie."

Rosalie said with extraordinary emphasis, leaning forward on the chair in which she sat facing Keggo. " *Why* is it, Keggo? "

If Keggo had answered, the thing would not have happened. Keggo did not answer. She was sitting with her hands crossed, one palm upon the other, and resting on her lap, her eyes to the ground. Quite a long time passed. Rosalie said, " You're drinking, aren't you, Keggo? "

" Yes, drinking, Rosalie."

" Oh, Keggo! "

It was then that Rosalie cried.

CHAPTER VIII

SHE cried. Her sympathies, though drying and slower now to be aroused, still then were such that she could weep for pity. It is a glimpse of her not to be seen again. There was she on her knees by Keggo, and with her arms about Keggo's waist, and with her head on Keggo's lap, crying for Keggo; and in the pauses of Keggo's unfolding of her story entreating her, as one that cried responses to a litany, "Don't mind, Keggo! Keggo, don't mind now! Dear Keggo, poor Keggo, it's all right now."

And presently all the tale told: what Mr. Ponders' medicine was; and all the humiliation suffered in keeping in with "that vile man"; and that vile man's betrayal of her to the Sultana, and her dismissal; and all the earlier dreadfulness of her first steps down into her dreadful malady; and all the dreadful secrecy of all those years; and all the horrible humiliation secretly to get her poison; and all the horrible humiliations when her poison got. All the dark tale of that presently told; and her head bowed down to Rosalie's, and Rosalie's wet face against her face, and her face also wet; and just her murmurs, murmured at intervals, as though her heart that had discharged its grievous load ran slowly now, slowly to rise and then to well with, "God bless you, Rosalie; oh, Rosalie, God bless you"; and for a long time just seated thus, cheek to cheek, hand to hand, heart to heart; weakness bound about with strength, sorrow in pity's arms, travail in sanctuary. . . .

It is desired that one should try to see that picture.

Its counterpart was not again in the life of Rosalie, hardening.

There were, after that, such happy evenings in Keggo's room. Keggo, with one to help her, fighting for herself; Rosalie, with one to help, elevated upon that high happiness that comes with fighting for another. For a short time there seemed to be no lapses in Keggo's struggle. When they came (as Rosalie knew afterwards) the practised cunning of years of secrecy had no difficulty in concealing them from the unsuspecting eyes of Rosalie. Ill that it was so! Rosalie was harder when came the lapse that cunning could not hide. She did not cry. Her eyes were hard. She said with thin lips, "Why, even all this time you have been deceiving me!" the which egged on, in that vile way in which exchanges of a quarrel are as knives sharpening one against the other, Keggo's enflamed retort, "The more fool you! Little fool!"

But at first, while the lapses were few and the cunning was equal to them, only a closer friendship was set afoot between the woman that was grown and the woman that was burgeoning, and there were such very happy evenings in the room in Limpen Street. Such jolly talks.

There was one talk that, forgotten with the very evening of its passage, afterwards very strongly returned to Rosalie and abode with her. It had in it rather vital things for Rosalie.

She loved to talk about her work with intelligent and sympathetic Keggo, and she had been on this occasion expounding to her the mysteries and interest of life insurance: in particular explaining the "romance" of vital statistics; in particular, again, the curious fact that, though women in the United Kingdom largely outnumbered men, many more male children were born than female. The disproportion "the other way about" in maturity, said Rosalie, was because the death rate among

men was much higher — due to risks of their occupations.
"A certain number of house painters," said Rosalie
sagely, "fall off ladders every year and are killed; women
don't paint houses, so they don't fall off ladders and get
killed. Similarly on railways, Keggo. The death rate
among railway men is much higher in proportion, over
an average, than the rate in any other occupation. Por-
ters doing shunting, for instance, are always getting
killed. Well, women don't shunt trains so they don't
get killed while shunting trains, so there you are again,
so to speak. The thing in a nutshell, Keggo, is that, by
contrast, men lead dangerous lives."

Keggo, who always was very alert in response, was
here very long in responding. Then she responded an
extraordinary thing that Rosalie afterwards remembered.
She said slowly, "Oh, but Rosalie, it's very dangerous to
be a woman."

Rosalie questioned her.

Keggo said, "Rosalie, you've great ideas, and I think
very shrewd and very striking ideas, about the difference
between men and women, but there's this difference I
think you haven't thought of — the danger that women
carry in themselves; right in them, here" — she had a
hand against her breast and she pressed it there — "born
in them, inerradicable, and that men have not. Men go
into dangers but they come out of them and go home
to tea. That's what it *is* with men, Rosalie. They can
always get out. They can always come back. They
never belong to a thing, body and soul and heart and
mind. Rosalie, women do. That's their danger. That's
why it is so very, very dangerous being a woman.
Women can't come back. They can't, Rosalie. Look at
me. They take to a thing and it becomes a craze, it becomes an obsession, it becomes a drug. Look at me.
They take to a thing — anything; a poison like mine,

or a pursuit like some one else's, or an idea like some
other's, or a — a career in life like, like yours, Rosalie,
— they take to it and go deep enough, and they're *its;*
they never will get away from it, they never, never will
be able to come out of it. *Never."*

She was extraordinarily vehement. It was embarrassing for Rosalie. Rosalie desired to contest, as vehemently,
these theories. She did not believe them a bit. They
were founded, she felt, on the tragedy of Keggo's own
case. Keggo was unfairly, though very naturally, arguing from the particular to the general, from the personal
to the abstract. But how could she reply to Keggo, " Of
course *you* say that? "

She was silent; but she betrayed perhaps her thoughts
in a gesture, her difficulty in some expression of her face.

Keggo said very intensely, " But, Rosalie, if you only
knew! With me it's drink and you'll say —. But I say
to you, Rosalie, never, never let *any*thing get the mastery
of you. With me it's drink and you'll say that is a matter
altogether different, with which parallels are not to be
drawn. Oh, do not believe it, Rosalie. A woman should
in all things be desperately temperate — watchfully, desperately temperate. A man — nearly every man — seems
somehow to have his life and all his interests in compart-
ments. He can be immersed in one while he is in it, and
can get out of it and distribute himself over his others
and close it and forget it. Rosalie, a woman *can't.* Men
have hobbies. They don't have attachments; they have
*de*tachments. They detach themselves and turn to a thing
and they detach themselves from it and turn back again.
Rosalie, women don't turn to a thing; they *go* to it. They
don't have hobbies, they have obsessions. They don't
trifle, they plunge. They cannot sip, they drain. It's
in their bone. They never would have occupied the place
they do occupy if it were not that from the beginning

they have given themselves over, or they were given over, to mastery. They are the weaker vessel. Rosalie, I tell you this, when a woman gives herself, forgets moderation and gives herself to *any*thing, she is its captive for *ever*. She may think she can come back, but she can't come back. For a woman there is no comeback. They don't issue return tickets to women. For women there is only departure; there is no return."

Rosalie said, "Keggo, I think I could argue, but I won't. But what I can't imagine is the application of it in hundreds of cases — in by far the great majority of cases. Take mine. You're not warning me, are you? I don't see the possibility — "

Keggo said, "Darling, I'm not warning you and yet I am. I am warning you because you are a woman; and because you are a woman you are susceptible to danger. It's what I've said; it's what I would have you remember for a day perhaps to come, that it *is* dangerous being a woman. I'm not warning you, because there's nothing to — well, but isn't there? You've got a theory of life and you are bent upon a career in life. There's — "

Rosalie cried, "Well, but there you are, Keggo. No comeback, no return tickets — well, I don't *want* to come back; I don't want a return ticket."

"You might. You never know. Suppose you ever did?"

"But you can't suppose it. Why ever should I?"

"Suppose you wanted to marry?"

Rosalie laughed. The thing immediately lost reality. "Well, suppose the incredible. Suppose I did. There'd be no comeback wanted there. I could perfectly well marry and still keep my theory of life; I could perfectly well marry and still keep on in my career — and most certainly I would still keep on. Why, that *is* my theory of life, as you call it, or a very outstanding principle of it. There's nothing to me more detestable in the whole business than the idea that because a woman marries she therefore must give up her work. That's what is the reason the boarding house and every boarding house and every home and street and city swarms with derelicts — with derelict women — just because their lives are all planned as blind alley occupations, marriage at the end of the alley, no need to do anything, no need to be anything because it's only a blind alley you're in. When you reach the end — you reach the end! That's it, Keggo. You reach the end. You're a woman, therefore for you — the end!"

She laughed again. She was returning Keggo's vehemence without embarrassment upon the subject that had made return difficult. She cried, "I've got you now, Keggo. I really have. You say they don't issue return tickets to women. No. Perhaps they don't; but I'll tell you where they book them all to — from the cradle: to a terminus."

Keggo smiled and would have spoken. But Rosalie was pleased with her adroit turning of metaphors. She repeated "To a terminus. Well, I've booked beyond, Keggo." She laughed again. "And then the idea of marriage for me! I've granted the preposterous just for the sake of the argument and just to floor the argument. But you know, you know perfectly well from all our talks, even so far back as at the Sultana's, that it's simply too grotesque! Marriage, for me! Why, if a million men came to me on their bended knees, each with a million pounds on their backs you know perfectly well that I'd just feel sick. Tame cats, tabby cats, tomcats, Cheshire cats, wild cats, stray cats, — I'm not going to set up a cats' home. No *thanks.*"

So Rosalie had the laugh of that evening.

CHAPTER IX

BUT this was not to continue. Keggo began to lapse; Rosalie began to weary of helping Keggo. She had herself to think of. Those who go down in life, whether by age or by misfortune, are prone, engulfed, to cry to those ascending, "You could help me!" There is a correct answer to this. It is, "I have done (or I do) a great deal for you. I cannot do more. It is not fair to ask me to do more. I have a duty to myself. I have myself to think of." Our generation endorses this.

Rosalie had herself to think of. By stages that need not be detailed, they are the common facts of life, the thing passes from that picture of those two with Rosalie's strong young arms about the other to a new picture, the last, between them.

The stages show Rosalie's enormous, ardent plans for the rescue and rehabilitation of Keggo, and they show the projection and the failure of the plans. They show work found for Keggo (through Simcox's scholastic side) and lost and found again and again lost and still again. They show Keggo's remorse and they show Rosalie's forgiveness. They show it repeated and repeated. They show by degrees the gradual, and then the rapid, staling of Rosalie's fond sympathies. They show her finally, immersed in her own purposeful interests, discovering to herself feelings in regard to Keggo on a plane with feelings discovered to herself in regard to her mother. It has been written: "Her mother was ageing rapidly. Rosalie could have wept to see the ageing signs; but somehow, seeing them, did not weep; was not moved;

received the impression but was not sensitive to it; felt the tug but did not respond to the pull. Rather, indeed, was apt to be a little impatient." It is not necessary to expand " Keggo was fast going downhill. Rosalie could have wept to see the downhill signs; but somehow, seeing them, did not weep; was not moved . . . rather, indeed . . . impatient."

She had herself to think of.

Youth's an excuse for youth as childhood's an excuse for childishness. Youth, still, like childhood, but unlike maturity, can be lost in its emotions, absorbed in them to the exclusion of all else, abandoned to them with all else pitched away as a swimmer discards his every stitch and joyously plunges in the stream. Youth is not accountable for its actions then: it is too happy or it is too sad. One oughtn't to blame youth, immersed.

There was outstandingly one such day of absorption in delight, of abandonment to ecstasy for Rosalie, and it was the day on which she made her third advance in the social grade of Miss Kentish's boarding house and moved into the two rooms en suite, furnished and decorated by herself to her own taste. She awoke to this great day, long anticipated; and with the vigorous action of throwing off the clothes and jumping out of bed, she plunged into it and was lost in it. The excitement and the elation of taking possession of that enchanting, that *significant* apartment of her own! She *was* excited; she *was* elated. Moving in was the cumulative excitement of all the long-drawn, anxious excitements of peering round the antique dealers and picking up the bits of furniture and of placing them and moving them a shade to this side and then a shade to that till was found the one and only exact position that suited them and that they suited; and the terrible excitements of watching the decorators

at work, her scheme developing beneath their hands, and
the awful knowledge that now it was being done it was
done for good or bad — no altering it now! and the
agonizing excitements of putting down the carpets —
how can you tell exactly how a carpet is going to look
until you see it actually down upon its floor and between
its walls? and the increasing excitement all the time of
the knowledge that everything was harmonising and was
looking just as in dreams of the ideal it had been made
to look; and now all ready! The bed-sitting-room slept
in last night for the last time; the two utterly perfect
rooms and all that their possession connoted, to be occupied that evening for the first time! Yes, in all the
tumultuous pride and engrossment of that, there was no
place — how could there be place? — for tiresome things
of other people's worlds, if such should offer.

And in this tremendous day there was stuff more tremendous yet. This also was the day on whose evening
was made the tremendous tribute to her work and to her
talent, the evening of the dazzling offer that, like a door
swung open on a treasure house, disclosed to her new
fields to which her career had brought her, new triumphs
that her career, in its stride, might make her own — the
evening when Mr. Sturgiss of Field's Bank leant across
the dinner table in his house (at his request only she and
himself left in the room) and said in his quiet voice,
"Well, look here — to come to the point — the reason
I've got you up here to-night — it's this: we want you,
Field and Company, the Bank, we want you to join us.
We want you in Lombard Street."

Lombard Street!

Cumulative also was this thrill, for it had begun some
few days previously when Mr. Sturgiss, calling at Simcox's for a chat with Mr. Simcox, an old friend, had
come into her room and after mysteriously fidgetting

with business and conversational trifles, had issued the invitation to dinner at his house at Cricklewood in language mysteriously couched. "My wife would like to meet you," said Mr. Sturgiss. "She's heard a lot from me, and from Field, of what an astonishingly clever young person we think you and she'd — she'd like to meet you. And more than that." Mr. Sturgiss's halting speech suddenly became direct and definitive like a flag that had been fluttering suddenly streaming upon the breeze. "And more than that. The fact is, there's a proposition I want to put up to you. A proposition. We could go into it quietly and discuss it. I rather think it would interest you. I'm sure it will. You'll come? Good. I'm very glad. Very glad."

A proposition! From Mr. Sturgiss! Of Field and Company! What could it be?

But Rosalie was not of the sort to tread the succeeding days on the enchanted air of fond surmises. She told herself that the mysterious proposition might be everything or might be nothing: the fact that outstood was that she had brought her aspirations to this — that a partner in a London bank recognised in her stuff sufficient to invite her to a confidential meeting, there to go into something with her "quietly together," to meet together over something and "discuss it." She had determined to establish herself and she *was* establishing herself. And was it not an omen propitious and significant that this recognition of her parts was to fall on the very day on which the exercise of those parts brought her into the dignity and comfort of that delicious, that *significant* apartment of her own?

This solid stuff, and no mere daydreams, was the delight absorbing her and the ecstasy to which she was abandoned when that great day came. In the morning she put the last of her possessions, the equipment of her

dressing table, into the new apartment; after the day spent
at Simcox's she returned to dress for the first time before the noble cheval glass purchased for the bedroom.
She decided to go up in a hat; it could be removed or
not for dinner as Mrs. Sturgiss might seem to indicate;
she put on an evening bodice of black silk and net with
a simple skirt in keeping. She gave last approving glances
about the delightful rooms and set out, immersed in
eager happiness, for Cricklewood.

One of those old red buses that vied with the white
Putney buses as being the best horsed on the London
routes took her there. Up the Edgware Road; past the
junction with the Harrow Road that led to Keggo's street
— she only had for it the thought that it was weeks since
she had seen Keggo, almost months; along broad Maida
Vale and past the turning that led to the Sultana's with
the corner where often the crocodile had huddled — and
she was so engrossed in her happy achievements that she
passed it without thinking of it. The bus terminated its
journey at the foot of Shoot Up Hill. Rosalie, called
upon to alight, came out of her thoughts into her surroundings. She realised that she must have passed Crocodile Corner without noticing and the realisation caused
her to give a little note of amused indifference. The
indifference was not directed precisely at the Sultana's; it was at the idea, which came to her, that,
normally to human predilections, she ought to have
given — ought now to give — a sentimental thought
to memories of the Sultana years. Well, she did
not. Funny! Yes, it *was* funny. As she sometimes
thought of her mother and of all her home ties; of
Miss Salmon and that cry of hers of never being able
to find another lover; of Keggo now so seldom seen and
known to be going from bad to worse, — so with memories of Crocodile Corner and the Sultana's: she could see

and appreciate the call of all these attachments, but somehow, seeing and appreciating, did not respond to them. What a very curious attitude! It was not unfeeling for she *could* feel. It was not insensibility for she was sensitive to such things. Sensitive! No, a better word than that. She was in such matters *sensible*. She saw, as one should see, these things in their right perspective. They were touching (as of her mother) or they were sad (as of Keggo) or they were appealing (as the happy schoolgirl memories) but they must not touch or sadden or appeal too closely. They must be estimated in their degree and in their place; they must not be assumed, be shouldered, be permitted to cumber. No *good* could be done to them by encumbrance with them. That was the point. What *good* could it do them? No good. Yes, that was *sensible*.

She abated, in these thoughts, nothing of the eagerness with which she was living this great day — the day whose points of suspension (on which it tumultuously revolved) were the taking over of the significant apartment from which she had just come and the entering upon the significant invitation to which now her feet were taking her. These thoughts, this analysis of her attitude to sentimental appeals, she tossed upon her eager happiness that was her being as an airball tossed upon laughing breath that yet is used, breathing, to support life. And she was aware that this was so. And she enjoyed a flash of approval of herself that it could be so; it was admirable, it was *sensible,* thus to be able to detach and look upon a portion of her mind while her main mind deflected not a shade from its occupation with the main chance. That faculty was perhaps the secret of her success, the quality, that, in exercise, had brought her to the significant apartment and to the significant invitation.

She was at the gate of Mr. Sturgiss's house and she most happily passed up the short drive, ascended the steps and rang the bell.

Mr. Sturgiss's house was almost on the summit of Shoot Up Hill. It was one of those houses standing a few miles along the main thoroughfares out of London that, now in decay or displaced by busy shops, packed villas, or monstrous flats, were then the distinctly impressive residences of distinctly well-to-do business people. Mr. Sturgiss was a distinctly well-to-do business person. The house, double-fronted, had that third sitting-room which confers such an immense superiority over houses of but two sitting-rooms — " Such a convenience in so many ways " as those newly promoted from two to three nowadays remark with languid triumph to visitors still immured in two. Houses — new, two sitting-roomed houses — extended beyond it and around it, and now stretch miles beyond and about, but Mrs. Sturgiss told Rosalie that when they first came there they actually had cows grazing and horses ploughing in fields adjoining their garden.

Mrs. Sturgiss told Rosalie this while personally attending Rosalie's removal of her hat (it was " no hat "; Rosalie felt so glad she had come dressed for either indication) and Mrs. Sturgiss sighed pleasantly as she said it. " Things are going ahead at such a pace now! " said Mrs. Sturgiss. " It's all very different from what it used to be. Why, the very fact of your coming here, not as my guest but as my husband's, ' on business! ' The idea of women being in business, or even knowing anything about business, when I was a girl, why, I can't tell you how, how positively shocking it would have been considered."

Rosalie laughed. She liked Mrs. Sturgiss, who was motherly and seemed to have her own dear mother's gentle ways — this personally attending her in her bed-room, for instance. "Oh, there are getting to be heaps of women in business now, Mrs. Sturgiss," she smiled.

Mrs. Sturgiss returned brightly, "Oh, I know it. I know it well." She paused and her voice had a thought-ful note. "But even then. . . . Use the long mirror, my dear; the light is better. Even then, there can be few as, — as much in it as you. You know, my husband has an immense idea of your abilities. He has spoken of you so much. Do you know, you are a great surprise to me, now I see you. I could only imagine from all John's idea of you a rather terrible looking blue-stocking, as we used to call the clever women." She came and stood by Rosalie, regarding the image in the glass that Rosalie regarded. She said simply, "But you are beautiful."

A very odd feeling, akin to tears — but for what on earth tears? — quickened in Rosalie. She turned sharply from the mirror. "I am quite ready now." She pre-tended she had not heard.

Mrs. Sturgiss said, "My dear, do you *like* it, being what you are?"

It was a great rescue for Rosalie to be able to spring away from that odd feeling (in her bosom and in her throat) by swift animation. "Oh, I love it. I simply love it. It is everything to me, everything in the world!"

Mrs. Sturgiss opened the door. "No, you go first, my dear. But if I had had a dear girl, such as you, I would have wished her to stay with me at home."

She had made with her hand the gesture of her wish that Rosalie should precede her from the room. Rosalie impulsively touched the extended fingers. "But, Mrs. Sturgiss, don't you see, that's just it, the idea there is now. If you had had a daughter and she had stayed at home — well, let that go, while you were with her. But

when you died and left her, what *would* there be — don't
you see it? — what would there be for her then?"

Mrs. Sturgiss pressed the warm young hand. "But
I would have left her married, a dear wife and a dear
mother."

"Oh, *that!*" cried Rosalie and her stronger personality
carried off the exchanges in a laugh. Mrs. Sturgiss
thought the expression and the tone meant, happily, that
marriage might happen to any one, in the market as
much as in the home. Rosalie, with all the fierce contempt
that her "Oh, *that!*" conveyed to her secret self, was ridden strongly away from emotionalism in the conversation. Her thought as they went downstairs was, "If I
were to instruct her in the cat-men! Her horror!"

There was downstairs a surprise that was very annoying, but that was made to produce compensations. An
unexpected fourth person, presuming — so Rosalie was
given to understand — on a long standing, indefinite invitation, had dropped in to dinner. She recognised him
directly they entered the drawing-room and could not
stop the emblem of a swift vexation about her mouth
and in her eyes. He caught it, she was sure; and she
hoped he did. It was Harry Occleve — Laetitia's futile
slave! He had already informed his host that he knew
her. She greeted him with a mere touch of her hand,
a touch made cold by intent, and with "With a free evening off one would have expected you would spend it with
Laetitia," said disdainfully. It was a rude and inept
thing to say (in the tone she said it) for the feeble creature, as she stigmatised him, had not yet screwed his
fatuous idolatry to the point of proposal of marriage.
But she intended it to be rude and to discomfort him and
she was glad to see some twinge at the flick pass across
his face. She hated his presence there. The presence of

any man, in the capacity of a monkey to entertain and to be entertained, was always, not to put too fine a point upon it, repulsive to her. This man was of all men obnoxious to her. When he approached her for their brief greeting (she turned instantly away at its conclusion) she savoured immediately that odd, nice smell there was about him, of mingled soap and peat and fresh tobacco smoke and tweed; and that annoyed her. It was a reminder, emanated from him and therefore not to be escaped, of a distinction he had different from, and above common men. She always granted him his distinction of looks, of air, of talent. It was why she so much disdained him. To be dowered so well and so fatuously to betray his dowry! Tame cat!

But she made him, through the meal, pay compensations for his presence. At the table of Aunt Belle, in his presence she was accustomed to sit largely silent. Beautiful Laetitia was there the star; and while he mouthed and languished in that star's rays Aunt Belle and Uncle Pyke, (stealing about him to capture him as a farmer and his wife with mincing steps and tempting morsel towards a fatted calf) fawned, flattered and deferred to him, he returning it. There was no place for her, and she would have shuddered to have held a place, in that society for mutual admiration. She sat apart. She was very much the poor relation (Aunt Belle could not comprehend her business success and Uncle Pyke would not admit it) and especially odious to her was the Occleve's polite interest in her direction when Aunt Belle, poor-relationing her, would turn to her from coquettish raillery of him with, " Dear child, you're eating nothing." He would smile towards her and, fatuously anxious to please, offer some remark that might draw her into the conversation. She never would be so drawn. She scarcely ever exchanged words with him.

She made herself to be unconscious of his presence. He was so occupied with his adoration of Laetitia that to be insensible of his presence was easy. When sometimes she glanced towards him it was with the thought, "Fancy being one of the rising young men at the Bar, being *the* rising young man — the Bar, with silk and ermine and, why not? the Woolsack before you — and being *that,* doing *that!* Fatted calf; dilly, dilly, come and be killed, goose; tame cat!"

Here, at the table of Mr. Sturgiss, it was very different. Intolerable that he should be here, but she was able to make him provide her compensation for his presumption. For the first time in her life she found herself with sufficient interest in a man to enjoy, nay, to seek, a triumph over him. And she had that triumph. She was as certain as that she sat there that Mr. Sturgiss, in the period before her arrival in the drawing-room, had been telling him of her abilities and of his high regard for her. There was an interest in his look at her across the table that assured her he had been informed. There was, much more, a conviction within her, from Mr. Sturgiss's manner and from his choice of subjects — confined almost entirely and to the absolute exclusion of Mrs. Sturgiss to the political situation and to markets, exchanges and the general tendency in the City — and particularly from the openings in these subjects with which continuously he presented her — a conviction arising out of these that Mr. Sturgiss, proud of her, of his discovery of her, was bent upon showing her off to his second guest, bent upon proving to his second guest what unquestionably he had said to him about her.

She most admirably responded. If she were indeed the subject of a challenge she most admirably flattered her backer. She is not to be imagined as a pundit excavating from within herself slabs of profound wisdom, nor yet as a pupil astoundingly instructing her masters, nor even as one of Mrs. Sturgiss's blue stockings, packed with surprising lore; Rosalie was nothing so foolishly impossible; but she displayed herself knowledgeable; she was profoundly interested in the matters under notice and therefore (for it follows) she was interesting in her contributions to them; she was fascinated — the old fascination of " Lombard Street " and of "The English Constitution " now intensified as desire intensifies by gratification — and therefore she fascinated; she was never silly — Rosalie could not be silly — but she was frequently in her remarks ingenuous, but her ingenuousness, causing Mr. Sturgiss more than once to laugh delightedly (Occleve, curiously grave, no doubt because surprised, did not laugh) was born out of a shrewd touch towards the heart of the matter, as the best schoolboy howlers are never the work of the dullard but of him that has perceptions. Of her in her childhood it has been said that she was never the wonder-child of fiction who at ten has read all that its author probably had not read at thirty. So now of her budding maturity she was not the wonder-woman of fiction, causing by her brilliance her hearers, like Cortez's men, to stare at each other with a wild surmise. No, nothing so unlikely. But she was intelligent and she was ardent; and there are not boundaries to the distance one may go with that equipment. She was admirable and she felt that she was effective. She had a consciousness of confidence amounting almost to a feeling of being tuned up and now let go; to a feeling of power, as of inspiration. And this strange animation that she had, came, she knew, from the triumph over that man, from the feeling, stated grimly, that she was giving him *one*.

It is much more important, all that, than, when it came, the great reason of the great invitation that had brought

Rosalie to take part in it. The great reason already has been disclosed — Mr. Sturgiss, bending across the table-cloth, they two left alone, " Well, look here — to come to the point — the reason why I've got you up here to-night — it's this : we want you — Field and Company, the Bank, — we want you to come to us — we want you in Lombard Street."

She was beautiful to see in her proud happiness at that. Startled and tremulous, she was; like some lovely fawn burst from thicket and at breathless poise upon the crest of unsuspected pastures; within her eyes the cloud of dreams passing like veils upon the gleam of her first ecstasy; upon her face, shadowed as she sinks somewhat back, the tide of colour (her rosy joy) flooding above her sudden pallor; her lips slightly parted; her hand that had been plucking at the cloth caught to her bosom where her heart had leapt.

It may be left at that. It is enough; too much. What, in the reconstruction of a life, are, in retrospect, its triumphs but empty shards, drained and discarded, the litter of a picnic party that has fed and passed along?

Mr. Sturgiss bent farther across the tablecloth, expanding his proposal : She knew, said he, what he represented, what the firm was. Field and Company. A private bank. Well, the days of private banks were drawing in. These huge joint-stock leviathans swallowing them up like pike among the troutlings. But not swallowing up Field and Company! Not much! If the old private houses were tumbling into the joint-stock maw, the greater the chances for those that stood out and remained. The private banks were tumbling in because they stood rooted in the old, solid, stolid banking business and the leviathans came along and pounced while they dozed. There was no dozing at Field's. They were very much awake. They were enterprising.

"Look at this very matter between us. The idea of bringing a woman into a bank! Even old Field himself was startled at first. Why? In America women are entering banking seriously and successfully. They're going to in England. At Field's. *You.*" He wasn't proposing to bring her in for fun or for a chance that might turn up, like the man who picked up a dog biscuit from the road on the chance that some one would give him a dog before it got mildewed; no, he was bringing her in to develop an enterprise that should be the parent of other and greater enterprises. Her knowledge of insurance, her knowledge of schools, these, with her sex, on the one side of the counter and all their clients — the Anglo-Indian crowd who were the backbone of the business — on the other side of the counter. Field's, for cash, and, while it was drawing, for advice, was always the first port of call of the wives and the mothers home from India, to say nothing of the husbands and the fathers, — " well, Field's, *you,* shall be the fount of all that domestic advice that is just what all those people, cut off from home, are constantly and distractingly in need of." She didn't suppose, as it was, that Field's did no more for them than bank their money? Field's were their *agents.* Field's saw that they booked their passages, and that their baggage got aboard; and when they arrived this end or the other, or when they broke their journeys coming or going, Field's representatives were there to meet them and take over all their baggage troubles for them. " Very well. Now Field's — *you* — are going to look after their domestic troubles for them — find them rooms, find them houses, find them schools for their children. When people know what we can do for them, people will come to us to bank with us *because* we can do it. When people come to us to bank with us — we go ahead."

Mr. Sturgiss ended and drew back and looked at her. He lit a cigarette and took a sip at his coffee. " We thought of offering you three — " he set down his cup and looked at her again — " four hundred a year."

She declined the post. She was girlish, and delighted him, in her expression of her enormous sense of the compliment he paid her; she was a woman of uncommon purposefulness, and increased his admiration for her by the directness and decision with which uncompromisingly she said him no. She owed a loyalty which she could never fully pay to Simcox's, to Mr. Simcox; that was the beginning and the end of her refusal. Simcox's was her own, her idea, her child that daily she saw growing and that daily absorbed her more: that was the material that filled in and stiffened out the joints of her refusal. " But if you knew how proud I am, Mr. Sturgiss! You don't mind my refusing?"

He laughed and rose to take her to the drawing-room. " I don't mind a bit. This is only what they call preliminary overtures. I shall ask you again. We mean to have you."

Between the two rooms he said, " Yes, mean to. It's a big thing. I'm certain of it. We shall keep it open for you. We shan't fill it." He put his hand on the drawing-room door and opened it. " We can't."

She went in radiant.

She was on the red bus again, going home. She had stayed but the briefest time after dinner. She was too elevated, too buoyant, too possessed possibly to remain in company; excitedly desirous to be alone with her excited thoughts, — especially to be alone with them in that significant apartment of hers. Significant! Why upon the very day of entering it had come this most triumphant sign of its significance! Significant! . . .

She had a front seat on the outside of the omnibus. She gazed before her along a path of night that the lamps jewelled in chains of gold, and streamed along it her tumultuous thoughts, terrible as an army with banners. It was very strange, and it vexed her, robbing her of her proud consciousness of them, that there obtruded among them, as one plucking at her skirt — as captain of them she rode before them — the figure of Laetitia's Harry. Similarly he had obtruded and been like to spoil the pleasure of her visit; but he had been made to provide compensations and he obtruded now only in rebirth of a passage with him that, rehearsed again, much pleased her even while, annoyed, she cut him down.

Taking her leave, she had been seen from the threshold by Mr. Sturgiss and by Laetitia's Harry. It was pitchy dark, emerging from the brightness of the interior, and he had stepped with her to conduct her to the gate. " It was an extraordinary coincidence, meeting you here," he had said.

She did not reply. His voice was most strangely grave for an observation so trite; he might have been speaking some deeply meditated thing, profound, heavy with meaning, charged with fate. Fatuous! It was extraordinary that there was not an action of his but aroused her animosity. This vibrant gravity of tone — an organ used for a jig, just as his gifts were used for his Laetitia moon-calfings — caused newly a disturbance within her against him. She would have liked to whistle or in some equal way to express indifference to his presence.

They were at the gate and he stooped to the latch and appeared to have some trouble with it. " Sturgiss has been telling me what a wonderful person you are."

Again that immense gravity of tone. She was astonished at the sudden surge of her animosity that it caused within her. She had desired to express indifference. She

desired now to assail. She made a sneer of her voice.
" I should have thought you had ears for the wonder of
no one but Laetitia."

" Why do you say that? "

She felt her lip curl with her malevolence. " To see
you raise your eyes and hear you breathe ' Ah, Laetitia ! ' "

He opened the gate and she passed out, tingling.

It astounded her to find herself a hundred yards gone
from the house, nay, now upon the bus a mile and more
away, recalling it, trembling and with her breath quickened. It was as if she had been engaged in a contest of
wills, very fierce; nay, in a contest physical, a wrestling.
She had not known, she told herself, that it was possible
to hate so. That man! These men! She put her eye
upon the bus driver, strapped on his perch so near to her
that she could have touched him, and absurdly in her
repugnance of his sex hated him and shrank farther away
from him.

It was enormously, sickeningly real to her, her repugnance. Even on detached consideration of her ridiculous
shrinking from the bus driver she could not have laughed
at it. People who had an uncontrollable antipathy to cats
did not laugh at the grotesque puerilities to which it carried them. Nor she at her antipathy. " Of course they're
beasts." Yes, the right word! It was the beastliness of
sex that bottomed her loathing.

She could not have laughed; but she could and did with
a conscious intention of her will put that intruder on her
animation finally out of her mind. This very joyous up-
lifting of her spirit, was it not because, in this world
dominated by men, based for its fundamental principle
upon play of sex as commerce is based upon the principle
of barter, she was assured of position, of privilege, and

of power that raised her independent of such conventions and such laws?

She was her own! All her proud joys, her glad imaginings, her delighted hopes, arose amain and anew, tuned to this cumulative paean as a flourish of trumpets at the climax of a proclamation. She was intoxicated on her happiness.

They were come to the lighted shops and the crowded pavements. The bus drew up at the thronged corner adjacent to the divigation of the Harrow Road and she leaned over and watched the scene, smilingly (for sheer happiness) looking down upon it, as smilingly (for her triumphant altitude) she felt that she looked down upon the world. She would not have changed place with any life living or that could be lived; she was so much abandoned to her happiness that she made the intention she would sit up in her significant apartment all that night, not to lose a moment of it. She grudged that even sleep upon her happiness should intrude.

There came one in the traffic beneath her that caught her attention: a woman whom people stood aside to let pass and turned to look upon with grins; two or three urchins danced about the woman, pointing at her and calling at her. Her dress was disordered, muddy all up one side as if she had fallen; her face flushed; her hat awry; her hair escaped and wisped about her eyes and on her shoulders. She was drunk. An obscene and horrible spectacle, the mock of her beholders. A horrible woman.

It was Keggo.

Rosalie caught her breath. She made to rise but did not rise. Keggo stopped and lifted all around a vacant gaze. Her eyes met Rosalie's straight above her. She lurched a step and stopped and swayed and looked again, battling perhaps with hints within her fumy brain of recognition. Rosalie made again to rise to go to her and again did not rise. The bus moved forward. That wretched woman, making as if to pursue her aroused befuddlement, turned about to follow and came a few steps, lurching like a ship that foundered. The light blazed down upon her upturned face. She lurched into some shadow and, as wreckage swallowed up in the trough of the sea, her face was gone.

Lurching . . . as a ship . . . that foundered. There was in Rosalie's mind some dim memory struggling. Lurching . . . as a ship . . . in the darkness . . . in the night. And her face . . . seen and gone . . . as a ship . . . labouring . . . as a ship . . .

Ah!

Ships that pass in the night, and speak each other in passing;
Only a signal shown and a distant voice in the darkness.

It came to Rosalie complete and word for word; and with perfect clearness, as though she saw and sensed them, all its attendant circumstances: the attic room at the Sultana's, the strange smell mingled with the smell of the oil lamp, Keggo in the wicker chair, she beside her, her head against Keggo's knee; and Keggo's voice reciting the lines and her young, protesting, loving cry, " O Keggo!"

She saw it, sensed it, heard it — and stonily regarded it. A thing to weep at, she knew it; but did not weep. A thing to stab her, it ought to; but did not stab. What *good* could she do? Suppose she had got up and gone down; suppose she now got up and went down and went back? What *good?* All sentimentality that. Be sensible! If a thousand pounds would do Keggo any good, and if she had a thousand pounds, freely and gladly she would give the last penny of it. But to get down, to have got down, what *could* she have done? Why *should* she worry about her? Keggo had had her chance. Everybody had their chance. She now had hers. Why *should* she . . .

She never saw Keggo again.

CHAPTER X

SHE had not good health in the week immediately following that great day. She did not feel well. She did not look very well. Mr. Simcox, profoundly sympathetic to every mood of her who was at once his protégé and his support, told her he thought she had been overdoing it. She seized upon that excuse and tried to persuade herself that perhaps she had; or, which amounted to the same thing, that she was suffering from the revulsion of those huge excitements. But she did not persuade herself. Her malaise, whatever it was, was not of that kind. Its manifestations were not in lassitude or sense of disability. They were in a curious dis-ease whose occasion was not to be defined; in a consuming restlessness beneath whose goad even the significant apartment had not power to charm and hold her; in a certain feverishness whose exsiccative heat, leaving her palms and temples cool (she sometimes felt them and had surprise) caused inwardly a dry burning that made her long for quiet places.

She could not settle to anything. Her limbs, and they had their way, desired not to rest; her mind, and it deposed her captaincy, would cast no anchor.

Mr. Simcox, as the week drew on, suggested a weekend at home. It had occurred to her, very attractively, but she had negatived it. Aunt Belle (before the idea had come to her) had written an invitation to one of the Saturday dinners in which she had "most *particularly,* my dear child" desired her presence. Something *most delightful* was going to happen and she *must be there.*

She had accepted and she later told herself she did not like to refuse. She knew, instantly as she read, what was the identity of this delightful thing that was to happen and she decided, with a sharp turn within her of some emotion, that certainly she would be there. To whet her scorn! She was thereafter much aggravated that her drifting mind, against her wish, swayed constantly towards it sometimes with that same sharp turn of that same emotion (nameless to her and without meaning) always with aggravation of her restlessness, of her fever, of her dis-ease. When came Mr. Simcox's suggestion of the week-end at home she decided, as swiftly as she had first accepted, to revoke her acceptance. She would not be there! She would not — waste her scorn!

Impatient for movement, she that evening went to the splendid house in Pilchester Square to tell her withdrawal. This most exasperating dis-ease of hers! Now that she was come to change her mind she did not want to change her mind. It was like going to the dentist with an aching tooth. On his doorstep the tooth does not ache. Her governance of herself was by her malaise so shaken that positively, as she came into Aunt Belle's presence, she did not know whether she was going to withdraw or to confirm her acceptance of the invitation.

Most comfortingly, Aunt Belle saved her the decision. " My dear child! How unexpected! How opportune! I was just writing to you. Our little dinner is put off! Sit here while I tell you. Now would you like anything, dear child? A piece of cake? Some nice fruit? To please me. Really, no? Well, now; our dinner that I so especially wanted you for — did you guess?"

She began to tell.

She told what Rosalie had perfectly well known. The delightful thing expected to happen was Harry Occleve's proposal of marriage to darling Laetitia. There had been certain signs and portents. They had come at last. Their meaning was perfectly clear. There was not the least doubt that at the next meeting Harry would ask Laetitia's hand. Not the shadow of a doubt! Aunt Belle knew all the signs! Every woman of Aunt Belle's experience knew them, dear child. So Harry had been asked for this dinner; a *meaningly* written letter, dear child, to encourage him, the dear, poor fellow! And had accepted, in terms so meaning too, the dear, devoted fellow. Then ——

"But, Aunt Belle —— "

"Listen, dear child. Then he suddenly wrote saying he found he had made a mistake —— "

"Made a mistake!" The words went out from Rosalie in a small cry.

"Dear child, it is nothing. How sweet to be so concerned! It is nothing, it is the best of signs. Made a mistake that he was disengaged for Saturday. The dear, devoted fellow was so absurdly vague about it. Unavoidable circumstances prevented him; that was all; his writing and all the appearance of his letter so delightfully distracted! How amused we were, your Uncle Pyke and I! How amused, and how we felt for the dear, devoted fellow! Screwing up his courage! How we remembered our own courtship! You should hear your Uncle Pyke tell how he had to screw up his courage to propose to me and how many times it failed him and he fled. Dear child, you've no idea how ridiculous these poor men are in their love! How timorous! How they suffer! The dear, poor fellows. Your Uncle Pyke wrote him at once a most kind and *meaning* letter — accepting his unforeseen circumstances (he had to, of course) and positively fixing him for Monday instead. *"Laetitia is expecting you,"* your Uncle Pyke wrote. The dear fellow! How happy it will make him! So it is Monday, dear child.

Monday, instead. We do so want you to be there. I do so want you, and so does my darling, to be the first to congratulate her. And you shall be a bridesmaid! Won't that be nice? Kiss me, dear child. I shall never forget your sweet concern before I told you his excuse meant nothing. Dear child, you look startled yet."

There was only a faint voice that came to Rosalie's lips. " Really nothing, Aunt Belle? "

" Dear child, nothing at all."

She went down to the Rectory on Saturday and found herself more glad to be there and to be with her mother than she had ever been. When she greeted her mother, " Kiss me again, dear, small mother," she cried and put her cheek against her mother's and held it there some moments, rather fiercely and with her eyes closed, as though there were in that contact some febrifuge that abated her inward fever, some mooring whereto, adrift, her mind made fast.

What beset her? *What* was the matter with her? *What* worked within her? Feverishly she inquired of herself, seeking to analyse her case; but she could by no means inform herself; her case was not within what diagnosis she could summon. *What?* Near as she could get she had the feeling, nay, the wild longing, to get *out:* out of *what?* She did not know. To get *away:* away from *what?* She could not say.

She found in herself a great and an unusual tenderness towards the home life. Only her mother and her father were now at home. Harold was at a branch of his bank in Shanghai. Robert was in Canada. Flora was in India, married, with two small children. Hilda was in Devonshire, married to a doctor. These things had happened, these flights been winged, and she had taken but the smallest interest in them. She had had her own af-

fairs. She had had herself to think of. She had lost
touch with her brothers and sisters. She scarcely ever
thought about them. Now she wanted very much to
hear about them. What news of them was there? How
were they getting on? She did want — she could fix
that much of her state, or it presented a relief for her
state — she did want to feel that she belonged to them
and they to her. She noticed with a large whelming of
pity how very small her mother seemed to have grown
She was always small, but now — much smaller, fallen
in, very fragile. She noticed with a quick pang how all
her father's violent blackness of hair, and violent red of
colouring, and violent glint of eye and violent energy of
gesture were faded, greyed, dimmed, devitalized to a hue
and to an air that was all one and lustreless, as if he
had gone in a pond covered, not with duckweed but with
lichen, and had come out, not dripping, but limp and
shrouded head to foot in scaly grey. Was it possible
that all this had been so when she was last here? She
had not noticed it. She noticed that both her dear mother
and her father walked on the flat soles of their feet, and
touched articles of furniture as they trod, heavily, across
the room. A most frightful tenderness towards them
possessed her. She wanted like anything to show them
devotion and, most frightfully, to receive from them
signs of devotion to her — to be able to feel she was
theirs, and they hers. She wanted it terribly.

But what *else* did she want? *What?* They gave her
all the home talk, but soon it flagged and whatever in her
desired satisfaction still gnawed within her and was un-
satisfied; she ministered to them and they were pleased
but they seemed very quickly tired; they had their accustomed hours and habits, and whatever it was in her that
found relief in solicitude still tossed within her and was
not relieved. What beset her? *What?*

Monday came. She was at this dinner, this festival for the consummation and celebration of the betrothal of beautiful Laetitia and Laetitia's darling Harry. That sick dis-ease of hers had wonderfully vanished when she came into the house, when she was hugged fit to crack her to Aunt Belle's bosom with "Dear child! Dear child! He's just arrived! He's with your uncle downstairs. Look at Laetitia! Lovely! Isn't she lovely? Kiss me again, again, dear child!" When she was floated to by Laetitia, exquisitely arrayed, pink and white, doll-faced, doll-headed, squeaking with coquettish glee, "Rosalie! Darling! Isn't this awful? Imagine it for me, Rosalie! It oughtn't to have been planned like this, ought it? Do tell darling mamma it ought not to have been! I'm trembling. Wouldn't you be?"

Yes, gone that sick dis-ease. How at this spectacle suffer dis-ease, or any other disturbance of the emotions save only disgust, contempt at such a horrid preparation for such a horrid rite. Excited responsiveness to their most friendly excitation was not needed in her for it was not expected. "The shy, quiet thing you always are, dear child," Aunt Belle often used to say to her and said now. (And within the week was to beat her breast in that same drawing-room and cry with an exceeding bitter cry, "Shy! We thought her shy! Sly! Sly! Sly to the tips of her fingers, the wicked girl!")

So she need respond with no more than her normal quiet smile, her normal tone, in their presence, of poor-relation deference and awe. So behind that mask could curl her lip and shudder in the refinements of her views at this most horrid preparation for this most horrid rite. And did. That dis-ease strangely fled, there came to her the swift belief that here, and she had not known it! — was that dis-ease's cause. It was the anticipation of this exhibition of all the things she hated most, of the most glaring presentiment of outrage of all her strongest principles. This Laetitia, embodiment of useless womanhood, launching herself on that disgusting dependence on a man that soon would strand her among the derelicts; and that Laetitia's Harry, that might have been a man among men, coming to the apotheosis of his languishing to — oh, wreathed, fatted calf with gilded horns!

Yes, it was this had vexed her so; and suddenly informed of the seat of her injury she turned upon it disgust and scorn such as never before had she felt (and she had felt it always) for the whole order of things for which it stood. She felt her very blood run acid, causing her to twist, in her acid contempt for the subservience of women, and most of all for that Laetitia's subservience, floated on that ghastly coquetry like a shifting cargo that in the first gale will capsize the ship; she felt her very temples throb, and almost thought they must be heard, in her fierce detestation of all the masculinity of men and most of all — yes, with a flash of eye she could not stay and hoped that he could see — that fatuous Harry's masculinity.

He came into the room — looked pale — poor calf! — and went, with a nervous halt in his walk — sick fool! — to his Laetitia; and looked across at Rosalie and made a half-step to her; and she thought with all her force, to send it to him, her last words to him: that most malevolent, " to see you raise your eyes and hear you breathe, ' Ah, Laetitia ' "; and surely sent it, for on that half-step towards her he stopped, hesitated, and turned and engaged Laetitia again.

She had told herself, leaving the Sturgiss's house that night a week ago, that she had not believed it possible to hate a man so. Now! Why that was not hate; that, compared with the inimity that now consumed her, was a mere chill indifference. And it had made her tremble!

She was rigid now. Stiff with hate! He personified for
her all in life against which she was in rebellion, all in
life that her soul abhorred; and while, in the moments
before dinner, grunting Uncle Pyke and rallying Aunt
Belle and coquetting Laetitia crowded about him, leaving
her alone and far apart, she, for the reason that it gave
to her hate, and for the example that stood before her
eyes, reviewed again her theories of life and again pledged
herself in their support. . . .

"Dinner is served." That group went laughing to the
door, she followed. "No, no, my boy. Don't stand on
ceremony. Pass along as we come. Why, hang it, man,
we regard you as one of the family! Ha! ha! haw!"
Down the stairs in a body, she following. There is, from
their conversation, something the wreathed calf is to get
from his coat to bring to show them, a letter or a token
or something. The dining-room is to the front on the
ground floor. The coats hang in the hall, a narrow passage there, that runs back to Uncle Pyke's study. They
are down. "Shall I get it now?" "Yes, bring it along;
bring it along, my boy." "And Rosalie" (Aunt Belle),
"my fan, dear child. Dear child, I left it on the table
in Uncle Pyke's den. You will? Dear child!"

They pass in. The gilded calf turns from them for
what it is he is to fetch from his coat; she slips by him
to the study and takes up the fan and comes with it again.

It is dim in the passage. A condition on which generous Uncle Pyke years before installed this wonderful
electric light that you flick on and flick off as you require
it was that it should always be flicked off when you did
not require it. Now as Rosalie came from the study the
passage was lit only by the shaft of light that gleamed
from the dining-room door; its only sound Aunt Belle's
noisy chatter from the waiting table.

He was fumbling at the coats, standing there sharply

outlined against the stream of light, his face cut on it in
a perfect silhouette. She had to pass him. That hateful
he. She was seized with a fit of that same trembling
that had shaken her after the passage between them at
the gate on Shoot Up Hill. It shook her now, dreadfully. Her knees trembled. She felt faint. Awful to
hate so! She was quite close, almost touching him. It
was necessary he should move, forward or back, to give
her room. But he did not move. His hands, outstretched
before him on the coats, and sharp against the light, appeared to her to be shaking; but that was the hallucination of this frightful trembling that possessed her. She
tried to say, "If you please — ," but, dreadfully, had
no voice; but made some sound; and he, most slowly,
drew back. It was before him that she had to pass.

She advanced; and felt, as if she saw it, the intensity of
the gaze of his eyes upon her; and saw, as if the place
were light and her look not averted, his " marching " face
and those lines radiating to his temples (horizon tracks)
where the faint touch of greyness was; and suddenly
had upon her senses, with an extraordinary pungency,
causing them to swim, that odd, nice smell there was
about him of mingled peat and soap and fresh tobacco,
of tweed and heather and the sea.

She caught her breath . . .

The thing's too poignant for the words a man has.

She was caught in his arms, terribly enfolding her.
He was crying in her ears, passionately, triumphantly,
" Rosalie! Rosalie! " She was in his arms. Those
long, strong arms of his were round her; and she was
caught against his heart, her face upturned to his, his
face against her own; and she was swooning, falling
through incredible spaces, drowning in incredible seas,
sinking through incredible blackness; and in her ears his
voice, coming to her in her extremity like the beat of a

wing in the night, like the first pulsing roll of music enormously remote, " Rosalie! Rosalie! "

The thing's too poignant for the words one has. This girl's extremity was very great, not to be set in words. Words cannot bring to earth that which, ethereal, defies our comprehension as life and death defy it and, like life and death, to our comprehension only sublimely *IS*. Words only can say her spirit, bursting from bondage, streamed up to cleave to his; how tell the anguish, how the ecstasy? Words only can say her spirit, like a live part of her drawn out of her, seemed to be rushing upwards from her body to her lips: words cannot tell the anguish that was bliss, the rapture that was pain. Only can say that she was in his arms, her heart to his, his lips against her own: and cannot tell —

But also it is to be accounted to her for her extremity that herein all her life's habit was delivered over by her to betrayal.

CHAPTER XI

HE was saying, "We must go in. Can you go in?"
She breathed, "I can."

That dinner! That after-dinner in the drawing-room
upstairs! It is a nightmare to be imagined, not to be
described. Imagine walking from the darkness and the
frightful secret of the passage into the blazing dazzle and
the glittering eyes of the resplendent dinner party! They,
in Harry's absence, have been exchanging the last private
nods and flashes. "Soon! Soon!" they have been nodding to one another. Uncle Pyke, licking his chops an-
ticipatorily of his bath in his soup, has been licking them
also in relish of working off his daughter in this excellent match; Aunt Belle, kind, kind Aunt Belle, with a last
satisfied eye about the appointments of the table, has patted her Laetitia's hand and conveyed to her, "Soon, soon,
darling; soon, soon!" Beautiful Laetitia has given a
gentle, glad squeeze to the patting hand and smiled a
lovely, happy, certain smile. "Soon! Soon!" has gone
the jolly signal — and it is not going to be soon, nor
late; it is never, never going to happen; and worse than
never happen!

Worse than never happen! That's it. That is the
awful knowledge of awful guilt with which Rosalie sits
there and freezes in guilty agony at every pause in the
conversation and could scream to notice how the pauses
grow longer and longer, more frequent and more frequent yet. There's a frightful constraint, a chilly,
creepy dreadfulness steals about the party. They go

upstairs — Aunt Belle and Rosalie and beautiful Laetitia — and the constraint goes with them. They sit and
stare and hardly a word said. Something's up! What's
up? What's the matter with everything? Why is everything hanging like this! What's up? And the men come
in — Uncle Pyke swollen with food, swollen with indi-
gestion, swollen with baffled perplexity and ferocious ir-
ritation; and Harry — she dare not look at Harry — and
the thing is worse, the awfulness more awful. Glances
go shooting round the awful silences — Uncle Pyke's
atrabilious eye in the burning fiery furnace of his swollen
face is a stupendous note of interrogation directed upon
Aunt Belle; Aunt Belle's eyebrows arch to scalp and appear likely to disappear into her scalp and remain there
in the effort to express, "*I* don't know! *I* can't
imagine!"; Laetitia — Laetitia's eyes upon her mother
are as a spaniel's upon one devouring meat at table.

Frightfulness more frightful, awfulness more awful;
in Rosalie almost now beyond control the desire to
scream, or to burst into tears or wildly into laughter.
Then she knows herself upon her feet and hears her
voice: "Aunt Belle. I must go, I think. I think I am
very tired to-night."

They suffer her to go.

That's all a nightmare; but, when the door is closed
upon them, like a nightmare gone. She was alone upon
the staircase and then down in the hall — by those coats!
— and, as though no ghastly interval had been, the amazing and beloved moment was returned to her. Out of a
nightmare into a dream! She stood in her dream a
moment — two moments — three — by the hall door.
Who till that evening never had thought of love, astonishingly was invested with all love's darling cunning.
She felt somehow he would see her again before she left;
and love's dear cunning told her right. He came swiftly

down the stairs. She never knew on what pretext he had left the room. He came to her. Love loves these snatched moments and always makes them snatched to breathlessness. She opened the door and must be gone. She said to him, speaking first, " Oh, we were vile in there! How vile we were!"

It was, the intimacy and the abruptness of it, the perfect comprehension that their thoughts were shared, as if they had known and loved for years.

He caught her hand. " My conspirator! My secret-sharer!"

She gave him her heart in her eyes.

He said, " To-morrow, I will come to you."

She disengaged her hand.

He gave a swift look all about and caught her in his arms. "You must tell me, my Rosalie. Tell me."

She breathed, " You knew, before I knew, that I loved you."

When she was home and got to her room she undressed, suffering her clothes to lie as they slipped from her. She got into bed, moving there and then lying there as one in trance.

Cataclysm! All she had been, all she had determined — all, all gone; all nothing, surrendered all. At a touch, in a moment, without a cry, without a shot, without a stroke, all her life's habit swept away. All she had been, all she'd designed, all she had built within herself and walled about herself, all she had scorned, all that with a violent antipathy she had shuddered from or with curled lip spurned away, — all, all betrayed, breached, mined, calamitously riven, tumultously sundered, burst away.

She turned her face to the pillow and began to cry — most frightfully.

It was very terrible for Rosalie.

PART THREE

HOUSE OF CHILDREN

CHAPTER I

THERE'S none so sick as, brought to bed, that robust he that ever has scorned sickness; nor any sinner like a saint suddenly gone from saintliness to sin; and there can be no love like love suddenly leapt from repression into being.

Rosalie, that had abhorred the very name of love, now finding love was quite consumed by love. She loved him so! Even to herself she never could express how tremendous a thing to her their love was. She used deliberately to call it to her mind (as the new, rapt possessor of a jewel going specially to the case to peep and gloat again) and when she called it up like that, or when, in the midst of occupation, her mind secretly opened a door and she turned and saw it there, a surge, physically felt, passed through her, and she would nearly gasp, her breath taken by this new, this rapturous element, as the bather's at his first plunge in the cold, the splendid sea.

She loved him so! She looked at him with eyes, not of an inexperienced girl blinded by love, but of one cynically familiar with the traits of common men, intolerantly prejudiced, sharply susceptible to every note or motion of displeasing quality; and her eyes told her heart, and what is much more told her mind, that nothing but sheer perfection was here. Harry was brilliantly talented, Harry was in face and form one that took the eye among a hundred men. But she had known all that and freely granted him all that before. What she found as she came to know him, and when they were married what she continued to find, was simply, that he was perfect.

He was perfect in every way and there was no way in which, inclining neither to the too much nor the too little, he was not perfect.

The labour of a catalogue of her Harry's virtues is thus discounted. Name a virtue in a man and it was Harry's. Declare too much perfection is as ill to live with as too much fault, and it is precisely just before too much is reached that Harry's dowry stopped. Suggest she was blind to defects, and it is to be answered that there was no man who knew him that ever had a thought against him (except Uncle Pyke, Colonel Pyke Pounce, R.E., who, justifiably, was warned by his physician never to think upon the monster lest apoplexy should supervene) nor any fellow man in his profession (and that is the supreme test) that ever grudged him his success. Disgruntled barristers, morosely brooding upon the fall of plums into other mouths than theirs, always said, when it was Harry's mouth: " Ah, Occleve; yes, but he's different. No one grudges Harry Occleve what he gets."

Different! In Rosalie's fond, fondest love for him she often used to hug her love by making that catalogue of all his parts that has been shown not to be necessary. And it was the little, tiny things wherein he differed from common men that especially she cherished. By the deepest part of her nature terribly susceptible to the grosser manifestations of the male habit, it was extraordinarily wonderful and delicious to her that Harry of these had none. In an age much given to easy freedom of language it will not be appreciated, it perhaps will cause the pair of them to be sneered at, but it demands mention as illuminating a characteristic of hers (and of his), that she had, for instance, especial delight in the fact that Harry never even swore. The impossible test in the matter of self-command is when a man hits his thumb with a hammer. What does a bishop say when he does that? But she saw Harry catch his thumb a proper crack hanging a picture in the house they took, and, " Mice and Mumps! " cried Harry, and dropped the hammer and the picture, and jumped off the stepladder, and did a hop, and wrung his hand, and laughed at her and wrung his hand and laughed again. " Mice and Mumps! "

" Mice and Mumps! " It always seemed to her to characterise and to epitomise him, that grotesque expression. It always made her laugh; and the more serious the accident or the dilemma that brought it to Harry's lips, the more, by bathos, one was forced to laugh and the seriousness thereby dissipated into an affair not serious at all. Yes, that was the point of it and the reason it epitomised him. There was none of life's dilemmas — little dilemmas that irritate ordinary people or in which ordinary people display themselves pusillanimous; or tragic dilemmas that find ordinary people wanting and leave them in vacillation and despair — there was none of any sort that Harry, receiving with his comic, " Mice and Mumps! Mice and Mumps, old girl! " did not receive with the assurance to her that, though this was a nuisance, he had metal and to spare to settle such; that, though this was a catastrophe, a facer, he'd too much courage, too much high, brave spirit for it to discommode him; there was no fight in such, he was captain of such, trust him!

" One who never turned his back but marched breast forward."

That was Harry!

" Mice and Mumps! " On the evening of the day following that astounding betrothal of theirs, affianced as it were at a blow — a day spent together in the park complete, without a break for food or thought of occupation — on the evening of that day he must go, he declared, to the horrific castle in Pilchester Square and break the awful news, proclaim his villainy.

She was terrified. "They'll kill you, Harry. Write."

"No, no. I've been a howling cad. It's true, a howling cad, not of guile, but of these astounding things that have happened to us outside ourselves, but nevertheless a howling cad as such conduct is judged, and will be judged. So I must go through it. I must. That's certain. I couldn't hide behind a letter. They are entitled to tell me to my face what they think of me. They must have their right. Oh, yes, I've got to give them that. To-night. Now."

A howling cad, but of forces outside themselves ("Too quick for me," he had explained), not of guile.

He had explained, in those enchanted hours in the park, that it was really by resolve to do the right thing, and not to do the caddish thing, that he had presented himself the howling cad that they would hold him. That night at the Sturgiss's at Cricklewood had charged him ("Oh, Rosalie, like bursting awake to breathe from suffocation in a dream.") what for many days, only looking at her, never speaking to her, suffering her not veiled contempt, he had felt as one feels a premonition that is insistent but that cannot be defined — that night had charged him that he loved her. He was no way definitely committed to poor Laetitia. Was he more wrong if, now knowing his heart was otherwise, he maintained and carried to its consummation the intimacy between Laetitia and himself, or if he stopped while yet he had not gone too far? He had decided to break while yet it might be broken. There was an invitation from Mrs. Pyke Pounce he had accepted. He wrote, endeavouring to give a meaning to his words, excusing himself from it.

She murmured, "I remember." ("Nothing in it, dear child; nothing in it!")

There came back a letter from Colonel Pyke Pounce in which Colonel Pyke Pounce also had endeavoured to give a meaning to his words, and had succeeded. Now Harry knew his problem of moral conduct in a fiercer form; now, resolving to do what he told himself was the right thing and not the caddish thing, he took the step that made him be the howling cad that they would think him. ("But, Rosalie, gave me you!")

He had resolved that he must accept the invitation, present himself at the house — and let the hour decide. As the situation revealed itself so he would accept it. If it was made clear to him, as the Pyke Pounce letter much gave him to believe, that proposal for Laetitia's hand was expected of him, he would "do the right thing" and stand by what his behaviour apparently had led them to expect; if the way still seemed open, the door not shut behind him, he would very frankly explain to Laetitia's grisly father that he thought it best his visits to the house from now should cease. The hour should decide! But there was in the hour, when it came, one terrible, one lovely element that he never had expected to be there. In all his visits to the house Rosalie never had been met on any other day than Saturday. This dinner was on the Monday, and arriving to face and carry through his ordeal, he was startled, he was utterly shaken to see her there. ("To see my darling there.")

O forces outside themselves! "When you had to pass me in the passage nothing mattered then — except I could not let you pass."

So it was that now, the right thing not having been done on that night, the right thing in this new position must be done to-day. They were entitled to tell him to his face what they thought of him and they must have their right. That was his view and he would not abate it.

" They'll kill you, Harry."

They had come by this to the corner of Pilchester Square and there he bade her wait. She said again, part laughing, most in fear, " They'll kill you."

" I've got to give them the chance to do their best."

And off he went, strongly, erect. One who never . . . but marched breast forward.

Waiting for him, she really was terrified for him. Ferocious Uncle Pyke! Terrific Aunt Belle! Swollen and infuriated Uncle Pyke! Bitter and outraged Aunt Belle!

In twenty minutes came the crash of a slammed front door that clearly and terribly was Uncle Pyke Pounce slamming it as if he would hurl it through its portals and crash it on to Harry down the steps.

Harry reappeared, uncommonly grave.

She put out a hand to him, dreadfully anxious.

" Mice and Mumps!" said Harry. " Mice *and* Mumps!"

You couldn't help laughing! But also, squeezing the strong arm beneath which he tucked her hand, you felt, with such a thrill, from that grotesque expression, and from his face as he said it, that this, like every forward thing, had in it nothing that could discommode that high, brave spirit: no fight in such; he was captain of such, trust him!

Thus also her delight in another form, and yet in the same form, in that grotesque expression, when it was ejaculated as his sole expletive when he caught his thumb that frightful crack while hanging a picture in what was to be his study in their newly taken house.

Any other man in the world, even a bishop, would have sworn; would have sworn no doubt harmlessly and with an honest heartiness to which the most pious prude could not have taken exception. Agreed! But the point was — that Harry didn't!

She loved him so! She insisted she must bind up the thumb with her pocket handkerchief, and did, Harry protesting; and for years, still loving him with the old, first love, she often would be reminded by the picture of the incident and of her joy in it.

Yes, the only expletive she ever heard him use; and, lo, in that very room, years on, he seated beneath that very picture, she was to come to him with news (and hers the guilt of it) that for the first time was to strike him between the joints of his harness, visibly ageing him as she spoke, and for the first time cause him to groan his pain. She was to glance at the picture as she spoke and very terribly its merry association to be recalled to her. She was to recall him young, gay, tremendously splendid, wringing his damaged hand, laughing, "Mice and Mumps!" She was to see him, grey ascendant upon the raven of his hair, shrinking down in his seat, wilting as one slowly collapsing after a stunning blow. and at her news (and hers the guilt of it) to hear his voice go, not exclamatorily, but in a thick mutter, as one dazed, bewildered, in a fog, "My God, my God, my God, my God!"

How could one ever have foreseen that?

CHAPTER II

SHE loved him so! On that first day together in the park she told him everything about herself, about all her ideas and theories and principles, particularly where these touched his sex, even about that terrible fit of crying of hers in bed an hour after she had left him. And Harry understood everything and agreed with her in everything. O rapturous affinity!

They met early when business London was rushing to business. They stayed late, with no thought of food or of their occupations, till business London was returning, and night, in lamps below and stars above, was setting out its sentinels.

She told him everything; and even if she had wished not to open all her heart, there would have been the immense selection of *everything* — every single thing about herself — from which to choose to tell him. For there never had been such a betrothal as theirs; done at a blow with no single intimate thing ever before passed between them! Her very first words to him as they met, her greeting of him as they came together, showed how preposterous and never-before-imagined was their affiancement. "You know, it's incredible," she greeted him. "It's incredible, it's grotesque, it's flatly impossible — I've never before seen you except in your dress clothes or at afternoon tea!"

Harry took both her hands in his. "But I think I've wanted you," said Harry, "ever since I was in long clothes. I know I've wanted you ever since first I saw you."

One knows another, in her place, would have bantered this off in that modern attitude towards love which is a horror, boisterously expressed, of admitting love as an emotion. Rosalie, that had scorned the very name of love, and that, because betrayed by love, had turned her face to her pillow and cried most frightfully, received it with a sound that was between a sigh and a catching of her breath. She loved him so!

And then they talked; and the thing between them, that had come so wonderfully, was so wonderful that they were as it were transfigured by it, as awe and spirituality and mysticism would fill the dwellers in a house visited by a miracle of God. So wonderful, that conversation, they would have felt, was not possibly a word for all that occupied them in those rapturous hours: not conversation, no, — a sublime engagement of their spirits wherein (possessing the keys of all the wonders), seas, continents and worlds of thoughts were traversed by them, in every clime most exquisite affinity discovered.

As at a blow they had become affianced, so, with no stage between, but in immediate sequence perfectly natural to them both, the natural repercussion of the blow, they talked immediately of betrothal's consummation, of marriage, of their marriage.

About marriage Rosalie had immensely much to tell Harry. It was what she had principally to say, and this is how and why and what she told him.

When from her first terrible dismay — that frightful crying, her face turned to the pillow — she had recovered; when to the lovely ardour of her love — stealing about her, soothing her, in the night; bursting upon her, ravishing her, in the morning — she had passed on; she remembered her second line of her defences and she fell back upon it. " If ever I fell in love," she had often said, alike to Keggo and to Miss Salmon, " if such an impossible thing ever were to happen to me, I'd marry as marriage should be. I'd enter a partnership. I would live my life; he would live his life; together, when we wanted to, when we were off duty, so to speak, we would live *our* life. A partnership, a mutually free and independent partnership."

The second line of her defences! Oh, strong and reassuring thought! Of course, of course the first line, breached and swept away, had never really mattered. Foolish to have wept for it! It was built against love and she knew now, by her darling and her terrible experience, that against love —— ! Nay, in that whelming admission's very tide, sweeping upon her from envisagement of Harry and bearing her deliciously upon its flood, there had come a thought as strong with wine as that was sweet with honey. Built against love! Why, in seeking to build against love, to shut away love from her life, was she not perpetrating against herself the very act — denial of anything a free life might have — that it was her life's first principle to oppose? A man's place, a man's part, everything that a man by conventional dowry is given, hers should be as freely as a man's it is! That was her aim; that at once the basis of her standpoint and the target of her shaft; and lo, at the very outset of her independence, she had sought to deny herself that which (as now she knew) was life's most lovely gift. She was steadfast, and she was caparisoned, to obtain and to possess the things that, of her sex, commonly a woman might not have, and she was shutting herself from that which, if it offers, not all the man-owned world can deny the woman lowliest in office, heaviest in chains, deepest in servitude!

O senselessness! She could see, as looking upon an individuality not her own, that foolish girl that for such had turned her face to her pillow and cried out her heart;

and at that very moment, and no other, of smiling pity for that mistaken grief, there came to Rosalie a sudden sense of womanhood attained; of much increase of years and wisdom; of growth of stature; of transportation, as from one world to another, from the character and the presence that had been hers to a personality and a body that looked down upon that other as, tenderly, a mother upon the innocence of her small child.

That poor, brave, foolish Rosalie that was! Did she protest, that foolish girl, that she was right in what had been her attitude to love? Did she with would-be bitterness recall those views laid down upon the women in the boarding house — that they were derelicts precisely through this love business, abandoned of men, relict of men, footsore and fallen in pursuit of men?

Ah, small, misguided creature! The principles were right but all askew the application. Love! Consider other attributes of life. Consider learning; consider food. Learning and food — were they not bounties of life's treasure, to be absorbed and used for sustenance in order, by their nourishment, to give to live this life more fully? Why, so with love! Derelicts, those women, because receiving love (that loveliest gift of all!) not as a means but as an end — the end of all: that attained, everything attained; that won, all finished. That was it! That the misapplication! Learning, or food, or love — the same with all! How dead the life that only lived in scholarship; how gross the life that only lived to eat; how derelict that she that only lived to love, to marry — then ceased to live!

And equally, O small, misguided girl, how starved the life that has no books; how weak the frame that has no food; ah, dear (thus smiled she to herself), how dead the life that knows not love!

The second line of her defences! Nay, as now through

this mature and happy cogitation she saw it, the first and last and only line! In her aloneness, in that girl's single life, there had been nothing against which to defend. She had fought phantoms, that girl; resisted shadows. Now was the necessity, now the test; and now, because with Harry, because she loved him so, because he was every way and in all things perfect, now should be the triumphant exposition.

And she told Harry: marriage that should be a partnership — not an absorption by the greater of the less; not one part active and the other passive; one giving, the other receiving; one maintaining, the other maintained; none of these, but instead a perfect partnering, a perfect equality that should be equality of place, equality of privilege, equality of duty, equality of freedom. "Harry, each with work and with a career. Harry, each living an own life as every man, away from home, shutting his front door upon that home and off to work, leads an own and separate life. Harry —— "

Oh, wonderful beneath this imperturbable sky, amongst these common, passive things — these paths, those trees, that grass, this bench — within this seclusion of that murmurous investment of this city, the ceaseless roar of London, standing like patient walls, eternal and indifferent, about her quietudes. Oh, wonderful in these accustomed and insensible surroundings thus to be calling "Harry," as he were brother, him that a day and night away virtually was unmet; to be exposing, as to a gracious patron, all her mind's treasury of thought; to be revealing, as in confessional, her inmost places of her heart; to be receiving, as by transfusion, the glow of affirmation on her way and in her trust. Oh, wonderful!

Wonderful, because remember for her that she was still beneath the shock of her dismay at her betrayal of herself; still breathless at that rout from her prepared positions; not yet assured her banners were unsullied in their withdrawal to her second line; not yet convinced it was no rout but a withdrawal, wise and strategical, ranks unbroken, to the true point of her defence.

Do try to imagine her, tremulous in this her vital enterprise, tremulous in this wonder that her armies found. It is very desirable to remember what can be remembered for that girl.

CHAPTER III

HARRY assured her! Harry convinced her! Harry was here upon the battlements, come with her in her retirement, joined with her as her ally. All her ideas were his ideas. He, too, had these new views of marriage. He said they always had been his. He hated, as she hated, that old dependence notion: all the privileges the man's, the woman's all the duties. That was detestable to him, said Harry. Marriage in his view ——.

"I'll tell you this," was one thing Harry said. "I'll show it to you this way, Rosalie. I don't exactly know what a reciprocating machine is, but I know what it sounds like, and what it sounds like is what a marriage ought to be, — a perfect fitting together, a perfect harmonising, a perfect joining of two perfect halves that everywhere reciprocate."

The word delighted her. A reciprocating machine! Yes, yes! Each an own part; each with own and separate interests; and their parts, and the production arising out of their interests — their individual selves — approached together, by free will, to join towards a mutual benefit, a shared endeavour, a common advancement, a single end.

She was desperately in earnest and so was he. There was a mill near his people's home in Sussex, a water mill, and his illustration by it of the design they had showed her how earnestly her own ideas were his. There were two wheels to this mill, Harry told her, one on either side. Each ran in its own stream, each was entirely independent of the other; they worked alone, but each helped the other's work; the mill joined them and they joined to make the mill.

That was it!

And she was not talking any generalities, and Harry was not, either. They weren't, either of them, playing with this idea of mutual independence. There would "of course" be a business basis to it, Rosalie said. She was earning her own income and she would pay her half of the upkeep of their home together. It was a stipulation that she advanced with a definite fear that here, at last, she might be taking Harry from his depth; that by natural instinct of generosity, or by instinct of immemorial custom to endow the wife with all the husband's worldly goods, he would here reveal a flaw in his till now flawless duplication of the views that were her own.

But Harry (the never failing rapture of it!) was every way without spot or blemish. He was looking straight and close into her eyes while she put forward this, and there moved not the least dissentient shade across his own while he received it. She need have had no fear. He said, "I agree absolutely with that, Rosalie. There's only one point — " and his expansion of this point wholly entranced her because it established conditions even more matter-of-fact and businesslike than her own broad principle.

"There's only one point," Harry said. "It can't be half and half in terms of actual bisection. Look, Rosalie, in this matter of running the home we're making a contract between two parties and — don't forget I'm a lawyer — it has to be an equable and just contract, and to be that it has to be based for each party's liability — Do you like me to use the law jargon?"

She nodded. "I do, I do!" This was frightfully, entrancingly serious for her. This was a survey of the fortifications of her second line of her defences. "I do, I do!"

"Well, has to be based for each party's liability on each party's interest, on the extent to which each party is involved. I'm making more — an uncommon good bit more — than you are, Rosalie. My interest, therefore my liability, that is, my share, has to be allowed to be proportionately the more. Put it in another way. We're going to run an establishment as an establishment might be run by two or more people of different incomes who wish to join forces for mutual pleasure, two or three relatives, two or three friends. Well, there's a regular principle governing that kind of arrangement. You don't all pay the same. If you did, you'd reduce the scale of living to the level of what the poorest can afford, and half the idea of the combination is to enjoy a very much better scale. No, you run the show on the level the wealthiest is willing to go to, and to the total charge each one contributes in the proportion of his income. If one party has a thousand a year and the other five hundred, and the thousand-pounder wants to live at the rate of nine hundred a year, he pays six hundred and the other three hundred. Each is paying his just share — that's the point. That's how we'd arrange it, Rosalie."

She loved him so! If that were said a thousand times (as already perhaps too often for the robust) it still would not approach the volume of its swelling in the heart of Rosalie, for that was ceaseless. His attitude in this matter now between them, as in every matter, might have been the perfect agreement with her own view that it was and yet might so have been presented as to be much antipathetic to her. His attitude might have made her feel she ought to say, " Thank you, Harry, for agreeing to that "; it might have had the note, " I know exactly how you feel about marriage; I want to make everything just as you wish." Quicksands! Principles to be received as grants, bases of her defences to be accepted as concessions! Quicksands! At either attitude, as at a foreign flavour in a cup, she would have drawn back, suspicious; at either sense within herself, of winning a favour, of accepting a hazard, she would have taken alarm, dismayed. But it was why she loved him so that here, as everywhere, his standpoint was her standpoint's own reflection. She was, as she would have said, deadly in earnest; deadly in earnest to a depth that she could let go to absurdity and never know it for absurdity; and so was he.

Approving this plan of computation of the share that each would pay, " It would have to be done strictly," she said, " as though it were strictly business. And — you don't know, perhaps — I'm making, or soon shall be, just on five hundred a year."

He smiled the nice smile of his she loved, more with his eyes than with his lips. " I'm afraid mine's a good bit more than that. Money's rather pushed at you at the Bar once it starts. You'd have to put up with that."

Her fondness in her eyes reflected him. " I know how famous you are getting. I'd not be stupid about that, Harry. It would be the just share, each according to our means; that's understood. Only, for me, it would have to *be* the just share, that's what I'm saying; not a matter of form, a strict proportion."

" If you liked," said Harry, " we'd give the figures to the costs clerk at my chambers and let him work the contributions out."

" Absurd! " she might have laughed; and as an absurdity he might, with a laugh, have presented it. But quite gravely he made the suggestion, and quite gravely, after a moment's grave thought, " I don't think that would be necessary," she returned.

His earnestness in this thing so vital to her matched her own, and therefore she loved him; and he yet could bring to it lightly a touch which, though light, yet was profoundly based; and therefore, newly, she loved him. She knew she talked with immense profligacy of words in her endeavour to make clear the principles this second line of her defences must maintain. "Each with work and with a career, each with an own and separate life." She kept repeating that. "Equal in work and in responsibility, Harry, and therefore equal in place, in privilege, in freedom."

And Harry, with a light touch but a grave air, a happy setting for a profound meaning, put it in a sentence. "Things which are equal to the same thing are equal to one another," said Harry.

She loved him so!

But there ought here to be explained for her what, loving him so and he so loving her, she could not have known for herself. This plan of maintaining their establishment by contribution of share and share was maintained by Rosalie from the beginning — to the end. She never had cause to doubt that in all the earnestness of that close conversation Harry was utterly sincere. She often recalled that steady gaze with no dissentient shade across it with which his eyes received her statement of her case and knew that only truth was in that gaze. He *did* believe what she believed. It only was afterwards she discovered that also he believed that, both for her and him, the thing would mellow down as mellows down the year, her heady Aprils burnt in June, her burning Junes assuaging to September; that it would pass; that time —

Yes, it must be explained. It was not active in his mind, this reservation. It was passive, underlying, subconscious, as beneath vigour's incredulity of death lies passively admission of death's final certitude. He believed what she believed; but he believed it as are believed infinity and eternity: wherein mankind, believing, reposes upon that limitation of the human mind which cannot conceive infinity but sees ultimately an end, and can pretend eternity through myriad years but feels ultimately a termination. Harry believed what she believed but only by stabilisation of a man's inherent articles of faith. He was of the male kind; and observe, by an incident, what inherent processes of thought the male kind has:

When they were looking over the house which ultimately they took — an all ways most desirable house in Montpelier Crescent, Knightsbridge — Rosalie had only a single objection: it was far too big.

" Miles too big," cried Rosalie, coming up to the second floor where Harry had preceded her. " What *are* you doing there, Harry? Miles too big, I was saying. It really is. Of course I realise you must have a house suitable to your fame but — What *are* you doing, Harry? "

" Fame, yes," breathed Harry, desperately occupied. " I've turned on this tap and I can't turn it off again. Eternal fame. After me the deluge! "

She was looking around. " But, Harry, really! Look at this floor. Two more huge rooms. What can we — "

" Mice and Mumps! " groaned Harry, straining at the tap. " Mice and Mumps! "

He came to her wiping his hands on his handkerchief. " Too big! Look here, supposing this house isn't washed away by that tap. Suppose it's still standing here tomorrow. Take a broad, courageous view of the thing. Suppose this isn't the beginning of the Great Flood of London, and that we're going to live in a house and not an ark. Well, what you've got to remember is that we're not coming in here for a week. We've got to look ahead. Take these two rooms. Why, you can see what they're for, what they've been. Opening into one another, and those little bars on the windows, and that protected fireplace. Nurseries. Day nursery and night nursery."

Rosalie laughed.

CHAPTER IV

THAT's all done. The thing traverses the waters of the years, as across seas a ship, and makes presently a new shore, a new clime, wherein are met occasions new and strange, not anticipated by Rosalie.

Here is one.

Habitant in the new continent across these years, she is wife and, though she had laughed, is mother, and on a day is with her Harry, and Harry is saying, not at all with any hardness in his voice, but very gravely:

" I have a right to a home."

She replies, as grave as he, as one debating a matter that is weighty but that is before the arbitrament, not of feeling, but of reason, " Harry, you have a home."

A gesture of his head, much comprehensive, is made by him: " Is this a home? "

" It's where we live."

" Ah, where we live, Rosalie! "

She did not reply to this. Himself, and not she, spoke next; but his note was as though she had answered and he were speaking in his turn. " I have a right to a home. The children have a right to a home."

She said, " Then, Harry, give yourself a home. Give the children a home."

He said, " Rosalie, I am a man."

She answered, " Harry, I am a woman."

Harry was smoking and he indrew an inhalation from his pipe with a long sibilant sound: her answer was very well understood by him.

No, she never had anticipated this.

Yet might not she have seen? Astounding how in life one's suddenly engulfed in depths and never has perceived the shoals from which they led; suddenly entombed in night and never has perceived the gradual declination of the day! Why, when she looked back, so far away as in those days of choosing their house had been in seed this thing that now was come to fruit. And ¹ she had watched it grow from seed to seedling, and on to bud and blossom, and never had suspected.

But had she not? Then it was curious, she knew, that, alone of all her thoughts, all her beliefs, all her theories, her observations and her deductions from her observations, curious that of them all only a certain observation, made when choosing their house, she never had told to Harry.

Choosing their house! She had gone back to her rooms from the third day of their house-hunting gently amused at an addition to her compendium of lore on the male habit. It was in a way like the cat idea; at least it was, like that, reversal of a common opinion on distinguishing traits as between men and women. It went in her mind like this and, because it arose out of Harry, she laughed softly to herself as like this she shaped it:

"They say a woman marries for a home. Wrong, wrong! It's man that marries for a home — a home that, having got it, superficially he cares little enough about, and superficially uses as a good place to get away from; but that's just how he uses his business, how he uses everything. Oh, he wants it, he wants it, and he marries for it far more than a woman wants it or marries for it. How plain it is! A man marries to settle down, a woman for just precisely the opposite: to break up; to get away from the constraints of daughterhood and of Miss-hood, as a schoolgirl, holiday-bound, from the constraints of school; to enlarge her life, not to restrict it; to aerate her life, not to compose it. Why, it's inherent in a man, the desire for a home; it's in his bones. Look at little boys playing — it's caves and tents and wigwams they delight to play at; a place they can in part discover and in part construct, and then arrange their things in, and then go off exploring and then, all the time, be coming back to the delicious cave and creep in and block up the door! Girls don't play at that; they play at shops and being grown up, at nursing dolls and not themselves being nursed. But that's your man — a hunter with a cave, and the return to the cave the best part of the hunting. That's what he marries for — a home; a pitch of his own; a place to bring his things to and wherein to keep his things; an establishment; a solid, anchored base; a place where he can have his wife and his children and his dogs and his books and his servants and his treasures and his slippers and his ease, and can feel, comfortably, that she and they and it are his, — his mysterious cave with the door blocked up, his base, his moorings, his settled and abiding centre. Dear Harry!"

"Dear Harry" because all this had come to her while with secret, fond amusement she had watched Harry delightedly and entrancedly fussing about the houses they explored. The boy with a cave! The man with a home! She liked the idea of a new home, and a home with Harry, but, given outstanding features obviously essential, almost any home would have satisfied her. She was animated and interested in the choosing, but not with Harry's interest and animation. Hers were the feelings with which she had established herself in the two-room suite at the boarding house. There any two rooms would have done; here any pleasant house would do. It was not the rooms; it was the significance of her entry into their possession. It was not the house; it was the significance of all connoted by the house. The rooms had been a stepping-off place to independence larger and to triumphs new; the house was a stepping-off place to independence, to triumphs, to battle of life and to joy of life, lifted upon a plane high above her old world as the stars, as bright and keen as they.

But for Harry it was a stepping-in place.

It was Harry that fussed and examined and measured and opened and shut and tested and tried and must have this and must have that. It was Harry who saw everything with the eye that was going to see it and live with it permanently and for all time. It was Harry who invested every square yard of every interior with the attributes that should be there when they therein were domiciled. Harry who said, "This front door! Rosalie, we're going to have a front door that will hit you in the eye and make you say 'Mice and Mumps, there's a distinguished couple that live behind a door like that!' None of your wretched browns and greens and blacks and reds for our door, Rosalie! We'll have a yellow front door, gamboge. I've seen it on a house in Westminster. I'll take you there. You wait till you see it. Imagine it, Rosalie, beneath that lovely old fanlight overhead. And then yellow window boxes tinted to match in every window and crammed with flowers. It'll be a house you'll run to get into directly you catch sight of it. Then inside here, in the hall, there'll be the thickest rugs money can buy and the brightest light and the warmest stove. You'll step in and shut the yellow door and, 'Mice and Mumps,' you'll say, 'this *is* home!' Now, look here; here'll be my study; I'll have bookshelves built in all round there and there and there. Pictures there. This nook — I'll fix a little cupboard there and keep my tools in. I'll spend half my time our first weeks pottering about with a hammer and a pair of pliers. This place just here on the landing. Looks like a dungeon. We'll knock out a window there and fit it up with hot and cold water as a cloak room. Now here's your room, your —— "

" *My* study," she had interpolated, a little apprehensive lest for her private room he should use another word.

" Yes, your study, rather. Each of us with our own study! A lark, eh? And Rosalie, in mine there'll be a special chair for you and in yours a special chair for me. We'll stroll in on each other's work — "

She loved him for that. " Like two men in chambers," she said.

His reply was, " We'll rip out this fireplace and put you in one in oak; the walls something between gold and brown, eh? Now come into the drawing-room. This'll be *the* room. Let's start with the hearth and imagine it's winter. This is where we'll have tea the days when I get back in time — "

" And when I get back in time."

" Of course, I'd forgotten that. Why, then whichever of us is back first will be all ready with the tea and waiting to welcome the other. Can't you see the room? Warm, shadowed, glowing here and there, here and there gleaming, and the tea table shining? Won't it be a place to rush back to? I say, Rosalie, it's going to be rather wonderful, isn't it? "

Dear Harry! Yes, men that married for a home.

So she had known that from the start; and, the significant thing (as later perceived) she never had mentioned it to Harry. There was not a line of her life, as lived before she knew him, that she had not revealed to him; there was not a passage of her life, when joined to his, that was not handed to him to write upon; but this, that she knew he'd married for a home, was never revealed, never inscribed upon the tablets submitted daily for his annotation.

Yes, significant!

But how could its significance have been perceived? Look here, there had been a night — a thousand years ago! — when a girl had turned her face to her pillow and cried, most frightfully. Significant! Why, that girl's world had lain in atoms at the significance of that girl's grief. And she that now looked back had been born out of those tears, as the first woman drawn from the side of the first man, and fondly had chid that child that no significance was there at all. There was none. There was nothing to fear. A natural joy of life that had been stifled had been embraced, a shattered world had been remoulded on foundings firmer and, ah, nearer to the heart's desire. Significant! It had been so disproved that not more possibly could fears arise from those, her lovely dissipations of those fears, than from its watchful mother's reassuring candle and her soothing words new terrors to a frightened child at night.

Then how, she used to ask herself, could significance have been perceived in not admitting Harry to her smiling thought on men and home? Significance — then? Nay, memory bear witness, much, much the contrary! Bear witness, memory, it was that very thought of Harry as boy with cave, as man with home, had suddenly suffused her with . . .

"Dear Harry!" she had thought, and with the thought . . .

Anna! That cry of Anna's upon that frightening night, striking her hands against her bosom, "I have a longing — here!" Never till then its meaning nor even thought upon its meaning.

Then! Upon that thought — "Dear Harry!" — had come, with a catch at the breath as at an obscure twinge of pain, a tremor of the sense that was its meaning: thereafter flooding all her being as floods a flood a pasture. A longing to be mother, Anna's longing was! A longing to be mother, to hold a tiny scrap against her breast; to have her heart, bursting for such release, torn out by baby fingers; to have her design of God, insufferably overpacked within her by the remorseless pressure of instinct through a million ages, relieved, discharged, fulfilled by motherhood. Poor Anna! Ah, piteous! " Oh, God, thou knowest how hard it is to be a woman." Poor, piteous Anna, and poor, piteous every woman that, made vessel of this yearning, must have it unfulfilled.

Not she!

The coronet of love, denied poor Anna, was hers. He'd said " These rooms — the nurseries "; the crown of love; and she had laughed!

Oh, stubborn still! Oh, still not cognisant of nature's dower to her sex. To wear the coronet and to refuse the crown! To be wife and not to be mother! To think of baby fingers and to think to put away the offer of their baby clutch!

That girl that turned her face to her pillow and began to cry, most frightfully, cried next again when she again lay abed and had a tiny scrap, an ugly, exquisite, grotesque, miraculous scrap, a baby boy, a baby man, along her arm and watched it there. Those had been passionate and rending tears; these did not even flow. Those burned her eyes; these stood within her eyes a lovely welling up of pride and adoration, drawn from her by this newly risen wonder as by the sun at his arising moisture in lovely mists is drawn from earth.

Motherhood! When later he was christened, she and Harry named him Hugh; but it was a caressing diminutive she made out of his name by which he was always

known. Her tiny son! His tiny arms hugged you as
never tiny arms possibly could have hugged before and
so she called him "Huggo."

"Harry, if you could feel how he's hugging me! It's
absurd he can have such strength! It's ridiculous he
can love me so! And how can he possibly know that
hugging's a sign of love? Harry, how can he? Take
him and hold him up like that and see if he hugs you the
same. He is! He is! Isn't he?"

"Mice and Mumps," said Harry, "he is; he's throttling me, the tiger."

"Ah, give him back, I'm jealous. There's never, never
been a hugger like him since the world began. He's
Huggo. That's his name. Creature straight out of
heaven, you're Huggo."

Her love for infant Huggo so maternal; her unity with
Harry so exquisitely one; how could she have known
were to be met across the waters of the years occasions
new and strange, as that already shown, or, onward yet
a further voyage, as this?

The matter between them touched the same as when, " I
have a right to a home; the children have a right to a
home," Harry had said. But their tones not the same;
in Harry's voice a quality of dulness as of one reciting
a lesson too often conned yet never understood; in hers
a certain weariness as with instruction too often given.

They had been talking a very long time. Harry hadn't
any arguments. He just kept coming back and coming
back to the one thing. He said again, the twentieth time,
in that dull voice, "We are responsible for the children.
We have a duty towards them."

The twentieth time! She made a gesture, not impatient, just tired, that was of repletion with this thing.
"Ah, you say 'we' have a duty. You say 'we'; but,

Harry, you mean me. Why I a duty more than you? Why am I the accused?"

Harry's dull note: "Because you are a woman."

Ineffable weariness was in the murmur that was her reply. "Ah, my God, that reason!"

No, she had never anticipated this.

CHAPTER V

How did it happen? Within her face abode the explanation of how it happened.

There was a mirage in her face.

If she were taken (for a moment) when she had been married ten years, her age thirty-two, and then taken again when she was forty-six, when she had done, when, in 1922, she said, " I have done," and her story ceases, it is material to a portrait of her that in those fourteen years her appearance did not greatly change. Events inscribed it; but these writings were in two scripts, rendered in the two natures that were hers, and, as it were, a balance was maintained between them; there remained constant the aspect that her face presented to the world; constant, that is to say, the spirit that looked out of her face.

That girl that at the door of the great house in Pilchester Square had breathed, " You knew, before I knew, that I loved you," had been called beautiful. This woman that now was wife and now was mother was beautiful with that girl's beauty and with her own, matured of years, set upon it. That girl, shaded in her colouring, commonly was sombre in her hue, but with a quick, impetuous spirit beneath her flesh that, flashing, somehow lightened all her tints; this woman, albeit dark, had somehow about her a deep golden hue as of dusk in a deep wood beheld against a sunset. Her face had always had a boyish look and still, with years, was boyish. There was a mirage in her face. The stranger glanced and saw a mother — extraordinarily shielding and maternal and

benignant things; and looked again and saw a boy —
astonishingly reckless and impetuous and rather boyish,
hard and mutinous things. Or glanced and saw a boy,
perhaps laughing and eager, perhaps obstinate and petu-
lant; and looked again and only much tenderness was
there.

There was a mirage in her face; and with its changes
her voice changed. When she was a boy her voice was
April; when she was a mother September was her voice.

There were two natures in her and those were their
reflections; two lodestars set above her that by turns
brightened and drew her gaze; two lodestones set within
her that claimed her banners as claim the moon and
earth the inconstant sea; one of head, one of heart; one
of choice, one of dower; one of will, one of nature.

In that tenth year her married life there stood for the
mother in her face three children: Huggo who then was
nine; Dora, whom she called Doda because in her first
prattle this heart's delight of hers — "A baby girl! A
beloved one, Harry, to be daughter to me, and to be a
tiny woman with me as little girls always are, and then
budding up beside me and being myself to me again,
my baby girl, my daughter, my woman-bud, my heart's
own heart!" — had thus pronounced her name, who then
was seven; and last Benjamin, then five, whom she named
Benjamin because, come third, come after cognizance of
confliction within herself, come after resentment of his
coming — called Benjamin because, come out of such,
there were such happy tears, such tender, thank-God,
charged with meaning tears to greet him, the one the last
of three, the little tiny one, so wee beside the lusty, tod-
dling others. Benjamin she told Harry he must be
named; Benji she always called him.

Huggo and Doda and Benji! Her children! Her
darling ones, her lovely ones! Love's crown; and, what

was more, worn in the persons of these darling joys of
hers (when they were growing up to nine and seven and
five years old) in signal, almost arrogant in her disdain
of precedent to the contrary, that woman might be
mother and yet work freely in the markets of the world
precisely as man is father but follows a career.

Children! There had been a time when, speaking from
the boy that would stand mutinous and reckless in her
face, and with her April voice, she had expressed her view
on parentage in terms of the old resentment at the old
disability, encountered, bedrocked, wherever into life
she struck a new trail; in terms of the old invertion of
an old conceit wherever with her principles she touched
conventional opinion. The catlike attributes, the marriage for a home, here the familiar saw on parenthood —

"They talk about hostages to fortune," she had expressed her idea, "they talk about a man with young
children as having given hostages to fortune. You know,
it's quite absurd. He doesn't. I don't say a man to
whom the support of children is a financial anxiety hasn't,
by begetting them, placed himself in a position of cap-
tivity to fortune, or to the future, or whatever you like
to call it. He very much has. He's backed a bill that
any day may fall due and find him without means to
meet it; he's let himself in for blackmail, always over him
a threat. But I'm talking about men above the struggle
line. They don't, in their children, give hostages. It's
the woman does that. Men don't give nor forfeit anything. It's the woman gives and forfeits. Why, when
his friends meet a man who was last met a bachelor a
couple or three years ago, what change do they see in
him? They don't see any change at all. There isn't any
change to see. He has to tell them; and he always tells
them rather sheepishly or rather boisterously. 'I'm married, you know,' he says. 'Yes, rather. Man alive, I've

got two kids!' The other says, 'My aunt!'— more probably he says 'My God!'—'My God, fancy you!' And they both laugh — laugh!

"Hostages to fortune! To a man and amongst men it's just a joke. It's no joke to a woman. Do you suppose a married girl, meeting old friends, has to tell them she's a mother, or, if she had to tell them, would tell them like that? Can't they see it at a glance? Isn't she changed? Isn't she, subtly perhaps, but unmistakably, altogether different from the unfettered thing she used to be? Of course she is. How otherwise? She's given hostages to fortune and she's paying; she's being bled. She's giving up things, she's not going out so much, she's not reading so much, she's not playing so much, she's not interested so much in what used to interest her. How can she? There's the children. How can she? She's given hostages to fortune. Oh, happy is the man that hath children for they are as arrows in the quiver of a giant. But it's the woman is the arrowbearer! It's the woman pays."

Lo, there had come to this intolerance the longing — "Here!" — that Anna's bosom had, the urge to hold a tiny scrap against her breast, to have her heart, bursting for such release, torn out by baby fingers. It had o'erborne the other. She had thrown herself upon its flood; not yielded to it as one drawn in by rising waters, but tempestuously engulfed by it and borne away upon it as swallowed up and borne away in Harry's arms when "Rosalie! Rosalie!" he had cried to her.

That which the subsidence revealed, adoringly she called her Huggo.

There was a mirage in her face. When, turned again towards the star to which she showed her boyish and impetuous look, and, following, she felt again the call that set the mother in her face, she this time reasoned. That idea that, having children, it was the woman who gave hostages to fortune! Deadly and cruelly true it was, but only by convention. Why should it be so? Why should motherhood that was the crown of love, of woman's life, be paid for in coin that no man was called upon to pay? Unjust; and need not be! She perfectly well had carried on her work with Huggo. Sleeping was the adored creature's chief lot in life. If she had ever thought (which she never had) of giving up her work and staying at home on his account, what could she have done but twirl her thumbs and watch him sleep and in his lovely lively hours superintend the nurse who required no superintendence? As it was she was about him in the delicious exercises of transporting him from cot through toilet and refreshment to readiness to take the air. His lordship was off in his lordship's perambulator by nine o'clock every morning. She did not herself leave, with Harry, till shortly before ten. There, in instance, was an hour at home with not the smallest benefit to Huggo. It would have been the same, had she remained at home, with three in four of all the other hours. Ridiculous to lay down that a mother, having a good nurse and a well-ordered house and a husband out all day, must tie herself there, abandoning her own life, to attend her children! Children! Darlings of her own! Ease for this yearning in her heart, assumption of this lovely glory that was her natural right! Yes, she had proved love not to be incompatible with her freedom; she would show motherhood as beautifully could be joined.

It seemed to her a blessing upon, and an assurance in, her purpose that in the precious person of a little daughter came the embodiment of this reasoning and of this design. A baby girl! A tiny woman-bud to be a woman with her in the house of Harry and of Huggo! A woman treasury into which she could pour her woman love! Her self's own self, whose earliest speech chose for herself her name — her Doda!

It all worked splendidly. Winged on the eager pinions of their individual lives these two nested their joined life in a home that for every inmate was a perfect home; perfect for a husband, perfect for a wife, perfect for the babies, perfect for the servants. The peace of every home in civilized society rests ultimately on the kitchen, and the peace of half the homes known to Harry and to Rosalie was in constant rupture by upheavals thence. Not so behind the gamboge door. Rosalie always granted it to men that, as was commonly said, servants worked better for men. Men kept out of the irrational creatures' way; that was about it. The conduct of her life gave her the like advantage. Giving her orders before she left the house, she was out all day and never unexpectedly in. Positively the servants welcomed her on her return at five o'clock!

The babies, to whom then she flew, were with a perfect nurse. Harry had helped in her appointment. She had come one evening, early in the life of Huggo, when a change had to be made from the nurse who specialised only up to the point then reached by Huggo, and she had presented herself to them, seated together in Harry's study, a short body, one shape and a solid shape from her shoulders to her shoes, who announced her name as Muffett.

" Miss Muffett, I hope," said Harry gravely.

" Unmarried, sir," said Muffett with equal gravity and with a sudden drop and then recovery of her stature as though some one had knocked her behind the knees.

" There's nothing to do," said Harry when she had gone, "but to buy her a tuffet and engage her "; and there was nothing to do, when she was installed, but enjoy the babies and delight in them just as a man enjoys and delights in his tiny ones, — in the early mornings before Rosalie left for her work, in the evenings when she returned home.

It all worked splendidly. In those early years, when two were in the nursery and as yet no third, there wasn't a sign that Harry who had married for a home ever could say, " I have a right to a home." He had, and he was often saying so, the most perfect home. He came not home of a night to a wife peevish with domestic frets and solitary confinement and avid he should hear the tale of them, nor yet to one that butterflied the day long between idleness and pleasures and gave him what was left. He came nightly to a home that his wife sought as eagerly as he sought, a place of rest well-earned and peace well-earned. That was it! " Things which are equal to the same thing are equal to each other." They had discovered and had removed the worm of disparity that eats away the heart of countless marriages. They not infrequently had friends in to dinner, not infrequently dined at the tables of friends, made a point of not infrequently attending a theatre or a concert; but however the evening had been passed — and the evenings alone were always agreed to be the best evenings of all — there was none but they ended sitting together, not in the drawing-room, but in Harry's study or in hers, just talking happiness. Equal in endeavour, they were thereby made equal on every plane and in every taste. A reciprocating machine. That was it!

At least that was how, profoundly satisfied with it, she thought it was.

Then Benji came.

CHAPTER VI

THERE were attendant upon the expectation and the coming of Benji certain processes of mind that had not been with Huggo or with Doda. When it was in prospect she had vexation, sometimes a sense of injury, that again her work was to be interrupted. It would make no difference to Harry. It happened that the days of her trial were timed to fall on the date when a criminal prosecution of sensational public interest was due for hearing at the Old Bailey. Harry, for the defence, had added immensely to his brilliant reputation when seeing it through the preliminary stages before the magistrate. The Old Bailey proceedings were to be the greatest event, thus far, in his career. He had told her — how proud and delighted to hear it she had been! — that if he pulled it off (and he had set his heart on pulling it off) he would really begin to think about " taking silk."

Well, but she also had her heart, in no single or sensational climax of her work, but in its every phase and every hour. It absorbed her. Two years earlier Mr. Simcox had begun disturbing signs of health that, begun, developed rapidly. His brisk activity went out of him. His walk had the odd suggestion of one carrying a load. His perky air went dull. His mind was like a flagging watch, run down. He could not concentrate, he suffered passages of aphasia, he began more and more to " give up the office," more and more to leave things to her. The agency in both its branches, scholastic and insurance, developed well. She was its head and it absorbed her. She had a sense, that was like wine to her, of increasing swiftness of decision, of power, of judgment, of vision, of resource. She used to hurry to her office of a morning as an artist urgent with inspiration will hurry to his colours, or a poet to his pen, — avid to exercise that which was within her.

Well, it was to be stopped. Childbed. For a month at least, for two months more likely, all was to be set aside, to go into abeyance, to drift. Whereas Harry's work. . . . Yes, vexatious! These laws that gave men the desirable place in life were not laws but conventions and she had proved them such; but with all proved there yet remained to the man privileges, to the woman restraints, that were ordinances fundamental and not to be escaped. Yes, injurious!

Thus in those weeks of the coming of him that was to be Benji, solely the boy of aspect mutinous and impetuous was in her face; and when within a month stood her appointed time came an event that stiffened there that aspect, turned it, indeed, actively upon the child within her waiting deliverance. This event in its momentous incidence on her career placed its occasion on parity with Harry's anticipations of the Old Bailey trial. Mr. Simcox died.

There's no use labouring why the emotions that at this loss should have been hers were not hers. That girl whose eyes had gathered tears at the picture of the little figure with flapping jacket peering through the curtains at the postman's " rat-tat-flick " was not present in the woman whose first thought at the sudden news, brought to her seated in her office, was, " At such a time! Just when — Now what is to be done? " True for her that there followed gentle feelings, and gentler yet in her attendance on her patron's obsequies, in the discovery that all of which he died possessed he'd left to her, but it is the duller surfaces that are slowest to give refraction, the least used springs that are least pliant. She was come a long road from her first signs of hardening. She was past, now, the stage where, when grieving for the little old man, she would have felt contrition that her first thought at his death had been, not of him, but of his death's effect upon her work.

And there supervened, immediately, interests that caused the passing of Mr. Simcox merely — to have passed.

Mr. Sturgiss, of Field and Company, attending the funeral with her, said to her as he was taking his leave, "One would say this isn't a moment to be talking of other things, business things, but after all — In a way it is the moment. You'll be making new arrangements and rearrangements now. Before you start settling anything I want you to have in mind the old proposition. You've been loyal to poor Simcox to the end. This business is your own now. We want it. We want you. We want you in Lombard Street."

This, cut and dried, glowingly enlarged in long interviews with Mr. Sturgiss and Mr. Field, succinctly reduced to writing by the firm that it might be fairly studied, was before her, not demanding, but eagerly absorbing, her most earnest attention when she was a fortnight from her trial. This was the event whose momentous incidence on her career placed the days then in process and immediately in prospect on parity of importance with their meaning to Harry, absorbed in preparation for his case. There was so much to weigh; and like a threat, a doom, banked her impending banishment from affairs, distracting her, haunting her, hurrying her. There was so much to do, to settle, to wind up (for she found herself arranging for the change even while she debated it); and in the midst of it she was to be cut off as by term of imprisonment! There was so much to scheme, to plan, to dream (her mind already elevated among the high places of her new outlook); and between now and action she was to go — out of action.

Whereas Harry. . . . Whose child it was also to be. . . .

Yes, injurious!

Not injurious as between dear Harry and herself; but injurious as between his sex and hers. There were moments of thinking upon the difference when she could have conceived a grudge against the child she was to bear.

And Harry could not perceive the difference! Immersed in his preparations and, when the case opened, lost to all else in his case, he presented precisely that faculty (and that permission by convention) of complete detachment from his home that long she had known to be man's most outstanding and most enviable quality. He had no attention to spare for the consideration of her own problem and ambition, and she was too honourable to his interests, and too devoted to him in his interests, to bother him with hers. But, more significantly to her feelings than that, he was also too immersed to offer her, in her ordeal of childbirth, the sympathy and the anxiety that, unengrossed, he would have shown. It was there, profound and loving, beneath the surface; but his work came first. He was a man, capable of detachment, permitted by convention to practise detachment, by gift of nature not inhibited from detachment. A man, he could put it beneath the surface. A woman, in conflict of her instincts and her ambitions, it was her ambitions that she must sink. That was it! Yes, injurious.

And he did not even understand.

On what proved to be the evening before her delivery, and was the third day of Harry's case, she was lying, as she had lain some days, on the Chesterfield in the drawing-room, loosely robed. Harry had thought he could get back to tea, and got back. He came to her with tenderest concern, and with immense tenderness at once was talking to her. But she could see! The apparent deepening of all the lines of his dear, striking face, as of one who for hours has been under enormous concentration; the slight huskiness of his voice, from hard service; the repressed excitation in his air; the frequent glint behind the soft regard of his eyes, as of one that has been hunting high and hunting well — she could see; she could tell where was his spirit!

Her own went lovingly to meet it where it was. " Ah, never mind all that, Harry. Tell me all that's been happening to you. How is it going, Harry? "

Dear Harry! Most mannish man! She laughed (and he laughed too, knowing perfectly well why she laughed) to note the delight, like a dog from chain, with which he bounded off into his mind's absorption. He sat upright. He grabbed for a cigarette and inhaled it tremendously. " It's going like cutting butter with a hot knife. I started cross-examining today. I gave him three and a half hours of it, straight off the ice, and I'm not through with him yet. Not half. If he had as many legs as a centipede he'd still not have one left to stand on when I'm through with him. I doubt he'll have his marrow bones to crawl out on, the way he's crumpling up. Even old Hounslow at his worst can't possibly misdirect the jury, the way I've gummed their noses on the trail. I'll tell you — "

He told her.

She had put out both her hands and taken one of his. " It's splendid, Harry. It's too splendid. How delighted I am, and proud, proud! No one would have imagined it at the beginning. What a triumph it will be for you! "

His grasp squeezed hers in fond response. "Why, it won't do me any harm," he agreed. His tone was light. He released his hand and took up a cup of tea, and his tone went deep. "Mind you, I'm glad about it," he said, and stirred the spoon thoughtfully within the cup. He had come into the room declaring he was dying for some tea, but he had touched none, and he now replaced the cup untasted on the table and she saw on his face the deep "inward" look that she knew (and loved) for the sign of intense concentration of his mind. "Yes, glad," he spoke; his voice, as was its habit when he was "inward," sounding as though it was the involuntary, and not the intentional, utterance of his thoughts. "I've gone all out over this case. I saw, the minute they briefed me, that one tiny flaw, his neglect to take up that option — you remember, I told you — right down at the bottom of the whole tangle, and I went plumb down for it and hung on to it and fought it up like, like a diver coming up from fathoms down."

She had a quickness of imagery. It constantly delighted him. "Yes, that's good," she declared. "Up like a diver, Harry. Not with goggles and a helmet and all that, but shot up like a flash, all shining and glistening and triumphant with the jewel aloft. What a shout there'd be! Dear Harry! You're splendid!"

He smiled most lovingly. "As a matter of fact, I feel I ought to make a mess of it. It'll be the first big case since we've been together that, while it's been on, we haven't had talks about. You couldn't, of course, with this so near to you. It would be significant, and proper, if I drowned in it."

She shook her head. "Absurd! Why, the thing I'm most glad about, Harry, is that all this" — she indicated with a gesture her pose, her dress, her condition — "that all this hasn't in the least upset your work. It might have. It hasn't — and when it happens, it won't, will it? "

Harry said, " I'm rather ashamed to say it hasn't, in the least. I've thought of you, often, but I've simply put the thought away. And when it happens, I shall think of you — terribly — going through it; and of the small thing. But we shall be in the crisis of the case and I shall have to forget you. I'll have to, Rosalie, as I have had to. The work must go on."

She agreed emphatically. " Of course it must." She then said, " Whereas mine — "

He did not attend her. The " inward " look was deep upon his face. There was the suggestion of a grimmish smile about his mouth. One could have guessed that he was rehearsing, with satisfaction, his enormous application while the work was going on.

She gave a sound of laughter, and that aroused him. " What's the joke? "

" Why, just how this does rather illuminate the point — "

" The point . . . ? "

" Your work and mine — a man's and a woman's."

" Yes, tell me, dear."

" Why, Harry, I do think of it sometimes. We've planned it and arranged it and settled it so nicely, these years, and you see the big thing in marriage comes along and shatters it to bits. Your work goes on precisely as if nothing at all were happening; mine has to stand by."

" Ah, but this," Harry said, and in his turn indicated her condition. " This — this is different. We agreed, before Huggo, that if we had children it need make no difference to you, to your work, in a way. And it hasn't, and needn't now — when it's over. But this time, this period, why, that's bound to interfere."

" But it doesn't interfere with you. It shows the difference."

" Oh, it shows the difference," he assented.

His tone was conspicuously careless, conceding the difference but attaching to it no importance at all; and with it he rose — she had instantly the impression of him as it were brushing the difference like a crumb from his lap — and announced, " I'm going to my study now for a couple of hours before dinner. I must. Our solicitor's coming in." He bent over her and kissed her lovingly. " You understand, I know."

And he went.

Yes, it showed the difference! And was not seen by him! Yes, injurious. Yes, could conceive a grudge. . . .

There was a mirage in her face. Her face, that had been boy's and mutinous these weeks, was Mary's and was lovely in maternal love when it was turned towards the scrap that on a morning lay against her breast; her thoughts, that had been stubborn, hard, resentful while her days approached, welled in remorse, compassion, yearning, joy, when they were past and this was come. She'd grudged him, this littlest one! Grudged his right, put her own right against it, this tiny, helpless one! When, added to these thoughts, Huggo and Doda, those lovely darlings, were permitted to see him, asleep beside her, he was so wee, so almost nothing against their sturdy limbs, and had come so unwanted — yes, unwanted, this cherishable one of all! — that she knew instantly what name he must be given. Her Benjamin!

Lying much alone in the succeeding days, contrite, adoring; with frequent happy tears (she was left weak); with tender, thank-God, charged with meaning tears, she found a vindication of her self-reproach that immensely bound her up, forgave her, gave her comfort. She could give up her work! She could leave all and be with her darlings! Of course she could! At any time! She had grudged the right to come of this defenceless scrap. She had set against his right her own right. Ah, dangerous! A long road lay that way! In conflict of his coming, with her own rights she had been much engaged. Here, on the sheet beside her, and in the nursery, overhead, were other rights. Well, when they claimed. . . . Of course she could! She had not thought enough about these things. . . .

There is to be said for her that she thought not very widely nor very deeply upon them now. Her resolution that she could, when it was necessary, give up her work, scattered them. It came to her as comes to a man, beset by poverty, scheming by this way and by that to abate it, news of a legacy. He ceases, in his relief, his present schemes; he has " no need to worry now." Or came to her as comes a sail to one shipwrecked and adrift, painfully calculating out his final dregs of food and water. He ceases, at that emblem, his desperate plans to stretch his days. He's all right now.

It was like that with Rosalie.

While only she had realised her resentment of this baby's claims, and only now her contrite yielding to them; before she had conjectured deeply on all the problem thus revealed; there came to her, like way of escape to one imprisoned, like instantaneous lifting of a fog to one therein occluded, the thought, " I can give up the work."

Of course she could! At any moment; by a word; by the mere formulation of the step within her mind, she could abandon her career. Not now. It was not necessary now. But if or when — she used that phrase, in set terms propounding her resolution to herself — if or when the call of her children, of her home, came and was paramount, she could give up everything and respond to it. Oh, happy! Oh, glad discharge of her remorse! When the children wanted her she could just — come

back. Field and Company, her career, her successes —
what of them? She had done well in her career, she
still would do well. Let the claim of home and children
once come into the scale against the claim of those ambitions and — she would just come back!

Oh, happy!

"Come back"? Who was it had said something about
that, something about "come back" for a woman, making the expression thus dimly familiar in her mind?
Who? Laetitia? No, Laetitia was always associated
with another phrase: striking because in terms identical
with accusation previously delivered against her. Well
she remembered it! On the day following Harry's visit
to the house to take his deserts from poor Aunt
Belle and Uncle Pyke, she also had gone there, following his high idea of what was right. She had been
refused admittance. There had come for her as the
last voice out of that house a quivering letter from
Aunt Belle, seeming to quiver in the hand with the passionate upbraiding that had indited it, and a forlorn sentence from Laetitia. "I have done everything for you,
everything, everything, and this is how you have re-
warded me," had pulsed the pages of Aunt Belle; Laetitia
only had written:

"Oh, Rosalie! You could have had any one you liked to
love you, but you took my Harry and I shall never, never
have another."

Miss Salmon's cry again! Twice identically accused.
Once grotesquely accused; once, on the surface, rightly
accused. Both times aware how poignant and pathetic
was the cry; not moved the first time, not moved the
second. Recurring to her now, she knew again how
broken-hearted sad it was, and knew again it ought to
move, but did not. Well, not strange now. She was

a long way out of those too soft compassions. No, not
Laetitia had made "come back" familiar to her. The
phrase, as she seemed to recollect its context, was too profoundly practical for the Laetitia sort; and that was why,
of course, it moved her nothing. She had learnt, jostling
off corners in the market place, what formerly she had
only conjectured, — that there was in life no room for
sentiment, it clogged; it hampered; it brought sticky un-
reality into that which was sharply real. "Come back?"
No, not Laetitia. Who? Keggo? Yes, it was Keggo;
and immediately with the name's recovery was recovered
the phrase's context. This very matter! "Rosalie, a
woman *can't* — come back."

Absurd! But, yes, how she remembered it now!
"Very dangerous being a woman," Keggo had said.
"Men go into dangers but they come out of them and
go home to tea. That's what it *is* with men, Rosalie.
They can always get out. They can always come back.
They never belong to a thing, heart and soul, body and
mind. Rosalie, women do. That's why it is so very,
very dangerous being a woman. Women can't come back.
They take to a thing, *any*thing, and go deep enough, and
they're *its;* they never, never will get away from it; they
never, never will be able to come back out of it. Rosalie,
I tell you this, when a woman gives herself, forgets
moderation and gives herself to *any*thing, she is its captive for *ever*. She may think she can come back but she
can't come back. For a woman there is no comeback.
They don't issue return tickets to women. For women
there is only departure; there is no return."

Poor Keggo!

Poor Keggo had of course founded her theory upon
her own bitter plight. How she had given her case away
when she had said, "Look at me!" It applied to her,
of course, or to any woman — or man for that matter —

who drank or drugged. It applied not in the least to such a case as this of her own. Keggo had tried to apply it. She had said, " You have a theory of life. You are bent upon a career in life. Suppose you ever wanted to come back? "

She had laughed and declared she never would want to come back. Well, look how absurd all poor Keggo's idea was now being proved! It had suddenly occurred to her that it might at some future time be required of her to come back; and all she had to do was just — to come back. No difficulty about it whatsoever! No struggle! Indeed, and fondly she touched that by her side which had called up these thoughts, she would come back joyously. Of course she would! Field and Company, ambition, *that* for it if and when her darlings called her! Yes, wrong every way, that poor Keggo. Dangerous being a woman, she had said, and it was not dangerous. It could be, and she had proved it, a state that could be lived full in every aspect, — full in freedom, full in endeavour, full in love, full in motherhood. Dangerous! A week ago, inimical to this advent, injurious; now, in this advent's presence, and with this resolution gladly dedicated to it, only and wholly glorious.

This one! Come after confliction, come in contrition, come to call her back when she should need to be called, the little tiny one, the belovedest one, the Benjamin one — her Benji!

CHAPTER VII

THOSE children were brought up with every modern advantage. Wisdom is judged by the age in which it flourishes, and everything that the day accounts wise for children those children had. Their father was of considerable and always increasing means; their mother was of great and untrammelled intelligence: anything that money could provide for children, and that intelligent principles of upbringing said ought to be provided for children, those children enjoyed. When they were out of the care of Muffet, who was everything that a nurse ought to be, they passed into the care of a resident governess, Miss Prescott, who was a children's governess, not for the old and fatuous reason that she " loved children," but for the new and intelligent reason that she was attracted by the child-mind as a study and was certificated and diplomaed in the study of children as an exact science, — Child Welfare as she called it. Miss Prescott had complete charge of the children while they were tiny and while they were growing up to eleven and nine and Benji to seven years old. She taught them their lessons (on her own, the new, principles) and on the same principles their habits and the formation of their characters. It might roundly be said that everything troublesome in regard to the children was left to Miss Prescott, and, left to her, came never between the children and their mother. Their mother only *enjoyed* her children, presented to her fresh, clean and happy for the purpose of her enjoyment; and the children only *enjoyed* their mother, visiting them smiling, devoted, unworried, for the purpose of their happiness.

It was a perfect, and a mutually beneficial arrangement. As there had been, before the children came, two independent lives behind the gamboge door, so, with the occupation of the nurseries, there were, as it might be, three independent households, mingling, at selected times, only for purposes of happiness.

It was perfect. In the summer a house was taken at Cromer by the sea and there, all through the fine weather, Miss Prescott was installed with her charges. Their mother had three weeks from Field's in the summer and she and their father would spend the whole of it, and often week-ends, at Cromer idling and playing with their darlings. That was jolly. The children associated nothing whatever but happiness with their parents.

In the other months of the year their mother was immensely occupied with her work at Field's, developing beyond expectation; and their father early and late with his work in the Temple, his esteem by solicitors and by litigants almost beyond his time to satisfy. Their father was much paragraphed in the social journals, and their mother also. The paragraphs said their father was making a " princely fortune " at the Bar and never told of him without telling also of his wife. They described her as " of Field's Bank " and always drove the word " unique " hand in hand with every mention of her parts. " Unique personality "; " unique position "; " unique among professional women "; " unique," said one, " in combining notable beauty and rare business acumen; an office which she attends daily and a charming home; a profession, three beautiful children, and a brilliant husband."

The syntax is weak, but the truth is in it and those children were to be envied in their mother.

Miss Prescott, when she came, did not displace the Muffet. She was installed additional to the Muffet; and as touching the modern principles relating to children she very soon told Muffet a thing or two not previously dreamt of in the Muffet philosophy but having, thenceforward, occasional place in the Muffet nightmares.

The Muffet, however, was of lymphatic character, with, as her most constant desire, the desire not to be " plagued." She was one of those people who are for ever declaring that they never eat anything, who at meals, indeed, appear to eat very little, but who between meals, are eating all day long. At all hours of the day the Muffet jaws, like the jaws of a ruminant, were steadily munching, munching. When Benji was three Muffet was getting distinctly fat. On a corner of the night nursery mantelpiece she had a photographic group of her parents and of an uncle and aunt who lived with her parents. These four were very fat and one evening the children's father made a remark about this portrait that made their mother laugh delightedly.

Benji was in his cot. Huggo had just come from his bath and was having his toes wiped by his mother because he declared Muffet had not dried them properly. He said Muffet groaned when she stooped.

His mother said, " You know, Harry, Muffet *is* getting fat. Have you noticed it? "

Their father was bent almost double swinging Doda between his legs, the stomach of Doda reposing on the palms of his joined hands and Doda squealing ecstatically.

Their father said, " I have. Go and look at that photograph, Rosalie, and you'll see why. Look at what her people are. Muffet's broadening down from precedent to precedent."

It made their mother laugh. The children didn't know why it made her laugh, but they laughed with her. They always did, or with their father when he laughed. And there was always lots of jolly laughter when their father and mother came up to the nurseries.

Those children, as they passed through early childhood, never saw their parents but happy and good-spirited. They never saw them worried nor ever saw them sad. That was, as one might say, Rosalie's chief offering to her darlings. It was splendid to Rosalie that her way of life, far from causing her (as prejudice would have prophesied) to neglect her children, enabled her to consider them in their relations with herself as, by their mothers, children in her childhood never were considered. That they should associate nothing — nothing at all — but happiness with her was the basis of it. Children, she held, ought not to see their parents bad-tempered or distressed or in any way out of sorts or out of control. For a child to do so has in two ways a bad effect on the child mind. In the first place, it is harmful for children to come in contact with the unpleasant things of life; in the second, parents should always be to their children models of conduct and of disposition. They should in themselves present ideals to their children. A man should be a hero to his son; a woman an ideal to her daughter. Why is no man a hero to his valet? It is simply because his valet sees him, as do not those whose esteem he desires to win, in his off moments. Children should never see their parents in their off moments.

This principle was not Rosalie's alone. It is the modern principle. The point, to Rosalie, was that, by her way of life, she was able to apply it. Children were too much with their parents. That was the fault: in her childhood the universal fault, even now the fault among the unenlightened. Parents, being human, must have off moments; are not off moments, indeed, in the total of the day, of greater sum than moments of circumspection?

It follows that if children are always with their parents, the more unlovely side cannot fail to be perceived, and, arising out of it, must follow injury by example, harm by environment, smirching of idealism, loss of respect. In those homes where the mother (in Rosalie's phrase) is the children's slave, why has the father the children's greater respect? Why is it fine to do what father does? Why jolly and exciting to be with father? It is only because the father commonly is away all day, only seen by them when, shedding other affairs, he comes to see them specially.

Her life — oddly how well for everything and every one her attitude to life fell out! — obtained for her and for them the same wise and happy restriction from too free familiarity. She was able to come to her children only when all her undivided attention and whole hearted love could be given to them. They never saw her vexed, they never saw her angry, they never saw her sad. It was not a commonplace to them to see their mother. It was an event. A morning event and an evening event — and unfailingly a completely happy event. She looked back upon her own childhood with her own mother and reflected, fondly but clearly, affectionately but not blinded by affection, how very different was that. She was always with her mother. Her mother was often sad, often worried, often, in distraction of her worries, irritable in speech. Often sad! Why, she could remember time and again when her dear mother, hunted by her cares, was broken down and crying. She would go to her mother then and cry to see her crying, and her mother would put her arms around her and hug her to her breast and declare she was her " little comfort." Was it good for a child to suffer scenes like that? She used to be with her mother all day long, from early morning till last thing at night. With what result? That she saw

and suffered with her, or suffered of her, all that her
mother suffered; that she was sometimes desolated to
feeling that her heart was broken for her mother. Could
that be good for a child? Her Huggo, her Doda and her
Benji never saw her anything but radiant; and because
that was so (as she told herself) she never saw them
cry, either on her account or on their own.

Therein — grief in her presence on their own account
— another point arose. With as her ideal that only
happiness should be associated with her, she found her
way of life beneficial to the preservation of that ideal
in that it prevented her from being the vessel that should
convey the restrictions, the reproofs and the instruction
that are troublesome to small minds. All that was left
to Miss Prescott. She remembered lessons with her
mother; she remembered the irksome learning of a hundred " don'ts " from her mother; and though they were
tender and pathetic memories she remembered also the
reverse of the picture, — being glad to escape from her
mother, resentful against her mother when stood in the
corner by her mother, when stopped doing this that and
the other by her mother, when made to learn terribly
hard lessons by her mother and to go on learning them
till she had learnt them. Only childish resentment, of
course, swept up and forgotten as by the sun emerging
out of clouds the shadow from a landscape. But why
should children ever have the tiniest frown against their
mother? There must be frowns, there must be tears.
Let others bear the passing grudge of those. Let Miss
Prescott.

Miss Prescott was willing and able to bear anything like
that. She delighted in such. She told Rosalie, when
Rosalie engaged her, and after she had seen the children,
that her only hesitation in accepting the post was that
the children were too normal. " By normal," said Miss

Prescott, speaking, as she always spoke, as if she were a passage out of a book given utterance, " By normal, Mrs. Occleve, I do not, of course, mean commonplace. Any one can see how attractive they are, how gifted; any one can know how distinguished, with, if I may say so, such talented parents, their inherited qualities must be. No, when I say normal, I mean showing no disquieting signs, constitutionally tractable, not refractory. In that sense of normality it is much more the abnormal child to whom I would have liked to devote myself. I have specialised in children. The harder the case the more I should be interested in it. That's what I mean. But I never could have hoped to find a household where, though there can be no difficulties, I should have such opportunities of helping children to be perfect men and women; nor a mother to whose children I would more gladly, proudly, devote myself; nor a place with which I should feel myself so entirely in sympathy. If you feel, on reflection, that I should suit you, it will be, I am sure — why should I not say so — an auspicious day for those little ones."

How happy was Rosalie thus by provision to destiny her darlings!

Miss Prescott was thirty when engaged by Rosalie. She had a way of looking at people which, if described, can best describe her appearance. She was once in an omnibus in London and the conductor, standing against her, and about to serve a ticket to a passenger seated next her, had some trouble with his bell-punch. It would not work and he fumbled with it, angry. Everybody in the bus watched him. It is not nice to be watched when baffled and heated in bafflement but the only gaze to which attention was given by the conductor was the gaze of Miss Prescott. He glanced constantly from the obdurate machine to the face of Miss Prescott. Suddenly he said:

" 'Ere, suppose you do it, then," and pushed the bell-punch at her. Miss Prescott took it, did it, astoundingly and instantaneously, and handed it back with no word. The conductor seemed more angry than before.

It was like that that Miss Prescott looked at people.

There is a right way of doing everything. Miss Prescott had an uncanny instinct for finding it; and, applying this faculty to her training of the child-mind, she presented herself as a notable exponent of the system in which, as has been said, she was certificated and diplomaed. She taught children how to play in the right way, how to learn in the right way, and above all how, in every way and at every turn, to reason. By the old, ignorant plan children were instructed, speaking broadly, by love or by fear. It was by pure reason that Miss Prescott instructed them. The child was treated as an earnest physician treats a case. Ill temper or wrong behaviour in a child was neither vexing nor sad. It was profoundly *interesting*. There was a right and scientific way to treat it and that right and scientific way was thought out and administered. The child was " a case."

It was taught nothing but truths and facts. Its mind was not permitted to be befogged with fairy stories, with superstitions, with Father Christmases and the like, nor yet with religious half-truths and misty fables. These entailed not only befogging at the time, but disillusionment thereafter. Disillusionment was wicked for a child. It further was taught nothing at all (in the matter of lessons) at the grotesquely early age at which children used to be taught. It was taught first to reason.

In general the whole system lay in developing the child's reasoning powers and then, at every turn and particularly at every manifestation of indiscipline, appealing to its reason. " I am here to be happy " — that was the first, and surely the kindest and easiest, knowl-

edge to fix in the child. From that foundation everything was worked. It never was necessary to punish a
child. It only was necessary to reason with it. In the
old phraseology a child meet to be punished was a naughty
child. In the terminology of Miss Prescott such a child
was a sick child or an unreasoning child: a case presenting an adverse symptom. But take the older term, — a
naughty child. A naughty child was an unhappy child.
The treatment went like this, " I am here to be happy.
I am not happy. Why am I not happy? Because I have
done so and so and so and so. . . ."

Kind, wise, simple, effective, easy. Rosalie in her
childish misdemeanours would have been prevailed upon
by the unhappiness her conduct caused her mother. All
wrong! A faulty process of reasoning; indeed not a
process of reasoning at all: a crude appeal to the emotions.
Those three children who on the one part never saw their
mother sad and were constrained to comfort her, on the
other never were bribed to good behaviour by the thought
of grieving her. They only associated happiness with
her and they enjoyed happiness simply by reasoning away
unhappiness.

Kind, wise, simple, effective, easy.

Happy Huggo, happy Doda, happy Benji, happy Rosalie!

CHAPTER VIII

It has been said of Time, earlier in these pages, the cloak-and-dagger sort he is, that stalks and pounces. One seeks only to record him when he thus assails, and there is this result; that it is necessary to pare away so much. In instance, there's to be inserted now a note on Rosalie's advance in her career. It's cut to nothing. This is because all that career ultimately was known to her never to have really mattered. And so with other things. That girl, all through, pressing so strong ahead, rises to the eye not cumbered with other importance than her own. There might be asked for (by a reader) presentation of Harry's parents; of what was doing all this time to her own parents in the rectory, to Harold, Robert, Flora, Hilda; of friends that Rosalie and Harry had. That girl's passage is not traced in such. Whose is? The chart where such are marked is just a common public print, stamped for the public eye. They're not set down upon that secret chart all carry in the cabin of their soul, and there, in that so hidden and inviolable state-room, poring over it by the uncertain swinging lamp of conscience, prick out their way.

Her installation in the bank had been a notable success. She dealt with all the insurance advice and with income-tax advice and business; and it was remarkable to her, at first, how many of Field's clients were as children in the mysteries of income tax, and as children alike in their ignorance of the possibilities of life insurance and in their pleasure at the discoveries she set before them. But further than this (and more important, said Mr. Sturgiss and Mr. Field) was the quick response of the clients to the various domestic advice that it was Rosalie's business to give. Husbands and wives from the East, or returned thither from London and writing from the East, consulted her on innumerable matters. When, in instance, an army officer wrote to her from India, very diffidently wondering if she could help him in the matter of some Christmas presents for his wife and children at home, Mr. Sturgiss was uncommonly pleased.

"I knew it!" said Mr. Sturgiss. "That's the kind of thing. You watch how side lines like that will develop. That's what these people want — some one at home they can rely on. I tell you, Mrs. Occleve, you, that is to say your department of Field's, is what the Anglo-Eastern has been wanting ever since Clive and Warren Hastings went out — a link with home. You see."

She did see. Mr. Field saw. The clients saw. The friends of the clients saw — and became clients.

All of her position reposed, and was developed by her, on the cruel disabilities of those who earn their bread in the East. For all such, married, comes, in time, the sad and the costly business of the divided home, — the two establishments, the sundering of children and parents, of husband and wife. By the age of seven at latest the children have to be sent home for health and education. Then the sundering, the losing of touch, the compulsion upon the man, that those at home may be promptly supported, to deny himself year after year the longed-for visit home. The losing of touch. . . . Invaluable to them to have in Field's, in "that Mrs. Occleve" a link, known personally or by reputation, that was useable as relations (capricious, "touchy," interfering) often are not useable; and dependable as relations, unpractical, certainly are not always dependable. Invaluable to the clients; declared by Mr. Field and by Mr. Sturgiss to be invaluable to the bank; absorbing and splendid to Rosalie. "And still," Mr. Sturgiss was always saying, "still capable of much bigger development."

He sketched one day a development that would be a stride indeed. It began to be discussed by the three. It connoted so absolute a recognition of Rosalie's worth that she decided — lest it should fall through — she would not mention it to Harry till either it was fallen through or was afoot. Then!

It made her busy. She told Harry once, when they'd been talking of how much at office she was kept, of her work, and of the place she was making for herself, "Well, it's not bad, Harry," she told him. "It's not bad. I'll admit that. What pleases me is that it's only a beginning; well as it's going, and long as I've now been at it, only a beginning. I can't, as I've often said to you, be doing all this without getting a long insight into the actual banking business. Oh, don't you remember my telling you about that appalling evening when I told poor Uncle Pyke that I wanted to be a banker? How outraged he was! Poor person, how rightly outraged! The ridiculous notion that I ever could be a banker! A grotesque dream!" She gave a small laugh as if tenderly smiling at image before her of that innocent, eager girl at the Pyke Pounce table. She said softly, "A grotesque dream. Now, with patent limitations — not a dream."

It was like that that Time (disguised as triumph) kept out of the way; and similarly disguised, showed no sign either on the children's side. All splendid there! Growing up! Huggo set to school!

Huggo learnt with Miss Prescott till he was nine, then attended daily a first-rate school for little boys in Kensington, at eleven started as a boarder at a preparatory school for Tidborough. Next he was to go to the great public school itself, afterwards to Oxford and the Bar. All's well! Time had nothing at all to say during the first two stages of the programme. It was in Huggo's first holidays from the preparatory school that Time whipped out his blade and pounced.

On a day that was a week before the end of that holidays the great new scheme for Rosalie at Field's rose to its feet and walked. It was a special mission on behalf of the bank.

It necessitated. . . .

She came once or twice to a bit of a stop like that while waiting their evening talk together in which she should tell Harry. It necessitated a departure from the established order of things; but what of that? Was not the way bill of her life all departures from things established, and all successful, and were not all contingencies of this particular departure fully insured against? She very easily cantered on, on this rein. That bit of a stop was scarcely a check in the progression of her thoughts.

Seated with Harry in Harry's room that night she was about to tell him her great news when, " I'd an unusual offer made to me today," said Harry.

Almost the very words herself had been about to use! " Why so had I to me! " she cried.

They both laughed. " Tell on," said Harry.

" No, you. Yours first."

" Toss you," cried Harry; and spun a coin and lost and went ahead: " Well, mine doesn't exactly shake the foundations of the world with excitement because I refused it. It was to go out to defend in a big murder case in Singapore! "

She exclaimed, " In Singapore! "

" Yes, Singapore. Why do you say it like that? "

She did not answer.

The prisoner, Harry went on, was a wealthy trader, immensely wealthy, and immensely detested, it appeared, by the European settlement; had native blood in his veins; was charged with poisoning an Englishman with whose wife he was supposed to have been carrying on an amour. "A wretched, unsavoury business," said Harry, and went on to say that, though the fee offered was extraordinarily handsome, he had declined the proposal. It was doubtful he would actually make more money over it than in his normal round at home, more than that it went against the grain to be defending a man of native origins who had pretty obviously seduced a white woman if not murdered her husband. "No, no ticket to Singapore for me, thanks," said Harry.

Rosalie turned to him with a sudden, direct interest. "Harry, suppose you had accepted, how long would you have been away?"

"Not less than six months in all. Certainly not less. That's another point against — "

"Yes, against the idea, because in any case you don't want to go. But suppose the circumstances had been different; suppose it was a case that for various reasons very much attracted you; would you have gone?"

Harry said indifferently, "Oh, no doubt, no doubt."

"Although it would have taken you from home six months — or more? You'd not have minded that?"

He laughed delightedly. "Ah, ha! I was beginning to wonder what you were driving at. You're a regular lawyer, Rosalie; you led me on and then caught me out properly."

His amusement was not reflected by her. She said with a certain insistence, "But you wouldn't have minded?"

He laughed again. "The judge ruled that the question was admissible and must be answered. Well, minded —

I'd have minded, of course, very much in a way. I'm a home bird. I'd have hated being away the best part of a year. But there you are. If the call was strong enough, there you are; it would have been business."

She indrew a long breath. "That's it. It would have been business."

There was then a pause.

Harry, who had been talking lightly, then said slowly, "Rosalie, is there something behind this?"

She turned towards him with a very nice smile. "Harry, I've been doing a very shocking thing. I've been making you commit yourself."

"Commit myself?"

She nodded. "Been taking down your statement without warning you that it may be used in evidence against you."

He said gravely, "Somehow I don't like this."

She told him, "Ah, stupid me! I'm making a small thing seem big. Listen, Harry. It was curious to me this about you and Singapore — "

"Yes, I noticed that. Why?"

"Because there's an idea of *my* going out to Singapore."

He was astounded. She might have said to Mars. "You? To Singapore?"

"To the East generally. To Bombay, to Rangoon, to Singapore. For about a year."

He was all aback. "For about a year? Rosalie, I can't — Why on earth — ?"

She did not like this. The great scheme! Her special mission! It necessitated. . . . Here was the necessity at which she had checked but confidently ridden on, and Harry was pulled right up by it. His astonishment was not comfortable to her. Was there to be a check then?

He said again, " You? A year? But, Rosalie, what on earth — "

She pronounced a single word, his own word:
" Business."

He was standing before her on the hearthrug. He made a turn and at once turned back. " Are you thinking of this seriously? "

" Most seriously."

" Of going? "

" Of going. It's business."

" For a year? "

" Harry, yes."

He began to fill his pipe with very slow movements of his fingers, his eyes bent down upon her. " And you called this — just now — a small thing? "

She said with a sudden eagerness, " Harry, it's a very big thing for me, for Field's. I meant a small thing in the sense not to be made a fuss about."

He made very slowly a negative movement with his head. " I don't see it like that."

" Let me tell you, Harry."

She told him how the great possibilities of the department she had established in the bank rested on the personal touch established between herself and the clients. The scheme was that those possibilities should be developed to their fullest extent. While she was in London that personal touch could be established with clients by dozens. If she visited the branches in the East, at Bombay, at Rangoon, at Singapore, it was by hundreds that the touch could be established. That was it. Field's customers would talk to her, and when she was returned they would talk of her, and would tell others of her, as one met, not during the jolly freedom of leave when the impulse was to feel that, after all, nothing mattered much, but met out there when they were in the yoke and the harness of the thing, — met as one fresh out from home in their particular interests and shortly, charged with their special interests, returning home. That was it! A novel mission, a valuable mission, *her* mission. About a year. To start in about six weeks. " There, Harry, that's the plan."

" And you are going? "

" I have agreed to go."

He said slowly, " It astonishes me."

There was then a pause.

She spoke. " I think I do not like your astonishment, Harry."

" It is justified."

" No, no; not justified. When you told me of a possibility of Singapore for you I was not astonished. I made no difficulty."

" Different," he said. " Different."

" Not different, Harry. The same. How different? If you could go, I can go. The same. Aren't things with us always the same? "

He shook his head. " Not this. If I had to go — "

" Yes, yes. It's the point. If you had to go you'd have to go. Well, I have to go."

" Rosalie, if I had to go I could go. A man can."

She cried, " But, Harry, that — This isn't us talking at all. You mean a man can leave his home because his home can go on without him. But our home — it's just the same for me in our home. We've made it like that. It runs itself. The kitchen — I don't know when I last gave an order. The children — there's never a word. The thing's organised. I'm an organiser." She laughed, " Dear, that's why they're sending me. Isn't it organised? "

He assented, but with an inflexion on the word " It's — organised."

She did not attend the inflexion. " Well, that's no organisation that can't, in necessity, run by itself. This can. You know, quite well, this will. You know, quite well, that you will not be put about a jot."

" Oh, I know that," he said.

" Well, then. Astonished — why astonished? "

He looked at her. " Let's call it," he said, " the principle of the thing."

Oh, now astonishment between them. Her voice, astounded, had an echo's sound — faint, faint, scarcely to be heard, gone. " The prin-ci-ple ! "

This room was lit, then, only by a standard lamp remote from where they were beside the fire. She was in a deep armchair; its partner, Harry's chair, close by. He sat himself on the arm, looking towards her. The firelight made shadows on his face.

She presently murmured, her voice as though that echo, lost, was murmuring back, " Oh, it is I that am astonished now. The principle! It's like a ghost. Harry, how possibly can there come between us the principle? "

His voice was deep, " Are we afraid of it, old girl? "

She put out a hand and touched him and he touched her hand. They were such lovers still. That was the thing about it. There never had been an issue between them, not the smallest; the bloom of their first union never had dissipated, not a rub. But there was in Harry the intention now to take her, and there was in her the apprehension now of being taken, to a new dimension of conversation, not previously trod by them. As they proceeded it was seen not to be light in this place; a place where touch might be lost.

She said, " But to bring up the principle in this! It can't be possible you've changed. It isn't conceivable to me that you have changed. Then how the principle? "

" It is the situation that has changed, Rosalie. It never

occurred to me; I never dreamt or imagined that a thing like this could arise."

She moved in her chair. " Oh, this goes deep. . . ."

He put a hand on her shoulder. " We're not afraid."

" But I'm so strong in this. So always certain. In our dear years together so utterly assured. Nothing within the principle could touch me. I am steel everywhere upon the principle. I might hurt you, Harry."

" I'll not be hurt."

" Well, say it, Harry."

He was silent a moment. " There isn't really very much to say. To me it's so clear."

She murmured, " And to me."

He said, " We've made this home — eleven years. It's been ideal. You have combined your work with your — what shall I call it? — with your domestic arrangements — your business with your domesticity — You've done it wonderfully. We've never had to discuss the subject since we agreed upon it."

She murmured, " That is why — agreed."

" Agreed in general. But when you take the home as between a man and a woman, there are bound to be responsibilities which, however much you share, cannot be divided. The woman's are the — the domesticity."

" What are the man's? "

" To maintain the home."

" I share in that."

" Well, grant you do. I do not claim to share the other."

" You are not asked to, Harry."

" No, but, Rosalie, I've the right to ask you to provide the other."

Her murmur said, " Oh, do not let us bring up rights. I am so fixed on rights."

" Rosalie, let's keep the thing square. A man can leave

his home; he often has to. I think not so a woman; not a mother; not as you wish now to leave it. It can't, without her, go on — not in the same way."

" Yes, ours. Ours can."

" Not in the same way. You can't take out the woman and leave it the same, — the same for the man, the same for the children. We're married. The married state. With children. Doesn't the whole fabric of the married state rest on the domesticity of woman?"

She murmured, " No, on her resignation, Harry."

As if he had touched something and been burnt he very sharply drew in his breath.

She said, " Ah, you'd be hurt, I told you. Dear, I can't be other than I am on this. Upon her resignation, Harry. Men call it domesticity. That's their fair word for their offence. It's woman's resignation is the fabric of the married state. She lets her home be built upon her back. She resigns everything to carry it. She has to. If she moves it shakes. If she stands upright it crashes. Dear, not ours. I've stood upright all the time. I've proved the fallacy. A woman can stand upright and yet be wife, be mother, make home. Dear, you are not to ask me now — for resignation."

Therein, and through all the passage of this place where the footway was uneven, the light not good, the quality of her voice was low and noteless, sometimes difficult to hear. There is to say it was by that the more assured, as is more purposeful in its suggestion the tide that enters, not upon the gale, but in the calm and steady flow of its own strength.

The quality of Harry's voice was very deep and sometimes halting, as though it were out of much difficulty that he spoke. He said, deeply, " That you stand upright does not discharge you from responsibilities."

She said, " Dear, nor my responsibilities discharge me from my privileges."

There was then a silence.

He spoke, " But I am going to press this, Rosalie.   I say, with all admitted, this thing — this ' I could go but you should not go ' — is different as between us.   I am a man."

She made a movement in her chair.   " Ah, let that go. I have a reply to that."

" What reply? "

" I am a woman."

He began — " It's nothing —."

She said, " Oh, painful to give you pain.   To me — everything."

He got up from his position beside her and went to his chair and seated himself.   He sat on the edge of the chair, bowed forward, his forearms on his knees, his hands clasped; not smoking; his pipe between his fingers, his eyes upon the fire.   Once or twice, his hands close to his face, he slightly raised them and with his pipe-stem softly tapped his teeth.

CHAPTER IX

He had called it the principle. She watched him. That attitude in which he sat was of a profundity of meditation not to be looked upon without that sense of awe, of oppression, of misgiving that is aroused by the suggestion in man or nature of brooding forces mysteriously engrossed. There came to her, watching him, a thought that newly disturbed her thoughts. He had called it the principle. She had been astonished but she had not been perturbed. Upon the principle as between man and woman, husband and wife, she was, as she had said, so strong, so confident, accustomed and assured, that there was nothing could be said could touch her there. But it was not the principle. This was the knowledge brought to her by the new thought suddenly appeared in her mind, standing there like a strange face in a council of friends, unbidden and of a suspect look. What if she communicated that knowledge to Harry brooding there? He had called it the principle. What if she put across the shadowed room the sentence that should inform him it was not the principle but was an issue flying the flag of ships whose freights are dangerous? What if she put across the shadowed room the sentence, " Men that marry for a home "?

Ay, that was it! The thing she had always known and never told. Those are keepsakes of our secret selves, those observations, vows, conspiracies with which romantically we plot towards our ideals. This the sole keepsake of her treasury she never had revealed to Harry. Significant she had not. Some instinct must have stayed her. Yes, significant! He had called it the principle. It was not the principle. He was sincere upon the principle and in the examination of eleven years had proved his sincerity. It was not the principle. It was that herein, in her intention to exercise her freedom in a new dimension, she had touched him, not through the principle, but upon the instinct that led him, as she believed men to be led, to marry for a home, a settling-in place, a settling-down place, a cave to enter into and to shut the door upon.

Oh, this was dangerous! There were no lengths to which this might not lead! If at her first essay at that which countered his idea of home she was to be asked to pause, what, in the increasing convolutions of the years, might not she be asked to abandon? Let him attempt restriction of her by appeal to principle and she could stand, and win, unscathed. Let him oppose her by his wish within his home to shut the door, and that was to put upon her an injury that only by giving him pain could be fought. Oh, dangerous! Not less an injury because by sentiment and not by reason done! Much more an injury because so subtly done! Much more! Dangerous! Ah, from this the outset to be withstood!

He spoke and his first words were confirmation of her fears.

"Rosalie, do you feel quite all right about the children?"

Yes, she could see where this was set to lead. He could leave her with the children; but she — men that married for a home — could not leave him with the children.

She said gently, "Dear, there'll not be the least difficulty. Everything's perfectly arranged. Everything will perfectly well go on."

He had not moved his pose and did not move it. His voice presented in tone the profound meditation that his pose presented. He said, "I don't quite mean that. I mean, do you always feel everything's quite all right with them?"

How setting now? She answered, "Dear, of course I do."

His eyes remained upon the fire. "Rosalie, d'you know I sometimes don't."

Her motion — a lifting of her face, a questing of her brows — was of a helmsman's gesture, suspicious to catch before it set a shifting of the breeze. "Harry, in what way? They're splendid."

"You feel that?"

"Dear, you know they are."

He put his pipe to his mouth and with that meditative tapping tapped his teeth. "Splendid, yes, in health, in appearance, in development, in all that kind of thing. I don't mean that." He turned his face towards her and spoke directly. "Rosalie, have you ever thought they're not quite like other children?"

Oh, setting from what quarter this? She said, "They're better — miles and miles."

He got up. "Well, that's all right. If you have noticed nothing, that's all right."

"But, Harry. I am at a loss, dear. Of course it's all right. But what have you noticed, think you've noticed?"

He was standing before her, his back against the mantelpiece, looking down at her. "Just that — not quite like other children."

"But in what way?"

"It's hard to say, old girl. If you've not noticed it, harder still. Not quite so childish as at their age I seem to remember myself with my brothers and sisters being childish. A kind of — reserve. A kind of — self-contained."

She shook her head, "No, no."

"You think it's fancy?"

" I'm sure it is."

He was silent a moment. " It's rather worried me. And of course now — If you are going to be away — "

Stand by! She had the drift of this!

She said simply, " Harry, this can't be."

" You can't give up the idea? "

Her hand upon the helm that steered her life constricted. " It is not to be asked of me to give it up." She paused. She said softly, " Dear, this is a forward step for me. You are asking me to make a sacrifice. I would not ask you."

He began, " There are sacrifices — "

" They are not asked of men."

He said, " Rosalie, you said once, when Benji was born, that, if at any time need be, you would give up, not a thing like this, but your work entirely."

As if to shield or to support her heart she drew her left hand to it. " Would you give up yours, Harry? "

He said quickly, " I'm not suggesting such a thing. It is ridiculous. I'm only showing you — "

She began to say her say, her voice reflective as his own had been. " But you have shown me frightful things, shown me how far and oh, how quick, a thing that starts may go. Oh, my dear, know the answer before it ever is suggested. Sacrifices! It is sacrifice for the children that you profess to mean. Well, let us call it that. Have you ever heard of a father sacrificing himself for his children? There's no such phrase. There's only the feminine gender for that. ' Sacrificed himself for his wife and children.' It's a solecism. If grammar means good sense, it isn't grammar because it's meaningless. It can't be said. It's grotesque. But ' Sacrificed herself for her husband and her children,' — why, that the commonest of clichés. It's written on half the mothers' brows; it

should be carved on half the mothers' tombs — upon my
own dear mother's." She stood up and faced him.
" Harry, not on mine." She put a gentle hand on his.
" I love you — you know what our love is. I love the
children — with a truer love that they have never been
a burden to me nor I on a single occasion out of mood
with them. But, Harry, I will not sacrifice myself for
the children. When I ask that of you, ask it of me. But
I never will ask it of you."

She was trembling.

He put an arm about her shoulders. " It's over. It's
over. Let's forget it, Rosalie."

Of course she did not forget it. Of course she knew
that Harry could not. Men that marry for a home!
Already in his mind the thought that for his home she
should give up, not only this present forward step, but —
everything! Oh, man-made world! Oh, man-made men!
" It's over. It's over," he had said. Of course she knew
it was not over. Men that marry for a home! Secret
she had kept it and in the same moment that she had realised the significance of her secrecy it had been enlarged.
Now it stalked abroad.

But what is to be observed is the quality of the love
between them. It was through the children that he had
made this claim that he had sought to impose upon her.
She had told him, as she believed, that what he thought
he saw was fancy. It never occurred to her to imagine
so base a thing as that he, to give himself grounds, had invented or even exaggerated his fancy; but it had been
excusable in her (threatened as she saw herself) to avoid,
in the days that followed, discussion of that fancy, much
less herself to bring it forward. Her love for Harry was
never in that plane. It could admit no guile. It happened
that within the week she was herself a little pained by

matter with the children. She took her pain straight to her Harry.

On his last day of the holidays before he returned for his second term at his preparatory school, Huggo was noisy with excitement at the idea of returning. It rather pained Rosalie that he showed not the smallest sign of regret at leaving home. Miss Prescott had done all the necessary business of getting his clothes ready for school but Rosalie took from Field's this last afternoon to do some shopping with her little man (as she termed it) in Oxford Street; to buy him some little personal things he wanted, — a purse of pigskin that fastened with a button, a knife with a thing for taking stones out of horses' hoofs, and a special kind of football boots. Since there had come to her the " men that marry for a home " significance, that mirage in her face had much presented that mutinous and determined boy it often showed. Only the mother was there when she set out with Huggo. And then the sense of pain.

Oxford Street appeared to be swarming with small boys and their mothers similarly engaged. All the small boys wore blue overcoats with velvet collar and looked to Rosalie most lovably comic in bowler hats that seemed enormously too big for their small heads. Huggo was dressed to the same pattern but his hat exactly suited his face which was thin and, by contrast with these others, old for his years. Rosalie wished somehow that Huggo's hat didn't suit so well; the imminent extinguisher look of theirs made them look such darling babies. And what really brought out the difference was that all these other small boys invariably had a hand stretched up to hold their mothers' arms and walked with faces turned up, chattering. Huggo didn't. She asked him to. He said, " Mother, why? "

" I'd love you to, darling."

He put up his hand and she pressed it with her arm to her side, but she noticed that he was looking away into a shop window while he did as he was asked, and there came in less than a dozen paces a congestion on the pavement that caused him to slip behind her, removing his hand. He did not replace it.

In the shop where the knife was to be bought an immense tray of every variety of pocketknife was put before them. Huggo opened and shut blades with a curiously impatient air as though afraid of being interfered with before he had made his choice. Immediately beside Rosalie was another mother engaged with another son upon another tray.

" It's got to have a thing for levering stones out of horses' hoofs," said Huggo, brushing aside a knife offered by the assistant and rummaging a little roughly.

Rosalie said, " Darling, I can't think what you can want such a thing for."

The lady beside her caught her eye and laughed. " That's just what I'm asking my small man," she said.

Her small man, whose face was merry and whose hat appeared to be supported by his ears, looked up at Rosalie with an engaging smile and said in a very frank voice, " It's jolly useful for lugging up tight things or to hook up toffee that's stuck."

They all three laughed. Huggo, busily engaged, took no notice.

He found the knife he wanted. Rosalie showed him another. " Huggo, I'm sure that one's too heavy and clumsy."

The voice of the little boy with the hat on his ears came, " Mummie, I'd rather have this one because you chose it."

Rosalie said to Huggo, " It will weigh down your pocket so."

" This one! This one!" cried Huggo and made a vexed movement with a foot.

Rosalie, sitting with Harry before the fire in Harry's room that night said, " Harry, tell me some more of what you said the other day about the children."

He looked up at her. He clearly was surprised. " You've been thinking about it?"

" I've been with Huggo shopping for him this afternoon and been at little things a little sad. Harry, when you said ' not like other children ' did you mean not — responsive?"

He said intensely, " Rosalie, it is the word. It's what I meant. I couldn't get it. I wonder I didn't. It's my meaning exactly — not responsive. You've noticed it?"

" Oh, tell me first."

" Rosalie, it's sometimes that I've gone in to the three of them wanting to be one with them, to be a child with them and invent things and imagine things. Somehow they don't seem to want it. They don't — invite it. Your word, they don't — respond. I want them to open their hearts and let me right inside. Somehow they don't seem to open their hearts."

She said, " Harry, they're such mites."

He shook his head. " They're not mites, old girl. Only Benji. And even Benji — It was different when they were wee things. It's lately, all this. They don't seem to understand, Rosalie — to understand what it is I want. That's the thing that troubles me. It's an extraordinary thing to say, but it's been to me sometimes as if I were the child longing to be — what shall I say? — to have arms opened to me, and they were the grown-ups, holding me off, not understanding what it is I want. Not understanding. Rosalie, why don't they understand?"

She had a hand extended to the fire and she was slowly

opening and shutting her fingers at the flames. This, coming upon the feeling she had had that afternoon with Huggo, was like a book wherein was analysed that feeling. But, " I am sure they do understand, dear," she said. " I'm sure it's fancy."

" I think you're not sure, Rosalie."

" Oh, yes, I am. If it's anything it's just perhaps their way — all children have their ways. What I thought about Huggo this afternoon might perhaps be something what you mean. Harry, if it is, it's just the little man's way."

" What was it you thought? "

She maintained that movement of the fingers of her hand. " Why, only things I noticed; tiny things; nothings, I'm sure. Out shopping with me, Harry. Well, it was his last day and I would have expected somehow he would have been fonder for that. He wasn't and I rather felt it. Things like that. I would so like him to have held my arm. He didn't want to. Not very grateful for the things we bought. But there, why should he be, dear Huggo? But just his way; that's what one ought to think. But I felt it a little."

Harry said, " I know. I know. It's that that I have felt — not responsive. It's what I've thought I've noticed in them all."

Telling him perhaps enlarged, as telling does, her sensibilities. She said very quickly, " Not Benji! "

" Well, Benji's so very young. But even — But in the other two — "

She said as quickly as before, " Ah, Doda's responsive! "

" You've seen it, dear, in Huggo."

" Oh, Harry, nothing, just his way. I'm sorry now I mentioned it."

He had been watching the flexion of her hand. He

said, " I'm glad you have. When I spoke of it the other
day you said you didn't see it. I think it's generous in
you to admit you have."

She murmured, " Generous? "

" It brings up — Rosalie, does this affect a little, alter
perhaps, your decision?"

She shut her fingers sharply. " No." She kept them
shut. " There's nothing at all could alter that, Harry."

He turned aside and began to fill his pipe, with slow
movements.

It has been warned that it was in this holidays of
Huggo's from his preparatory school that Time, that
bravo of the cloak-and-dagger school, whipped out his
blade and pounced. These, since that warning, were but
the doorways and the lurking posts he prowled along.

He now was very close to Rosalie.

Rosalie and Harry both were home to lunch next day.
In the afternoon they were to take Huggo to Charing
Cross to see him off in the saloon specially reserved for
his school. All the children were at lunch for this occasion. Benji in a high chair just like the high chair that
had been Rosalie's years back — what years and years! —
at the rectory. Huggo was in boisterous spirits. You
would think, you couldn't help thinking, it was his first
day, not his last day home. Rosalie observed him as she
had not before observed him. How he talked! Well,
that was good. How could Harry have thought him reserved? But he talked a shade loudly and with an air
curiously self-opinionated. But he was such a child, and
opinions were delightful in a child. Yes, but something
not childish in his way of expressing his opinions, something a shade superior, self-satisfied; and she particularly
noticed that when anything in the way of information
was given him by Harry or by herself he never accepted

it but always argued. She grew very silent. She felt she would have given anything to hear him, in the long topic of railways with his father, and then of Tidborough School, say, "*Do* they, father?" or, "*Does* it, father?" He never did. He always knew it before or knew different. Once on a subject connected with the famous school Harry said, a shade of rebuke in his voice, "My dear old chap, I was at Tidborough. I ought to know." Rosalie felt she would have given anything in the world for Huggo to reply, "Sorry, father, of course you ought." Instead he bent upon his plate a look injured and resentful at being injured. But in a minute she was reproaching herself for such ideas. Her Huggo! and she was sitting here criticising him. Different from other children! Why, if so, only in the way she had affirmed to Harry — miles and miles better. Opinionated? Why, famously advanced for his years. Superior? Why, bright, clever, not a nursery boy. She had been wronging him, she had been criticising him, she had been looking for faults in him, her Huggo! Unkind! Unnatural!

Listen to him! The meal was ended. His father was bantering him about what he learnt, or didn't learn, at school; was offering him an extra five shillings to his school tip if he could answer three questions. The darling was deliciously excited over it. How his voice rang! He was putting his father off the various subjects suggested. Not Latin — he hadn't done much Latin; not geography — he simply hated geography. Listen to him!

"Well, scripture," Harry was saying. "Come, they give you plenty of scripture?"

"Oh, don't they just! Tons and tons!" Listen to him! How merry he was now! "Tons and tons. First lesson every morning. But don't ask scripture, father. Father, what's the use of learning all that stuff, about the Flood, about the Ark, about the Israelites, about Samuel, about Daniel, about crossing the Red Sea, about all that stuff; what's the *use?* "

Time closed his fingers on his haft and took a stride to Rosalie.

She sat upright. She stared across the table at the boy.

Harry said, " Here, steady, old man. ' What's the *use?* ' "

" Well, what *is* the use? It's all rot. You know it isn't true."

Time flashed his blade and struck her terribly.

She called out dreadfully, " *Huggo!* "

" Mother, you know it's all made up! "

She cried out in a girl's voice and with a girl's impulsive gesture of her arm across the table towards him, " It isn't! It isn't! "

Her voice, her gesture, the look upon her face could not but startle him. He was red, rather frightened. He said mumblingly, " Well, mother, you've never taught me any different."

She was seen by Harry to let fall her extended arm upon the table and draw it very slowly to her and draw her hand then to her heart and slowly lean herself against her chair-back, staring at Huggo. No one spoke. She then said to Huggo, her voice very low, " Darling, run now to see everything is in your playbox. Doda, help him. Take Benji, darlings. Benji, go and see the lovely playbox things."

When they had gone she was seen by Harry to be working with her fingers at her key-ring. In one hand she held the ring, in the other a key that she seemed to be trying to remove. It was obstinate. She wrestled at it. She looked up at Harry. " I want to get this " — the key came away in her hand — " *off.*"

He recognised it for her office pass-key.

Caused by that cry of hers to Huggo and by that gesture with her cry, and since intensifying, there had been a constraint that he was very glad to break. He remembered how childishly proud she had been of that key on the day it was cut for her. They had had a little dinner to celebrate it, and she had dipped it in her champagne glass.

He said, " Your pass-key? Why? "

She said, " I'm coming home, Harry."

" Coming home? "

She was sitting back in her chair. She tossed, with a negligent movement of her hand, the key upon the table. " I have done with all that. I am coming home."

He got up very quickly and came around the table to her.

PART FOUR

HOUSE OF CARDS

CHAPTER 1

THERE is a state wherein the mind, normally the court of pleas where reason receives and administers the supplications of the senses, is not in session. Reason is sick, suspends his office, abrogates his authority, withdraws to some deep fastness of the brain, and suffers the hall of judgment to be the house of license or of dreams: of dreams, as sleep, as vanity of reverie; of license when there is tumult in the body politic, as fever, as excesses of the passions, as great shock. Reason is sick, withdraws, and there is strange business in that place.

If that is just the way one writes, not susceptible of easy comprehension, and not enough explanatory of Rosalie's condition, it goes like this in Rosalie's own words. Drooped back there in her chair before that littered disarray of lunch, and that key lying there, and Harry stooping over her and holding both her hands, she said, "Oh, Harry! Oh, Harry! I feel deathly sick."

She said it had been a most frightful shock to her, what Huggo had declared. She said, "Oh, Harry, I feel all undone."

Undone! We'll try to feel her mind with that; to let that explain her when she said this else, and when she wrote some things that shall be given.

She said she had suffered, in that moment of crying out to Huggo and of stretching out her arm to him, the most extraordinary — what was the word? — the most extraordinary hallucination. "Harry, when Huggo said that frightful thing! Oh, Harry, like an extraordinary dream, I was a child again. It wasn't here it was happening; it was the rectory; and not you and the children but all us children that used to be around the table there. No, not quite that. More extraordinary than that. Robert was there; Robert, I think, in Huggo's place; and all the rest were *me* — me as I used to be when I was ten; small, grave, wondering, staring. And yet myself me too as I was then — oh, horrified as I'd have then been horrified to hear the Bible stories called untrue; jumped up and crying out, 'It isn't! It isn't!' as I would then have jumped up and cried out; and all the other Rosalies staring in wonder as I'd have stared. Oh, extraordinary, extraordinary! Within this minute I have been a child again. The strangest thing, the strangest thing!

"I was a child again, Harry, in a blue frock I used to wear and in a pinafore that had a hole in it; and all those other Rosalies the same. Those other Rosalies! To see them! Harry, I've not seen that Rosalie I used to be — not years and years. That tiny innocent! It is upon me still. I feel that small child still. Oh, I feel it! I remember — dear, did I ever tell you? — when my father once . . . had been talking about Cambridge . . . and suddenly cried out, it was at breakfast, 'Cambridge! My youth! My God, my God, my youth!' There was coffee from a cup that he'd knocked over came oozing, and I just sat there huge-eyed, staring, a small, grave wondering child. . . .

"Oh, Harry, my youth, my childhood — and now the children's! The difference! The difference!"

Harry talked to her. He ended, "The teaching, all the ideas, dear girl, you mustn't worry, it's all different nowadays."

"Harry, to hear it from a child like that!"

"It's startled you. It needn't. We'll talk it out. We'll fix it. It's just what he's been taught, old girl."

She said, "Oh, it is what he's not been taught!"

Then there were things that, while was still upon her
this shock, this sense of being again the small, grave child
in the blue frock and in the pinafore with the hole in it,
she wrote down. She dismissed Miss Prescott. She
thought, when the interview of dismissal opened, that she
would end by upbraiding Miss Prescott, but she was
abated all the time in any anger that she might have felt
by Huggo's other frightful words, "Well, mother, you
never taught me any different." She did not want to hear
Miss Prescott tell her that. She told Miss Prescott simply
that she was giving up her business and coming now to
devote herself to the children. She thought, she said, their
education had in some respects been faulty, and told Miss
Prescott how. Miss Prescott, speaking like a book, told
her it had not been faulty and told her why. "Truth,
knowledge, reason," said Miss Prescott. "Could it con-
ceivably be contested that these should not be the sole food
and the guiding principle of the child mind?"

It was after that interview that Rosalie, sitting long
into the night, wrote down some things. She is to be
imagined as wrenched back, as by a violent hand, across
the years, and in the blue frock and the pinafore with a
hole in it again, and awfully frightened, terribly unhappy,
at the thing she'd heard from Huggo. That was the form
her shock took. Beneath it she had at a blow abandoned
all her ambitions as when a child she would instantly have
dropped her most immersing game and run to a frightening cry from her mother; as once, in fact (and the
incident and the parallel came back to her), she had been
building a house of cards, holding her breath not to shake
it, and her mother had scalded her hand and had cried
out to her, frighteningly. "Oh, mummie, mummie!"
she had cried, running to her; and flap! the house of cards
had gone. Her inward cry was now, "The children!

The children!" and what amiss the leaving of her work? Her work! Oh, house of cards!

Her state of mind, the imaginings in which that shock came to her, is better seen by what she wrote down privately, to relieve herself, than by the talk about it all that she had with her Harry. She wrote immediately after Miss Prescott had stood up for " truth, knowledge, reason," and by combating truth, knowledge, and reason more clearly expressed herself than in her talk with Harry. It was in her diary she wrote — well, it wasn't exactly a diary, it was a desultory journal in which sometimes she wrote things. As she wrote, her brow, in the intensity of her thought, was all puckered up. She still felt " deathly sick; all undone." She wrote:

" Of course it's as she says (Miss Prescott). That *is* the kind of thing to-day. Knowledge, stark truth — children must have in stark truth all the knowledge there is on all the things that come about them. It's strange; yes, it *is* strange. No parent would be such a fool as to trust a child with all the money she has nor with anything superlatively precious that she possesses; but knowledge, which is above all wealth and above all treasure, the child is to have to play with as it likes. Oh, it *is* strange. Where is it going to stop? If you bring up a child on the fact that all the Old Testament stories are untrue, a bundle, where they are miraculous, of obviously impossible fairy tales, what's going to happen to the New Testament? The Immaculate Conception, the Resurrection, the Ascension — what's your child-mind that knows the old stories for inventions going to say to those? Are they easier to believe? The Creation or the Conception? The Flood or the Resurrection? God speaking out of a burning bush or the Ascension to Heaven? The pillar of cloud and the pillar of fire or the Three in One of the Trinity? Oh, I wonder if Modern Thought has any thought to spare for that side of the business — or for its results in a generation or two?"

Then she wrote:

"I've never taught them any different."

Then she wrote:

"Mother, I am a child again to-night. *Darling,* in that blue frock I used to wear. Darling, all that I to-night am thinking is what you taught me. Oh, look down, beloved! I've been so wrong. I thought everything was infinitely better for them than you made it, beloved mother, for me. I didn't *realise.*"

Then she wrote:

"It just means losing everything in God that's *human.* It must mean that. All our intelligence, if materialism may be called intelligence; all modern teaching, if this new stuff that they pontificate may be called teaching, offers us God the Spirit but, as it seems to me to-night, denies us God the Father and God the Son. It may be — reasonable. But things spiritual demand for their recognition emotions spiritual, and there's a pass that thousands reach when the spirit is a dead thing. If they are to believe in God only as a Spirit, a Force, a Power; an Essence to be felt but not seen; an Element to be absorbed into but not to be visualised — if this, if these, there needs in them some spirit, some force, some power of themselves to lift themselves to meet it. They must be of themselves responsive as hath the sea within itself that which respondeth to the sublimation of the sun. Well, there are thousands (am I not one?) that have it not. It once was theirs. Now it is not theirs. If there is for them only God the Spirit then is there for them only that to which they have no more power to reach than has one bedridden power to rise and find a mile away what may restore him. They have only that, their breaking heart, which would cast itself, ah, with what bliss of utter abandonment, before

God the Father, a human and a personal Father, quick
to succor, and before God the Son, a human and a personal Son, ardent to intercede. And that is denied them.
That God that existed and that was taught to exist for
my mother and for her day to this day may not exist. It
may be — reasonable. Oh, it is offering a stone where
bread was sought."

She also wrote:

"Oh, mother, if you could have been here, how you
would have loved my darlings, and how you would have
given them all that you gave to me! I will now, mother.
Mother, I've come back home to them, in the blue frock,
and in the pinafore with a hole in it."

That was the spirit in which she came back home to
the children, that and all that went with it and that arose
out of it. It was nothing at all to her when she did it, the
frightful break with Field's. Harry was distressed for
her, but there was no need at all for him to be distressed,
she told him. There wasn't a sigh in her voice, nor in her
inmost thoughts a sigh, when, telling him of the interview
with Mr. Field and with Mr. Sturgiss at her resignation
of her post, she said with a smile, "Carry on? Of course
the department can perfectly well carry on. Dear, it's
just the words I said to you a fortnight back on the matter
so very different. 'The thing's organised. It runs itself.
That is why it is the success it is, *because* it's organised.
That's why I can come away and leave it, because I'm an
organiser. Aren't I an organiser?"

He held her immensely long in his arms. "You are
my Rosalie," he said.

Immensely long he held her, immensely close; oh, men
that marry for a home! Until, come home, she saw
Harry's tremendous happiness in the home that now she
gave him, she never had realised the longing that must

have been his for the home for which he had married, and never till now had had. It was poignant to her, the sight of his tremendous happiness. "Always to find you here!" he would cry, in the first weeks of the new life, coming home to tea and coming in to her in the drawing-room where she would be, all ready for him, with Doda and with Benji. "Always to leave you here!" he would say, taking leave of her in the morning, and she and Doda and Benji coming with him to the hall door to see him off. "Mice and Mumps," he used to add in codicil, "Mice and Mumps, I'm a happy chap!" and was for ever bringing home trifles for her and for the children, or plans and passes for how and where the Saturday and the week-end should be spent, all four together. "Mice and Mumps, I'm gorged with happiness! And you, Rosalie?"

"Oh, happy!" she used to say.

And was. It was poignant to her, his tremendous happiness, and it brimmed up the cup of her own happiness. She was doing virtuously and she had of her virtue that happiness which, as the pious old maxims tell us, comes of being good.

That should have been well; but virtue is a placid condition and the happiness arising out of it placid. It brims no cups, flushes no cheeks, sparkles no eyes. It is of the quality of happiness that one, loving a garden, has from his garden, the happiness of tranquillity, not of stir; of peace, not of thrills; of the country, not of the town. There was more heady stuff than this that Rosalie had out of her new condition, and that was dangerous. She was doing virtuously and she had out of her virtue an intoxication of joy that, in so far as it is at all concerned with virtue, arises, not from virtue's self, but from the consciousness of virtue. That was dangerous. The danger point in stimulants is when they are resorted to, not as concomitant of the pleasures of the table, but be-

cause they stimulate. Rosalie, come to her children and
her Harry and her home, to the thought of her renunciation and of her happiness constantly was turning for the
enormous exhilaration of happiness that there she found.
" How glad I am I gave it up! How glad! How glad!
How right I'm doing now! How right! How right!
How happy I am in this happiness! How happy! How
happy!"

Is it not perceived that thus it was not well assured, this
great joy that she had, this cup of hers that brimmed?
She *started* from that danger point at which the drug is
drunk for stimulant. On the very first day of her new
life she was saying, " How glad I am! How glad I am!"
and going on radiant from her gladness. But she in her
resort to this her stimulant suffered this grave disparity
with the drinker's case: he must increase his doses —
and he can. She, living upon her stimulant, equally was
compelled — but could not. The renunciation that
brimmed her happiness on the first day was available to
her in no bigger dose on the succeeding days, the
hundredth day and the three hundredth and the five
hundredth. It never could increase. It had no capacity
of increase. Is it not perceivable that it had, on the contrary, a staling quality?

It would have been all right if it had been all right.
It would have been all right if it had not been all wrong.
If these absurd premises can be understood her case can
be understood. She used them herself in after years.
" It would have been all right," she used to say to herself,
twisting her hands together, " if it had been all right."
" It would have been all right," she used to say to herself,
" if it had not been all wrong." What she meant, and
what here is meant, requires it to be recalled that it was
in that spirit of that glimpse of herself back a child again
in the blue frock and in the pinafore with a hole in it that

she came back to the children, came back home to them. Shocked by the thing that had come to pass, penitential by influence of the old childhood influences that had stirred within her, most strangely and most strongly transported back into that childhood vision of herself, it was in the guise of that child and with that child's guise as her ideal for them that passionately she desired to take up her children's lives. Her Huggo, her man child, her first one! Her Doda, her self's own self, her woman-bud, her daughter! Her Benji, her littlest one, her darling! She longed, as it were, to throw open the door, and in that blue frock and in the spirit of that blue frock most ardently to run in to them and hug them, blue frocked, to her breast, and be one with them and tell them the things and the things and the things that were the blue frock's mysteries and joys, and hear from them the things and the things and the things that were the blue frock's all-enchanted world again.

That was what most terribly she wanted and with most brimming gladness set about to do — and there was borne in upon her, hinted in weeks, published in months, in seasons sealed and delivered to her, that there was among her children no place for that spirit. They did not welcome the blue frock; they did not understand the blue frock; they were not children as she had been a child. It was what Harry had said of them, they somehow were not quite like other children; it was what she herself had noticed in Huggo; they did not respond. They'd gone, those children, too long as they'd been left to go. She came to them ardently. They greeted her — not very responsively. They didn't understand.

What happened was that, coming to them great with intention, she was, by what she did not find in them, much dispirited in her intention. What followed from that was that she turned the more frequently to the stimulation of the thought of her renunciation, to the sensation of happiness that arose in her by consciousness that she was doing what she ought to be doing. She would be puzzled, she would be a little pained, she would be a little tired at the effort, fruitless, to call up in the children those lovely childish things that as a child had been hers. She then would feel dispirited. She then would think, "*But* how glad I am that I gave it all up; *but* how right I am to be at home with them; *but* how happy I am that I am now doing that which is right." That stimulated her. That made her tell herself (as before she had told Harry) that it was just fancy, this apparent difference, this *in*difference, in the children.

But the more she found necessary that stimulus the less that stimulus availed; and she began to feel, then, the first faint gnawings after that which had been stimulus indeed, her work, her career.

Of course this is making a case for her, this is special pleading for her, but who so abandoned that in the ultimate judgment a case will not for him be prepared? Try to consider how it went with her. First intoxication of happiness; and must not intoxication in time wear off? Then immense intention and then dispirited in her intention. Then frequent resource to the stimulus of her realisation of virtue and then the natural diminution of that cup's effect. Is she not presented prey for her life's habit's longings? Is she not shown dejected and caused by that dejection (as caused by depression the reclaimed victim of a drug) to desire again that which had been to her the breath of life?

That was how it went with her.

Doda was nine when she began; Huggo, when he was home for his holidays, eleven, rising twelve; Benji only seven. They seemed to her, all of them, wonderfully old for their years and, no getting over that, *different*. She tried to read them the stories she used to love. They didn't like them. Doda didn't like " The Wide Wide World " and didn't like " Little Women." Huggo thought " The Swiss Family Robinson " awful rot, and argued learnedly with her how grotesque it was to imagine all that variety of animals and all that variety of plants in one same climate. " But, Huggo, you needn't worry whether it was possible. It was just written as a means of telling a family of children natural history things. They didn't have to believe it. They only enjoyed it. I and your uncle Robert never worried about whether it was possible; we simply loved the adventure of it."

" Well, I can't, mother," said Huggo. " It's not possible, and if it isn't possible I think it's stupid."

And Doda thought Ellen in the " Wide Wide World " silly, and Beth and Jo and the others in " Little Women " dull.

She read them Dickens, but it was always, " Oh, leave out that part, mother. It's dull." And so was Scott. Lamb's "Tales from Shakespeare" never had a chance at all. They had heard from Miss Prescott, or Huggo had heard at school, that Shakespeare was a lesson. " Oh, not a thing out of lessons, mother." What they liked were what seemed to Rosalie the crudely written stories, and the grotesque and usually rather vulgar comic drawings, in the host of cheap periodicals for children that seemed to have sprung up since her day. They called these exciting or funny and they revelled in them. They *were* different. Benji was no more than a baby, but he was extraordinarily devoted to Doda, liked only the things that Doda liked, and did not like the things that Doda didn't like, or, in the language sometimes a little unpleasantly emphatic that always was Doda's and Huggo's, that Doda " simply loathed." Rosalie had some old bound

numbers of treasured juvenile periodicals of the rectory
days. Even Benji didn't like them. They were markedly
different from the books the children did like. Their
illustrations were mainly of children in domestic scenes.
"Don't they look stupid?" was Doda's comment; and
Benji, copying, thought they were stupid too.

All this was a very small thing and of itself negligible;
even, as Rosalie told herself, natural — naturally children of succeeding generations changed in their tastes.
It only is introduced as conveniently showing in an
obscure aspect what was noticeable to Rosalie, and felt
by her, in many aspects, whose effect was cumulative.
"A kind of reserve," Harry had said of them: "a kind
of — self-contained." It was what she found. She
wanted to be a child with the children; they didn't seem
to understand. She wanted to open her heart to them
and have their hearts opened to her; they didn't seem to
understand. She was always seeing that vision of Rosalie
in the blue frock among them, rather like Alice, the real
Alice, Tenniel's Alice. She was always feeling that Rosalie, thus guised, was held off from their circle, not welcomed, not understood, as certainly they did not care for
the demure, quaint Alice of Tenniel.

She began to have sometimes when she was with the
children an extraordinary feeling (just what Harry had
said) that she was younger than the children, that it was
she who was the child, they that were the grown-ups.

When the step of her renunciation was first taken,
ardent to devote herself to them in every moment of the
day, she began to give their lessons to Doda and to Benji.
It was not a success. The methods of teaching, as the
text-books, had changed since she was a child. The
Prescott methods were here and to her own methods the
children did not respond. There it was again — did not
respond. There was obtained a Miss Dormer who came

in daily and who confined herself, Rosalie saw to that, solely to lessons; the walks and all the other hours of the day were Rosalie's.

That's all for that. The picture has been overdrawn if has been given the suggestion that Rosalie was unhappy with the children or the children openly indifferent to her. All of that nature that in fact arose was that, whereas Rosalie had expected an immense and absorbing occupation with the children, she found instead an occupation very loving and very happy but not relieving her of all the interest and all the affection she had desired to pour into it. It was rather like to a hungry person a strange dish that had looked substantial but that, when finished, was found not to have been substantial; still hungry. She had thought the children would have been entirely dependent on her. She found them in many ways independent and wishing to be independent. It would have been all right if it had been all right. That was it. It would have been all right if it had not been all wrong. That was it.

She began to think of Field's.

When first she began to think of Field's, which was when she had been nine months away from Field's, she would let her mind run upon it freely, as it would. One day, thus thinking upon it, she brought up her thoughts as it were with a round turn. She must not think so much about Field's — not like that. She sighed, and with the same abruptness of mental action checked her sigh; she must not regret Field's — not like that.

It was a fateful prohibition. It was the discovery to herself, as to Eve of the tree by the serpent, of a temptation seductive and forbidden. Thereafter " like that " her mind, missing no day nor no night, was often found by her to be there. The quality that made " like that " not seemly to her, increased, at each return, its potency.

It became very difficult to drag her mind away. It became impossible to drag her mind away.

Her governance of her mind became infected and it became not necessary to think it necessary to drag her mind away.

She had not visited Field's since she had left. Mr. Sturgiss and Mr. Field had written to her reproaching her for carrying to such lengths of neglect her desertion of them, and she had responded banteringly but without a call. One day (she had lain much awake on the previous night) she at breakfast told Harry she had the idea of going that afternoon to see how Field's was getting on.

She was surprised at his supplement to his reply. The children had left the room. He first agreed with her that the idea was good. " Yes, rather; why not? " was the expression he used. He then said, surprising her, " Rosalie, you've never, have you, regretted? "

Her surprise framed for her her reply. " Why ever should you ask that? "

" I've thought you've not been looking very well lately."

" But what's the connection, Harry? "

" Fretting? "

She smiled. " I'm not the fretting sort."

He was perfectly satisfied. " I knew you'd tell me if you were. Everything going well? "

" Fine."

He shot out his arms with a luxurious stretching gesture. " Mice and Mumps, it's been fine for me, I can tell you. Fine, fine! "

How happy he looked! How handsome he looked! Her thought was " Dear Harry! "

He got up and began to set about his departure. She went with him into the hall and she called up the stairs, " Children, father's going." They came bounding down

He joked and played with them. He loved this custom, now long established. She brushed his hat, also a rite she knew he loved. He kissed her with particular affection. " Yes, you go up to Field's and give old Sturgiss and old Field my love. You'll almost have forgotten the way there. I say, it's funny, isn't it, how time changes things and how it goes? We couldn't have imaged this once, and here it is the most established thing in the world. Do you know, it's almost exactly a year since you chucked it ? "

" Chucked it ! " The light expression smote her. O manlike man that thus could phrase divorce that from her heart's engrossment had cut her life asunder !

In the afternoon she set out upon her intention. It meant nothing, her visit, she assured herself. It had no purpose beyond the exchange of courtesies. But when she was leaving the house she paused. Should she go? She went down the steps and through the gate, then paused again. She returned to the house. She had an idea. She would take the children with her. She called them, and while they gleefully dressed for the outing she repeated to herself the word in which the idea of taking them with her had come to her.

" A bodyguard ! " she said.

The note of laughter she gave at the word had a tremulous sound.

Tremulous would well have described her manner when they were at Field's. She was asking herself as they went towards the City what it was that she wanted to hear — that Field's was doing very well without her? That her department was not doing very well without her? Which?

She would not let her mind affirm which it was that she desired.

It appeared, when they arrived, that it was neither, nor anything at all to do with the Bank. Her first words to the partners were of smiling apology at bringing to precincts sacred to business, " a herd of children." That was a natural introduction of herself; it *was* an unusual thing to do. But not natural the way in which she maintained the subject of the children. It seemed that she had come to talk of nothing else. Tremulous she was; talking, of the children, with the incessant eagerness, and with the nervous eagerness, of one either clamant to establish a case or frightened of a break in the conversation lest a break should cause appearance of a subject most desperately to be avoided.

Her bodyguard!

Mr. Field and Mr. Sturgiss were delighted to see her and expressed themselves delighted to see the children. There was plenty in the bank, coffers and strong-rooms and all sorts of exciting things, said Mr. Field, that would amuse the small people, and when tea was done they should be taken around to see them. In an inner holy of holies behind the partners' parlour a very exciting tea was made. A clerk was sent out for a parcel of pastries and returned with an enormous bag, and there was no tablecloth, nor no proper tea-table, and the children, much excited, were immensely entertained.

Easy, while they were there, to make them the conversation's centre. But the meal ended and then became most evident her anxiety to keep the chatter on the children. They became impatient to be off on the promised exploration. She delayed it. Twice the clerk who was to conduct the tour was about to be summoned. By a new gathering of general attention she stopped his coming. When at last he came she said she would be of the party. The partners did not want that. The children did not want it. "Mother, it will be much more exciting by ourselves."

She insisted. She was aware for the first and only time in her life of a feeling of nerves, of not being quite in control of herself, of making of her insistence rather more than should be made.

"Well, stay," said Mr. Sturgiss, "at least for a minute's chat before you join them."

That was not possible, unless she was going to become hysterical, to resist. The children trooped away. Her bodyguard!

She turned aside and it is to be remembered for her that, her face concealed from the partners, she gave the tiniest despairing gesture with her hands.

When, with the children, she was returning home, she was trying to determine whether, while it was in suspense, she had or had not desired to hear of the partners that which she had heard from them. They had talked with her generally of the business. They had talked particularly of the work of her department of the business. There was approaching all the time the thing that sooner or later they must say. She was trembling all the time to know how she would receive it. In whichever of its two ways it came would she be glad or would she be sorry? She simply did not know. She suddenly herself projected the point. She could not endure any longer its delay. "And Miss Farmer," she said. "How's Miss Farmer doing?" Miss Farmer, formerly one of her assistants, had on her resignation taken her place.

Miss Farmer, replied Mr. Sturgiss, was estimable but — he opened his hands and made with them a deprecatory gesture. "She's not you. How could she be you, or any one be you? We could replace Miss Farmer. What's the good? It's you we've got to replace. We can't replace you."

Her heart had bounded.

CHAPTER II

THAT happened in the Christmas holidays, in January. In February was Doda's eleventh birthday. The child had friends rather older than herself, neighbours, who for a year had been boarders at a school in Surrey. She was desperately eager to join them there and it was a promise from Rosalie that she should go when she was twelve, earlier if she were good. On this eleventh birthday, which brought birthday letters from the neighbours at the school and thus again brought up the subject, "Oh, haven't I been good?" cried Doda at the birthday breakfast. "Oh, do let me go next term, mother. Father, do say I may." Her eagerness for school had been much fostered by Huggo's holiday stories of school life; and Huggo, as Doda now adduced, was leaving his preparatory and starting at Tidborough next term; couldn't she, oh, *couldn't* she make also her start then?

Harry said, "O grown-up woman of enormous years, think of your sorrowing parents. How will you like to leave your weeping mother, Doda? How will you like to leave your heart-broken old father?"

"Oh, I'd love to!" cried Doda.

The ingenuousness of it made her parents laugh.

"She'll have her way, won't she?" said Harry, when Doda, conscious, by that laugh, of tolerance, had danced out of the room.

"I think she'd better," said Rosalie.

The school was very well known to Rosalie. It was exclusive and expensive; was limited to seventy girls, of whom twenty, under the age of thirteen, were received in the adapted Dower House of the ancient estate which was its home; and the last word in modernity was, in every point of administration, its first word. It had been established only eight years. The motto of its founders and of its lady principal was " Not traditions — precedents! "

The subject came up again between Rosalie and Harry that evening and it was decided that Doda should be placed there after the next holidays, at the opening of the summer term. Harry declared himself, " in my bones " as he expressed it, against boarding schools for girls, " But that's my old fogeyism," said he. " It's the modern idea that girls should have the same training and the same chances in life as their brothers, and there's no getting away from the right of it."

Rosalie said in a low voice, " To what end? "

He did not hear her. She had got out from the accumulation of papers of her business life prospectuses and booklets of the school and he was amusedly browsing over the refinements and advantages therein, not by traditions but by precedents, set forth. " Mice and Mumps, Rosalie," said he, " they not only do riding as a regular thing but ' parents are permitted, if they wish, to stable a pupil's own pony (see page 26).' Oh, thanks, thanks! ' Mr. Harry Occleve, barrister-at-law, availing himself of your gracious permission on page twenty-six, is sending down for his daughter a coach and four with 'ostlers, grooms, coachmen, and outriders complete.' Ha! "

She was just watching him.

He said after an interval: " Yes, there's a lot of sound stuff here, Rosalie. It's convincing. Not that any one needs convincing on the point less than you and I." He quoted again. " ' And advance them towards an independent and a womanly womanhood.' And it talks further back about how ' Idle women ' will soon be recognised as great a term of reproach as ' an idle man.' It's sound. I like this booklet here that each girl's given, ' To the Girl of the Future.' It tells them all about an independent career, makes no fancy picture of it, tells 'em everything. Did you read that ? "

" A long time ago. It probably doesn't tell them one thing."

" What ? "

" That they can always — chuck it."

He looked up quickly. " Hull-o ! "

She gave him no response to his expressed surprise and he laughed and said, " D'you know, Rosalie, I don't believe I've ever before heard you use slang."

" You taught me that bit, Harry."

" Oh, I sling it about. When did I ? "

" One day last holidays when it was just on a year since I'd left Field's. Just a year, you said, since I'd — chucked it. O Harry — "

There was a quality in her voice that might, from what she saw upon his face, have been a tocsin's roll. His face was as a place of assembly into which, as it might be a people alarmed, there came crowding in emotions.

He said, " What's up ? "

She said, " O Harry, you look out for yourself ! "

There was much movement in his face. " Look out for myself ? "

She said, " That came out of me. I didn't know I was going to say it. It's a warning. It shows the fear I have."

" Rosalie, of what, of what ? "

" Harry, for you."

" You're going to say something you think will hurt me ? "

" No, something you'll have to fight — if you want to

fight it. Harry, perhaps I can't go on like this. I want
to go back to my work."

He expired a breath he had been holding. " I was
guessing it."

" Before just now? "

" No, while you've been speaking. Only now. I
asked you weeks ago if you ever felt you regretted — "

She leant forward from the couch whereon she sat, and
with an extended hand interrupted him. She said intensely, " Look here, Harry, if it was just regret I'd not
mind and I would tell you No a hundred times, just not
to disturb you, dear. But when you asked me that you
spoke, a minute afterwards, of my having — chucked it,
as if it was giving up sugar or stopping bridge. Well,
that's why I'm warning you to look out for yourself.
Because, Harry, I don't *regret* it. I'm *craving* to go back
to it, craving, craving, craving! " She stopped. She
said, " Do you want me not to go back, Harry? "

He looked steadily at her. " Rosalie, it would be a
blow to me."

She said, " Well, then! " and she leaned back in the
couch as though all now was explained.

He very gravely asked her, " Are you going back, Rosalie? "

" Would it be a crime, Harry, to go back? "

He said to her, " I believe in my soul it would be a
disaster."

She got up. " Come over here to me, Harry.

He went to her and took the hands that she extended
to him. " If you think that, a disaster, and if to you it
would be what you said, a blow; then that's what I mean
by saying, Harry, you look out for yourself. I don't
know if I'm going back. I want to go terribly, oh, terribly. There was a woman I once knew told me that if
a woman once gives herself to a thing, abandons all else

and gives herself to it, she never never can come back from it. 'They don't issue return tickets to women,' she said to me. 'If you *give yourself*,' she said, 'you're *its*. You may think you can get away but you never will get away. You're *its*.' She was right, Harry. I believe I've got to go back. If you don't want me to, well, you look out for yourself." She drew herself towards him by her hands. "Harry, when I went down to Field's with the children that day last holidays I took them to be a body-guard to me, to prevent me from being captured. When they left me there alone for a few minutes I turned away and wrung my hands because I knew I was going to be terribly tempted. I *am* terribly tempted. I'm being dragged." She went into his arms. "Harry, hold me terribly tight and say you don't want me to go back."

He most tenderly embraced her. "Don't go back, Rosalie."

She disengaged herself, and made a sound, "Ah!" as if, while he had held her body, herself had held the fort of her solicitude for his desires against the horde of her own cravings that swarmed about its walls.

How long?

There was a mirage in her face. While Easter came and Doda, in huge spirits, made her start at school, and Huggo, boisterously elated, his start at Tidborough, and Benji, much dejected at Doda's going, his start at Huggo's former day school; and while the long summer term and the holidays passed on, there was never again seen nor heard by Harry the tenderness that had been in her face and in her voice when she had warned him, "Well, Harry, you look out for yourself," and when she had asked him, "Harry, hold me terribly tight in your arms and say you do not want me to go back." There thenceforward did fill up her countenance the boy, mutinous and defiant, that was her other self. It was almost upon the morrow of that passage with him (whose poignancy the written word has failed to show) that she had a revulsion from the attitude she had then exposed to him. Avid now to go back to the life she had abandoned, she was ferocious to herself when she remembered she had asked him, " Would it be a crime, Harry, to go back? " A crime! " Horrible traitor to myself that I was " (her thoughts would go) " to question it a crime just to take up my life again! A crime! Horrible fool that I was to be able, with no sense of humour, to give to so natural a desire an epithet so ludicrous as crime! A crime! A right, a right! "

Worst of all, she had invited, she had implored, Harry when her longings were manifest to reason with her. Her longings now always were manifest; but when he reasoned with her it was out of the scorpions of her revulsion that she answered him.

He once said, " It appears to me that your attitude is changed from the night you first mentioned this."

She said, " Harry, what's disturbing me when we talk about it is not my own case, it's the general case. Here's a woman — never mind that it's me — here's a woman that has made a success in life, that has abandoned it and that wants to go back to it. You argue she mustn't. I could say it's monstrous. I don't say that. I choose to say it's pitiful. If it was a man he'd go. He wouldn't think twice about it. And if he did think twice about it every opinion and every custom that he consulted would tell him he was right to go. It happens to be a woman, therefore — well, that's the reason! It's a woman — therefore, No. That's the beginning of the reason and the end of the reason. A woman — therefore, No. Oh, it's pitiful — for women."

Harry questioned: " Every opinion and every custom would tell a man to go? No, no. You're taking too much for granted, Rosalie. He wouldn't go, necessarily, and he wouldn't be advised to go, if he had duties that pulled him the other way."

She gave a note of amusement. "But that's the point. He never *would* have such duties. It's notable that a man always makes his duties and his ambitions go hand in hand. Yes, it's notable, that."

"Well, put it another way. Suppose it wasn't necessary for him to go. . . . Suppose nothing depended on his going, much on his staying. That makes the parallel, Rosalie."

She said to him, "Ah, I'll agree to that. Let that make the parallel. They'd tell a man in such a case, 'Man, take up your ambitions. You are a man. You have yourself to think of.' That's what they'd say. Well, that's what I'm saying. 'I am a woman. I have myself to think of.'"

He asked, "And shall you, Rosalie?"

She said, "I'm thinking — every day."

The more she thought the more she stiffened. This was the thought against whose goad she always came — *Why* should she be hesitant? What a position! What a light upon the case and upon the status of woman that, just because she was a woman, she must not consider her own, her personal interests! For no other reason; just that; because she was a woman!

"I've shut a gate behind me," she on another day said to Harry. "That's what I've done. I've come out of a place and shut the gate behind me and because I am a woman I mustn't open it and go back. That's what a woman's life is — always shutting gates behind her. There aren't gates for a man. There're just turnstiles. As he came out so he can always go back — even to his youth. When he's fifty he still can go back and have the society of twenty and play the fool as he did at twenty. Can a woman?"

" That's physical," said Harry. " A man much longer keeps his youth."

She said then the first aggressively bitter thing he ever had heard her say. " Ah, keeps his youth! " she said. " So does a dog that's run free. It's the chain and kennel sort that age."

She hardened her heart.

She looked back upon the days when she had discovered for herself the difference between sentiment and sense, between sentimentality and sensibility. She then had made her life, and therefore then her happiness, by putting away sentiment and using sense for spectacles. She told herself she now was ruining her life, and certainly letting go her happiness, by suffering herself to bear the sentimental handicap.

The summer holidays came. It had been her obvious argument to Harry that, now the elder children were at school, and Benji soon to be the same, that reason for her constant presence in the home no longer was advanceable. It had been Harry's argument to her that there were the holidays to remember. The holidays came. Huggo wrote that he wanted to go straight from school to a topping time in Scotland to which he had been invited by a chum; when that was over he had promised, and he was sure he would be allowed, to have the last three weeks with another friend whose people had a ripping place in Yorkshire. Doda came home and Doda's first excitement was that nothing arranged might interfere with an invitation from mid-August to a schoolfellow whose family were going to Brittany. So much for her holiday necessity! Rosalie thought. So much for Harry's idea of how the children would naturally long to spend the vacation all together! Doda did not seem to have a thought for Huggo, nor Huggo a thought for when he should see

Doda. Neither of them, she could not help noticing, had the faintest concern to be with Benji. She and Harry with Benji went down to a furnished house in Devonshire, and the other two, their plans in part curtailed, were brought to join them. It was jolly enough. It would have been more truly jolly, she used to think, if Doda had not largely divided her time between writing to apparently innumerable school friends and counting the days to when she might be released for the Brittany expedition; and if Huggo had not for the first few days openly sulked at the veto on the Yorkshire invitation. How independent they were, how absorbed in their friends, how — different!

She hardened her heart.

The reopening of the schools drew on and return was made to London. Huggo and Doda were made ready for school and returned to school. The Law Courts reopened and Harry took up again his work. October! You could not take up a paper without reading of the inauguration of the new Sessions at all the universities and seats of education. October! The newspapers that for months had been padding out vapid nothings became intense with the activities of a nation back to the collar. October! The first brisk breath of winter in the air! She could not stand this! Could not, could not!

She said suddenly one evening: "Harry, I was down at Field's to-day. They want me."

Ever since, by that simile of hers of the dog chained and kenneled, she had put a bitter note into this matter between them, he had by this means or by that contributed no share to it when she had presented it. He once had referred to the dog incident. "I can't talk to you when you talk like that, old girl," he had said. "That's not us. We don't talk like that. You know how I feel about this matter. Talking only vexes it."

"Harry, I was down at Field's to-day. They want me." It was now to be faced.

He put down the paper he had been reading and began to fill his pipe. "This wants a smoke," he said and smiled at her; and he then told her that which the level quality of her voice, a note from end to end of purpose, had informed him. "I think we're getting to the end of this business," he said.

Her voice maintained its quality. "Yes, near the end, Harry."

"Field's want you. What are you going to do?"

"Going back."

"I want you."

"I'm not leaving you. I am with you, as I came to you!"

"The children want you."

"I am not leaving the children."

"It's a question of home, Rosalie. It's the home wants you."

She shook her head.

"What are you going to do?'

"Going back."

"You've thought of everything?"

"Everything."

"The children?"

"Harry, the children don't want me in the way that children used to want their mothers when I was a child. They don't display the same affection, not in the same way, that we used to. I wish they did. I came back for it. It wasn't there. They're darlings, but they're self-reliant darlings, self-assured, self-interested."

"They've a right to a home, Rosalie." He paused. "And, Rosalie, I have a right to a home."

She said, "Have I no rights?"

"There are certain things —" he slowly said and paused again — "established."

She said quickly, "Yes, men think that. They always have. Well, I believe that nothing is."

He looked steadily before him. "If it's not established that woman's part is the home part; if that is going to change, I wonder what's going to happen to the world?"

She said, "Men always do. They always have — wondered, and the future always has changed right out of their wondering. I believe that the future is with woman. I believe that as empires have passed, Rome, Greece, Carthage, that seemed to their rulers the pillars of the world, so will pass man's dominion. Woman's revolt — it's no use talking of it as that, as a revolt. Women aren't and never will be banded. They're like the Jews. They're everywhere but nowhere. But the Jews have had their day; woman — not yet. They work, not banded, but in single spies. In every generation more single spies and more single spies. In time. . . . In every generation man's dominion, by like degree, decreased, decreased. In time. . . . I'm one of this day's single spies, Harry."

He said with a sudden animation, "Look here, let's take it on that level, Rosalie. In your case what's the need? Call it dominion. I've never exercised nor thought to exercise dominion over you."

"But you've not *understood*, Harry. I gave up what was my life to me. To you I'd only — chucked it. Oh, but that hurt! That man's supreme indifference, that is dominion."

He said, "I'll know it, dearest, for your sacrifice."

She put out a hand as if to hold that word away. "Oh, trust not that. They talk of the ennoblement of sacrifice. Ah, do not believe it. It can go too long, too far, and then like wine too long matured . . . just acid, Harry.

I never said a bitter thing to you until — thus sacrificing. It is the kennel dog again. If I went on I'd grow more bitter yet, more bitter and more bitter. It's why women are so much more bitter than men. It's what they've sacrificed. I'm going back, Harry. I've got to. You ask me if I've thought of everything. I have; but even if I had not this outrides it all. I have gone too far. She was right, that woman I told you of, who said that for a woman, once she has given herself to a thing, there is no comeback from it. I have tried. It is not to be done."

There was a very long silence. She said, " It's settled, Harry."

He said, " Nothing's been said, Rosalie, that gets over what I have said. There's no home here while both of us are working. I have a right to a home. The children have a right to a home. Nothing gets over that."

She answered, " Then, Harry, give yourself a home. Give the children a home."

He said, " I am a man."

She answered, " I am a woman."

CHAPTER III

THE thing goes now at a most frightful pace for
Rosalie. One hates the slow, laborious written word
that tries to show it. There needs a pen with wings or
that by leaping violence of script, by characters blotched,
huge and run together, would symbolise the pace at which
the thing now goes. There's no procession of the days.
Immersed in work or lost in pleasure, there never is procession of the days, so hurtling fast goes life. They
crowd. They're driven past like snow across a window
pane. The calendar astounds. It is the first of the month,
and lo, it is the tenth. It's the sixteenth — half gone! —
while yet it scarcely had begun; a day after the twentieth
is the date; it's next the twenty-fifth; it's next — the
month has gone. . . . The month! It is a season that
has flown. Here's Summer where only yesterday the
buds of Spring; here's Winter, coming — gone! — while
yet the leaves seem falling.

It was like that the thing now went with Rosalie.

They call it a race. It isn't a race, living like that. It's
a pursuit. Engaged in it, you're not in rivalry, you are
in flight. You're fleeing all the time the reckoning; and
he's a sulky savage, forced to halt to gather up what you
have shed, ordered to pause to note the things that you
have missed, and at each duty cutting notches in a stick.

That is his tally which, come up, he will present to you.

Well, best perhaps to take that tally stick to try by it
to show the pace at which the thing now went. Rosalie,
when all was done, could run the tally over (you have to)
in thought, that lightning vehicle that makes to crawl the

swiftest agency of man's invention: runs through a life-time while the electric telegraph is stammering a line; reads memory in twenty volumes between the whiff and passing of some remembered scent that's opened them; travels a life again, cradle to grave, between the vision's lighting on and lifting from some token of the past.

All's done; some years rush on; she sits in retrospection, that tally stick in hand; and thought, first hovering, would always start for her from when, returned to her career, the thing at frightful pace began to go; and then, from there, away! from scene to scene (the notches cut by reckoning in his stick) rending the womb of memory in dread delivery, as it were flash on flash of lightning bursting the vault of night from east to west across the world.

Her thoughts first hovering: There's Huggo and there's Doda and there's Benji! Her children! Her darling ones! Her lovely ones! Love's crown; and, what was more, worn in the persons of those darling joys of hers in signal, almost arrogant in her disdain of precedent to the contrary, that woman might be mother and yet live freely and unfettered by her home, precisely as man is father but follows a career. Ah. . . .

Away! The womb of memory is rent, and rent, delivers.

Look, there they are! She's down with one or other at some gala at their schools. It's Founders' Day at Tidborough, or it's at Doda's school on Prize Day. Aren't they just proud to be with her and show her off, their lovely, brilliant mother so different from the other rather fussy mothers that come crowding down! All the masters and all the mistresses know the uncommon woman that she is. The children, growing older, know it. " You must be very proud of your mother." It has been said (the self-same words) to each of them by their respective principals. Nice! Nice to have your children proud of you!

Look, there's Huggo telling her how the headmaster had said the thing to him (she's just walking with her Huggo across the cricket ground on Founders' Day). "And a sloppy young ass that heard him," says Huggo, "oh, an awful ass, asked me why the Head had said I must be proud of you, and I told him, and I said, 'I bet you're not proud of your mother.' And he said, 'Of my father, I am. He got the V. C. in South Africa.' So I said, 'Yes, but proud of your *mother?*' So this frightful ass said — what *do* you think he said? 'No, I'm not *proud* of my mother. I don't think I'd want to be. I only love her.'"

Huggo mimicked the voice in which the frightful ass had said this; and Rosalie, at the words and at his tone, had across her body a sudden chill, as it were physical. She wanted to say something. But it was the kind of thing you couldn't, somehow, say to Huggo, at fifteen. But she said it. "Huggo, you *do* love me, don't you?"

He turned to her a face curiously thin-lipped. "Oh, I say, mother, do look out, some one might hear you!"

Her Huggo! (She wants to stop the passing scenes and to stretch out to him across the years her arms.) Her Huggo! The one that first along her arm had laid; the scrap that first within her eyes adoring tears had brimmed; her baby boy, her tiny manling, her tiny hugging one, her first born! It is in retrospection that she sits and there's expelled for ever from her face that aspect mutinous, intolerant, defiant, that used to visit there. That, when she housed it, was the aspect of the young man Ishmael whose hand was against every man. She is like Hagar now to be imagined, sitting over against these things a good way off, as it were a bowshot.

Strike on!

Her Huggo! Look, that's the day they got that bad report of him from school. She had questioned Harry about a letter in his post and, naming the headmaster of Tidborough, "Yes, it's from Hammond," he had answered her.

"About Huggo?"

"Yes, it's about Huggo."

Nothing more. They were beginning to have exchanges terse as that.

She said presently, "I suppose it would interest me, wouldn't it?"

His face was very hard. "Do you want to know the answer I feel like giving to that?"

"I've asked for it, haven't I, Harry?"

"You shall have it. The answer is that I think what the letter says implicates you."

She preserved her composure. She by now had had practice in preserving her composure. "What's the matter, Harry?"

"Hammond says — as good as says — that Huggo will have to be withdrawn from Tidborough."

She knew perfectly well that this was only leading up to something. "May I hear?"

"You may." He took up the letter and read from it. "'Apart from that, and it would of course be the reason given — the other, I am confident, is susceptible of change — apart from that, the boy has now twice failed to keep his place in the school. If he does not get his remove in the coming term I shall be compelled to ask you to remove him.'" He put down the letter and looked at her. "That'll be nice, won't it?"

She made an appeal. "Harry, don't. I mean, don't talk like that. It won't happen."

He softened in no degree. He said sternly: "It will happen."

She persevered. "I'm quite sure it won't. You've only got to talk seriously to Huggo. This coming holidays you can get him some coaching. He's got brains."

There was a steely note in Harry's voice: "Oh, he's got brains. He can have coaching. It's what he hasn't got and what he can't get that's going to get Huggo withdrawn."

"What is it you mean?"

"A home."

She slightly raised the fingers of her hands and dropped them. This subject!

Harry said: "Hammond says more than I've told you."

"I supposed he did. 'Apart from that.' Apart from what?"

"It's Huggo's character he's writing to me about. This is what he says. 'The boy, though young, has not a good influence in his house. If I may suggest it, he does not, during the holidays, see enough of his home.'"

He folded the letter and returned it to its envelope. "Does it strike you that is going to be easy for me to answer?"

"It might be easier, Harry, if your tone made it possible for us to discuss it."

He gave a sound that was glint, as it were, of the blade in his voice: "Our discussions! I am a little tired of that blind alley, Rosalie."

She said sombrely, "And I."

"Will you suggest how the letter is to be answered?"

She said: "It's plain. If you agree with Mr. Hammond, it's plain. You can say you will stop Huggo's invitations. Harry, we're not by any means the only family that doesn't spend the whole of its holidays together. It's rather the practice nowadays, young people visiting their friends. If you think Huggo shouldn't — you can say so."

"Yes, I can say that. Tell me this. Is it going to give him a home?"

Her voice sprung from a sudden higher note. "Oh, you insist, you insist!" she cried. "You speak of blind alleys, but you insist."

He touched the letter. "This gives me ground for my insistence. This is an outsider, a stranger, appreciating how we live. This is my son, at my old school, condemned by how we live."

She interjected, "A schoolmaster's primeval animosity — blame the parent."

"Rosalie, a parent's primeval duty. We are responsible for the children. We have a duty towards them."

She softly struck her hands together. "Ah, how often, how often, and always worse! You said just now that I am implicated. It's always I. You say we have a responsibility towards the children. But you don't mean us, you mean me. Why I more than you? Why am I the accused?"

He began, "Because you — "

"Ah, don't, don't!"

But he concluded. "Because you are a woman."

Her voice that had gone high went numb. She made a gesture, as to the same reason and with the same words she'd made before, of weariness with this thing, "Ah, my God, that reason!"

Strike on!

Look, there's Huggo, failing again to get his remove, superannuated, withdrawn. There's Harry having a scene with the boy. There ought to be tears. There are tears. But they're in Harry's voice and twice he wipes his eyes. They're not in Huggo's.

Harry says to Huggo: "I say, I'm not going to be harsh; but, I say, can't you understand the disgrace; can't you understand the shame, old man? You've been at the finest school in England and you've had to leave. You're sixteen. Old man, when I was sixteen I got my footer colours. I was the youngest chap in the team. You're sixteen and you've never even got a house cap and you've had to leave. Huggo, I've never missed going down to a Founders' Day since I went to Oxford. It's always been the day of the year for me. I don't say I've ever done much in life, but every time I've been down to Founders' Day I've thought over, in the train, any little thing I may have pulled out in the year and I've felt, I've felt awfully proud to be taking it down to the old school, so to speak. Old chap, the proudest, far the proudest of all, was the year I went down when first you were there. I *was* proud. I'd given a son to the place. I'd got a boy there. Another Occleve was going to write the name up on the shields and rolls and things. It was the year Garnett first came down as a Cabinet Minister. Huggo, I looked old Garnett in the face with a grin. Whatever he'd done I'd got this much up on him — he hadn't given a son to the place. He hadn't got a boy there. That's how I always felt. Well, old man, it's all over. I can't go down to Founders' Day ever again. I've never missed. Now — I've had to withdraw my boy. I can't go again. I couldn't face it."

He wiped his eyes. No tears in Huggo's eyes. On Huggo's face only a look sullen and aggrieved; and sullen and aggrieved his mutter, "Well, perhaps it was different for you. I couldn't stick the place."

She gasped out, "Huggo!" but Harry had heard, and Harry, perhaps in offset to the emotion he had displayed, smashed his hand down on the table before him and cried out, " Well, keep your mouth shut about it then! Couldn't stick it! What can you be? What can be the matter with you? Couldn't stick it! Tidborough! The finest school in the world! Couldn't stick it!"

She interposed, " Harry, dear! Huggo; Huggo, tell your father you didn't mean that."

Huggo's mumble: " I'm sorry, father."

Harry's deep, kind voice: "I'm sorry too, old man. It rather jarred. Look here, this is all over. It's just been a side-slip. I've forgotten it. So has your mother. You just think over sometimes what I've said, my boy. We're fixing up this tutor's for you. You start in fresh and go like steam. Finest thing in the world a fresh start. Makes a side-slip worth while. I'm going to be — I *am* — prouder of you than anything on earth. My eldest boy! Like steam from now, old chap, eh?"

Strike on!

After that interview and when the boy had left the room — shambled out of the room in that sullen, aggrieved air he would always assume under correction — after that she and Harry had talked, most fondly. It was all, the talk, that poignantly affecting " fresh start " business that he'd begun with Huggo. Poignantly affecting because Harry, piling upon his love for Huggo and his pride in Huggo, which she shared, his love for his old school and his pride in it, which she could understand but could not share, had been so bravely, cheerfully earnest and assured about the future. " One who never turned his back but marched breast forward." The boy would be all right. Mice and Mumps, old lady, he'd be all right! It was just a mistake, just a side-slip. He'd got the right stuff in him, Huggo had, eh, old lady? They must just pull together to help the boy, eh?

He paused the tiniest space at that and pressed her hand and looked at her. She knew his meaning. If only. . . .

He went on: This was a good place, this tutor's down in Norfolk they were sending him to, Harry was sure it was. It was a pity, of course, he couldn't go to another public school; but of course he couldn't; they wouldn't take him; no use worrying about that. This tutor, this man they were sending him to, was a first-class chap. Only took six pupils. Was a clergyman. Understood boys and youths who hadn't quite held their own and wanted special coaching and attention. Huggo was keen on the idea. After all, why shouldn't he have disliked Tidborough? There were such boys who didn't like public-school life. There, there! Perhaps it was the best thing that could have happened. Bet your life this was going to be the making of old Huggo, this change. This tutor and the quiet, self-reliant life there, each chap with his own jolly little bed-sitting room, would prop him up and get him into Oxford when the time came and make him no end happy and splendid.

"There, there, old lady," said Harry, and patted her and kissed her (she'd been affected). "There, there, it's going to be fine. The rest is just up to us, eh? We know the boy's weaknesses. We know what Hammond's told us about him — home life and home influences and all that stuff, and that's easy; we'll see the boy gets that, won't we?"

She used to wring her hands at that, and crying "If only!" cry again in desperation of excuse: "If only the war hadn't come! If only the war hadn't come!"

The war was on then. It was 1915. "You see," she used to appeal to the arbitrament before which, watching these pictures, she found herself, "you see, the war made everything so difficult, so impossible, so frightful, so confused, so blinding. Sturgiss had left the Bank to do war service in the Treasury. More than half the clerks had gone. We were understaffed and badly staffed at every turn. How could I give it up then? I don't say I would have. I'm on my knees. I've thrown in my hand. I'm not pretending anything or anyway trying to delude myself. I don't say I would have given it up and come home to make home life for the boy and for them all. I don't say I would. I'm only saying how infinitely harder, how impossibly harder, the war conditions made it. There was the understaffing — that alone. There was the cry about releasing a man for the front — that alone. I was releasing half a dozen men. Field said I was. I knew I was. How could I go back and be one of the women sitting at home? That alone! How could I? And there was more than that. It wasn't only the understaffing. It was Sturgiss going. I'd been absorbing the banking business for years. It was meat and drink to me. I'd had a bent for it ever since the Bagehot 'Lombard Street' days. I'd nourished my bent. I'd been encouraged to nourish my bent. The work was just a passion with me. Sturgiss went. I went practically into his place. I'd a position in banking that no woman had ever held, nor no banker ever imagined a woman ever holding, before. It was Sturgiss, a partner, I'd released for war service. It was Sturgiss's, a partner's, place I'd got. How could I give that up? How could I? How could I? If only the war hadn't come. If only. . . ."

Strike on!

It isn't all going as it should with the boy at the tutor's. But wasn't it impossible to observe, at the time, that it wasn't all going as it should? Of course (her thoughts would go) it was her fault; but was not the world, spiritual and material, in conspiracy against her, and against Huggo, and against her other darlings, to make easy her fault? Ah, that war, that war! Didn't it unsettle everybody and everything? Naturally it unsettled the boy down at the tutor's. Naturally one did not notice or foresee the trend of his unsettlement. Naturally it made plausible the excuses that he made.

There he is, down there at the tutor's. He wanted to do war work, not sitting there grinding lessons. All the tutor's pupils did. Naturally they did. The boy couldn't go in the army. He was too young. He was in a rural district. He got doing land-work. They all did. It was supposed to be done in leisure hours. Naturally it encroached on, and unfitted for, work hours. "After all," as the tutor wrote, "how can you blame the boys? After all, it's very hard to seem to try to check this patriotic spirit." After all! Oh, why do people say "after all" when they mean quite the contrary? This was *before* all, this seductive escape from uncongenial duties, precedent of all, influencing to all that happened — after all. Naturally it interfered with scholastic work. That was condoned. As naturally it interfered with discipline. That was not mentioned by the tutor. If he was cognisant of it was not domestic discipline everywhere relaxed "on account of the war"?

There Huggo is. These are his holidays. After the setback at Tidborough he was to have spent all his holidays at home. He was not, for the future, to go away on invitations. That war! He never spent any of his holidays at home. How could the boy be tied down in London with this war on? He made his land-work his excuse, most plausible. He spent all his holidays with friends whose homes were in rural districts.

Then it turned out that he had not, as he had given out, been always at the house of friends. He was found in cottage lodgings living with a friend, a fellow-pupil at the tutor's; on land-work truly, but in gross deception, and in worse.

It came out quite by chance and in a way very horrible. Harry discovered it. Harry, early in 1915, had been absorbed into the Home Office. His work was very largely in connection with a special secret service body dealing with spies. He examined in private arrested suspects. He advised and he directed on criminal matters therewith connected. He was working, under immense pressure, terrible hours. He was hardly ever in to dinner. He often was away all night. He frequently was away travelling for days together. When he was seen he showed signs of strain to Rosalie.

He came in one evening about nine o'clock. It was early in 1916. Huggo was then seventeen. Rosalie heard him in the hall and heard that some one was with him. She heard him, by the dining-room door, say, " You'd better go in there and get something to eat. I'll attend to you presently."

His voice was iron hard. Who was with him? What was the matter?

He came in to her. His face was iron hard. He shut the door. " Do you know who I've got here with me? Do you know where I've been? Do you know what's happened? "

His manner was extraordinary. His voice was like heavy axes, thudding. His face was dark and passionate, menacing. Happened? Things were always happening in these appalling days. She said, " Oh, what is it, Harry? "

" It's Huggo."

" Huggo? "

" Huggo! "

Like axes! It seemed that, of his passion (and she

never before had seen passion in his face), he scarcely could speak. He fought for words. When they came out they thudded out.

"Do you know where Huggo's been this past month?"

"With the Thorntons, his friends."

"He's not. He's lied. He's been living with some blackguard friend in rooms in Turnhampton, in Buckinghamshire."

"Harry! Doing what? Land-work?"

"Land-work! Loafing! Drinking!"

"Drinking? Huggo?"

"Listen to me. This is what I've come to. This is what that boy's come to. I had to go down to this place Turnhampton about a spy they'd arrested. He was to come up in the police court there this morning. They took the other cases first. Court going to be cleared for my man. I sat there, waiting. The second case — this is what I've come to — was my son, my boy, Huggo, brought up from the cells where he'd spent the night. My son! Drunk and disorderly. He didn't see me. The police gave him a character. I sat there and listened to it. My son! A visitor, the police described him. Supposed to be working on some farm. Not a desirable character in the village. My son! Always loafing about. Always in the inn. Last night drunk. Assaulted the landlady. My son! Arrested. My son!"

He turned away.

She cried, "Harry! What happened?"

He turned on her in a violence renewed. "I declare to you that if he had gone to prison I would not have raised a hand to stop him. He'd had the grace — or he'd all the time had the guile — to give an assumed name. Would I have confessed, to save him, that he was my son? I believe I couldn't. He got off with a fine. I got hold of him. I've brought him back. He's here."

She went to the bell. " I must get you some food."

He stayed her. " Food! I'll tell you what to get me. I'll tell you what to get that boy. Get me a home. Get him a home. That's what's caused this. Do you know what he said to me coming up in the train? I said to him, 'Why are you always away like this? Why, in the holidays, are you never at home?' He said, ' What home is there for me to come to? Who's ever there?' He's right. Who is? Are you?"

She said quietly, " Harry, not now. Dear, you are not yourself."

He was not and continued not to be. " Well, answer my question. Are you ever in the home?"

She implored, " Oh, my dear!"

He was not to be placated. " Where is the home?"

" Harry!"

" Where's Doda?"

She began in her spirit to move. " Staying with friends."

" Where's Benji?"

" You perfectly well know. Staying with friends."

" Where are you?"

She put her hand to her bosom. " Oh, beware me, Harry. Here."

" For the night. Are you ever in the children's home?"

" Are you?"

" That sophistry! I have my work!"

" I've mine."

He smote his hand upon the mantelshelf by which he stood and turned and left the room.

Strike on!

Of course it healed and was obliterated and all passed over. Of course Harry forgave the boy. Of course he

was handsome to the boy's excuses. Drunk! Of course
it was just a slightly tipsy ebullition. Had been in the
hot sun in the fields all day and was affected by a too
long slake of beer. Assaulted the landlady! She'd been
rough mannered and objected to his noise and got in
the way and he had pushed her. " The boy's all right,"
Harry said to Rosalie after, the boy forgiven, he sat
and talked with her. " He's got no vice. How could he
have? It was wrong, it was deceitful, going off like
that to that place without telling us. But he meant no
harm. He's explained. He's genuinely sorry. He's
just got out of hand a bit. They all have, the young
people, in this war time. The boy's all right. He's eighteen in a few months. I'll see if I can speed it up a bit
getting him into the army. He's magnificently keen.
He'll do fine, God bless him. Think no more about it,
old lady. In the whole business I'm only sick with myself that I lost my temper with him as I did — and with
you, my dear, and with you." And he put out his hand
to her.

" One who never turned his back but marched breast
forward."

" And with you." Of course he was distressed he had
been violent with her. Of course that painful outbreak
was healed, obliterated, put away. He had expressed
his utter regret. He'd been badly rattled with this infernal war all that week; this business on the top of it
had been a most frightful shock to him. What had he
said? Forgive, Rosalie, forgive! Of course she had
nothing to forgive. Forgiveness also was for her to
ask. As to the point thus violently raised, he saw, didn't
he, the clear impossibility of her giving up her work, war
work as much as his own, at such a time? Not to say
the unnecessity of it — the children were growing up . . .
it clearly could be done now. The position she held . . .

He said, "I know, old lady." He said, "I know, I know," and sighed.

Ah, from that vision of him saying, "I know," and sighing, and from the mute appeal that then was in his eyes, from that—strike on!

Most retentive to her, as it had passed, of Huggo's share in all that episode had been that she from her expostulation with Huggo had not come away with the same satisfaction as seemingly had Harry. She put before the boy how terribly his father had felt the shame of it, how almost broken-hearted he had been. "He idolises you, Huggo. You're always his eldest son. He thinks the world of you."

Huggo took it all with that familiar air of his of being the party that was aggrieved. He listened with impatience that was not concealed and he had no contrition to display. "Well, mother, it's all over. What *is* the good of going on and on about it? I've had it by the hour from father. He's understood. What *is* the good?"

She very lovingly talked to him. He all the time had an argument. He kept up his own case. He presently said, "And I do wish, mother, especially now I'm going into the army soon, I do wish you'd drop that 'Huggo.' You can't tell how I hate it. You might just as well call me Baby. It's a baby's name."

"Oh, Huggo, it was the name we loved you by."

"Well, I can't stick it. My name's Hugh."

Strike on!

There he is. He's in the army. He's utterly splendid in his uniform. How proud of him she is! They no longer gave commissions direct from civil life; but he'd been in the cadet corps at Tidborough and Harry was able to get him direct into an officer cadet battalion. He's off to France in what seems next to no time. He's home on leave and there's nothing that's too good for him and her purse at his disposal when he's run through Harry's generous allowance. He seems to get through an immense amount of money on leave. He's never at home. He's often out all night. Well, he's on leave. He's fighting for his country. You can't be anything but utterly lenient with a boy that's fighting for his country. He went back. Three days after he was supposed to have gone back Rosalie came face to face with him in Piccadilly. He was with some flapper type of girl, in the detestable phrase (as she thought it) by which the detestable products of the war (as she thought them) were called. He was just getting into a cab. She called out to him, astounded. She heard him swear and he jumped into the cab and was driven away. She didn't tell Harry. Harry found out. It came out that the boy for overstaying his leave was to be court-martialled. She did not know what Harry did. She noticed in those days what a beaten look Harry's face was getting. It was, of course, the war strain; but it only was first evident to her in that time of the court-martial. He scarcely spoke to her. She did not know what he did, but she knew he had much influence and exerted it at no sparing of himself. The boy got off with a severe reprimand and was returned to France. And to be in France, out there, in that ever-present shadow of death, was to be excused everything and to be forgiven everything.

Miraculously the war ended. The boy had had rather more than two years of it. He applied for immediate demobilisation as being a student, and he was one of the batch that got away immediately on that ground. He was nearly twenty then. Now what was he going to do? Oxford, of course, Harry said, and then the Bar, as always intended. Huggo, larking about in uniform long after he ought to have been out of it, was in immense feather with himself. He didn't say No and he didn't say Yes to the Oxford idea. All he said was that he voted all that wasn't discussed the very day he got back (it was more than six weeks since he had got back). He surely, he said, was entitled to a bit of a holiday first, after all he had been through. London seemed to be swarming with thousands of young men who claimed they were entitled to a bit of a holiday first after all they had been through. Huggo was never in the house. He had picked up with a man, Telfer, whom he had met in France, a big business man, Huggo described him as, and he seemed to spend all his time with this man. Telfer was a much older man than Huggo. Huggo brought him to dinner one night. It was rather a shock to Rosalie, meeting the man of whom she had heard so much. Huggo had never said anything about his age. He must have been quite forty. He had dull, cloudy eyes and a bad mouth. He called Huggo " Kid," using the word in every sentence, and it was easy to see from Harry's manner that Telfer was repellent to him. Easy, also, and not nice, to see Telfer's dominion over Huggo. Not nice to hear Huggo's loud, delighted laughter at everything addressed to him by Telfer. Harry spoke less and less as the meal advanced. The two left early; they were going to a music hall. When they had gone Rosalie and Harry looked at one another across the table and by their look enchanged a great deal.

" That's a detestable companion for Huggo," Harry said. " Rosalie, there's been enough of this. The boy must get to work."

It appeared, in interviews following that evening, that Huggo was not a bit keen on the Oxford idea. He wanted to go into business. He was not clear as to precisely what kind of business, but he wanted the freedom

and the excitement of earning his own living, not to be
cooped up at the 'Varsity " like back at school again."
Harry took a firm line. The boy resented the firm line.
Well, anyway, he argued, he couldn't go till October, it
was only June now; all right, he'd go in October — if he
had to. Harry made arrangements for some reading
through the summer preparatory to Oxford. It upset
plans made by Huggo. He thought it " uncommonly
hard " that he should have to spend the whole summer
" swotting." Oh, well, if he had to, he had to. He had an
invitation for a month for that immediate time to Scotland. The reading was arranged to start a month ahead.
He didn't in the least want to be out of London just
when there was so much going on and all his pals here;
but anything was better than sticking this kind of life
at home, father always at him; so he'd go to Scotland;
he supposed he was entitled to a bit of country holiday
before they cooped him up? He went to Scotland.

Twice during that month Rosalie thought she saw
Huggo in the West End. But London was full of young
men of the Huggo type. It wasn't likely.

It turned out to have been very likely. It turned out
that Huggo had never been in Scotland at all but in
London all the time. And much worse than that. One
evening towards the end of the so-called Scotland month
Huggo unexpectedly walked into the house. Rosalie
was sitting with Harry in the dining-room over the end
of dinner. Doda was upstairs putting last touches to herself before going out to a dance. Doda was eighteen then
(it was 1919), had left school, and, with a large circle
of friends, was going out a great deal. Benji was still
at school, at Milchester. Harry had never resumed relations with beloved Tidborough.

The door opened and Huggo walked in. His face was
very flushed and his articulation a little odd. When,

after greetings, he sat down, he sat down with a curiously unsteady thud and gave a little laugh and said, " Whoa, mare, steady! "

It appeared, after explanations, that he had come to talk about " this Oxford business." " I really can't very well go to Oxford now, father. I really ought to start in some money-making business now and I've got a jolly good opening promised me. I really ought to take it."

The decanters were on the table. He had already taken a glass of port. He filled another and drank it.

" The fact is, I'm — married."

There were some hard and bitter things said between his father and the boy. The boy fumbled — he obviously had been drinking — between would not or could not say very much as to who it was that he had married.

Harry said, " Who are her people? That's a plain question, isn't it? "

Huggo, very red, increasingly difficult to understand, said, " It's a plain enough question. It's a plain enough question. I've come here to be perfectly frank and plain and plain enough question. The fact is I don't know very much about her plain enough people."

Rosalie broke out of the frozen stupefaction that had numbed her. " Huggo, you must know. You must know who her people are."

Huggo turned a very slow gaze around from his father to his mother. He looked at her. He said with astonishing violence, " Well, I tell you I don't. People! What have her people got to do with it? I haven't married her people. She's my little girl and I've married her, not her people. Isn't that enough for you? "

Harry got up and went over to him. " Look here, you'd better run along. You're not in a fit state to talk to your mother. I'm not sure you're in a fit state to talk to anybody or to know what you're saying. You'd better go, my boy. We'll go into this in the morning. Come round early in the morning. We'll settle it then."

He was passing with Huggo through the door when Doda, equipped for her dance, came running down the stairs. " Hull-o, Huggo! Why, I haven't seen you for weeks. Where *have* you been?"

Huggo, standing unsteadily, unsteadily regarded her. " Point is, where are you *going?* All dressed up and somewhere to go! I'll bet you have! I've seen you jazzing about the place when you haven't seen me, Dods. And heard about you! There was a chap with me watching you at the Riddle Club the other night told me some pretty fierce — "

"Oh, dash, I've left my fan," cried Doda, and turned and ran back up the stairs.

Huggo called, " I say, Dods. I'm in a row. So'll you be one day, if you don't look out for yourself."

Doda's voice: " Oh, dry up — you fool!"

Strike on!

CHAPTER IV.

Her Doda! The one that was her baby girl, that was her tiny daughter! The one that was to be her woman treasury in which she'd pour her woman love; that was to be her self's own self, her heart's own heart, her tiny woman-bud to be a woman with her in the house of Harry and of Huggo! Her Doda!

Look, there she is! There's lovely Doda! She's fourteen. It's early in 1915, in the first twelve months of the war. (That war!) She's at that splendid school. She's been there nearly three years. She loves it. She's never so happy as when she's there, except, judging by her chatter, when she's away in the holidays at the house of one of her friends. It's at home — when she is at home — that she's never really happy. She's so dull, she always says, at home. She always wants to be doing something, to be seeing something, to be playing with somebody. She can't bear being in the house. She can't bear being, of an evening, just alone with Rosalie. "Oh, dear!" she's always saying. "Oh, dear, I do wish it would hurry up and be term time again."

"Darling, you are a restless person," Rosalie says.

"Well, mother, it *is* dull just sticking here."

"You know how Benji loves to have you home, Doda. Benji simply lives for you. I've never known a brother so devoted. You ought to think of Benji sometimes, Doda."

"Well, I can't be *always* thinking of Benji. I'm surely entitled to be with my own friends sometimes. I don't *ask* Benji to be devoted to me."

She's strangely given to expressions like that : " I didn't *ask* for " — whatever circumstance or obligation it might be that was irksome to her. " Not traditions — precedents ! " The watchword of the school was strangely to be traced in her attitude, still in her childish years, towards a hundred commonplaces of the daily life. She was always curiously older than her years. She seemed to have a natural bent away from traditionally childish things and towards attractions not associated with childhood. She did excellently well at the school. She was, her reports said, uncommonly quick and vivid at her lessons. She was always in a form above her years. Her friends, while she was smallish, were always the elder girls, and the elder girls gave her welcome place among them. " Perhaps a shade precocious," wrote the lady principal in one of the laconic, penetrating sentences with which, above her signature, each girl's report was terminated : and, in a later term, " Has ' Forward ! ' for her banner, but should remember ' not too fast '."

" Cripes ! I know what she's referring to," said Doda, seeing it ; and laughed, obviously flattered.

" Your expressions, Doda ! "

" Huggo uses it."

" They're wretched even in Huggo. But Huggo's a boy. You're a girl."

" Well, mother, I didn't *ask* to be a girl."

" Doda, that's merely silly."

" A lot of us say it, that's all I know."

" Then, darling, a lot of you are silly."

" Oh, I *shall* be glad when next week I go to the Fergussons. It *is* dull."

Look, there she is. She's sixteen. She's beautiful. She's pretty as a picture, and she knows she is. She's grown out of the rather early fullness of figure that had been hers. She's slim and tall and straight and supple and slender as a willow wand. If she had her hair up and her skirts lengthened (skirts then were only starting on their diminution to the knees), she'd pass for twenty anywhere, and a twenty singularly attractive, curiously self-possessed, strikingly suggestive in her pale and beautiful countenance, and in an alternating sleepiness and glinting in her eyes; strikingly suggestive of, well, strikingly suggestive according to the predilictions and the principles of the beholder.

This was in 1917. She was beginning rather to hate school now. She wanted to be out and doing some war work of some kind. Oh, those sickening scarves and things they were eternally knitting, that wasn't war work. It was fun at first. They were fed to death with doing them now. She didn't much want to go into a hospital or into any of these women's corps. They were a jolly sight too cooped up in those things from what she'd heard. She wanted to go into one of the Government offices and do clerical work. Several of the school Old Girls who had been there with her were doing that and it was the most ripping rag. Of course you had to work, and of course it was jolly good patriotic work, but you had a topping time in many ways. That was what she wanted to do. Oh, mother, do let her chuck school now and get to it! Not till she was seventeen? Well, it *was* sickening. Well, it was only another term, thank goodness.

It was in the holidays — in her brief days at home of the holidays — in which these wishes were expressed, that Rosalie found Doda was corresponding with officers at the front.

Doda was appallingly untidy in her habits. She was out one evening to a party — she managed to get a considerable number of parties into her dull days at home. Rosalie, come in from Field's, peeped into her bedroom to find her. She had not known that Doda was going out. The bedroom cried aloud that Doda had gone out. Drawers were open and articles of dress hanging out of them. One drawer, no doubt stubborn in its yieldings, was bodily out in the middle of the room. Clothes were on the floor. Clothes strewed the bed. Powder was all over the mirror. It was as if a whirlwind had passed through the room.

" Powder ! " murmured Rosalie.

The state of the room dismayed her. The intense orderliness of her own character forbade her ringing for a maid. She simply could not look at untidiness like that without tidying it. She started to tidy. Doda's box was open. Its contents looked as if a dog had burrowed in it, throwing up the things as he worked down. If anything was to go in, everything must first come out. Rosalie lifted out an initial clearance.

There lay scattered beneath it quite half a dozen photographs of officers in khaki.

There were all inscribed. " To the school kid." " Wishing you were here." " With kisses." " Till we meet." And with slangy nicknames of the writers. There lay with them a number of letters, all in their envelopes. There lay also a sheet of paper covered in Doda's bold handwriting. It began " Wonderful Old Thing."

Rosalie had not touched these evidences of an unknown interest in Doda's life. She stooped, staring upon them, the lifted bundle of clothes in her hand. The stare that took in " Wonderful Old Thing " took in also the first few lines. They were not nice. But she oughtn't to read it. One didn't do that kind of thing. She replaced the bundle and closed the box. Then she tidied the room and wiped the mirror.

Early next morning, immediately on coming out of her bath, she went in to Doda. She opened the door softly and she distinctly saw the lids of Doda's eyes flash up and close again.

" Doda! "

Doda pretended to be asleep. Rosalie had sat up for Doda the previous night but had said nothing to her either of her discovery or of going to an invitation without having told her. Doda wasn't pretending to be asleep because she feared trouble. She was pretending to be asleep just because she had no wish for an early talk with her mother.

There was a little pang at the heart of Rosalie.

But it was just that the child wasn't demonstrative of her affections. None of them were. Even Benji not really what you would call demonstrative. How beautiful the child was! Her Doda! How little she ever saw of her!

She called her again.

Doda opened her eyes. " Hullo, mother."

Just that. No more. They *were* different, the children.

She sat down on Doda's bed and began to talk to her. Tidiness! " Doda, your room as you left it last night when you went out was simply terrible. How can you? "

" Oh, I can't be tidy," said Doda. " I simply can't. It's no good trying."

" Darling, you ought to try. It's so odd. I'm so fearfully tidy. It's almost a vice with me. One would have thought you'd have had it too."

Doda said indifferently, " I don't see why." She said, " Oh, I am sleepy. It's a matter of teaching when you're a kid, that sort of thing. You're tidy, but you never taught me to be tidy."

Rosalie said some more of encouragement to tidiness. She then said, " And there's another thing, Doda. I think you ought not to have rushed off like that to the Trevors last night without telling me."

"Mother, you knew where I was. I told the maids."

"You should have consulted me, Doda."

The child assumed the Huggo look. "Mother, how could I? They only asked me on the telephone at tea-time. How *could* I have consulted you?"

"In the same way as you were invited. On the telephone."

"Well, I never thought about it. Why should I if I had? I knew you'd have agreed. You wouldn't have stopped me, would you? It's dull enough, goodness knows."

"Doda, what I've come in to talk about is this. When I was tidying your room last night—"

Doda sat up. "Did you tidy my room?"

"I couldn't possibly leave a room like that. Well, I went to tidy your box—"

"I'll get up," said Doda. She jumped very quickly out of bed and put on a wrapper and her slippers. "Yes, well?"

"Are you writing to men at the front, Doda?"

"Every girl is. It's a thing to do. It helps them."

"Are they friends of yours, dear? Personal friends."

"They're brothers of girls I've stayed with."

"All?"

"Practically all. There're not more than two or three. Lonely soldiers, they're called. They used to advertise. It helps them. There's no harm in it, is there?"

"I haven't suggested there is, Doda."

"I can see you're going to, though. If you ask me—" She stopped.

"I don't think I like the idea, quite. I never did when I heard of it being done. Why should they send you their photographs?"

"But what's the harm? Why shouldn't they?"

"Darling, it's I am asking you. I'm your mother."

"Well, if you ask me —" Doda walked over to the window. She stood there a moment looking out. She suddenly turned. "If you ask me, I don't think it's right to — Of course if you think it right to — if you've been reading my letters —"

"Doda, I haven't. I just saw them there. But I'd like to read them, Doda. May I?"

"They're private letters. I don't see how you can expect me to show you private letters."

Rosalie went over to Doda and stood by her and stroked her hair. "Doda, I think we'll look at it like this. Let me read the letters and we'll talk about them and see if it's nice to go on writing to the men, in each individual case. That certainly you shall do, continue writing, if it all seems nice to us, together, Doda. If you won't show them to me — well, let us say if you'd rather not show them to me — then I'll ask you just to burn them and we'll forget it."

Doda stepped violently away from the hand that stroked her hair. "No. I *won't* show them."

"Then it's to burn them, Doda."

Doda looked slowly around the room. Her face was not nice. She said sullenly, "There's no fire here."

"Bring them down with you to the breakfast-room. Your father will have gone. We'll see Benji's not there."

She went to Doda and kissed her on the forehead. Doda shut her eyes. Her hand on Doda's shoulder could feel Doda quivering. She went to the door and at the door said, "And the photographs, dear. I should bring them too."

She had long finished breakfast when at last Doda came down. The tall, slim, beautiful and pale creature appeared in the doorway. She walked towards the fire, her head held high, her brown hair in a thick tail to her waist. She had a packet in her hands. As she began to stoop over the fire she suddenly uprighted herself and turned upon her mother. She said violently, " Perhaps you'd like to count them ? "

Rosalie said very softly, " Doda ! "

Doda bent to the flames and pressed the packet down upon them. She stood watching them mount about it. A half-burnt photograph slid onto the hearth. She gave a sound that was a catching at her breath and swiftly stooped and snatched the burning fragment up and cast it on its fellows. The leaping flames died down. She turned violently towards Rosalie, seated at the table watching her, her heart sick. That tall, slim, beautiful creature whose face had been pale and was habitually pale was in her face crimson, her slight young bosom heaving, her eyes, so often sleepy, flashing, her young hands clenched. " I call it a shame ! " Her voice was high and raw. " I call it a shame ! I call it wicked ! I call it abominable ! I call it an — an outrage ! "

Rosalie said, " Doda ! Doda, I haven't reproached you. I haven't reproved you. If they had been letters you could have shown me, yes, then a shame — "

The child called out, " I'm nearly seventeen ! I call it an outrage ! "

Rosalie got up and went to her. " Darling, they couldn't be shown. They're just burnt. They're forgotten." She put out inviting arms. " My poor Doda ! "

That child, almost touched by her arms, brushed herself from the arms. " *Why* should I have things like this done to me by you?"

" Doda, I am your mother. You have a duty — "

" Well, I won't have a duty ! Why should I have a duty ? I didn't ask to be born, did I ? You chose for me to be born, didn't you? I didn't choose it. I'll never forget this. Never, never, never!"

Tears rushed into her eyes and leapt from her eyes. She gave an impassioned gesture. She rushed from the room.

Strike on!

Look at her. There she is. She's only eighteen but she's woman now. Grown-up. "Out," as one would have said in the old and stupid days, but out much wider than the freest budding woman then. It's 1919. They've caught, the rising generation, the flag of liberty that the war flamed across the world; license, the curmudgeons call it; liberty, the young set free. It's 1919. She's been a year war-working in one of the huge barracks run up all over London for the multitudes of women clerks the Government departments needed and, the war over, not too quickly can give up. She loves it. She's made a host of friends. Her friends are all the girls of wealthy parents, like herself, or of parents of position if not of means; and all, like her, are far from with complaint against the war that's given them this priceless avenue away from home. She loves it. Of course she doesn't love the actual work. Who would? What she loves is the constant titillation of it. The titillation of getting down there of a morning and of the greetings and the meetings and the rapt resumptions of the past day's fun; the titillation of watching the clock for lunch and of those lunches, here to-day, to-morrow there, and of the rush to get back not too late. The titillation of watching the clock for tea, and of tea, and then, most sharpest titillation of them all, watching the clock for — time!; for — off!; for — out! away! That is the charm of it in detail. The charm in general, as once expressed to Rosalie by one of Doda's friends brought in to tea one Sunday is, " You see, it gets you through the day."

That's it. The night's all right. There's nearly always something doing for the night. It's just the day would be so hopeless were there not this lively way of " getting through the day." That's it, for Doda.

Until she found her feet — not in her office, but at home at first emergence from her school — until she found her feet she often used to be kept uncommonly late at office. In a very short while she found her feet and that excuse no longer was put forward. Every girl of Doda's association was on her feet in 1919; and for Doda very much easier, at that, than for the generality, to establish her position in the house. By 1920, when she was nineteen, she was conducting her life as she pleased, as nineteen manifestly should. In 1921, when she was twenty, the war work was over and she was " getting through the day " much as she lived the night. It was pretty easy to get through the day in 1921. That which the curmudgeons called license, and liberty the free, was in 1921 held by charter and by right prescriptive.

Look at her. There she is. She's lovelier yet, if that which was her budding loveliness could bear a lovelier hue. She's always out somewhere, or she's always off somewhere, or she's always coming in from somewhere. Her eyes, in presentation more pronounced, have always got that sleepy look or got that glinting look. She never talks much at home. She seems to keep her talking for her friends and she never brings her friends home. She's on good terms with Rosalie. That's the expression for it. She was to have been a woman treasury into which was to be poured by Rosalie all her woman love. She was to have been a woman with her mother in the house of Harry and of Huggo. But that's all done. She's not a daughter to her mother. She never asked to be born to her mother,

as once she told her mother, and though that never now
again is said it is the basis of her stand. She owes no
obligations. They just meet. They get on very pleasantly. She's on good terms with Rosalie.

It is odd — or else it isn't odd but only natural — that
in all the pictures seen by Rosalie there scarcely is a
picture that ever shows the children all together. They
hardly ever, within the compass of her pictures, were
together. As in their schoolhood, so much more in
adolescence, they never showed a least desire for one
another's company. They had their friends, each one,
and much preferred their friends. You'd not, it's true,
say that of Benji; but Benji in fraternal wish had to
take what was offered him and there was nothing offered
him by Doda; by Huggo less than nothing.

Benji!

Look, here's the Benji one; the good, the quiet, gentle
one; the one that never gave a thought of trouble, Benji.

Her Benji! The one that came after disfavour, after
remorse; that came with tears, with thank God, charged-
with-meaning tears. The littlest one. The one that was
so tiny wee beside the big and sturdy others. Her last
one! Her Benji!

Look, there he is. Always so quiet, gentle, good.
Always, though snubbed, so passionately fond of Doda.
Look, there he is. He's at Milchester, in his spectacles,
the darling! He's always in his books. He isn't good at
games. He does so well at school. Oh, isn't Harry proud
of him and fond of him! Oh, doesn't Harry often sigh
and wish he could have gone to Tidborough to win those
prizes and those honours there. But Tidborough's closed
to Harry, Harry says. Look, there goes Benji! It's
1919. He's sixteen. It's Speech Day at Milchester. He's
in the Sixth. He's won all those prizes. She's holding

two and Harry's holding three, and there he goes to take the Heriot Gold Medal. All the great hall is simply cheering Benji! The Head is saying that he's the youngest boy that's ever won the Heriot. Look, there's the Bishop handing it, and shaking Benji by the hand, and patting Benji on the back, and saying something to him. You can't possibly hear what it is, every one is cheering so. Look, here he comes with the medal, in his spectacles, the darling! She can scarcely see, her eyes are brimming so. Harry's quite shameless. Harry's got tears standing on his cheeks and he's set down the prizes and is stretching both his hands out to the boy. Feel, that's his hand — her Benji's hand — snuggled a moment in hers, and then he turns to his father and is eagerly whispering to his father, his spectacles rubbing his father's head, the darling! He's more demonstrative to his father than he is to her. She feels it rather sometimes. He's awfully sweet to her, but, you can't help noticing it, it's more his gracious manner than the outpouring she'd give anything to have. It's funny how he always seems the tiniest atom strange with her as if he didn't know her very well or hadn't known her very long. It sometimes pains a little. He's different with his father. He loves being with his father. And doesn't Harry love having the boy with him! Harry idolises the boy. Of course Huggo is Harry's eldest, and whatever Huggo's disappointments, these men — at least these perfect Harry type of men — have for their eldest boy within their hearts a place no other child can quite exactly fill. There's some especial yearning that the eldest seems to call. There's some incorporation of the father's self, there's some reflection that he sees, there's some communion that he seems to find, that makes " My eldest son " a thing apart. But, with that reservation, and that's ingrained in men, it's Benji that's the world to Harry. He's going to Oxford. He's going to have the Bar career that Huggo wouldn't take. But Harry thinks there's some especial wonders going to come to Benji. He says the boy's a dreamer. He says the boy's a thinker. "Benji's got something rare about him, Rosalie," he says. "That boy's got a mark on him that genius has. You wait and see, old lady. It's Benji's going to make the old name shine!"

Strike on!

It *is* odd, sad, significant, that there is scarcely a picture that shows together those three children, or even two of them. It's 1921 now and drawing very close to Finis; but always the old detachment, the seeming want of mutual love, appears to hold the three apart. Doda is sometimes glimpsed, no more, with Benji, always putting off or chilling off her brother for her friends; sometimes she's seen with Huggo, meeting him and he her, more like an acquaintance of their sets than like fruit of the same parents; familiar, apparently, with one another's lives; referring to places of amusement by both frequented, as had been done, in instance, on that night of Huggo's announcement of his marriage when with a note that rung sinister he had bantered Doda and she had turned and run upstairs. But no more than that. The children seem to have no mutual love. They're different.

It's 1921. Huggo was scarcely ever seen now. He had married in haste and had in haste repented. He also had played a trick, involving a sum of money, on his father. His wife, as it appeared, had been met at some dancing club and the brief courtship had continued anywhere but at her home. Of her home Huggo knew only what she told him; and what she told him was only what she could invent. She was then, at their first meeting, in the uniform of a war service corps to which she belonged. She said her father was a clergyman.

"A clergyman's daughter!" cried Huggo bitterly, acquainting Rosalie only three months after his marriage of his marriage's failure. "A clergyman's daughter! That's what they all say — those! Wasn't I a fool to be caught out by that! Oh, wasn't I a fool! If you want to know what she really was, she was a teashop waitress, in the city somewhere. If you want to know what her reverend father in the country was, is, he doesn't live in the country; he lives in Holloway, and he doesn't live in a rectory in Holloway, he lives in a baker's shop. That's what he is, a baker! That's what I've done for myself, married a waitress! Yes, and then you, you and father, when she comes whining here and complains I ill-treat her and keep her without money, you two take her part and send her back to me with your championship and get me here to pijaw me about my duty to my pretty young wife! Well, now you know, now you know, and you can tell father what my pretty young wife is — how she deceived me. Deceived me! Now you know."

Rosalie said, "Huggo, you deceived her."

Huggo had been leaving and now very violently went. "That's your tone, is it? I might have known! That's all you can say, is it? To see me ruin my life and then reproach me! Ruin my life! It's not I that's ruined my life. It's you. There, now I've told you! I can see things now. What sort of a chance have I ever had? What sort of a home have I ever had? Have I ever had a mother? When I was a kid did I ever have a mother like other kids have? I can see things now. A mother! I can't ever remember a time when I wasn't in the charge of some servant or governess or other. You said this afternoon before father that I didn't love you. Did you ever teach me to love you? By God, I can't remember it. By God, I can't."

Strike on!

Also that trick, touching a sum of money, upon his father. When he first made known his marriage, and it was obvious he must have his way and be set up to start in life, he had also, as he had said, the chance of a lucrative business. It was the kind of thing he liked. It was the kind of thing he was keen on. It was a motor-car business. There was a little syndicate that was putting a new car on the market. They'd got works, just outside London somewhere. They'd got show-rooms in the West End. And they'd got an absolutely first-class article. That chap Telfer was one of the directors; a first-class chap called Turner was another; they'd let him in for eight thousand pounds and he'd be absolutely set up for life and be pulling in an immense fortune in no time. You will, won't you, father?

Of course Harry forgave the boy, his eldest son. The marriage was done, what was the use of being unkind or stupid about it? Of course Rosalie welcomed the wife, Lucy, the prettiest creature, a tiny shade common, perhaps, but a sweet little soul with always about her a pathetic air of being afraid of something (of when it should come out precisely what she was, as the event proved). Of course Harry paid over the eight thousand pounds. Huggo took, " to start with," as he said, a tiny furnished flat in Bayswater. Rosalie installed him and his bride therein and left him, on their first night there, ever so gay, so confident, so happy. Her Huggo!

In two months it all came out. Lawyers are notoriously lax in making their own wills. Harry, who could master a case quicker than any man at the Bar, and could see to the soul and beyond it of a hostile witness a minute after getting on his feet to cross-examine, was fooled blind by the syndicate that was going to put the absolutely first-class article on the market. Whether it was that there never had been a business, and that Harry's inspection of works, visits to show-rooms, and examination of books, was all part of an elaborate swindle carried out with the aid of some one who possessed these accessories; or whether it was that the whole thing was bought up cheap merely to sell at a profit, was never clearly known to Harry and to Rosalie. Harry was too grieved to pursue the shock. "I'll take not a step further in the matter, Rosalie," Harry said. "I can't bear to find the boy out deeper. It's done. There's no sense in being stupid or unkind about it."

What happened was that the car enterprise never was an enterprise at all except an enterprise to get eight thousand pounds into the possession of the syndicate. Nothing ever was properly announced by Huggo. It just "came out." It "came out" that the syndicate was not established in the West End show-rooms but in three rather dingy offices in the city. It "came out" that the syndicate was not running a motor-car business but a business cryptically described as "Agents." Huggo said disaster had overtaken the car enterprise and that the syndicate, rescuing what remained of the smash, had pluckily set up on another line. He thought he could scrape along. It was a knockout of course, but he thought he could scrape along.

"But what I can't make out, old man," said Harry, when Huggo had stumbled through an entirely non-explanatory explanation of the syndicate's business in its new capacity as agents, "What I can't make out, old man, is why you should trade under another name. Why, ' So-and-So, and So-and-So, and So-and-So, Agents ' — I can't ever remember the names? Why not ' Telfer, Occleve and Turner '? "

"Well, as a matter of fact, father — I want you to know everything without any concealment — "

"I know you do, old man. I know you do."

" Well, as a matter of fact, that's just a bit of useful swank. The names we're trading under are swagger names and we think it sounds better."

" Occleve sounds pretty good to me, Huggo. We've been a good long way on Occleve, the Occleves."

" Well, that's what they think, father, and of course, as I've told you, they know infinitely more about business than I do. They'll explain the whole thing to you any time you like. It's all absolutely above-board, father."

" My dearest old boy, don't talk like that. Of course it is. We're only so grieved, your mother and I, that you should have had such a setback so early. But remember, old man, the great thing is not to let your wife suffer. No pinching or screwing for her, Huggo. Always your wife first, Huggo. We'll give you at the rate of three hundred a year just until all's going swimmingly, and that's to keep Lucy merry and bright, see? "

It was shortly after that it all came out that the thing was a ramp, the motor-car business never in existence; shortly after that it came out Huggo was neglecting his wife; shortly after that the high words to Rosalie, telling her how his wife had deceived him; shortly after that that the syndicate, amazingly prosperous, moved into offices better situated and handsomely appointed; shortly after that it came out that the business of the syndicate was in some way connected with company promotion.

Harry, seen among these developments, was not the man he used to be. He was at the crest of his career at the Bar, working enormously and earning richly, but the old bright, cheery way had gone from Harry. There was permanently upon his face, and there was intensified, the beaten look that Rosalie first had seen on that night, in the war, when there had been the Huggo drinking business and when for the first and only time he had spoken passionately to Rosalie. When he now was at home he used to sit for long periods doing nothing, just thinking. When sometimes, home earlier than he, Rosalie saw him coming up the street towards the gamboge door she noticed, terribly, the bowed shoulders, the weary gait, the set, careworn face. She used to run down then to the famous gamboge door and open it and greet him and his face used to light up in the old way, but it was not the same face, and the effect of its radiation therefore not the same. It was not that the face was older. It was that its aspect was changed.

He used to look up from that chair where he sat just thinking, when Doda, butterflied for the evening, butter-flied across the room, and used to say, " Out again, Doda? " He then would relapse back into his thoughts. He had a habit of getting up suddenly and rather strangely wandering about from room to room of all the principal rooms of the house, just standing at the door of each, and looking in (they were all empty of inhabitants), and then coming back and sitting again in the chair and just sit, thinking.

It used to pain the heart of Rosalie.

She said more than once when he returned from such a tour, " Dear Harry, looking for anything? "

He'd say rather heavily, " No; no, dear. Just having a look around."

It used to pain the heart of Rosalie.

But he used to be enormously brightened up when Benji came home. Benji was just at Oxford then, eighteen. He was a different man when Benji was at home. He used to say, " Rosalie, that boy's going to make a name for himself in the world. My heart's wrapped round that boy, Rosalie. Ay, me! I wish he'd been our eldest, Rosalie."

That was because he couldn't tear away the wrappings of his heart from about his eldest. Men can't.

It used to pain the heart of Rosalie.

Of course, with everything now known, Huggo was forgiven. Huggo was prosperous now, almost aggressively prosperous. He kept a car. The syndicate, whatever it actually did, was obviously doing enormously well. What was the good of being stupid and unkind to the boy now that, at last, he had found his feet? But Huggo scarcely ever came to the house. He had virtually left Lucy. Lucy lived on in the originally-taken furnished flat in Bayswater. Huggo had rooms somewhere, no one quite knew where, and lived there. Rosalie used to get Lucy to the house sometimes, but Lucy was never at her ease on these visits, and Doda, who sympathized entirely with Huggo in the matter, very much disliked her and would not meet her. Lucy was in bad health and she was going to have a baby. Her health and her condition made her look much more common than she used to look.

Then the baby was born; a little girl. Poor, grateful Lucy called it Rosalie. She told Rosalie that Huggo said he didn't care what the baby was called. He was very angry about the baby. " He was worse than usual when he was here last week," said Lucy. " I think he's got something on his mind. I think he's worrying about something. Oh, he *was* sharp."

Lucy was very ill with the birth of her baby. She didn't seem able to pick up again from her confinement. She kept her bed. Then, suddenly, she developed pneumonia. The maternity nurse, paid by Rosalie, was still in attendance. Rosalie sent in another nurse, and on that same night, going straight to the sick bed from Field's, and then coming home very late, told Harry, who was waiting up for her, that the worst was feared for Lucy. She then said, " Harry, if anything happens, I think we'll have that baby here. It will practically be a case of adopting the child."

Harry agreed.

"I'd get in a nurse for her, the new little Rosalie."
She sighed.

"Yes, yes," said Harry.

She said after a little, "Harry, the nurseries in use
again!"

He sat there as he was always sitting, thinking.

She went over to him. "Dear, won't you like the
nurseries to be in use again?"

He said slowly, "I will, very much, Rosalie. It's
lonely, these empty rooms. I will very much — in some
ways."

Rosalie knew what Harry meant. She touched his
hand. "Dear, I think it can be made different."

Harry knew what Rosalie meant. He pressed the hand
that touched his own. "That's all right, Rosalie. That's
all right, dearest."

Rosalie was down early next morning. She desired an
early breakfast and to go on to see Lucy before Field's.
It might be necessary to stay the day with Lucy. There
was also Huggo. What was Huggo doing? Overnight
Rosalie had seen Doda, come in late from an evening with
a very intimate friend of hers always known, through
some private joke of Doda's, as "the foreign friend."
The foreign friend, not in the least foreign but English,
was a young married woman living apart from her husband. Doda had brought her to the house once. She was
very pretty and a cheery soul. She would have been called
fast when Rosalie was a girl. In 1921 she would almost,
in the manner she presented to Rosalie, have been called
slow. Doda and she were greatly attached.

Doda, overnight, going straight upstairs to bed, had
said, "Have you seen Huggo to-day? He's in a scrape of
some sort."

" Oh, Doda, what kind of a scrape? "

" He didn't tell me. I ran into him quite by chance coming away from a theatre with the foreign friend. We both thought he was rather badly rattled."

" Was he going on to Lucy? Did he know Lucy was very ill indeed? "

Doda said, " I don't know. He didn't tell me. Is she? " and indifferently passed upstairs.

Rosalie at her early breakfast was thinking what news the day would give of Lucy and of Huggo. She was suddenly, by Huggo in person, brought intelligence of both. She heard the door bell ring and in a minute Huggo surprisingly broke into the room. He had kept his hat on. He looked white, drawn and very agitated. He shut the door behind him. " Lucy's dead."

Tears sprang into the eyes of Rosalie, " Oh, my poor Huggo! "

He made a gesture. " Oh, that's no good! Look here, mother, will you look after things over there for me? That's all I've come in to say. Will you see to everything and will you take the kid? I can't stop."

He made to go.

" Huggo, of course I will. But you'll be there? Are you going there now? "

" I'm not. I'm going away."

" Going away? "

His hand was on the door. " Yes, going away. Look here, there's another thing. If any one comes here for me will you say you haven't seen me? It's important. It's vital."

" Huggo, what is the matter? "

" You'll jolly soon know. You may as well know now. Then you'll realise. If you want to know — the police are after me."

He was gone.

CHAPTER V

In the Book of Job it all happened, to Job, in the apparent compass of one piece of time not broken by diurnal intervals, not mitigated by recuperative cessations between blow and blow. It seemed to Rosalie that it was like that it happened also to her. There seemed no interval. It seemed to her wrath on wrath, visitation upon visitation, judgment upon judgment.

It seemed to her that she was no sooner come down out of the Old Bailey — her hand touching at things for support, her vision vertiginous, causing the solid ground to be in motion, her ears resonant, crying through her brain the words she saw in Huggo's look as they removed him; it seemed to her she was no sooner out from there than she was at the telephone and summoned by the foreign friend and was there with Doda and was in process of "Oh, Doda!" — "Oh, mother!"; it seemed to her she was no sooner out from that than she was with that burly messenger, going with him, returning from him. There were days and nights walled up in weeks and months between these things, but that is how they seemed to Rosalie.

The syndicate was laid by the heels, one here, one there, Huggo in France, very shortly after the warning that had put Huggo in flight. The syndicate went through the police court where was unfolded a story sensational with surprising sums of money, captivating with ingenuity of fraud covered up by fraud to help new fraud again. The syndicate stood in the dock at the Old Bailey. Those

two of the syndicate described by the prosecution and by
the judge as the principals were sentenced to three years'
penal servitude. "You," said the judge, addressing with
a new note in his voice the third prisoner, "You, Occleve,
stand in a different — "

Rosalie began to pray.

Harry would not attend the trial. He had done all that
could be done, and of his position there was very much
that he was able to do, and had attended the police court
during the initial proceedings. He would not go to the
Old Bailey. He would not go out. He would not read
the papers. He used to sit about the house. "My son a
felon. . . . My boy a felon. My son. . . . My eldest
son. . . ."

Rosalie was given a seat in the floor of the court on
the first days of the hearing. On the day when the verdict
was to be given and sentence passed she could not bear
that. An usher, much pitying, obtained her a place in
the gallery. She looked down immediately upon her
Huggo. Her hands, upon the ledge before her, were all
the time clasped. Her eyes alternately were in her hands
and on her Huggo. Her heart moved between her Huggo
and her God.

"You, Occleve, stand in a different position. . . ."

She began to pray. All of her being, all of her soul, all
of her life, with a spiritual and a physical intensity
transcending all that her body and her mind had ever
known, was in apotheosis of supplication. "O God the
Father! O God the *Father!* O God the *Father!*"

Her Huggo! Those words that only in snatches she
heard were being addressed to her Huggo.

" . . . Your counsel has most eloquently pleaded for
you. . . . You bear an honoured name. . . . You bear
a name held in these precincts in honour, in esteem, in
love, in admiration. . . . You have had a good home, a

great and a noble father, a distinguished and devoted mother. . . ."

That suppliant crouched lower in her supplication.

". . . You have been the dupe, you have been the tool, you have been in large part, as your counsel has pleaded, and as I believe, the unsuspecting agent. . . . Nevertheless, the least sentence I can pass on you — "

"O God the Father, the *Father!*"

". . . is six months' imprisonment."

That boy, whose head had been hung and eyes downcast, lifted his head and raised his eyes and gave one look into the eyes of that suppliant for him that sat above him. There was recalled by that suppliant a look that had passed from the place of accusation to the place of assembly in the place called the Sanhedrin.

Her Huggo!

They took him away.

Doda didn't stop going out. She seemed to go out more. The pain within that house, brought there by Huggo, seemed to make that house more than before unbearable to Doda. She often spent the night, or the week end away, staying with the foreign friend, she generally said. She would have nothing whatever to do with the baby now installed in the house. She never would go near it. Once she passed it in the hall in its perambulator. She stopped and stooped over the face of lovely innocence that lay there and gazed upon it with an extraordinary intensity. She drew back with a sharp catch at her breath and sharply stepped away and turned and ran very quickly upstairs. After that when she chanced to pass the child she turned aside and would not look upon the child. She began not to look well, Rosalie thought. There often was upon her lovely face a pinched and drawn expression, disfiguring it. On the rare occasions when she was in to dinner she sat strangely moody. There only was a moodiness about that table then; but the moodiness of Doda was noticeable to Rosalie. She ate hardly at all. She sometimes would get up suddenly before a meal was ended and go away, generally to her own room. Very many times Rosalie would seek anxiously to question her, but apart from the independence which commonly she maintained towards Rosalie, Doda seemed very much to resent solicitude upon her health. " What *should* be the matter? I look perfectly well, don't I? "

"Doda, you don't. I've noticed it a long time."

" Well, I *am* perfectly well. If I wasn't I'd say so."

Strike on!

Rosalie was called up on the telephone by the foreign friend. It was the evening, about ten o'clock. Doda was away for a week at Brighton with the foreign friend. She was due back to-morrow. Harry was out with Benji. Benji was nineteen then and was home on vacation from Oxford. Harry never could bear Benji out of his sight when Benji was home. In the affliction that had come upon them he seemed to cling to Benji. Rosalie had persuaded him that evening to go with Benji to a concert. Harry said the idea of anything like that was detestable to him, but Rosalie had pleaded with him. Just a little chamber concert was different. It would do him so much good to have an evening away and to hear a little music and Benji would love it. Harry allowed himself to be persuaded and went off arm-in-arm with Benji. He always put his arm in Benji's when he walked with Benji.

Rosalie was waiting for them when the telephone bell rang and she was spoken to by the foreign friend.

It then happened like this.

The voice of the foreign friend was very alarmingly

urgent. " Would she come and see Doda at once, *at once, at once?* "

The voice struck a chill to the heart of Rosalie. " But where are you? You're at Brighton, aren't you? Are you speaking from Brighton? "

" No, no. At my flat. At my flat."

" But what is it? What is it? Why don't you tell me what it is? "

" It's an — it's an —." The voice stammered and hesitated.

" Oh, speak! Oh, speak."

She could hear the voice gulping.

" Oh, please do speak! "

" Doda isn't very well. Doda's very ill. It's an — it's an accident."

" I'll come. I'll come."

" Is Mr. Occleve there? "

" He isn't. He's out."

" Can you get him? "

" No. Yes. I don't know. I can't think. Oh, tell me. Tell me."

" Will you leave a message for him to come at once? "

" At once. At once."

She wrote a message for Harry and she picked up a wrap and she ran out hatless to find a cab.

She found a cab and went to Doda.

This all happened as quickly as bewilderingly. It was not like a dream and it was not like a nightmare. It was like a kind of trance to Rosalie.

The foreign friend was not seen at the flat. She was in some other room and did not appear. She said afterwards, and proved, that she had been away the previous night, leaving Doda at the flat, and had returned to find her — as she was found; and had immediately called the nearest doctor and then Doda's mother.

It was the doctor that opened the door to Rosalie. He was a Scotchman; a big and rugged man, all lines and whiskers and with a rugged accent.

He said, " You'rre her mother, arren't ye? Where's her father? "

" He's coming. Where is my child? "

The doctor jerked his head towards a wall. " She's yon."

" Tell me, please."

He pushed a chair towards her but she shook her head. " Please tell me."

" Ye'll want your courage." He again indicated the chair. She again shook her head. " It'll try ye. She's dying."

The lips of Rosalie formed the words: " Tell me." There was no sound in her.

The doctor said, " I cannot tell ye. It is for your husband to hear."

The heart of Rosalie stood still. She put both her hands upon her heart and she said to the doctor, " Tell me. I am strong."

The doctor looked upon Rosalie intently and he said (he was perhaps dexterously giving her time that she might weld herself) he said, " Ye'll need be strong. Ye look sensible. Ye'll need be sensible." He said, " There's been before me here another — There's been a creature here before me. There's been blackguarrd work here. There's been — that poor child there . . ." He told her.

She moaned : " O God, be merciful! "

That child, as that night went, was in delirium. She seemed to lie upon a bed. She lay, in fact, upon the altar of her gods, of self, of what is vain, of liberty undisciplined, of restless itch for pleasure, and of the gods of

Rosalie, a piteous sacrifice to them. You that have tears to shed prepare to shed them now. Or if you have no tears, but for emotion only sneers, do stop and put the thing away. It is intolerable to think to have beside that bed, beside that child, beside that Rosalie, your sneers. It's not for you and you do but exacerbate the frightful pain there's been in feeling it with them.

Rosalie was all night with that child. Harry was there upon the other side upon his knees and never raised his head. Benji was there that loved his sister so. Across the unblinded window strove a moon that fought with mass on mass of fierce, submerging clouds as it might be a soul that rose through infinite calamity to God. That child was in much torment. That child was in delirium and often cried aloud. That child burned with a fever, incredible, at touch of her poor flesh, to think that human flesh such flame could hold and not incinerate. That child in her delirium moaned often names and sometimes cried them out. Nicknames that in the sexless jargon of her day and of her kind might have been names of women and might be names of men. Darkie, Topsy, Skipper, Kitten, Bluey, Tip, Bill, Kid. Names, sometimes, more familiar. Once Huggo; once father; once loud and very piteously, " Benji, Benji, Benji, Benji, Benji! "

She never once said mother.

She calmed and a long space was mute. The moon, its duress passed, stood high, serene, alone. The doctor breathed, " She's passing." That child raised her lids and her eyes looked out upon her watchers.

Rosalie cried, " Oh, Doda! "

That child sighed. " Oh, mother! "

There was no note of love. There was of tenderness no note. There only was in that child's sigh a deathly weariness. " Oh, mother! " That child passed out.

They came home in the very early morning. Rosalie was in her working room. She had some things to do. She wrote to Mr. Field a letter of her resignation from Field's Bank. She only wrote two lines. They ended, " This is *Final*. I have done."

She sealed that letter and she moved about the room unlaying and as she unlaid, destroying, all evidences, all treasures, all landmarks, all that in any way referred to or touched upon her working life. There were cherished letters, there were treasured papers. She destroyed them all. From one bundle, not touched for years, dust-covered and time-discoloured, there came out a battered volume. She turned it over. " Lombard Street." She opened it and saw the eager underlinings and saw the eager margin notes, and ghosts . . . (it's written earlier in these pages). She rent the book across its perished cover and pressed it on the fire and on to the flames in the fire. " I have done."

But she was not done with and she had the feeling that she was not done with. She said to Harry, " This is not the children's tragedy. This is my tragedy. These were not the children's faults. These were my transgressions. Life is sacrifice. I never sacrificed. Sacrifice is atonement. It now is not possible for me to atone."

She was on her knees beside his chair. He stroked her hair.

There was an inquest. Harry went. She stayed at home and Benji stayed with her to be with her. Benji was not to be consoled. His mood was very dreadful. A report was printed in the evening paper before Harry came home. Benji read it and told Rosalie a witness, a man, had been arrested on the coroner's warrant. Benji said, " I think I'll go out now, mother, for a little."

Later in the afternoon when Rosalie was with Harry a

maid came into the room and looked at Harry and saw how sunk he was in his chair and so went to Rosalie and whispered to her. Rosalie went out. There was a man wished to see the master. Rosalie spoke to him. He was a large, burly man with a strong face. He looked like, and was, a police officer in plain clothes. Rosalie heard what he began to say and said she would go with him. In the cab the man told her about it. All his sentences began with or contained " The young gentleman."

" The young gentleman . . . the prisoner, when the young gentleman came rushing in, happened to be in the charge-room writing out a statement. . . . The young gentleman, before any one could stop him, rushed at this prisoner and caught him by the throat and threw him and the table over and banged the man's head against the floor, fair trying to kill him. They got the young gentleman off. They ought to have arrested the young gentleman, and they did most earnestly wish they had of arrested him, and blamed themselves properly that they didn't arrest him. But they felt cruelly sorry for the young gentleman and they got him outside and let him go and no more said. Of course, as madam knew, the police office wasn't very far from Gower Street station, the underground station with them steep stairs leading straight down from the street to the platform, as madam might be aware. . . . The young gentleman was seen by witnesses, whose names were took, to come rushing down these stairs on to the platform as if some one was after him. . . . The young gentleman come rushing down and there was a train just coming in, and whether he couldn't stop or whether he. . . . There's some say one thing and some say the other. . . . Whichever way it was the young gentleman. . . ."

Rosalie did her errand with the man and then came back to Harry. She had to tell Harry.

He was sitting in his chair. He had an open book on his knees. She saw, as one notices these things, it was a Shakespeare. She stood up there at the door before him and she said, " Harry — Benji! "

He saw it in her face.

He groaned.

He took the book off his knees and fumbled it, and with a groaning mutter dropped it: " ' Unarm, Eros, the long day's work is done.' "

She came to him and saw, as one sees things, above his head the picture he had hung when raven was his hair and radiant his face, and had hit his thumb, and jumped, and cried out, " Mice and Mumps! " and had laughed and wrung his hands, and cried out, " Mice and Mumps! " and laughed again. She came to him and saw him wilt and crumple in his chair, and could have sworn she saw the iron of his head, that had been raven, go grey anew and greyer yet. She came to him and she said, " Harry — Benji — an accident — not an accident — on the railway — killed. "

His voice went, not exclamatorily, but in a thick mutter, as one agrope, in sudden darkness, befogged, betrayed. " My God, my God, my God, my God, my God! "

She fell on her knees; and on her arms and on his lap she buried then her face.

He suddenly stooped to her, and caught his arms about her, and raised her to him, and pressed his face to hers, and held her there; and his cry was as once before, passionately holding her, his cry had been; then from his heart to her heart, now from the abysses of his soul to her soul's depths, " Rosalie! Rosalie! "

POSTSCRIPT.

There was to have been some more of it; but there, they're in each other's arms, and one has suffered so with them one cannot any more go on. One's suffered so! One has looked backward with her. The heart must break but for a forward glimpse: —

They're all right now. Huggo's in Canada. He writes every week. They're all right now. That other Rosalie that they brought in is looking after them. She's looking after them, that elf, that sprite, that tricksy scrap, that sunshine thing. She calls Harry father and Rosalie she calls mother. She has all her meals with them. There's no nurse. It's breakfast she loves best. She's on the itch all breakfast. When breakfast's done she's off her chair and hopping. She trumpets in her tiny voice, "Lessons! Lessons!" She trumpets in her tiny voice, "Lessons, lessons! On mother's knee! On mother's knee!"

THE END